PENGUIN

THE BEST OF MO

Edward L. Ferman has been
Magazine of Fantasy and Sci
twenty years. He has edited many anthologies, including
Final Stage, *Arena: Sports SF* and *The Best from
Fantasy and Science Fiction* series. He lives in Cornwall,
Connecticut, with his wife Audrey.

Anne Jordan is a writer, editor and children's book critic
and authority. She is the magazine's former managing
editor.

CONTENTS

ACKNOWLEDGMENTS

"Window" by Bob Leman. Copyright © 1980 by Mercury Press, Inc. By permission of the author.

"Insects in Amber" by Tom Reamy. Copyright © 1977 by Mercury Press, Inc. By permission of the author's agent, Virginia Kidd.

"Free Dirt" by Charles Beaumont. Copyright © 1955 by Fantasy House, Inc. Copyright renewed 1983 by Mercury Press, Inc. By permission of the author's agent, Don Congdon Assoc.

"Rising Waters" by Patricia Ferrara. Copyright © 1987 by Mercury Press, Inc. By permission of the author.

"The Night of the Tiger" by Stephen King. Copyright © 1977 by Mercury Press, Inc. By permission of the author and his agent, Kirby McCauley, Ltd.

"Poor Little Warrior" by Brian W. Aldiss. Copyright © 1958 by Mercury Press, Inc. Copyright renewed 1986. By permission of the author.

"Nina" by Robert Bloch. Copyright © 1977 by Mercury Press, Inc. By permission of the author.

"Werewind" by J. Michael Reaves. Copyright © 1981 by Mercury Press, Inc. By permission of the author.

"Dress of White Silk" by Richard Matheson. Copyright © 1951 by Fantasy House, Inc. Copyright renewed 1979 by Mercury Press, Inc. By permission of the author's agent, Don Congdon Assoc.

"Gladys's Gregory" by John Anthony West. Copyright © 1962 by Mercury Press, Inc. By permission of the author.

"By the River, Fountainebleau" by Stephen Gallagher. Copyright © 1986 by Mercury Press, Inc. By permission of the author.

"Pride" by Charles L. Grant. Copyright © 1982 by Mercury Press, Inc. By permission of the author.

"Longtooth" by Edgar Pangborn. Copyright © 1969 by Mercury Press, Inc. By permission of the author's agent, Richard Curtis Associates.

"Glory" by Ron Goulart. Copyright © 1986 by Mercury Press, Inc. By permission of the author.

"Bug House" by Lisa Tuttle. Copyright © 1980 by Mercury Press, Inc. By permission of the author.

"Hand in Glove" by Robert Aickman. Copyright © 1978 by Mercury Press, Inc. By permission of the author's agent, Kirby McCauley, Ltd.

"Stillborn" by Mike Conner. Copyright © 1981 by Mercury Press, Inc. By permission of the author and his agent, Frances Collin.

"Balgrummo's Hell" by Russell Kirk. Copyright © 1967 by Mercury Press, Inc. By permission of the author.

"The Old Darkness" by Pamela Sargent. Copyright © 1983 by Mercury Press, Inc. By permission of the author.

"The Night of White Bhairab" by Lucius Shepard. Copyright © 1984 by Mercury Press, Inc. By permission of the author.

"Salvage Rites" by Ian Watson. Copyright © 1986 by Mercury Press, Inc. By permission of the author.

"Test" by Theodore L. Thomas. Copyright © 1962 by Mercury Press, Inc. By permission of the author.

"The Little Black Train" by Manly Wade Wellman. Copyright © 1954 by Fantasy House, Inc. Copyright renewed 1982 by Mercury Press, Inc. By permission of Frances Wellman.

"The Autopsy" by Michael Shea. Copyright © 1980 by Mercury Press, Inc. By permission of the author.

INTRODUCTION

A friend of mine—who is a writer of horror tales—becomes immobile with fear at the idea of having to ride in one of those glass-sided elevators. He has missed out on a number of things because he is literally unable to get into such an elevator. Me, I'm not too keen on snakes and bugs, and the larger they are, the faster I move—in the opposite direction. Do I *really* believe that the spider dangling before my windowpane, which is possibly one millimeter in size, will suddenly turn feral, charge toward me, and wipe me from the face of the earth? Intellectually, no. Well . . . maybe.

The engine of fear is relentless, subjective, and fueled by the imagination. We all can imagine "what if" situations, but it takes a true literary talent to craft that "what if" into a story of quality and worth. While I'm skittering away from a bug, a writer like Lisa Tuttle is crafting that bug into a complete and *very* creepy tale such as "Bug House." When it comes to horror stories, one person's nightmare is another's inspiration, and nowadays the subject of a tale of horror is constrained only by the limits of a writer's imagination.

The horror story has come of age in the twentieth century. It is no longer merely the recitation of an eerie event or ghostly happening, but rather it is a tale of people—people reacting to the dark and the dark side of the soul, where control has been eliminated and chaos threatens. Horace Walpole created the "Gothic" in 1765 with his ghostly tale, *The Castle of Otranto*, giving us the tone and mood of the modern horror story. Each successive writer of horror has added something more to the genre so that today we can be frightened anywhere, anytime, by anyone . . . or thing. Horror has crept out of the castle and into *any* shadowy corner.

But "it"—whatever "it" is in a story that frightens us—must be believable. That takes skill. Anyone can make a person shudder (picture sliding down a banister that transforms into a razor blade—small, internal shudder?) but to create a story around that shudder and bring the story and characters to life takes unusual talent. At *The Magazine of Fantasy & Science Fiction* we take great delight when we encounter such talent. When we read a manuscript we look first and foremost for quality writing, for craftsmanship; gore is not important. Too often a beginning writer, perhaps overly influenced by the slash and stab "horror" movies of today, equates rivers of blood with what makes horror work. The best horror stories make a play for our minds and fears, not our queasy stomachs.

Since its inception, *The Magazine of Fantasy & Science Fiction* has published tales of horror that have been among the best in the genre, and the stories chosen for this collection are the best of these best. In putting together this collection we have tried to include tales for every taste. Russell Kirk's "Balgrummo's Hell," for example, has an old-fashioned flavor to it. It uses many of the conventions of the traditional Gothic horror story, yet is set in today's world. It is one of the most chilling stories ever written. On the other hand, "Gladys's Gregory" by John Anthony West will have you laughing—although it may be a nervous laugh.

While John Anthony West makes you chuckle uneasily, there are other stories here of the more look-over-your-shoulder-and-lock-the-door variety. Patricia Ferrara's "Rising Waters" is an elegantly written tale of eerie ghostliness, while Pamela Sargent's "The Old Darkness" may send your electric bill sky-high. For those preferring a bit more science and science fiction mixed with their terror, Michael Shea's "The Autopsy" provides that—and much more. Yet the primary thing the tales in this very diverse collection do have in common is that they are all of exceptional quality, written by extremely talented people, with the express purpose of scaring you out of your socks.

Horror tales, and these twenty-four tales in particular, are artfully crafted reminders to "take care!" Even the tiniest thing in our world can turn on us, can black out the light, douse the fire, and leave us alone in the dark, waiting. . . .

So—lock the doors, turn on all the lights (keep that flashlight handy, though), get comfortable, turn the page, read . . . and enjoy the creeping shadow of fear.

Take care!

—ANNE DEVEREAUX JORDAN

THE BEST
HORROR STORIES
FROM THE
MAGAZINE OF FANTASY AND
SCIENCE FICTION

WINDOW

BOB LEMAN

Bob Leman is one of *F & SF*'s most valued and interesting
contributors; he often takes a realistic, contemporary nar-
rative and introduces a chilling wrinkle, turning the usual
into the unusual and, at times, the deadly. "Window" was
first published in *F & SF* in May 1980 and is a fine example
of Bob's technique. It is a gripping story about a military
project that is investigating telekinesis and which experiences an incredible accident: the disappearance of an entire
building, along with one researcher, and the appearance,
in its place, of something terrifyingly different from what
it appears to be.

"**W**e don't know what the hell's go-
ing on out there," they told Gilson in Washington. "It may be pretty
big. The nut in charge tried to keep it under wraps, but the army was
furnishing routine security, and the commanding officer tipped us off.
A screwball project. Apparently been funded for years without anyone
paying much attention. Extrasensory perception, for God's sake. And
maybe they've found something. The security colonel thinks so, anyway.
Find out about it."

The Nut-in-Charge was a rumpled professor of psychology named

Krantz. He and the colonel met Gilson at the airport, and they set off directly for the site in an army sedan. The colonel began talking immediately.

"You've got something mighty queer here, Gilson," he said. "I never saw anything like it, and neither did anybody else. Krantz here is as mystified as anybody. And it's his baby. We're just security. Not that they've needed any, up to now. Not even any need for secrecy, except to keep the public from laughing its head off. The setup we've got here is—"

"Dr. Krantz," Gilson said, "you'd better give me a complete rundown on the situation here. So far, I haven't any information at all."

Krantz was occupied with the lighting of a cigar. He blew a cloud of foul smoke, and through it he said, "We're missing one prefab building, one POBEC computer, some medical machinery, and one, uh, researcher named Culvergast."

"Explain 'missing,' " Gilson said.

"Gone. Disappeared. A building and everything in it. Just not there anymore. But we do have something in exchange."

"And what's that?"

"I think you'd better wait and see for yourself," Krantz said. "We'll be there in a few minutes." They were passing through the farther reaches of the metropolitan area, a series of decayed small towns. The highway wound down the valley beside the river, and the towns lay stretched along it, none of them more than a block or two wide, their side streets rising steeply toward the first ridge. In one of these moribund communities they left the highway and went bounding up the hillside on a crooked road whose surface changed from cobblestones to slag after the houses had been left behind. Beyond the crest of the ridge the road began to drop as steeply as it had risen, and after a quarter of a mile they turned into a lane whose entrance would have been missed by anyone not watching for it. They were in a forest now; it was second growth, but the logging had been done so long ago that it might almost have been a virgin stand, lofty, silent, and somewhat gloomy on this gray day.

"Pretty," Gilson said. "How does a project like this come to be way out here, anyhow?"

"The place was available," the colonel said. "Has been since World War Two. They set it up for some work on proximity fuzes. Shut it down in forty-eight. Was vacant until the professor took it over."

"Culvergast is a little bit eccentric," Krantz said. "He wouldn't work at the university—too many people, he said. When I heard this place was available, I put in for it, and got it—along with the colonel, here.

Culvergast has been happy with the setup, but I guess he bothers the colonel a little."

"He's a certifiable loony," the colonel said, "and his little helpers are worse."

"Well, what the devil was he doing?" Gilson asked.

Before Krantz could answer, the driver braked at a chain-link gate that stood across the lane. It was fastened with a loop of heavy logging chain and manned by armed soldiers. One of them, machine pistol in hand, peered into the car. "Everything O.K., sir?" he said.

"O.K. with waffles, Sergeant," the colonel said. It was evidently a password. The noncom unlocked the enormous padlock that secured the chain. "Pretty primitive," the colonel said as they bumped through the gateway, "but it'll do until we get proper stuff in. We've got men with dogs patrolling the fence." He looked at Gilson. "We're just about there. Get a load of this, now."

It was a house. It stood in the center of the clearing in an island of sunshine, white, gleaming, and incongruous. All around was the dark loom of the forest under a sunless sky, but somehow sunlight lay on the house, sparkling in its polished windows and making brilliant the colors of massed flowers in carefully tended beds reflecting from the pristine whiteness of its siding out into the gray, littered clearing with its congeries of derelict buildings.

"You couldn't have picked a better time," the colonel said. "Shining there, cloudy here."

Gilson was not listening. He had climbed from the car and was staring in fascination. "Jesus," he said. "Like a goddamn Victorian postcard."

Lacy scrollwork foamed over the rambling wooden mansion, running riot at the eaves of the steep roof, climbing elaborately up towers and turrets, embellishing deep oriels and outlining a long, airy veranda. Tall windows showed by their spacing that the rooms were many and large. It seemed to be a new house, or perhaps just newly painted and supremely well-kept. A driveway of fine white gravel led under a high porte-cochère.

"How about that?" the colonel said. "Look like your grandpa's house?"

As a matter of fact, it did: like his grandfather's house enlarged and perfected and seen through a lens of romantic nostalgia, his grandfather's house groomed and pampered as the old farmhouse never had been. He said, "And you got this in exchange for a prefab, did you?"

"Just like that one," the colonel said, pointing to one of the seedy buildings. "Of course, we could use the prefab."

"What does that mean?"

"Watch," the colonel said. He picked up a small rock and tossed it in the direction of the house. The rock rose, topped its arc, and began to fall. Suddenly it was not there.

"Here," Gilson said. "Let me try that."

He threw the rock like a baseball, a high, hard one. It disappeared about fifty feet from the house. As he stared at the point of its disappearance, Gilson became aware that the smooth green of the lawn ended exactly below. Where the grass ended, there began the weeds and rocks that made up the floor of the clearing. The line of separation was absolutely straight, running at an angle across the lawn. Near the driveway it turned ninety degrees and sliced off lawn, driveway, and shrubbery with the same precise straightness.

"It's perfectly square," Krantz said. "About a hundred feet to a side. Probably a cube, actually. We know the top's about ninety feet in the air. I'd guess there are about ten feet of it underground."

" 'It'?" Gilson said. " 'It'? What's 'it'?"

"Name it and you can have it," Krantz said. "A three-dimensional television receiver a hundred feet to a side, maybe. A cubical crystal ball. Who knows?"

"The rocks we threw. They didn't hit the house. Where did the rocks go?"

"Ah. Where, indeed? Answer that and perhaps you answer all."

Gilson took a deep breath. "All right. I've seen it. Now tell me about it. From the beginning."

Krantz was silent for a moment; then, in a dry lecturer's voice he said, "Five days ago, June thirteenth, at eleven thirty A.M., give or take three minutes, Private Ellis Mulvihill, on duty at the gate, heard what he later described as 'an explosion that was quiet, like.' He entered the enclosure, locked the gate behind him, and ran up here to the clearing. He was staggered—'shook-up' was his expression—to see, instead of Culvergast's broken-down prefab, that house there. I gather that he stood gulping and blinking for a time, trying to come to terms with what his eyes told him. Then he ran over there to the guardhouse and called the colonel. Who called me. We came out here and found that a quarter of an acre of land and a building with a man in it had disappeared and been replaced by this, as neat as a peg in a pegboard."

"You think the prefab went where the rocks did," Gilson said. It was a statement.

"Why, we're not even absolutely sure it's gone. What we're seeing can't actually be where we're seeing it. It rains on that house when it's sunny here, and right now you can see the sunlight on it, on a day like this. It's a window."

"A window on what?"

"Well—that looks like a new house, doesn't it? When were they building houses like that?"

"Eighteen seventy or eighty, something like—oh."

"Yes," Krantz said. "I think we're looking at the past."

"Oh, for God's sake," Gilson said.

"I know how you feel. And I may be wrong. But I have to say it looks very much that way. I want you to hear what Reeves says about it. He's been here from the beginning. A graduate student, assisting here. Reeves!"

A very tall, very thin young man unfolded himself from a crouched position over an odd-looking machine that stood near the line between grass and rubble and ambled over to the three men. Reeves was an enthusiast. "Oh, it's the past, all right," he said. "Sometime in the eighties. My girl got some books on costume from the library, and the clothes check out for that decade. And the decorations on the horses' harnesses are a clue, too. I got that from—"

"Wait a minute," Gilson said. "*Clothes?* You mean there are people in there?"

"Oh, sure," Reeves said. "A fine little family. Mamma, poppa, little girl, little boy, old granny or auntie. A dog. Good people."

"How can you tell that?"

"I've been watching them for five days, you know? They're having— *were* having—fine weather there—or then, or whatever you'd say. They're nice to each other, they *like* each other. Good people. You'll see."

"When?"

"Well, they'll be eating dinner now. They usually come out after dinner. In an hour, maybe."

"I'll wait," Gilson said. "And while we wait, you will please tell me some more."

Krantz assumed his lecturing voice again. "As to the nature of it, nothing. We have a window, which we believe to open into the past. We can see into it, so we know that light passes through; but it passes in only one direction, as evidenced by the fact that the people over there are wholly unaware of us. Nothing else goes through. You saw what happened to the rocks. We've shoved poles through the interface there —there's no resistance at all—but anything that goes through is gone, God knows where. Whatever you put through stays there. Your pole is cut off clean. Fascinating. But wherever it is, it's not where the house is. That interface isn't between us and the past; it's between us and— someplace else. I think our window here is just an incidental side-effect, a—a twisting of time that resulted from whatever tensions exist along that interface."

Gilson sighed. "Krantz," he said, "what am I going to tell the secretary? You've lucked into what may be the biggest thing that ever happened, and you've kept it bottled up for five days. We wouldn't know about it now if it weren't for the colonel's report. Five days wasted. Who knows how long this thing will last? The whole goddamn scientific establishment ought to be here—should have been from day one. This needs the whole works. At this point the place should be a beehive. And what do I find? You and a graduate student throwing rocks and poking with sticks. And a girlfriend looking up the dates of costumes. It's damn near criminal."

Krantz did not look abashed. "I thought you'd say that," he said. "But look at it this way. Like it or not, this thing wasn't produced by technology or science. It was pure psi. If we can reconstruct Culvergast's work, we may be able to find out what happened; we may be able to repeat the phenomenon. But I don't like what's going to happen after you've called in your experimenters, Gilson. They'll measure and test and conjecture and theorize, and never once will they accept for a moment the real basis of what's happened. The day they arrive, I'll be out. And dammit, Gilson, this is *mine*."

"Not anymore," Gilson said. "It's too big."

"It's not as though we weren't doing some hard experiments of our own," Krantz said. "Reeves, tell him about your batting machine."

"Yes, *sir*," Reeves said. "You see, Mr. Gilson, what the professor said wasn't absolutely the whole truth, you know? Sometimes something *can* get through the window. We saw it on the first day. There was a temperature inversion over in the valley, and the stink from the chemical plant had been accumulating for about a week. It broke up that day, and the wind blew the gunk through the notch and right over here. A really rotten stench. We were watching our people over there, and all of a sudden they began to sniff and wrinkle their noses and make disgusted faces. We figured it had to be the chemical stink. We pushed a pole out right away, but the end just disappeared, as usual. The professor suggested that maybe there was a pulse, or something of the sort, in the interface, that it exists only intermittently. We cobbled up a gadget to test the idea. Come and have a look at it."

It was a horizontal flywheel with a paddle attached to its rim, like an extended cleat. As the wheel spun, the paddle swept around a table. There was a hopper hanging above, and at intervals something dropped from the hopper onto the table, where it was immediately banged by the paddle and sent flying. Gilson peered into the hopper and raised an interrogatory eyebrow. "Ice cubes," Reeves said. "Colored orange for visibility. That thing shoots an ice cube at the interface once a second. Somebody is always on duty with a stopwatch. We've established that every fifteen hours and twenty minutes the thing is open for five seconds. Five ice cubes go through and drop on the lawn in there. The rest of the time they just vanish at the interface."

"Ice cubes. Why ice cubes?"

"They melt and disappear. We can't be littering up the past with artifacts from our day. God knows what the effect might be. Then, too, they're cheap, and we're shooting a lot of them."

"Science," Gilson said heavily. "I can't wait to hear what they're going to say in Washington."

"Sneer all you like," Krantz said. "The house is there, the interface is there. We've by God turned up some kind of time travel. And Culvergast the screwball did it, not a physicist or an engineer."

"Now that you bring it up," Gilson said, "just what *was* your man Culvergast up to?"

"Good question. What he was doing was—well, not to put too fine a point upon it, he was trying to discover spells."

"Spells?"

"The kind you cast. Magic words. Don't look disgusted yet. It makes sense, in a way. We were funded to look into telekinesis—the manipulation of matter by the mind. It's obvious that telekinesis, if it could be applied with precision, would be a marvelous weapon. Culvergast's hypothesis was that there are in fact people who perform feats of telekinesis, and although they never seem to know or be able to explain how they do it, they nevertheless perform a specific mental action that enables them to tap some source of energy that apparently exists all around us, and to some degree to focus and direct that energy. Culvergast proposed to discover the common factor in their mental processes.

"He ran a lot of putative telekinecists through here, and he reported that he had found a pattern, a sort of mnemonic device functioning at the very bottom of, or below, the verbal level. In one of his people he found it as a set of musical notes, in several as gibberish of various sorts, and in one, he said, as mathematics at the primary arithmetic level. He was feeding all this into the computer, trying to eliminate simple noise and the personal idiosyncrasies of the subjects, trying to lay bare the actual, effective essence. He then proposed to organize this essence into *words*; words that would so shape the mental currents of a speaker of standard American English that they would channel and manipulate the telekinetic power at the will of the speaker. Magic words, you might say. Spells.

"He was evidently further along than I suspected. I think he must have arrived at some words, tried them out, and made an attempt at telekinesis—some small thing, like causing an ashtray to rise off his desk and float in the air, perhaps. And it worked, but what he got wasn't a dainty little ashtray-lifting force; he had opened the gate wide, and some kind of terrible power came through. It's pure conjecture, of course, but it must have been something like that to have had an effect like *this*."

Gilson had listened in silence. He said, "I won't say you're crazy because I can see that house and I'm watching what's happening to those ice cubes. How it happened isn't my problem, anyhow. My problem is what I'll recommend to the secretary that we do with it now that we've got it. One thing's sure, Krantz: this isn't going to be your private playpen much longer."

There was a yelp of pure pain from Reeves. "They can't *do* that," he said. "This is ours, it's the professor's. Look at it, look at that house. Do you want a bunch of damn engineers messing around with *that?*"

Gilson could understand how Reeves felt. The house was drenched now with the light of a red sunset; it seemed to glow from within with a deep rosy blush. But, Gilson reflected, the sunset wasn't really necessary; sentiment and the universal, unacknowledged yearning for a simpler, cleaner time would lend rosiness enough. He was quite aware that the surge of longing and nostalgia he felt was nostalgia for something he had never actually experienced, that the way of life the house epitomized for him was in fact his own creation, built from patches of novels and films; nonetheless he found himself hungry for that life, yearning for that time. It was a gentle and secure time, he thought, a time when the pace was unhurried and the air was clean; a time when there was grace and style, when young men in striped blazers and boater hats might pay decorous court to young ladies in long white dresses, whiling away the long, drowsy afternoons of summer in peaceable conversations on shady porches. There would be jolly bicycle tours over shade-dappled roads that twisted among the hills to arrive at cool glens where swift little streams ran; there would be long, sweet buggy rides behind somnolent, patient horses under a great white moon, lover whispering urgently to lover while nightbirds sang. There would be excursions down the broad, clean river, boats gentle on the current, floating toward the sound from across the water of a brass band playing at the landing.

Yes, thought Gilson, and there would probably be an old geezer with a trunkful of adjectives around somewhere, carrying on about how much better things had been a hundred years before. If he didn't watch himself, he'd be helping Krantz and Reeves try to keep things hidden. Young Reeves—oddly, for someone his age—seemed to be hopelessly mired in this bogus nostalgia. His description of the family in the house had been simple doting. Oh, it was definitely time that the cold-eyed boys were called in. High time.

"They ought to be coming out any minute now," Reeves was saying. "Wait till you see Martha."

"Martha," Gilson said.

"The little girl. She's a doll."

Gilson looked at him. Reeves reddened and said, "Well, I sort of gave them names. The children. Martha and Pete. And the dog's Alfie. They kind of look like those names, you know?" Gilson did not answer, and Reeves reddened further. "Well, you can see for yourself. Here they come."

A fine little family, as Reeves had said. After watching them for half an hour, Gilson was ready to concede that they were indeed most engaging, as perfect in their way as their house. They were just what it took to complete the picture, to make an authentic Victorian genre painting. Mama and Papa were good-looking and still in love, the children were healthy and merry and content with their world. Or so it seemed to him as he watched them in the darkening evening, imagining the comfortable, affectionate conversation of the parents as they sat on the porch swing, almost hearing the squeals of the children and the barking of the dog as they raced about the lawn. It was almost dark now; a mellow light of oil lamps glowed in the windows, and fireflies winked over the lawn. There was an arc of fire as the father tossed his cigar butt over the railing and rose to his feet. Then there followed a pretty little pantomime as he called the children, who duly protested, were duly permitted a few more minutes, and then were firmly commanded. They moved reluctantly to the porch and were shooed inside, and the dog, having delayed to give a shrub a final wetting, came scrambling up to join them. The children and the dog entered the house, then the mother and father. The door closed, and there was only the soft light from the windows.

Reeves exhaled a long breath. "Isn't that something," he said. "That's the way to live, you know? If a person could just say to hell with all this crap we live in today and go back there and live like that. . . . And Martha, you saw Martha. An angel, right? Man, what I'd give to—"

Gilson interrupted him. "When does the next batch of ice cubes go through?"

"—be able to— Uh, yeah. Let's see. The last penetration was at 3:15, just before you got here. Next one will be at 6:35 in the morning, if the pattern holds. And it has, so far."

"I want to see that. But right now I've got to do some telephoning. Colonel!"

Gilson did not sleep that night, nor, apparently, did Krantz or Reeves. When he arrived at the clearing at five A.M. they were still there, unshaven and red-eyed, drinking coffee from thermos bottles. It was cloudy again, and the clearing was in total darkness except for a pale light from beyond the interface, where a sunny day was on the verge of breaking.

"Anything new?" Gilson said.

"I think that's my question," Krantz said. "What's going to happen?"

"Just about what you expected, I'm afraid. I think that by evening this place is going to be a real hive. And by tomorrow night you'll be lucky if you can find a place to stand. I imagine Bannon's been on the phone since I called him at midnight, rounding up the scientists. And they'll round up the technicians. Who'll bring their machines. And the army's going to beef up the security. How about some of that coffee?"

"Help yourself. You bring bad news, Gilson."

"Sorry," Gilson said, "but there it is."

"Goddamn!" Reeves said loudly. "Oh, goddamn!" He seemed to be about to burst into tears. "That'll be the end for me, you know? They won't even let me in. A damn graduate student? In *psychology*? I won't get near the place. Oh, dammit to hell!" He glared at Gilson in rage and despair.

The sun had risen, bringing gray light to the clearing and brilliance to the house across the interface. There was no sound but the regular bang of the ice cube machine. The three men stared quietly at the house. Gilson drank his coffee.

"There's Martha," Reeves said. "Up there." A small face had appeared between the curtains of a second-floor window, and bright blue eyes were surveying the morning. "She does that every day," Reeves said. "Sits there and watches the birds and squirrels until, I guess, they call her for breakfast." They stood and watched the little girl, who was looking at something that lay beyond the scope of their window on her world, something that would have been to their rear had the worlds been the same. Gilson almost found himself turning around to see what it was that she stared at. Reeves apparently had the same impulse. "What's she looking at, do you think?" he said. "It's not necessarily forest, like now.

I think this was logged out earlier. Maybe a meadow? Cattle or horses on it? Man, what I'd give to be there and see what it is."

Krantz looked at his watch and said, "We'd better go over there. Just a few minutes, now."

They moved to where the machine was monotonously batting ice cubes into the interface. A soldier with a stopwatch sat beside it, behind a table bearing a formidable chronometer and a sheaf of charts. He said, "Two minutes, Dr. Krantz."

Krantz said to Gilson, "Just keep your eye on the ice cubes. You can't miss it when it happens." Gilson watched the machine, mildly amused by the rhythm of its homely sounds: *plink*—a cube drops; *whuff*—the paddle sweeps around; *bang*—paddle strikes ice cube. And then a flat trajectory to the interface, where the small orange missile abruptly vanishes. A second later, another. Then another.

"Five seconds," the soldier called. "Four. Three. Two. One. *Now.*"

His timing was off by a second; the ice cube disappeared like its predecessors. But the next one continued its flight and dropped onto the lawn, where it lay glistening. It was really a fact, then, thought Gilson. Time travel for ice cubes.

Suddenly behind him there was an incomprehensible shout from Krantz and another from Reeves, and then a loud, clear, and anguished "Reeves, *no!*" from Krantz. Gilson heard a thud of running feet and caught a flash of swift movement at the edge of his vision. He whirled in time to see Reeves's gangling figure hurtle past, plunge through the interface, and land sprawling on the lawn. Krantz said, violently, "*Fool!*" An ice cube shot through and landed near Reeves. The machine banged again; an ice cube flew out and vanished. The five seconds of accessibility were over.

Reeves raised his head and stared for a moment at the grass on which he lay. He shifted his gaze to the house. He rose slowly to his feet, wearing a bemused expression. A grin came slowly over his face, then, and the men watching from the other side could almost read his thoughts: Well, I'll be damned. I made it. I'm really here.

Krantz was babbling uncontrollably. "We're still here, Gilson, we're still here, we still exist, everything seems the same. Maybe he didn't change things much, maybe the future is fixed and he didn't change anything at all. I was afraid of this, of something like this. Ever since you came out here, he's been—"

Gilson did not hear him. He was staring with shock and disbelief at the child in the window, trying to comprehend what he saw and did not believe he was seeing. Her behavior was wrong, it was very, very wrong. A man had materialized on her lawn, suddenly, out of thin air, on a sunny morning, and she had evinced no surprise or amazement or fear. Instead, she had smiled—instantly, spontaneously, a smile that broadened and broadened until it seemed to split the lower half of her face, a smile that showed too many teeth, a smile fixed and incongruous and terrible below her bright blue eyes. Gilson felt his stomach knot; he realized that he was dreadfully afraid.

The face abruptly disappeared from the window; a few seconds later the front door flew open and the little girl rushed through the doorway, making for Reeves with furious speed, moving in a curious, scuttling run. When she was a few feet away, she leapt at him with the agility and eye-dazzling quickness of a flea. Reeves's eyes had just begun to take on a puzzled look when the powerful little teeth tore out his throat.

She dropped away from him and sprang back. A geyser of bright blood erupted from the ragged hole in his neck. He looked at it in stupefaction for a long moment, then brought up his hands to cover the wound; the blood boiled through his fingers and ran down his forearms. He sank gently to his knees, staring at the little girl with wide astonishment. He rocked, shivered, and pitched forward on his face.

She watched with eyes as cold as a reptile's, the terrible smile still on her face. She was naked, and it seemed to Gilson that there was something wrong with her torso as well as with her mouth. She turned and appeared to shout toward the house.

In a moment they all came rushing out, mother, father, little boy, and granny, all naked, all undergoing that hideous transformation of the mouth. Without pause or diminution of speed they scuttled to the body, crouched around it, and frenziedly tore off its clothes. Then, squatting on the lawn in the morning sunshine, the fine little family began horribly to feed.

Krantz's babbling had changed its tenor: "Holy Mary, Mother of God, pray for us. . . ." The soldier with the stopwatch was noisily sick. Someone emptied a clip of a machine pistol into the interface, and the colonel cursed luridly. When Gilson could no longer bear to watch the grisly feast, he looked away and found himself staring at the dog, which sat happily on the porch, thumping its tail.

"By God, it just can't be!" Krantz burst out. "It would be in the histories, in the newspapers, if there'd been people like that here. My God, something like that couldn't be forgotten!"

"Oh, don't talk like a fool!" Gilson said angrily. "That's not the past. I don't know what it is, but it's not the past. Can't be. It's—I don't know—someplace else. Some other—dimension? Universe? One of those theories. Alternate worlds, worlds of If, probability worlds, whatever you call 'em. They're in the present time, all right, that filth over there. Culvergast's damn spell holed through to one of those parallels. Got to be something like that. And, my God, what the *hell* was its history to produce *those*? They're not human, Krantz, no way human, whatever they look like. 'Jolly bicycle tours.' How wrong can you be?"

It ended at last. The family lay on the grass with distended bellies, covered with blood and grease, their eyelids heavy in repletion. The two little ones fell asleep. The large male appeared to be deep in thought. After a time he rose, gathered up Reeves's clothes, and examined them carefully. Then he woke the small female and apparently questioned her at some length. She gestured, pointed, and pantomimed Reeves's head-long arrival. He stared thoughtfully at the place where Reeves had ma-terialized, and for a moment it seemed to Gilson that the pitiless eyes were glaring directly into his. He turned, walked slowly and reflectively to the house, and went inside.

It was silent in the clearing except for the thump of the machine. Krantz began to weep, and the colonel to swear in a monotone. The soldiers seemed dazed. And we're all afraid, Gilson thought. Scared to death.

On the lawn they were enacting a grotesque parody of making things tidy after a picnic. The small ones had brought a basket and, under the meticulous supervision of the adult females, went about gathering up the debris of their feeding. One of them tossed a bone to the dog, and the timekeeper vomited again. When the lawn was once again immaculate, they carried off the basket to the rear, and the adults returned to the house. A moment later the male emerged, now dressed in a white linen suit. He carried a book.

"A Bible," said Krantz in amazement. "It's a Bible."

"Not a Bible," Gilson said. "There's no way those—things could have Bibles. Something else. Got to be."

It looked like a Bible; its binding was limp black leather, and when the male began to leaf through it, evidently in search of a particular passage, they could see that the paper was the thin, tough paper Bibles are printed on. He found his page and began, as it appeared to Gilson, to read aloud in a declamatory manner, mouthing the words.

"What the hell do you suppose he's up to?" Gilson said. He was still speaking when the window ceased to exist.

House and lawn and white-suited declaimer vanished. Gilson caught a swift glimpse of trees across a broad pit between him and the trees.

Then he was knocked off his feet by a blast of wind, and the air was full of dust and flying trash and the wind's howl. The wind stopped as suddenly as it had come, and there was a patter of falling small objects that had momentarily been windborne. The site of the house was entirely obscured by an eddying cloud of dust.

The dust settled slowly. Where the window had been, there was a great hole in the ground, a perfectly square hole a hundred feet across and perhaps ten feet deep, its bottom as flat as a table. Gilson's glimpse of it before the wind had rushed in to fill the vacuum had shown the sides to be as smooth and straight as if sliced through cheese with a sharp knife; but now small landslides were occurring all around the perimeter, as topsoil and gravel caved and slid to the bottom and the edges were becoming ragged and irregular.

Gilson and Krantz slowly rose to their feet. "And that seems to be that," Gilson said. "It was here and now it's gone. But where's the prefab? Where's Culvergast?"

"God knows," Krantz said. He was not being irreverent. "But I think he's gone for good. And at least he's not where those things are."

"What are they, do you think?"

"As you said, certainly not human. Less human than a spider or an oyster. But, Gilson, the way they look and dress, that house—"

"If there's an infinite number of possible worlds, then every possible sort of world will exist."

Krantz looked doubtful. "Yes, well, perhaps. We don't know anything, do we?" He was silent for a moment. "Those things were pretty frightening, Gilson. It didn't take even a fraction of a second for her to react to Reeves. She knew instantly that he was alien, and she moved instantly to destroy him. And that's a baby one. I think maybe we can feel safer with the window gone."

"Amen to that. What do you think happened to it?"

"It's obvious, isn't it? They know how to *use* the energies Culvergast was blundering around with. The book—it has to be a book of spells. They must have a science of it—tried-and-true stuff, part of their received wisdom. That thing used the book like a routine, everyday tool. After it got over the excitement of its big feed, it didn't need more than twenty minutes to figure out how Reeves got there, and what to do about it. It just got its book of spells, picked the one it needed (I'd like to see the index of that book) and said the words. Poof! Window gone and Culvergast stranded, God knows where."

"It's possible, I guess. Hell, maybe even likely. You're right, we don't really know a thing about all this."

Krantz suddenly looked frightened. "Gilson, what if—look. If it was that easy for him to cancel out the window, if he has that kind of control of telekinetic power, what's to prevent him from getting a window on *us*? Maybe they're watching us now, the way we were watching them. They know we're here now. What kind of ideas might they get? Maybe they need meat. Maybe they—my God."

"No," Gilson said. "Impossible. It was pure, blind chance that located the window in that world. Culvergast had no more idea what he was doing than a chimp at a computer console does. If the Possible-Worlds Theory is the explanation of this thing, then the world he hit is one of an infinite number. Even if the things over there do know how to make these windows, the odds are infinite against their finding us. That is to say, it's impossible."

"Yes, yes, of course," Krantz said gratefully. "Of course. They could try forever and never find us. Even if they wanted to." He thought for a moment. "And I think they do want to. It was pure reflex, their destroying Reeves, as involuntary as a knee jerk by the look of it. Now that they know we're here, they'll have to try to get at us; if I've sized them up right, it wouldn't be possible for them to do anything else."

Gilson remembered the eyes. "I wouldn't be a bit surprised," he said. "But now we both better—"

"*Dr. Krantz!*" someone screamed. "*Dr. Krantz!*" There was absolute terror in the voice.

The two men spun around. The soldier with the stopwatch was pointing with a trembling hand. As they looked, something white materialized in the air above the rim of the pit and sailed out and downward to land beside a similar object already lying on the ground. Another came; then another, and another. Five in all, scattered over an area perhaps a yard square.

"It's bones!" Krantz said. "Oh, my God, Gilson, it's bones!" His voice shuddered on the edge of hysteria.

Gilson said, "Stop it, now. Stop it! Come on!" They ran to the spot. The soldier was already there, squatting, his face made strange by nausea and terror. "That one," he said, pointing. "That one there. That's the one they threw to the dog. You can see the teeth marks. Oh, Jesus. It's the one they threw to the dog."

They've already made a window, then, Gilson thought. They must know a lot about these matters, to have done it so quickly. And they're watching us now. But why the bones? To warn us off? Or just a test? But if a test, then still why the bones? Why not a pebble—or an ice cube? To gauge our reactions, perhaps. To see what we'll do.

And what *will* we do? How do we protect ourselves against *this*? If it is in the nature of these creatures to cooperate among themselves, the fine little family will no doubt lose no time in spreading the word over their whole world, so that one of these days we'll find that a million million of them have leapt simultaneously through such windows all over the earth, suddenly materializing like a cloud of huge carnivorous locusts, swarming in to feed with that insensate voracity of theirs until they have left the planet a desert of bones. Is there any protection against that?

Krantz had been thinking along the same track. He said shakily, "We're in a spot, Gilson, but we've got one little thing on our side. We know when the damn thing opens up, we've got it timed exactly. Washington will have to go all out, warn the whole world, do it through the U.N. or something. We know right down to the second when the window can be penetrated. We set up a warning system, every community on earth blows a whistle or rings a bell when it's time. Bell rings, everybody grabs a weapon and stands ready. If the things haven't come in five seconds, bell rings again, and everybody goes about his business until time for the next opening. It could work, Gilson, but we've got to work fast. In fifteen hours and, uh, a couple of minutes it'll be open again."

Fifteen hours and a couple of minutes, Gilson thought, then five seconds of awful vulnerability, and then fifteen hours and twenty minutes of safety before terror arrives again. And so on for—how long? Presumably until the things come, which might be never (who knew how their minds worked?), or until Culvergast's accident could be duplicated, which, again, might be never. He questioned whether human beings could exist under those conditions without going mad; it was doubtful if the psyche could cohere when its sole foreseeable future was an interminable roller coaster down into long valleys of terror and suspense and thence violently up to brief peaks of relief. Will a mind continue to function when its only alternatives are ghastly death or unbearable tension endlessly protracted? Is there any way, Gilson asked himself, that the race can live with the knowledge that it has no assured future beyond the next fifteen hours and twenty minutes?

And then he saw, hopelessly and with despair, that it was not fifteen hours and twenty minutes, that it was not even one hour, that it was no time at all. The window was not, it seemed, intermittent. Materializing out of the air was a confusion of bones and rent clothing, a flurry of contemptuously flung garbage that clattered to the ground and lay there in an untidy heap, noisome and foreboding.

INSECTS IN AMBER

TOM REAMY

Tom Reamy (1935–1977) first began publishing in 1974,
when his story "Twilla" appeared in *F & SF*. By the time
of his death in 1977, his writings had earned him considerable stature in the field of science fiction and fantasy and
established him as a writer of immense talent. His story
"San Diego Lightfoot Sue" garnered him the Nebula Award
in 1976, the same year in which he received the John W.
Campbell Award for best new science fiction writer. After
his death his short fiction was collected and published along
with his only novel, *Blind Voices* (1978). "Insects in Amber"
is a fine example of Tom Reamy's imaginative style. It is a
gripping story that opens with a haunted house scenario
and then turns into something quite different. . . .

The storm built in the southwest,
turning the air to underwater blue, making the flat land look like the
bottom of the sea. Lightning flickered in the approaching darkness and
threw fleeting shimmers on the rolling clouds. Thunder that had been
distant rumbles soon crackled across the Kansas prairie unhindered.

Tannie and I watched the spectacular display through the rear window
of the new Buick station wagon. The rain followed us like a vague, miles-
long curtain. It caught us in minutes and turned the late afternoon to
night.

My father grunted and flipped on the lights and windshield wipers. He braked the station wagon carefully and hunched over the steering wheel peering into the downpour. Thunder crashed and rattled around us. The lightning flashes were so brilliant that they left a white streak floating before your eyes. The windshield wipers snicked away merrily, but futilely.

Tannie sat beside me bright-eyed with excitement. She was seven and had one of those inquisitive minds that drove certain adults up the wall.

We were starting out on one of those vacations the auto manufacturers, the motel owners, the resort owners, the tire companies, Howard Johnson's and the curio sellers on Route 66 like to promote. We had piled into the station wagon for three weeks of butt-numbing travel. We left Lubbock that morning (my father was an associate professor of English at Texas Tech) planning to go up through Kansas, Nebraska, South Dakota, over to Wyoming and Yellowstone, then back through Colorado and home. It wasn't the kind of vacation I would have initiated, though I didn't mind it that much.

I was fifteen, not too far from sixteen, and if given a guilt-free choice, I would have probably stayed in Lubbock to goof around with my friends. But since I had a special relationship with my family, the trip was no sacrifice.

We had planned to make it to Dodge City by nightfall, but the rain seemed to have put the kibosh on that. Dad was creeping along about twenty miles an hour, barely able to see the road. It went like that for a while until we came up behind a couple of other cars going even slower. We were behind a red Firebird with Arizona plates, and it was behind an old pickup truck. Dad didn't try to pass, and the Firebird seemed content to stay where it was too.

Mom squinted at an Exxon roadmap. "The next town is Hawley, but it looks pretty small," she said. "It's an open circle, which means"—she shuffled the map, "ah . . . under a thousand."

"Let's hope it's not too small to have a motel," Dad said, giving up on Dodge City.

"I don't care about a motel," Tannie chirped. "I just hope there's someplace to eat." She sat with her nose pressed against the window, fogging up the glass with her breath and then drawing pictures in it.

"Eat?" I laughed. "You've eaten enough today to kill a horse." I knew she really was hungry, but she liked me to tease her.

Tannie turned from the window and surveyed me coolly, but with a twinkle in her eye. I knew she was about to devastate me. She leaned back in the seat and crossed her arms. "There's a little too much sibling rivalry in this seat," she said with an ultra-ladylike air.

I groaned. She was always saying something like that. Mom and Dad laughed. I could see Tannie's mouth beginning to twitch. She wouldn't be able to hold that lofty expression very long.

"It's your own fault, Ben." Dad chuckled. "You should never have told her she was precocious."

"Yeah." Tannie grinned. "I looked it up."

"Uh-oh," Dad said. He stopped laughing and slowed the station wagon. I leaned on the back of the front seat and looked over Mom's shoulder. Wooden barricades with amber flashers were in the road ahead. Two cars were already stopped: a yellow Volkswagen and a dark, sedate sedan that may have been a Chevrolet. The pickup stopped behind the sedan, the Firebird stopped behind the pickup, and we stopped behind the Firebird. Everyone sat there for a bit in a neck-craning session; then a man in a raincoat got out of the passenger side of the VW.

He hurried around to the driver's side of the sedan, apparently intending to get in without comment, but the guy in the pickup stuck his head out the window and said something. The man in the raincoat hesitated, rather reluctantly, I thought, then came back to the pickup and stood there talking.

"Guess I'd better get out and see what's going on," Dad said with a resigned sigh.

"Charles, you're gonna get soaked."

Dad twisted around in the seat. "Ben, can you get to the umbrella back there?"

I got on my knees in the seat and dug around in the back among the suitcases, blankets, cardboard boxes full of who knows what, and all kinds of vacation gear. I finally found it and handed it to him. As Dad got out in the rain, a girl got out of the VW, also with an umbrella. They met at the pickup. Then a guy got out of the Firebird and joined them. It was turning into a convention.

They stood there in the pouring rain, all four of them, talking and waving their arms and pointing this way and that. Mostly it was the man from the sedan and the guy in the pickup. He was the smart one—he was in out of the rain. Then, after a while, they dispersed.

"We gotta take a detour," Dad said when he got back in.

"What's wrong?" Mom asked.

"Highway's underwater up ahead."

"Could you see it?" Tannie perked up at the first sign of disaster.

"No. The girl in the VW said a highway patrolman in a yellow slicker told her the road was flooded. He stopped her, and then the old gentleman in the sedan came along. Seems they know each other."

"Did he say the detour was safe?" Mom asked, looking at the rain with a little frown.

"I don't know. The patrolman seems to have disappeared. The guy in the pickup lives around here. He said it was okay."

Tannie bounced in the seat. "Isn't this exciting?" she squeaked.

"You won't think so if we have to spend the night in the car stuck in the mud somewhere," I said.

Dad grimaced. "Hold that thought, Cheerful Charlie," he said, and started the motor.

The sedan pulled around the VW and turned left onto a gravel road that cut off the highway at the barricades. The VW followed him, then the pickup, then the Firebird, and then us. Just like a camel caravan. The road wasn't bad, a little rough with lots of standing puddles.

I turned around in the seat and looked back at the highway, but I couldn't see the flashers anymore. We must have gone over a rise, although I hadn't noticed doing so. I also thought I saw the headlights of a car go by on the highway, but with the rain I wasn't sure. It must have been lightning.

Mom and Dad didn't talk. The farther we traveled from the highway, the darker it seemed to get. Mom watched the road nervously, and Dad kept his attention on his driving. Even Tannie was quiet for a change. She had her nose against the window again, trying to see by the frequent flashes of lightning. I don't know how far we had gone. It probably seemed farther than it was because we were moving so slowly.

Then I pressed my nose against the window and looked out. I don't know if it was coincidence or not, but it couldn't have been better if it had been staged by Alfred Hitchcock. There was a tremendous rattle of thunder and a flash of lightning that lingered for an unaccountably long time. I saw a house some fifty yards from the road on top of a low hill. It looked quite old, a big, boxy shape with lots of tall chimneys and gables and a tower on one corner. The lightning faded slowly, and I turned my head to follow it, but the lightning wasn't repeated.

I turned as Dad braked the station wagon to a stop. The other cars in the caravan were stopped also, their brake lights flicking on and off.

"You think somebody got stuck in the mud?" Tannie asked with a faint current of desire under the question. I think she would gladly be attacked by tigers just to find out what it was like.

"Let's hope not," Dad grunted.

Somebody up the row honked his horn. "Looks like they're calling another conference," I said.

"Looks like you're right." Dad pulled out the umbrella.

I leaned my arms on the back of the seat and watched them gather around the pickup truck again. Then the rain slacked or something, and I could see by the headlights of the sedan a sheet of muddy water flowing across the road. Trash and debris swirled around on it, weeds and tree limbs.

After a bit they disbanded and Dad got back in, wrestling with the umbrella. "This road is flooded too," he said in a discouraged voice. "We'll have to turn around and go back."

"Doesn't look like there's room to turn around. You might get stuck in the ditch," Mom said matter-of-factly. She was worried but wouldn't show it; she didn't want to frighten Tannie and me.

"According to the guy in the pickup, we just passed, quote, the old Weatherly place, unquote. We're supposed to back up and turn around in the drive."

"Yeah," I said, "I saw it. Looked like something out of a horror movie."

"Terrific," Dad groaned.

"I want to see!" Tannie squealed, and scrambled on top of me, pasting her face against the damply cool window.

"Watch it!" I grunted. "You've got bony knees."

"Okay. Hold it down back there," Dad said, but he was smiling. He backed the car slowly, looking over his shoulder.

"Can you see where you're going?" Mom asked.

"Actually, no." He grimaced.

Dad had it the worst. The others could see by the headlights of the car behind them. Tannie and I had our noses against the window again, watching for the house. A flash of lightning came right on cue. Tannie let out a little sigh of appreciation.

Dad stopped the station wagon with a lurch. Brake lights flashed on sequentially down the row. Dad raised up in the seat and examined the drive critically with a little frown on his face. A culvert crossed the ditch of rushing water, though more water seemed to be going over the drive than under it. He looked at Mom. She looked at the water. Dad shrugged, rippled a tattoo on the steering wheel with his fingernails, and pulled slowly in.

The front end had nosed in about three feet, when it lurched suddenly sideways and slipped into the ditch.

"Are we stuck in the mud?" Tannie asked with cloying innocence.

"I wouldn't be at all surprised." Dad put the station wagon in reverse and tried to back out. The tires whined and the rear end slithered farther into the road. Dad cut the engine and settled back in the seat with a snort.

"Looks like it's time for another conference," I said when I saw the others converging on us.

"Don't be a wiseacre," he groaned. He grabbed the umbrella and got out. I scooted over to the other side and rolled down the window so I could hear.

"Sorry, folks," Dad said.

"Tough luck, Mr. Henderson." That was the guy from the Firebird. They had apparently introduced themselves at a previous conference.

The girl in the yellow Volkswagen was Ann Callahan. She was twenty and absolutely lovely. That was the first time I had had a good look at her. When I did, I couldn't keep my eyes off her.

The old guy in the sedan was Professor Philip Weatherly. That's right: Weatherly, as in "the old Weatherly place." He was sixty, with a kindly but slightly befuddled expression. I also caught, inadvertently, a certain amount of nervous strain, but I didn't think much about it under the circumstances.

Carl Willingham was the driver of the pickup. He was about fifty, with a slightly protuberant beer belly and a cigar that he worried about in his mouth. He was wearing boots and a sweat-darkened Stetson. I think he had been sent over by central casting.

The guy from the Firebird was Poe McNeal. He was about twenty-five, with a cheerful face and a quick smile. He had a stocky, muscular build and a pleasant rather than handsome face. I liked him immediately.

Ann Callahan and Carl Willingham went to the front of the car, as close as they could get without wading, and examined the mired wheels.

"It wasn't your fault, Mr. Henderson," she said with a voice that did funny things to me. "The pipe is clogged and the drive was badly undercut."

The others moved up to check on it. "Maybe we could put something under the wheels to give it some traction," Poe McNeal suggested.

"Won't do no good," Carl Willingham grunted. "Car's too heavy and in too deep. Have to get a tow truck." The brown water swirled around the bumper.

"Great," Dad said. "How do we do that?"

"I guess we could wait till another car comes along and send them," Poe said without much conviction.

"How will they turn around?" Trust Dad to put his finger on it. "We may have three hundred cars piled up here before the night's over."

Poe grinned. "The tow truck drivers will love it."

"What about that house there?" Dad asked, squinting through the rain. A flash of lightning and a roll of thunder punctuated his question. Much too convenient; more like William Castle than Alfred Hitchcock.

"I noticed some chimneys. Maybe there's a fireplace where we can dry out and get warm." That was Ann.

Carl looked up the hill with displeasure. "Nobody lived in that house for fifty years. Like as not, it's about to fall down."

"Guess we could check it out," Poe said doubtfully. "Do you think the owner would mind a band of pilgrims taking refuge?"

Professor Weatherly spoke for the first time. "I suppose I'm the owner. You have my permission." His voice had a tenseness in it, like somebody with a pat hand.

Carl's frown grew deeper. "Don't know that I'd fancy spending the night in that house."

"Don't tell me it's haunted!" Poe cried with suppressed excitement.

"Don't rightly know," Carl answered with no trace of humor, "though I've heard folks talk."

The professor looked at Carl with a little frown, as if he'd misread one of his cards.

"I'll get a flashlight," Dad said, and opened the door of the station wagon. He leaned in, trying to keep himself covered with the umbrella. "Ben, hand me the flashlight." He looked at Mom. "We're gonna check out that house to see if it's fit to spend the night in." Mom nodded and looked through the darkness, trying to see it.

I dug the flashlight out from behind the seat. "May I go with you?"

"No, you can't. If it's not fit, there's no point in your getting wet."

"Heck!" I said.

"Heck, yourself." Then he grinned. "Come on."

I got another umbrella from the backseat cornucopia and scrambled out. Poe was leaning in the window of the Firebird telling the other people what was happening. Then we all traipsed up the hill to the house.

With the darkness and the rain and trying to see where we were putting our feet, none of us really paid much attention to the house until we made it to the old-fashioned porch around three sides. Once out of the rain, we looked about without saying anything. The house was a little weather-beaten and badly needed paint, but it wasn't what one would call dilapidated. A few pieces of gingerbread were missing from around the top of the porch, and a few boards squeaked when stepped on, but I've seen people living in a lot worse.

Dad looked at the others and opened the wide front door with a fanlight over it. He shined the flashlight around, and the rest of us crowded in behind him. My arm bumped Ann's. She smiled at me. It was just one of those friendly but noncommittal smiles you give to strangers, but I felt my face getting warm.

We were in a large entry hall—I finally noticed. A wide stairway ascended to a second floor landing at the rear. We looked at each other with no small amount of bewilderment. Everything was clean and free of dust. The carpet running down the middle of the hall and up the stairs was faded but in good condition. The lace curtains over the windows on either side of the door, though somewhat yellowed with age, were clean. A tall grandfather clock at the top of the stairs suddenly rattled and struck six times. We all stared at it, hardly breathing, until it finished.

"When does Vincent Price arrive?" Poe muttered.

"What?" Ann said, turning her head suddenly toward him.

"Nothing." He grinned.

Dad looked at Carl. "Are you sure this has been empty for fifty years?"

He shrugged stoically. "Always thought it was. Musta been wrong."

We wandered into the living room (though I imagine it was called a parlor in its day) which opened to the left off the entry hall. "If this belongs to you, Professor," Ann said softly, "you should know if anyone's been living here."

He was genuinely confused. "Mr. Willingham's right. No one *has* lived here for fifty years. When I was last here, thirty-five years ago, I hired a man to look after the place. Apparently he's doing his job very well."

The living room/parlor was completely and neatly furnished in that blocky, ungainly style of the early twenties. Even so, it didn't actually look as if someone lived there; more like a display; the Sunday parlor kept spotlessly unused for company that never came.

"There's wood for the fireplace." Dad brightened. "I was afraid we might have to burn the furniture."

Poe wrinkled his nose. "Wouldn't hurt."

The professor came out of his mood. "Why don't you get the others from the cars and whatever else you might need while Mr. Willingham and I get a fire going?"

So we reentered the downpour and slogged back to the cars. Ann smiled at me as we went down the porch steps. I missed one with my foot and had to grab the railing. Damnation!

When we returned with the suitcases, blankets, and everything else we could carry, Weatherly and Carl had a crackling fire going. That and the half-dozen kerosene lamps scattered around the room made it almost cheerful. We all trooped in, bustling around, shedding raincoats and umbrellas, and looking around tentatively. Everyone was happily excited and seemed to regard the whole thing as an adventure.

"This is terrific," Linda McNeal said with delight. "I was expecting spiders and rats." Poe's wife was twenty-two, blond, pink, and pretty—and very pregnant. Poe helped with her raincoat. I liked Linda as much as I did Poe.

"Either that, or some farmer would be using it to store hay." That was Judson Bradley Ledbetter, known professionally as Jud Bradley—he thought Ledbetter sounded a bit too hayseed. It was easy enough to tell he was Linda's brother. He was also blond, pink, and pretty, but with a dark undercurrent missing in Linda. I thought he was a bit overdressed and had obviously swiped his shoes from Carmen Miranda.

"Where are the ghosts?" Tannie asked, ready to get down to business.

"They don't show up till midnight," I said with a straight face.

"Stop it, Ben," Mom said. "You know she believes everything you tell her."

"You okay, hon?" Poe said to his wife. "You oughtn't to catch cold."

"You're the one who looks like you've been swimming with your clothes on."

He grinned. "I was expecting Fred MacMurray to paddle by in a rowboat."

"*The Rains of Ranchipur!*" Linda cried gleefully.

"Right!"

Mom wasn't one to let things go untended. "I have some towels in the suitcases," she said, and fished out several. She handed one to Linda.

"Thank you." Linda smiled. "Just my hair and feet are wet."

"Is this your first?" Mom asked.

"Yes. It's all sorta terrific, isn't it?"

"Yes, it is." Mom laughed. "I felt the same way when I had my two. Here, sit by the fire and take off your shoes." She and Poe pushed one of the chairs closer to the fire and fussed over Linda. Then she gave Tannie and me each a towel with instructions to dry everything that was wet.

Mom was in high gear now that she had something to do. I guess that's one of the reasons she made such a good faculty wife. There are a lot of women who can't hack it. I've seen perfectly level-headed women go glassy-eyed at the thought of one more faculty tea, and assistant professors' wives seriously consider sticking their heads in the oven after being cut down by a *full* professor's wife—delicately and with no visible wounds, of course.

Mom says a faculty wife has to be one-quarter hostess, one-quarter scullery maid, one-quarter diplomat, one-quarter secret agent, and one hundred percent saint.

"If everyone is getting settled," the professor said in his role as reluctant leader of the castaways, "I'll get my suitcases. I also have some food."

"I'll go with you," Dad volunteered. "We have some coffee in the car."

"Thank you," Weatherly replied. "There's a stove in the kitchen but, I'm afraid, no hot water."

"Clare, will you put some water on?" Dad asked. "We'll be right back."

"Of course."

They left and everyone was snuggling in quite comfortably. I got dry socks for myself and Tannie from the suitcase. Mom and Poe still hovered over Linda. Carl Willingham and Judson Bradley Ledbetter rotated themselves in front of the fire, drying off. Jud soon gave it up and went into another room to put on dry clothes, after fussing around in several matched pieces of luggage.

"When is it due?" Mom asked, not quite having exhausted the topic of babies.

"Five weeks," Linda said.

"We were on our way to visit Linda's parents in Wichita before she got too big to travel." Poe smiled a proud and slightly mystified father-to-be smile. "We live in Flagstaff."

"Oh, Poe," Linda moaned. "They're gonna be so worried when we don't show up. We were supposed to be there by eight."

"I know, hon, but there's nothing we can do about it."

"Would you like a blanket?" Mom handed her one before she could answer.

"Thank you, Mrs.—" She laughed. "I don't know your name."

"Clare Henderson. I guess that's the first thing we ought to do. That was my husband, Charles, who just went for coffee. My son, Ben, and my daughter, Tannie."

Everyone had the slightly nervous fidgets you get when you introduce yourself to strangers. Except me. I was looking at Ann Callahan just coming into the room from an exploration foray.

"My name is Tania Henderson," Tannie announced proudly. "After my grandmother."

"That's a terrific name," Ann said as she joined us.

"Thank you very much." Tannie smiled at her.

"You're welcome," Ann beamed back at her. "I'm Ann Callahan. From Albuquerque."

"Poe McNeal. I won't mention what the Poe is short for. My wife, Linda."

"That's my brother in there," Linda said, inclining her head toward the closed door, "Jud Ledbetter. He lives in Hollywood."

Mom raised her eyebrows questioningly. "Is he an actor? He's handsome enough to be."

Linda's mouth quivered with a suppressed grin. "He'll probably tell you he is," she said, "but he's a model. You may recognize the back of his head." The grin broke through and Poe chuckled. "He's been in a lot of commercials, but the camera is always on the girl's shiny hair or her gleaming white cavity-free bicuspids. All you ever see of Jud is the back of his head. If you'd like to hear a choice account of the doubtful ancestry of TV commercial producers and directors, bring the subject up." She and Poe both smothered laughter.

"Why are you laughing?" Mom asked in confusion. "He seems fortunate to me."

"Oh, he is," Poe controlled himself. "He makes money hand over fist—a lot more than I'll ever make. You see, Mrs. Henderson, Jud and Linda and I grew up together in Wichita. Jud and I were in the same grade. It's just hard for us to take him seriously. We know too much about him."

Poe plucked at his sodden clothes, unsticking the fabric from his skin. "If you'll excuse me, I'll follow my beautiful brother-in-law's example and put on some dry clothes." He rummaged around in a suitcase and followed Jud.

"I take it your husband and brother don't get on too well," Mom said.

"No, it isn't that," Linda said, hitching the blanket higher around her shoulders. "They've seen very little of each other since high school, and Jud's changed a lot since then. I think the term is gone Hollywood. It's nothing serious. Jud's airs amuse Poe and Poe's amusement irritates Jud."

"Would you care to join me in the water-boiling detail?" Mom asked Ann, suddenly remembering.

"Sure," she said. They took a lamp and went in the direction opposite Jud and Poe.

"I wonder when they read the will," Poe said when they came back.

"Huh?" I asked, because my mind was still on Ann.

"In the movies," he explained, "when a bunch of people are gathered in a spooky old house like this, they generally read the will. But there's always the stipulation that they spend the night. And then the beneficiaries are murdered one by one."

"Poe." Linda frowned. "Don't talk that way. You'll scare Tannie."

"Nothing scares her," I said.

"Does too!" Tannie asserted.

"Either that," Poe continued, undaunted, "or they're lured there by a mysterious host, who then murders 'em one by one."

"*And Then There Were None* and *The Thirteenth Guest*," I supplied.

"Uh-oh." Linda laughed. "Poe's found a kindred spirit."

"Huh?" I said with another example of my brilliant repartee.

"Poe and Linda ask each other questions about old movies," Jud explained with no small amount of condescension. "If one can stump the other, he gets a point."

"It's a game we play on trips to pass the time," Poe said with a slight narrowing of his eyes.

"May I play?" I asked.

"Sure." Linda laughed. "I'm not much of a challenge."

"Be warned, young man." Poe grinned. "You are opposing a master."

"Okay, my turn," Linda said, and looked studious. "Let's see. Ah— how many times was Scarlett O'Hara married?"

Poe turned to me with mock exasperation. "You can see the kind of competition I have. You know the answer to that one?"

"Sure." I grinned. "Three."

"No points for Linda," he crowed. She made a face at him. "All right," he continued, preparing a zinger, "what famous star of B westerns once played the romantic lead opposite Greta Garbo?" He settled back with a satisfied smirk.

Linda looked at him suspiciously. "You're making that up."

"No, I'm not." He laughed.

"Johnny Mack Brown," Jud muttered.

An expression of abject betrayal settled on Poe's face. "How did you know?" he groaned.

Jud raised his pale eyebrows. "You mean that's right? I just said the most unlikely name I could think of."

"I was gonna say Lash LaRue," Linda said with a straight face. We were all laughing when Dad and Professor Weatherly came back. The professor had a suitcase and a picnic hamper. Dad had a cardboard box with instant coffee, Styrofoam cups, sugar, powdered cream, and a bunch of other stuff. We were helping them unpack it all, when Mom and Ann returned, looking smug.

"Water's on," Mom announced. "With a little native ingenuity, feminine intuition, and a lot of luck, we figured out how to work that antique kerosene stove."

"Professor," Ann said with a slight frown, "does your caretaker live here in the house? There's food in the kitchen. Not much, mostly canned stuff."

"I don't know," he said with a befuddled look. "The man I hired lived in Hawley with his wife."

"Maybe some hobo has taken squatters' rights," Jud said.

"Wouldn't be nobody from around here," Carl said with assurance. "Folks in Hawley stay away from this place."

"You're here, Mr. Willingham," Mom pointed out. "Have you changed your mind about the place being haunted?"

"Never said it was haunted," he stated phlegmatically. "Just said folks talk."

What happened then is difficult to explain. Poe and I had gone back to Linda at the fireplace. I was sitting in a chair next to Linda while Poe sat on the floor with his arms around his knees. Everyone else was at a table about ten feet away unpacking the professor's picnic hamper. I was thinking that he surely had brought a lot of food for some reason.

I felt it coming before it hit me, but I was so startled I didn't do anything to protect myself.

There was an impact. Then pressure, pressure that knocked the breath out of me. If I'd been standing, I think I would have fallen.

My head flopped back against the chair. It couldn't have lasted more than a second, but the residue of cold fear was overpowering. The sweet chill of fear, drenched, infused with icy sugar water.

My eyes closed and I shivered uncontrollably. My arms were so weak, I couldn't lift them. I never knew so much fear.

But not my fear.

One eternal second and it was gone, the pressure and the presence gone as suddenly as it came.

I could hear what everyone was saying, their tiny voices far away; and I knew what everyone was doing, not seeing them with my eyes.

In that chill second Ann gasped and looked around quickly, seeking a source. Of what? Everyone stopped talking and looked at Ann, Professor Weatherly with more interest than I could explain.

Then Linda looked at me. "Mrs. Henderson!" she shouted. "Something's wrong with Ben!"

Everyone gathered around me except Jud and Carl. Ann was shaken. They helped her to a chair. Tannie stared at me with eyes like saucers. Mom and Dad knelt beside me. Mom put her hands on my clammy face.

"Darling, what's the matter?"

I tried to open my eyes, but my eyelids fluttered like moth wings, and I couldn't focus.

"Ben!" Dad said, strain and worry harsh in his voice. "Son, say something."

"Mom?" I whimpered. I wasn't ashamed of whimpering. I was thankful I didn't scream.

Mom put her arms around my shoulders and pulled me against her breast, holding me like I was two years old. Dad had his hand on the back of my head. I opened up all the way, let down all the barriers. I sopped up their love and concern and compassion. I bathed in it, swam in it, drowned in it. I let the warmth of it wash over me, let it drive out the chill of that fear.

"What is it, Ben? Are you ill?" Mom asked softly.

"Oh, Mom, it was so scared," I moaned against her shoulder.

"What was scared?" Dad asked in confusion.

My eyes focused on Ann over Mom's shoulder. She was staring at me, staring with surprised recognition. But she was no more surprised than I. Professor Weatherly was looking from Ann to me and back again like a startled owl. Then I saw everyone else was staring at me, too, and I got a little embarrassed. I disengaged Mom's arms and leaned back in the chair because I wasn't sure I could stand up. But I didn't take my eyes off Ann.

"I don't know, Dad," I said, trying to answer his question. "Suddenly, I felt . . . I felt . . . it was like I had my breath knocked out . . . and . . . there was so much fear."

"That's what I felt . . . only not so strongly," Ann said calmly.

Tannie slowly and tentatively took my hand in hers and looked at me with big round scared eyes. I grinned at her and winked. Her little face sort of exploded and she grinned back. Mom turned to Ann.

"Are you feeling better, Ann?"

"Yes, I'm fine."

Tannie suddenly perked up and piped, "It must have been the ghost." A little wave of nervous laughter rippled around the room.

"I think she's right." Poe grinned. "I've seen enough movies to know a haunted house."

"I've heard folks talk," Carl said with a nod of his head.

"You keep saying that," Jud grumbled. "Exactly what do folks talk *about*?"

"This house and what happened here fifty years ago."

"I knew it!" Poe cried, and clapped his hands together sharply. "A house doesn't get a reputation for being haunted unless there's a story to go with it. What happened fifty years ago, a juicy murder?"

"First time I been in this place," Carl said, a little abashed at being the focus of attention. "Nobody I know's ever been inside. Seen it lots of times from the road. Used to be the main road before they built the highway."

"Well, what happened?" Poe squirmed.

Professor Weatherly was distinctly uncomfortable and wished he were somewhere else.

"Happened before I was born, but I've heard folks talk," Carl continued, warming to his subject. "The Weatherlys lived here. Had a right nice farm, folks say. That was before the Depression. Man, wife, two girls, and a boy. Real well liked, I hear, though folks say there was something peculiar about the boy. One night folks livin' close by saw the house all lit up kinda funny. Lights dancin' all over it and flames in one of the upstairs rooms. Thought the place was burning and rushed over to help. When they got here, there was nothin'. No fire, nothin'. They called. Nobody answered. They went inside and looked all over. Didn't find nobody. Just found that upstairs room where the fire was. They say it was the boy's room. The inside was all burned, but the fire was cold out. Nobody ever saw the Weatherlys or heard tell of 'em since."

"Hey!" Poe exhaled slowly. "That's even better than a juicy murder."

"Didn't they ever find out what happened?" Dad asked.

"Nope." Carl shrugged. "Not that I ever heard."

"Professor?" Ann turned to him. "You told me when we were stopped on the highway you used to live around here. In this house?"

"Yes, for a time." He fidgeted, then changed the subject. "Do you suppose the water's boiling, Mrs. Henderson? I'm ready for a cup of coffee."

"Oops!" Mom laughed. "I forgot about the water." She looked questioningly at me and I nodded. She hurried from the room. Ann continued to look speculatively at the professor but decided to let it drop for the moment.

"You said there were people living close by," Poe said hopefully. "Maybe we could walk to one of them and phone for a tow truck."

"And my parents," Linda added.

Carl shook his head. "Ain't there no more. Not many small farms anymore. Reckon there's not another house for four, five miles."

"Forget I mentioned it," Poe grunted, and settled back.

Mom returned with a steaming kettle and put it beside the coffee stuff. We made coffee and sandwiches from the copious picnic hamper and went back to the fireplace.

All of us except Carl; he was standing at the window looking through the rain toward the cars. He was more worried and nervous than the rest of us. Then he turned from the window and joined us. He was frowning and worrying his cigar to a frazzle.

"It's real funny," he said. "I've been kinda keepin' an eye on the road. Hasn't been another car along since we got here."

"Maybe the water went down," Jud said in a bored voice.

"Not likely." Dad frowned also. "It's still raining."

"The answer's very simple," Poe pronounced in mock gloom. "The ghosts lured us here for some diabolical reasons of their own and are now keeping everyone else away."

Professor Weatherly gave him a startled owl look. Well, well, the professor seemed to concur with that opinion. Linda laughed and shivered.

"Poe, stop! You're scaring *me* now."

"Not at all, young man." Weatherly rushed in to repair the breach. "Obviously, they've discovered the detour is also flooded and are turning the cars around."

Poe grimaced and laughed. "Spoilsport!"

Ann picked up the kettle and looked at me. "I'll put on some more water," she said, and left the room. I followed her, kicking myself for not getting her alone sooner.

The door to the kitchen was open. I leaned against the doorjamb and watched her fill the kettle from the hand pump. She had short dark hair—actually not much longer than mine. She was tall, with long, very good legs. With high heels she would be taller than I, but she was wearing sneakers. I was five-ten, but I hoped to make it to six feet in a couple of years. I know I didn't make a sound, and she had her back to me.

"Hello, Ben Henderson," she said without turning around.

The kitchen was dark and gloomy even though one of the kerosene lamps was burning. I had her alone and I didn't know what to say. So I pretended interest in the lamp.

"It's a wonder people didn't go blind with no more light than these things make." I gritted my teeth.

"They probably did," she said, and lit the burner under the kettle. Then she turned and looked at me. She had a faint, slightly impudent smile on her lips. I felt as if I were standing there stark naked. It came so suddenly and unexpectedly, I blushed like a virgin. Then I blushed because I was blushing. The sensation was so erotic, I had to do some fancy mental footwork to keep from really embarrassing myself.

She laughed, but there was only fondness in it. "I'm sorry. I didn't mean to embarrass you. I only wanted to see if you could pick it up."

"Loud and clear," I said, fighting the tingle in the pit of my stomach.

"You're a very good-looking young man," she said matter-of-factly. "You should be used to it."

"It was a little different this time. You *knew* I was picking it up."

She leaned back against the kitchen cabinets. Her voice was wistful. "Don't you sometimes wish you were like everyone else? Do you get sick to death of always knowing?"

"Yeah. Sometimes."

"You're very lucky, you know. Your family loves you very much."

"You don't have a family, do you?"

"No. My parents were both killed when I was little. I was adopted by an aunt. Did you see that?"

"No, not really. I felt sadness and a sense of loss when you mentioned my family. It had to've been something like that."

"My aunt and uncle are very good to me, but, unlike you, there's no warm, comfortable glow into which I can retreat when things get a bit overwhelming."

So I did something I'd been wanting to do since I'd found out Ann was like me. She looked at me with pleased surprise. "Thank you, Ben," she said softly, like white velvet flowing over burnished gold.

"Think nothing of it. Warm, comfortable glows supplied on demand."

"You're an idiot." She chuckled.

"It was real, you know."

"Yes, of course I know," she said simply. Then she laughed. "And watch it, I've picked up that one before."

"Sorry." I grinned. "Involuntary reflex. Besides, you started it."

"You're not a child to me, Ben." I had again that feel of white velvet.

"I know. It takes a little getting used to, I guess. I thought I was all alone."

"Seeing yourself as others see you is true with a vengeance in our case. I guess the worst part of it is so many things are boring."

"Like card games."

"And school. Did you skip a grade?"

"Yeah."

"Me too. I'm in my last year of college."

"One more year of high school. What will you do when you finish?"

She shrugged. "I'll probably.do postgrad work and get my doctorate in psychology." A smile. "That's one field we're very good in." I looked at her and she looked at me. It was good, so good. But we had a problem.

"What do you think Professor Weatherly is up to?"

She frowned. "I don't know. I have a feeling all this has been contrived somehow." I felt the same thing, but I didn't say so. She knew. "He's my psychology professor at the University of New Mexico. When I stopped at that roadblock and he pulled in behind me, I was surprised, to say the least. He said he was on his way to Hawley, that he had lived near there as a child, that he owned some property and had come to settle some affairs." She looked around the room. "This seems to be the property and we seem to be enmeshed in his affairs."

"How did you happen to be here?"

She shrugged. "No reason in particular. After classes yesterday I just decided to take a drive over the weekend. I don't know why. It seemed a good idea at the time, though I'm not so sure now." She looked at me and smiled. I felt the hum of violin strings. "No. It was a good idea." She lowered her eyes. "The water's boiling. We'd better go back."

She turned toward the stove with her back to me. "Ben? What you were thinking a moment ago. I didn't mind."

"I know," I said, and took the kettle. She turned off the burner and looked at me. It never even occurred to me to blush.

On the way back to the parlor we found Tannie sitting on the bottom step of the stairway with one of the kerosene lamps beside her. She had her elbows on her knees and her chin in her hands. She had that perplexed expression she would get when she ran up against something too complex for her to understand. She was obviously waiting for me to help her out.

"Tannie, what are you doing wandering around?" I asked.

"I wanted to see the burned room," she mumbled with her mind still on something else.

"Did you find it?" Ann asked.

"Yes, thank you," she said politely, then looked up at me with a little frown. "Ben, what do ghosts look like?"

"I don't know," I said, and laughed because she was so serious. "I've never seen one."

She looked at her toes and absently scratched her leg. "I always thought they wore sheets, or that you could see right through them. Now I think they look just like people."

"What did you see?" I asked seriously, because I knew she'd seen something.

"There was a lady in the burned room. She was about two hundred years old and wore funny clothes." She looked up at me again with a puzzled little squint. Tannie related all this to me very matter-of-factly, because she knew I never disbelieved her when she was telling the truth.

I put the kettle on the floor and sat beside her on the step. "What did the lady do?"

"Nothin'. She wouldn't talk to me."

I took her hand and stood up. "Come on back to the fire. Ann and I will go see."

Mom, Dad, Poe, and Linda were playing bridge. Carl was looking out the window again, and Jud was reading Rex Reed's *Conversations in the Raw*. Weatherly sat on the couch looking depressed.

"Mom," I said. "Tannie was exploring."

"What? I thought she was with you. Tannie, you know better than to wander off without telling us."

"Heck, Mom." Tannie sighed, expressing the triviality of her offense. "I was just talking to the ghost."

The reaction from Weatherly was so strong that I turned and looked at him. He was a severely startled man.

Mom smiled. "Sure you were."

"I'll be back in a minute," I said, still watching the professor. "Ann and I are gonna look around."

"Okay. Be careful."

"Sure." I retrieved the lamp from where Tannie left it on the stairs. "Tannie was telling the truth," I said. "She saw somebody."

"Yes, I know." Ann smiled.

I smiled back at her because it was the easiest and most pleasant thing in the world to do. "I keep forgetting. Professor Weatherly is definitely keeping secrets from us."

"I know that too. He wasn't telling the exact truth when he said he lived here as a child."

"Didn't he?"

"That part's true. He did. But he was evading the issue somewhere. Didn't you pick it up?"

"I wasn't thinking about it. I seldom read people without a good reason. It's usually too discomfiting and embarrassing. I just sorta close them out like a background noise you get used to and don't hear unless you listen for it—or unless it's very strong, like when Tannie mentioned the ghost. I picked up an extreme dose of surprise and confusion. I don't think the professor was expecting to find anyone here."

We checked out several upstairs rooms, all bedrooms, before we found the burned room. One door, which should have led to the tower if my memory of its position was correct, was locked. I raised my eyebrows questioningly at Ann. She shrugged. The burned room had been a bedroom as well. It looked as if no one had touched it since the fire fifty years ago. The furniture and walls were charred in places but only scorched in others, as if the fire had raged fiercely for a few minutes and then been instantly doused.

But there was no old lady with funny clothes.

When we got back downstairs, Tannie was facing the others defiantly, and near tears. She turned and ran to me. "Ben, would you please tell these people what I saw?" she said with a quiver in her voice.

I knelt and took her in my arms. She put her arms around my neck and valiantly kept from crying. "I'm sorry, honey," I said softly. "When we got there she was gone."

"Do you think I'm imagining things too?" The quiver had grown more pronounced at the thought that I, too, might be against her.

"Of course not," I said firmly. "She really did see someone," I said to the others. I stood up, but Tannie kept a grip on my hand.

"How are you so sure?" Judson Bradley Ledbetter asked with a supercilious sneer.

"Has the ghost made an appearance?" Poe asked with genuine interest.

"You'll have to ask Professor Weatherly about that," I said.

The professor frowned at me as if one of his own troops had turned on him. He fidgeted a bit and then sighed. "I can assure you there are no ghosts in this house," he snapped irritably. "However, you are due an explanation, as I see some of you are letting your imaginations run away with you. Before I explain anything, and I still can't tell you everything, I want to show you something." He went to the table where the bridge game had been abandoned.

"Why can't you tell us everything?" Dad asked, becoming a little bit irritable himself.

"You wouldn't believe me, Mr. Henderson." He sighed impatiently. "And there's no point in alarming you unnecessarily."

Poe grunted. "It's statements like that that alarm me unnecessarily."

"Mr. McNeal," Weatherly snapped, "there are no ghosts; you are in no danger. Please stop this wild speculation." Poe hunkered his head protectively between his shoulders and grinned at me. Ann and I cocked an eyebrow at each other. Weatherly was difficult. He was telling the truth, but I had a feeling it was only *technically* the truth. "Now, everyone," he continued and sat at the table, "gather around. Ben, you and two others sit down."

I sat opposite him, eager to cooperate and find out what was going on.

Ann stood behind me. Mom and Dad sat in the other chairs. Everyone else gathered around except Carl, who watched from the other side of the room. I had the impression he was staying close to the door, on the verge of bolting. Weatherly gathered up the cards and handed them to Mom. "Now, Mrs. Henderson, please shuffle the cards carefully and deal out four hands."

Mom gave him a quizzical frown but did as he asked. Weatherly picked up his cards and fanned them. The rest of us did the same. I had thirteen clubs neatly arranged in order, with the deuce on the left and the ace on the right.

"Now, Ben," Weatherly said, "tell us who has the winning hand if we were playing bridge."

"Dad," I said.

He nodded with satisfaction. "Correct," he said crisply, and laid his cards face-up on the table. He had thirteen hearts. Mom had thirteen diamonds and Dad had thirteen spades. "Explain how you knew."

"I can't explain," I said with a frown. "It's like . . . like explaining sight or sound or smell to someone lacking them. Dad knew he had the winning hand, and I . . . felt . . . sensed him knowing it."

"Did you know exactly which cards he had?" Weatherly asked intensely.

"No. But it wasn't hard to figure out when I saw mine."

"Read everyone in the room, Ben," he said like a wire stretched to the breaking point. He never took his eyes off mine. "Your parents."

"Concern. Love."

"Tannie."

"She's still mad."

"Poe."

"Interest. Wonder."

"Linda."

"Love. Incomprehension."

"Mr. Ledbetter."

"Disbelief. Annoyance."

"Mr. Willingham."

"Nervousness. Stoicism."

"Me."

"Determination." I narrowed my eyes a little, and he knew I read more than that, but I didn't say anything else.

"Ann."

I hesitated. How could I put Ann into words? I couldn't, and so I just grinned like a sap. Ann put her arm around my shoulder.

"Ben . . ." Mom said in a tight little voice.

I hadn't really wanted my parents to find out like this, though my father had known subconsciously for quite some time. He'd never said anything; he hadn't wanted to upset Mom and didn't really want to believe it himself. Now they were both confused and frightened. I started to say something, to try to ease their worries, but Ann beat me to it.

"Don't you see, Clare?" she said quietly. "You and Charles think of Ben as an adolescent. So he acts the part to please you. It's difficult for us to be ourselves and not just the reflections of others. I went through the same thing. No one likes an uppity kid." She ran her fingernails through the hair on the back of my neck.

All I could do was grin and turn red. She hit me lightly on the back of the head.

"Ben . . ." Mom said again.

"I know, Mom."

"So, there you are," Weatherly said, getting us back on the path of his purpose, whatever that was. "Ann could have told me the same things. They are both telepathic and empathic, though Ben is the more sensitive."

"Telepathic," Jud snorted, and poured himself another cup of coffee.

"Don't worry, Jud," Ann assured him. "We can't read your thoughts, only your emotions, your state of mind, and the like."

"But I also knew who had the winning hand," Weatherly barreled ahead. "I knew where every card lay, because I controlled the deal. If I hadn't, I wouldn't have known any more than . . . the man in the moon."

"I figured that," I said.

"How did you control the deal?" Dad had accepted everything completely.

"That, too, is difficult to explain." Weatherly sighed. "Ben and Ann are telepathic and empathic. My own ability is telekinesis, though I believe these days they are calling it psychokinesis."

There was a momentary silence. "What's that?" Linda asked, wide-eyed. Poe had his arm around her and she leaned against him. Poe was quiet, absorbing everything.

"The ability to mentally control physical objects," Weatherly explained tersely.

"You mean mind over matter?" Linda breathed.

"Yes," he sighed, "I believe that is the popular term."

Jud was pacing a short path on the faded carpet. "Let's see you make that shoe move," he snorted, and pointed to Poe's still damp sneaker on the hearth.

Weatherly leaned back in the chair and tiredly ran his hand over his face. He broadcast resignation to the constant interruptions. He nodded and the shoe rose into the air. Mom and Linda gasped. Tannie was watching bug-eyed. Carl Willingham eased a little closer to the door. The shoe made a circle of the room and plopped back on the hearth.

"There's more to it than moving shoes about, Mr. Ledbetter," Weatherly explained impatiently. "Matter can also be controlled on a molecular level. Mrs. Henderson, lift the top card, please, and look at it."

She gave him a curious look and turned the card. It was the three of hearts.

"Turn it face down again." Mom did so. "Now look at it." Mom exposed it once more. The hearts had been replaced by little yellow daisies. "It is now the three of daisies," Weatherly said without looking at it. "I could continue to perform carnival tricks until morning, but there are more important matters. There is something absolutely vital which I must do. I could not do it alone, not without the aid of a telepath. I have been searching for thirty-five years: I had just about given up hope. And then I found Ann. My dear, I must apologize for the way I maneuvered you here."

"Maneuvered?"

"Yes. I'm afraid it's turned into something of an imbroglio, however. I instigated your weekend drive by thinking it at you for the past two weeks. Naturally, you thought it your own idea. I created the rainstorm, the roadblock, and the flooded detour. Of course, I never intended the rest of you people to fall into my little charade. Yes," he sighed, "I seem to have botched it rather badly." He brightened. "But, actually, it has turned out rather well. If things had gone according to plan, I wouldn't have found Ben."

"I don't believe any of this!" Jud flopped onto the couch and stretched his long, fashionably sheathed legs in front of him. He looked away with a sour expression.

."Really, young man," Weatherly said in exasperation, "creating a rainstorm, a couple of wooden barricades, an animated yellow slicker, and a little water over the road differs from controlling a deck of cards only in degree. It's exactly the same principle."

"If you can do all that," Dad said suspiciously, "you could've gotten my car out of the ditch."

"Most assuredly, Mr. Henderson. But, you see—and I must apologize—it was I who put your car in the ditch."

"Why?" Mom asked.

"Oh, dear, isn't it obvious?" Weatherly whined. "In order to keep Ann here, I was forced to keep all of you."

"Why did you go through all these elaborate machinations, Professor?" Ann asked seriously. "Why didn't you just ask me to help you?"

"I couldn't take the chance. If you had refused . . . It was imperative that you come. I'm an old man, Ann. This is my last chance. If I'm unsuccessful again"—his shoulders slumped—"then God help us."

Stunned silence spread over the room like a blanket and lay there. Then Ann spoke softly. "What is it you want me to do?"

"Please be patient with me, my dear." He sighed and ran his hand over his face again. His eyes were bleary from nervous strain, and his skin had developed a putty-colored pallor. I still didn't know what he was up to, but he didn't appear to be in condition to subdue an irritated kitten. "There are preparations that must be made before I explain fully. Imagine"—he brightened—"after thirty-five years I find *two* telepaths."

"Just a minute," Dad said with a hardness in his voice I'd seldom heard before. "If Ann wants to help you with whatever you're doing, that's her affair, but Ben is not to be involved."

Weatherly's chin set firmly. He was about to argue, but Jud jumped up to pace again. He rubbed his hands on the fabric molding his hips and said with nervous volume, "I think you're all nuts! You're sitting around talking about telepathy, telekinesis, and created rainstorms and . . . and . . . as if you were talking about . . . about the weather. All I've seen is a man, whose sanity I am beginning to doubt, do card tricks." He stopped and fixed Weatherly with a pale blue glare.

"Jud, please," Linda whispered in embarrassment.

"Don't forget the shoe," Poe said brightly. Jud transferred the glare to his brother-in-law. Poe grinned and raised his eyebrows.

Jud turned back to the professor. "If you can do all this hocus-pocus, will you kindly turn off the rain, get Mr. Henderson's car out of the ditch, and let us get out of this freak show?" His voice rose a little in volume with each word.

Weatherly matched him decibel for decibel. "I am not a magician, Mr. Ledbetter. I can't snap my fingers and *turn off* the rain. It took two days of careful manipulation to create it in the first place. Besides"—his voice lowered to conciliatory tones—"there is no point in your leaving. You have to spend the night somewhere. It might as well be here. There are very comfortable bedrooms upstairs. If any of you wish to retire, I'll show you the way."

Jud wasn't giving up so easily. "You mean we stay whether we like it or not? My parents are expecting us tonight, and I want to leave!"

"I'm sorry, Mr. Ledbetter. Take my word. It is impossible."

Ann and I looked at each other. We had both caught the same thing.

He was telling the truth as he saw it. It *was* impossible for us to leave—and not because of the weather. But neither of us could get the real reason.

"Take it easy, Jud," Poe said sensibly. "We're so late now, a few more hours won't matter."

"Okay, okay." Jud shrugged elaborately and sat at the now empty table. He picked up the cards and shuffled them. "You go right ahead with your spook hunt. I shall sit right here and play solitaire all night. I don't care if twenty ghosts come traipsing through here rattling chains and moaning their heads off. I shall be totally oblivious to them." He dealt out a hand of solitaire and pointedly ignored us.

Everyone looked at him with some amusement for a moment. His shouting match with the professor had done quite a bit to break the tension in the air. Then Mom sort of shook her head and said, "I know one young lady who needs to go to bed."

"Do I have to?" Tannie groaned. "Things are much too interesting to go to bed."

"Yes, you do." Mom laughed.

She took one of the suitcases and led Tannie out. Tannie said good night to everyone, kissed Dad and me, then gave me a defeated look. I winked at her. They left and Tannie came back almost immediately. "Mom forgot the flashlight," she said. Dad was about to hand it to her, when we heard Mom gasp and drop the suitcase. We all scrambled into the hall. Mom was standing at the foot of the stairs with her hand over her mouth, looking up. The suitcase lay on its side at her feet.

"I saw someone standing at the top of the stairs," she said with a controlled voice.

Dad pointed the flashlight at the top of the stairs and turned it on. There was no one there. The grandfather clock suddenly rattled and struck eight o'clock. A startled squeak escaped from Linda. Dad moved the beam lower and caught a man descending toward us.

He was young, about the same age as Poe and Jud, dressed in rough clothes, with no expression on his dark, Slavic face. That's the way he appeared to my eyes. When I looked at him without using my eyes, he was a featureless shimmer. Dad kept the flashlight on him.

"It's Lester Gant," Carl Willingham said from behind us as if he were identifying a rabid dog.

The man reached the bottom of the stairs and stood looking at us, still with no expression. The clock stopped striking. For some reason, we all took a half-step backward.

"You know him?" Weatherly asked, slipping back into the befuddlement he had only recently escaped. I had the impression he couldn't take very many more interruptions or complications.

"Is this the caretaker?" Dad asked.

"What?" Weatherly turned to him with a slight jerk of his head. "Of course not. That was thirty-five years ago. Wait, yes, the man's name was Gant. What was it? Horace? Homer?"

"Lester's father was Harold Gant," Carl supplied. "Is that it?"

"Possibly." The professor nodded and turned back to the dark young man. "Mr. Gant, is your father the caretaker I hired?"

"Old man Gant's been dead over ten years," Carl said. "Least ways, him and his wife disappeared."

"Ah"—Poe widened his eyes—"more mysteries."

"You don't keep very close track of your caretakers, Professor," Dad grunted.

"What?" His head did another revolution. "Oh, the bank in Hawley handles all that. I suppose they gave the job to the boy when the father disappeared. Can't he talk, Mr. Willingham?"

"He can talk. Heard him myself," Carl stated.

And he did. Four words. I never heard him say anything else. "Missus will be down," he said in flat, colorless tones.

"Who else is here?" Jud groaned.

Weatherly sighed. "I imagine he means my mother, Mr. Ledbetter."

"Your mother?" Mom squeaked. "Why didn't you tell us your mother was living here?"

"I wasn't sure that she was." Weatherly sounded on his last legs. "I didn't expect she would still be alive."

Gant turned without another word and vanished into the darkness at the top of the stairs. Weatherly looked as if he had been kicked in the stomach. He had had one complication too many. After a moment Dad picked up Mom's suitcase and escorted her upstairs.

"You want to go to bed, hon?" Poe asked his wife. "You must be exhausted."

"If it's all the same to you," Linda laughed nervously, "I'll wait until you go. I couldn't sleep up there by myself."

Poe grinned and put his arm around her. They all drifted back to the parlor, but I gave Ann a signal and went out to the front porch. The rain had stopped. I could see stars in the west and a smudge of light where the moon hid behind clouds. Frogs were screaming in damp ecstasy, and a few bold crickets had emerged from their dry hidey-holes. The air had the fresh, clean smell it gets right after a rain, pointing up the slight mustiness of the house. I took a deep breath and leaned against the railing, looking at the cars on the road at the bottom of the hill.

"Did you see it?" I asked when I felt Ann behind me.

"Yes. I've run across it a few times before. Apparently some people have natural shields." She leaned on the railing beside me.

I turned when I heard the door open, but I knew who it was. Carl Willingham nodded to us and went down the porch steps.

"Where are you going, Mr. Willingham?" Ann asked politely.

He stopped and turned, looking up at us. "Leavin' ma'am. Rain's stopped and I'd rather walk four miles than stay in the same house with Lester Gant. I can take magicians and mindreaders"—he dipped his head—"no offense, and even flying shoes, but he's too much. I'd advise the rest of you to do the same."

"What's the matter with him?" I asked, because he was genuinely frightened.

"Folks say he killed his parents. Never found 'em, no proof he did it, but folks know just the same." He nodded again and started down the hill. We watched him for a moment.

"Folks around here sure say a lot," I observed wryly, and we went back in the house. Weatherly was sitting on the couch deep in gloomy thought. I had the impression of swirling, muddy water. Poe, Linda, Jud, and Dad were starting another card game. "Mr. Willingham just left," I said, certainly not expecting the reaction I got.

Weatherly jumped up and stared at me. "Left? What do you mean?"

"He said he was gonna walk to town," I said, completely mystified.

Weatherly was severely agitated. He moved around as if he couldn't decide which direction was the right one. "He can't leave!" he wailed. "He'll be killed! Stop him! Bring him back by force if you have to! Hurry! Hurry!"

Weatherly's anxiety was so strong and sharp that I ran from the room and out the front door. They all followed me, confused and frightened. Carl was almost to the bottom of the hill. I yelled at him. Dad and Poe were right behind me, not knowing what was going on. The others stayed on the porch.

Carl turned and looked at us curiously. His eyebrows rose in bewilderment at the sight of us bounding down the hill, floundering in the slippery mud, yelling like madmen.

Carl, the only one looking toward the house, was the first to see it. His eyes got big. He took a step backward.

Then I felt it, like static electricity in my head. I skidded to a halt on the muddy ground and fell to my knees with a grunt. I looked back at the house. Weatherly was waving his arms and yelling. The crickets stopped singing.

The house was surrounded by a glow, an iridescent nimbus, like a soap bubble growing larger and larger. Dad and Poe had stopped, looking at the house. Weatherly was screaming, waving us back. My head was singing with the sweet chill of fear, but not my fear. The air crackled with energy. I could feel the hair on my arms standing up. Sparks danced across the hill, flowing down it like a faerie river. I turned to look at Carl.

He stared at the house, backing slowly away. The static electricity in the air made his clothes cling to his skin. Then he whirled and ran. The energy pressure was growing unbearable.

Then there was light, an eye-burning flash, a fierce discharge. All the energy floating free in the air gathered at one point. It circled around like a whirlwind of fireflies, swept by me, contracted, converged at one point.

On Carl.

He screamed. Then he was covered with fire. He screamed and ran and burned. He beat at his clothes with his hands, beat at flames with flames. His glowing feet kicked through the damp grass and left little curls of steam that sizzled and disappeared.

Carl stopped his useless flailing and just ran, his arms stretching before him, seeking. Then he stumbled, staggered a few steps, and fell, still screaming. He kept moving, trying to crawl.

The screaming stopped.

Then the movement.

Carl was nothing but a shapeless lump, burning, sending a shaft of black smoke into the night air. The energy and the pressure was gone. The crickets started up again.

I had thrown up my tattered barriers, trying to shut him out, trying to block his agonies from my mind. Then, I think I felt the muddy ground hit me in the face.

I was moving, floating in warmth. Dad was carrying me as he had when I was three and had fallen asleep. I tightened my grip around his neck. Then he was prying me loose, putting me on the couch.

They were all crowded around, looking at me, except Jud. He was staring out the window, pale and shaken. Tannie, in her pajamas, was round-eyed with wonder. Ann put her hand on my forehead and pushed the hair out of my eyes.

Dad was standing a few feet away watching me. I had never known him to be so angry. "Professor Weatherly," he said in a low voice, "you told me there was no danger. I want you to explain exactly what's going on. No evasions. No promises. We'd like to make a few decisions for ourselves."

"I'm sorry, Mr. Henderson," he said with honest regret. "It's too late for independent decisions. There is only one course open to us."

"Did you hear what I said? *I want an explanation.*"

"Of course, Mr. Henderson." He fluttered like a moth. "Give everyone a chance to calm down and I'll tell you all I know."

"Jud. Come away from the window," Linda said. Her voice was hoarse and trembled a little. Jud turned without comment and sat in a chair.

"So the spirits are malignant after all, Professor," Poe said quietly.

"Be patient a few minutes, please. Let's get Ben back on his feet." He looked down at me with real concern on his face. "Are you feeling better?"

"Yes. I think so." I took Ann's hand in mine and squeezed it. Tannie looked at me with her little face pinched and pale. I grinned and winked at her.

"I absolutely refuse to give you a hug, Benjamin Henderson," she stated uncategorically. "You had me scared to death. I thought I was gonna be a widow."

Everyone laughed—more than it deserved, to be sure, but it broke the tension. Even Jud managed an anemic grin. Tannie sniffled. I sat up and held my arms out to her. She threw herself at me and sobbed on my chest.

"I'm sorry, honey," I said.

"Oh, Tannie!" Mom groaned, thankfully finding something practical on which to focus her attention. "Ben is covered with mud. You're getting it all over you." She extracted Tannie bodily. "Ben, go change your clothes and wash your face."

So I went to the suitcase and got clean blue jeans and a clean shirt. I was a bit wobble-kneed, but I tried not to show it. You can take just so much fussing. I went in a corner behind a chair and changed while they talked.

"Are you ready, Professor?" Dad asked, nearing the end of his patience.

"Yes, Mr. Henderson. Everyone get comfortable. I want to explain as well as I can what happened. Ben. Are you feeling it?"

"Yes."

"Describe it to me."

"There's really nothing to describe. It's just there. It's aware of us. And . . . it's just . . . there."

"That's right," Ann agreed.

"There's no hostility? No anger?" Weatherly asked as if he expected there would be.

"Not now," I answered. "It's frightened. I think it's always frightened. There was anger . . . no not anger . . . panic, when Mr. Willingham tried to leave." I finished changing clothes and joined the group.

I was so busy concentrating on Weatherly, I didn't sense her presence. Neither did Ann. No one knew she was in the room until she spoke in her brassy bellow. "Philip!" she brayed. "What are these people doing in my house?"

Everyone turned quickly. I felt Weatherly's resolve become as fragile as cobwebs. She stood in the doorway, surveying us. She wore a long black dress that reached the floor. It had a high collar that pushed her flesh into wrinkles around her sharp chin. The long-sleeved dress was unadorned but for a large cameo at her throat. Her hands rested on a silver-headed stick and her pewter-colored hair was piled on top of her head. Her skin was almost white and had a peculiar sheen—like a wax-works figure come to life. Lester Gant lurked behind her ramrod-straight figure, as inscrutable as ever.

"I'm waiting for an answer, Philip."

"It's good to see you again, Mother." He sounded like a little boy who had been caught doing something naughty in the bathroom.

"You're a fool, Philip," she stated in her clarion voice. "You've always been a fool."

"Yes, Mother, very good to see you again." He sighed.

She speared him with a look and sat regally in a chair near us. She moved as if her spine were of one piece. Gant remained in the doorway.

"You've come to try again, have you." It was a statement rather than a question. The rest of us sat there with our mouths open.

"Yes," he said. "I was about to explain to these people."

"It will kill you as it did the man just now. I knew you were fool enough to keep trying, but I didn't know you were so obsessed as to endanger others."

"They are not here by design, Mother."

"How long has it been since your last futility, Philip?"

"Thirty-five years."

"So long?" she said a little wistfully.

"Professor," Dad said through clenched teeth, "we're waiting."

"What?" He started as if he had forgotten the rest of us. "Yes. Excuse me, Mother." He turned away from her. "You heard how it began from Mr. Willingham. I was ten years old. It was in my room that fire was seen. I had for some time been aware of my powers, but I thought everyone had them. After almost disastrously finding out that wasn't the case, that I was unique, I kept them secret and practiced. However, as you heard Mr. Willingham say, I didn't do it in time to avoid getting a reputation in the area for being . . . ah . . . peculiar. My powers developed with practice, but I was so immature."

"You were a fool."

"Yes, Mother. It happened the night Mr. Willingham told you about. I unfortunately thought I knew all there was to know. You see, I had just read Wells's *The Time Machine*. I . . . ah . . . I'm afraid I attempted to travel in time." He looked at us with an ironic frown.

"Why?" Dad asked a bit dumbfounded.

Weatherly shrugged. "I was ten years old and it seemed like an excellent idea."

"What happened?" Poe asked in rapt fascination.

"My powers were quite strong," he continued, "but my control wasn't. I didn't know at the time exactly what I had done, but I believe, now, that in some way I warped space. And something came through. It was ferocious. All fire and energy. It attacked me the same way it did Mr. Willingham. I tried to fight it but was successful only in saving myself. I ran out of the house and didn't return for fifteen years."

"He ran away and left his family to be destroyed."

"There was nothing I could do, Mother."

"Why did nothing happen to you, Mrs. Weatherly?" Dad asked.

Her head swiveled toward him. "I do not know why I was not destroyed, but I was not. It kept me like a souvenir. Like an insect in amber. I often wish I had been . . . destroyed."

Dad inclined his head toward Lester Gant, still standing in the doorway regarding us impassively. "What about him?"

"Mr. Gant is in no danger," she said with a slightly upward twist of the corners of her thin mouth. "Mr. Gant comes and goes as he pleases. It knows he will return. Mr. Gant is a worshiper." I had the impression this was only a casual volley in an old war. Gant looked at her without expression.

"We were awakened by the commotion in Philip's room." Mrs. Weatherly picked up the story. "My husband and daughters reached it first. I saw them destroyed. I hid in the attic. When the neighbors searched the house, they didn't find me, and the thing didn't bother them. By the time I had recovered from my fright, it was too late. I was unable to leave."

"I returned fifteen years later. I was much stronger and completely in control."

"You should have seen the foolish expression on his face when he found me," his mother said with a slight pucker of her thin lips.

"You were here fifteen years?" Mom said in confusion. "How did you live?"

"Insects in amber require nothing," she answered flatly. "I do not eat. I do not sleep. I am not sure that I am even alive."

"The thing I brought here has no physical existence as we know it," the professor explained. "I think it sustains my mother with its own life energy."

"Is it the same for him?" Poe asked, and indicated Lester Gant. I looked at Gant, still standing immobile in the doorway. His eyes were slightly narrowed and focused on Ann. I didn't think much about it at the time.

"Mr. Gant is here for other purposes," Mrs. Weatherly said with that tightening of her mouth that seemed to denote amusement. "Mr. Gant is here voluntarily. Mr. Gant has secret appetites."

Gant gave her a malevolent look and turned on his heel. She watched him leave, her porcelain eyes twinkling. She turned back to us. "Mr. Gant is blasphemed."

"What did you do when you came back?" Dad asked Weatherly, getting back on the subject.

"I'll tell you what the fool did," his mother brayed as Weatherly opened his mouth. "He tried to destroy it. But it had grown stronger also. And he ran again. Then, rather than letting the house fall down as it deserves, he hired Mr. Gant's father to keep it in repair."

"I did it for you, Mother. I couldn't—" She stopped him with a snort.

"What happened to Mr. Gant's parents?" Ann asked.

"Mr. Gant and I talk of many things, but that is not one of them. They moved into the house when he was a baby. It didn't matter to me. I never left my room. When Mr. Gant was about that boy's age"—she pointed a bony finger at me—"the parents weren't here anymore."

"What are you planning to do now, Professor?" Ann asked.

"My mistake was in trying to destroy it." He frowned. "I know now it probably can't be destroyed. But it must be stopped before it moves out of this house. I don't know why it's still here. I must communicate with it, find out what it wants. That's why I brought you, Ann, to communicate with it. You can't imagine the elation I felt when I found you. Thirty-five years . . ." His voice faded.

"How did you spot me anyway?" she asked.

"Tests." He raised his forefinger. "That's why I became a professor of psychology, so I could test students. Tests of all kinds, to thousands of students. Most of them had been somewhat altered to my purposes rather than the original author's, of course."

"What will communication accomplish," I asked, "other than to satisfy your curiosity?"

"Isn't that enough?" His eyes widened. "But I expect to learn much more. Much more."

"If it can't be destroyed," I asked, "what do you plan to do?"

"I must warp space and sent it back where it came from," he said.

His mother looked at him speculatively. "Perhaps you are no longer such a fool." Then she shook her head. "No. You could have done it without involving the girl. You are still a fool." She stood and walked imperially toward the door. She paused and turned, both her hands resting on the silver-headed stick. "Do not let Mr. Gant know what you are doing." Then she went out the door and up the stairs like a wraith to disappear in the darkness.

"Mom," Tannie said droopily, "could I go back to bed, please? I'm sleepy."

Mom put her hand on Tannie's head. "Maybe you'd better sleep down here, dear."

"Why?"

"Isn't she frightened of anything?" Jud groaned.

Tannie looked at him, surprised at his ignorance. "My brother is here."

Jud grimaced and sighed. "I wish I had your confidence, kid. I really do."

"I guess we're as safe in bed as we are here," Poe said sensibly. "I'm ready myself."

I started for the door and Ann met me halfway there. I took her hand. We went back to the porch while the others bustled around preparing for bed. The sky had almost completely cleared. The night was bright out over the Kansas pastureland. I couldn't see Carl's body, if there was anything left to see. We sat on the railing.

"Ben," she said softly, "do you think we ought to be doing this? You know what happened to you when it killed Mr. Willingham."

"I've been working on that," I said, and turned to face her. "Read me."

She concentrated for a moment then looked at me in surprise. "You're completely shielded. I wouldn't even know you were there if I couldn't see you."

"When Mr. Willingham was killed"—the memory made my skin crawl—"I got the full blast. I've always had a shield of sorts. I don't pick up anything unless it's especially strong or I want to. Background babble doesn't get through at all. That's why I didn't spot you."

She nodded. "I wonder how many others there are, how many we've passed on the street and didn't recognize?"

"I've been trying to strengthen my shield," I continued. "It was relatively easy. It just never occurred to me to try. Here, concentrate on me. I'll let it down slowly. See how it works."

I showed her how it worked and she tried it. We practiced it for a while until she was as good at it as I was. She was quiet then, looking at me.

She stood up and stepped in front of me, facing me. She put her hands on either side of my neck. Tannie has nothing on me when it comes to looking wide-eyed.

"Ben . . ." she said solemnly. "I know what you're feeling about what you can do. You've never explored it before, never really tried to extend the limits of your ability. I know you're strong, stronger than I. But . . . be careful. Don't get in over your head with this thing. Don't get overconfident. Just . . . be careful."

I nodded, understanding. We looked at each other, not reading, just being physical. Then I slid my hands up her arms and interlaced my fingers behind her neck. I pulled her head down to mine slowly. She didn't resist. I kissed her very lightly on the lips, still not reading, enjoying the purely physical sensation. She pulled her head back and smiled at me. I stood up and let my arms slip lower down her back. I felt hers do the same thing. I kissed her again, harder. She kissed back.

We were sitting on the steps, not doing anything, not talking, just being together, when I felt it. It was like a hobnail boot in the groin. Fear and pain, but mostly rage and anger. Ann got it too. She jerked and grunted and looked at me with pain. We jumped up and ran inside. I knew who it was. I did a quick survey of the house. Only one was missing.

I stuck my head in the parlor, where the professor sat meditatively before the dying fire. "Where's Jud?"

He jumped at the sound of my voice and looked at me blankly. I repeated the question more insistently. "He's sharing a room with you," he said bewildered. "The second one on the right at the top of the stairs. What's the matter?" He rose and moved toward us.

"He's dead," I said over my shoulder as Ann and I ran up the stairs. We found him in the bathroom, on the floor, facedown. He was wearing only gold jockey shorts. Blood was still seeping along the crevices between the white floor tiles. His blond fairness was now a pallor. Judson Bradley Ledbetter wasn't beautiful anymore. His shaving kit was scattered about as if he'd had it in his hands when attacked. I knelt beside him and turned him over. I shouldn't have. His chest and abdomen had been thoroughly worked over with a large-bladed knife.

Ann gasped and Weatherly let the air hiss out between his teeth. "Who could have done it?" he whispered.

"Gant."

"Why?"

"We don't know. Perhaps your mother does. She's in the hall."

She was standing there watching us, looking exactly as she had earlier. Poe opened the door across from us and stepped sleepily into the hall wearing pajama bottoms. "What's the commotion?" he asked, rubbing his face. Ann went to him and talked quietly. He looked frightened and hurried into the room we had come out of.

"Mrs. Weatherly," I said. "Jud Ledbetter has been killed." She turned her porcelain eyes on me but said nothing. "We've read everyone in the house except Gant. He's the only one who could've done it. We need to know why."

She narrowed her eyes at me and then turned to her son. "Your foolishness is catching up with you, Philip. Mr. Gant is also a fool. He killed the wrong one."

"What?" Weatherly gasped.

"Don't be an idiot," she snapped. "Mr. Gant is protecting the thing." She turned back to me. "Young man, Mr. Gant will undoubtedly discover his error." She wheeled and walked away into the darkness.

"Ben," Ann hissed. "He meant to kill you."

"I'm trying to remember what we said while he was in the room. He knows that you and someone else are here to help the professor get rid of it, but you were sitting next to Jud when he mentioned it. That means he'll be coming after you next."

"We've got to find him," Weatherly whined. "He could ruin everything."

I gave him a disgusted look, but he didn't really mean it the way it came out. "I'll wake Dad," I said. Poe came back into the hall looking a little sick. Ann and the professor went to him.

Mom and Dad were both asleep. Tannie was on a daybed screwed up like a worm, the way she always slept. I put my hand on Dad's shoulder and his eyes popped open. He started to say something, but I put my finger to my lips and motioned him to come outside. He got out of bed, careful not to wake Mom, and put on his robe, looking at me questioningly.

In the hall we explained everything that had happened. "Do you think Linda and your mother will be safe?" Poe asked.

"Wake Linda and put her in with Mom. Ann, stay with them and bolt the door." She nodded.

Poe was worried. "Don't tell Linda what happened to Jud. Not yet." He went back in his room and closed the door.

"Professor," I said, "you know the house. Where could he be hiding?"

He shook his head. "I don't know. Lots of places. I suggest we start downstairs and work up to the attic. Ben, can you read him at all?"

"No."

We started in the cellar and searched every hidey-hole. He wasn't down there and he wasn't on the ground floor either. Dad had his flashlight, and I had one of the kerosene lamps so we could split up when necessary to prevent Gant from doubling back on us. Poe had a poker he took from the parlor fireplace. He grinned at me nervously and smacked it a couple of times in his palm.

We went back upstairs. Dad shined the flashlight down the hall. Gant was at the door of Mom's room crouched over the doorknob. He had a large butcher knife in his hand. He looked up at us and ran off in the opposite direction, through a door. When we got to it, it was locked.

"That's the stairway to the attic," Weatherly said.

Dad rattled the door a few times, frowning at it. It had one of those old mortise-type locks that could be locked from either side, but only with a key.

"Wait a moment," Weatherly muttered. The lock rattled and went *snick*. The door swung open about two inches with a lazy creak.

Dad glanced at Weatherly, then opened the door the rest of the way. He pointed the flashlight up the steep, narrow steps, but there was nothing except gloom and cobwebs. Dad took a deep breath and started up very cautiously. Poe was behind him with the poker, then the professor. I brought up the rear with the kerosene lamp.

The stairs entered the attic through a hole in the middle of the floor, a perfect place to get your head knocked off when you poked it up. Dad shined the flashlight around, keeping down as far as he could, ready to duck if Gant was waiting. When he motioned the rest of us up, I realized I'd been holding my breath.

The attic was a jumble of discards and had a fifty-year accumulation of dust. The floor was velvety smooth, disturbed only by Mr. Gant's footprints leading into the pile of rubble, and little stitcherylike marks made by crawling beetles. Dad followed Mr. Gant's footprints with the flashlight beam, but we couldn't see him.

Twenty people could have been hiding in all the clutter. I held the lamp high, trying to see into the darkness. It was practically useless; it lit everything beautifully—for three feet in every direction. And when one of us moved, he cast a shadow the size of Godzilla.

The rafters were draped with dusty cobwebs and spotted with little brown mounds made by mud daubers. The flashlight passed over a wasp nest the size of a dinner plate back in the corner. The yellow jackets stirred sluggishly, lethargic in the cool night air.

Dad kept swinging the flashlight around, covering as much of the attic as he could, but Mr. Gant was as invisible to my eyes as he was to my mind. He could have been hiding in any one of many places.

I was about to suggest we lock the attic securely and leave Mr. Gant to the spiders, when something toppled behind me.

We whirled in that direction. The flashlight caught Mr. Gant charging straight at us with the butcher knife drawn back. The whole thing couldn't have taken more than a couple of seconds, but I suddenly had a sensation of slow motion, of Gant running at me through a narrow aisle between stacks of cardboard boxes, of the knife glinting in the flashlight beam, of his shirt flaring out at each step.

I remember studying his face, remember feeling surprise that it was almost emotionless, surprise that he wasn't slavering like a madman. All of this must have been only in my mind because my muscles didn't correspond. I just stood there like a dummy, watching him.

Then he tripped. His toe caught in a picture frame leaning against the stack of boxes. A startled expression crossed his face as his body got ahead of his feet. Instead of getting me with the knife, he rammed into me bodily.

My arms went up and the lamp slipped smoothly from my fingers. I grunted as the wind was knocked out of me. Then Gant and I landed on the floor in a tangle, but the lamp stayed in my line of vision, arching up slowly, very slowly. The thin glass chimney hit a rafter and shattered, then the base, the wick still burning, smashed against a trunk engulfing one end of the attic in burning kerosene.

Mr. Gant lost no time in getting himself untangled; he had landed on top. I was flat on my back. The next thing I knew he was straddling my stomach with the knife drawn back. I twisted as he brought the knife down, and I heard it thunk into the floor beside my ear.

Then good old Poe swung the poker with both hands as if he were chopping wood. It caught Mr. Gant across the shoulders. He yelled and arched his back, his face twisting with pain. He lurched up, gasping for breath, and staggered into the darkness, the knife still in his hand. He upset several piles of uncertain junk, bringing them down with a clatter. Poe and Dad helped me up and I grinned thanks at Poe.

Mr. Gant was out of sight again, hidden by the darkness and the smoke. We turned to the fire. The whole end of the attic was burning furiously. The heat was rapidly becoming uncomfortable. We edged toward the stairs, but the professor was staring at the flames, deep in concentration. We stopped and watched.

A mist began forming in the attic, like heavy fog rolling in. It even smelled like fog. It grew thicker and thicker, closing in on the fire until, finally, it was completely obscured by the bank of white. The crackle of the flames gradually changed to a damp hissing, and then nothing. I could no longer feel the heat. Little beads of water stood on the hairs on my arms, like a heavy dew. The thick mist swirled away as if in a wind, and the fire was out. The end of the attic was blackened and charred, shiny with moisture. Drops of water fell from the rafters, thumping against the boxes and trunks and other debris. Weatherly sighed deeply.

"You're sure handy to have around, Professor," Poe said with a certain amount of awe.

"Carnival tricks." He perished the thought.

Dad swung the flashlight away from the burned area and started to say something. He stopped with his mouth open, looking at something. We turned. Gant was creeping toward us with the knife in his hand. Mr. Gant may have had his faults, but lack of determination wasn't one of them. He stopped when the light hit him. His eyes glittered like marbles. Weatherly was concentrating again.

I heard a harsh buzzing, and the wasp nest almost directly over Gant's head erupted in a yellow and black storm. I don't know what Weatherly did, but the yellow jackets swarmed all over Gant. He screamed and stumbled back, crashing through a pile of discards, swatting at the stinging insects. He kept yelling and threshing, and I guess Weatherly couldn't go through with it any longer because the wasps left Gant and settled back on the nest.

Then, unbelievably, Gant rose from the junk and started toward us again. His face and hands were solid with welts that grew redder and larger by the second. One eye was almost closed, but he came at us, staggering and stumbling, entangling himself in the clutter. He warded off the collapsing debris with one hand and held the knife in the other.

Professor Weatherly groaned. Then the knife in Gant's hand glowed a cherry red. Gant sucked air through his teeth and dropped it, clutching his hand with the other. The knife clattered to the floor. A curl of smoke rose from it. But before another fire could get started, Weatherly did something to it and it was cold once more.

Dad kept the flashlight on Gant. He backed away, still hunched over his burned hand. We moved toward him. His eye was now completely closed, and the other didn't look too good. He still hadn't given up. He grabbed the base of a piano stool with his good hand and drew back to throw it.

Then he froze. The piano stool slipped from limp fingers and bounced off a three-legged table. Gant sucked in air like a fish. He clutched at his chest. I looked at Weatherly, then back at Gant. He breathed in great, roaring gasps, tearing at his shirt. He dropped to one knee, then doubled up and fell sideways into a rusty bird cage. He didn't move. We went to him. He was unconscious but breathing evenly.

I looked at Weatherly. "You could have killed him."

"Yes."

"What do we do with him now?" Dad asked softly.

The professor didn't answer for a moment, then looked up. "The closet in the upstairs hall has a strong lock on it."

So we wrestled Gant down the steep, narrow stairs and locked him in the empty closet. The lock didn't seem to me any stronger than any of the others, but it worked and wasn't loose. The door opened outward, but there wasn't enough room for Gant to get much of a run at battering it down. If he tried, we would hear him. We propped a chair under the knob just in case and stood there looking at each other.

"Now what?" Poe finally said, plucking stray cobwebs from the hair on his chest.

"Everyone should go back to bed. There's nothing more to be done," the professor said.

Dad brushed dust from his robe. "How long do you plan to wait before you attempt to send your monster back where it came from?"

Weatherly glanced at me, then looked morosely at Dad. "I don't know," he sighed. "Tomorrow, in the daylight, after everyone's rested . . . I don't know." He glanced at me again. "We must make sure everything is right. I doubt if we'll have a second chance." He looked at the floor, then back at Dad. "I'm terribly sorry all of you were involved in this, Mr. Henderson. Mr. McNeal. Terribly sorry." He turned and walked slowly toward the stairs.

"Claire and Linda will be very curious about all this commotion," Dad observed.

"Don't tell Linda until in the morning . . . about Jud," Poe said in a strained voice. "She needs sleep."

"Ann has already satisfied their curiosity," I explained.

We moved Jud's body downstairs to the dining room and covered it with a sheet. None of us could think of anything else to do. Then we went back to bed.

I don't know how long I'd been asleep. I'm not at my most lucid when suddenly awakened. I found myself sitting in the middle of the bed wondering what woke me. Then I knew.

I ran into the hall, barefooted and in my underwear. The closet door was wide open. I never found out how Gant got it open without waking someone. I should have known his determination wouldn't have been dampened by a simple locked door.

I burst into Ann's room without slowing and skidded to a halt. Gant had his arm around her throat so she couldn't cry out. They stood near the foot of the bed. Ann was fighting him, but he was too strong for her. He had gone back to the attic for the knife and held it at her breast. His face and hands looked like raw hamburger. He didn't even look at me, though I imagine he could barely see. His good eye was almost swollen shut. But he was lost in some fantasy of his own, and I thought I could detect an expression of rapture on his swollen face. He wasn't holding Ann as a shield or a hostage, but as a sacrifice.

I stood petrified in the middle of the room as he drew back the knife. My face contorted in rage and hate and I screamed a silent mental scream. I don't know exactly what I did, and I've never tried to repeat it. I drew on something I hope never emerges again.

My mind raged at Gant, blasted him with primal hate. Synapses opened like floodgates. The knife froze in the air. My fingernails dug into my palms. My body trembled uncontrollably. Sweat popped out on my face. My eyes locked on his. The arm around Ann's neck fell away. The knife slipped from his upraised hand. He took a step backward, staring at me uncomprehendingly with his red slit of an eye, his mouth slack. Ann stumbled away from him and got behind me.

I didn't stop because Ann was free. The vision of the knife buried in her breast was too vivid. I could have rationalized it as the only way, but I wasn't thinking at the time, only hating.

Gant backed against the wall, but his legs kept moving, trying to get him farther away. His head jerked back and forth, as if he wanted to loosen something clinging to his face. He put his red, puffy hands over his ears and breathed through his mouth. A low moan began deep in his throat. The moan grew slowly in volume and pitch until it was a shrill keening, ending only when his lungs were empty.

I hammered at the bright mirror surrounding him, beat at it, battered against it until it shattered, and I plunged through into his mind.

I thought I screamed, but Ann said later it was a whimper.

I threw up my shields and fought my way out, ripping and tearing, clawing my way free, slashing through the bright chaos and blinding disorder of Gant's mind. As I broke free, I felt his mind dim and go black.

I felt like jelly and slumped to my knees. I couldn't get my breath. My arms hung limp and immovable. Gant was in a crumpled heap against the wall. Ann was beside me, kneeling beside me, her arms around me, feeling me.

A heartbeat began.

Oh, Ben.

Yes. My God! Do you know what I did?

I felt it. Part of it reflected off his shield.

Are you all right? Did he hurt you?

No. I was only frightened. You came.

We can do it now.

No. Not now. Later.

Yes.

The heartbeat continued.

They're all still asleep.

Yes. I never thought it could be so . . .

I know. I know.

I keep forgetting. Ann . . .

I know. Don't be sad.

We've lost something. But we've gained more, so very much more.

The heartbeat ended.

I put my arm around her. She leaned her head against mine and we went to my room. I closed the door behind me and leaned against it, looking at her. She stepped toward me. I met her halfway. We kissed, melded in mind and body. We undressed and moved to the bed, touching and loving. It wasn't only physical love, but I wasn't reading her. It was no longer necessary.

I was me.

I was Ann.

We were us.

When the sun came up we got out of bed and dressed. I went to my parents' room. Ann went to Poe and Linda's. "Dad. Mom," we said. "Poe. Linda," we said. "Wake up. Get dressed and ready to leave. Pack everything and go out on the porch."

"Ben?" Mom said.

"Ann?" Linda said.

"Everything's okay," we said. "We're ready to help the professor get rid of his monster. Hurry."

Ann and I met in the hall and went downstairs. Professor Weatherly was asleep on the couch, tired and gray, slipping into despair.

"Professor," we said with my voice.

"What?" He sat up suddenly, confused. "Oh. Ben. Is it morning?"

"Yes."

"We're ready," the Ann part of me said.

"What?" He stood up, rubbing his eyes.

"We're ready to help you exorcise your monster."

He looked at us. "Something has happened."

"Yes. Ann and I are telepathically linked. It's permanent."

"Describe it to me."

"I'm not sure I can. I know everything Ben's thinking; I remember; I feel everything he feels."

"But there's more than that," I said. "I'm both of us and we're one of us. We're . . . well, essentially we're one person in two bodies. Yet we still retain our separate egos. Perhaps a better explanation would be we're two people cohabiting two bodies. I don't know how it would be with two men, or two women, but with us, it's . . . it's love."

"Yes," he whispered. "Yes. It would have to be, wouldn't it? Total love or . . . total loathing. There could be no other way."

"There's no way to really know what it's like without experiencing it," Ann said. "People who know only physical love are missing so much." We grinned. "Though, I guess there is something faintly masturbatory about it."

"This is absolutely marvelous." He beamed like a child on Christmas morning. "Will you allow me to study this further?"

We smiled at him. "Of course, Professor," I said. "As soon as the others are ready to leave, we can contact your monster. Your mother will not leave. Mr. Gant is dead."

"Dead?" He blinked.

"I killed him," I said. I locked my muscles to stop the trembling I could feel about to begin. "I willed him dead and he died," I said numbly.

Ann put her hand on my shoulder. "We're ready," she said. Vocalizing was slow and clumsy, but it was an old habit.

"Wait here," I told him, and went to the entry hall. They came down the stairs with their suitcases and uncertain expressions, Linda crying, but trying to stop. Poe had told her about Jud. I herded them unresisting onto the porch. Mom and Dad turned and looked at me, frightened. I smiled. "Don't worry," I said. Tannie peeked back at me, saucer-eyed and solemn. I winked at her. She grinned and went on out. I closed the door and went back to the parlor.

"Are you ready?"

"Yes." Weatherly nodded.

"I hope what you find out justifies everything, Professor." We concentrated. A brilliant flash. A sheet of energy swirled around us, held away by the professor, and died out. "Take it easy," I said softly, "take it easy. It's almost insane with fright."

We touched that alien mind. Not entered, only touched. We would have been lost if we had entered. Its alienness was indescribable. There was no point of reference to human thought. We stared in awe at its great shining immature mind. Its alienness made details, even large details, impossible to grasp; but basic emotions, which must be common to all intelligent life, were clear to read. It was aware of our minds, but did not fear them. It feared only what was alien to *it*: Weatherly's *physical* assault.

A smile came involuntarily to our lips. "I'll be damned," I said aloud. "Do you know what we've got, Professor? It's a . . . a baby, if that's the right word. Its memory goes back millions, billions of years; so far it can't remember its origin, but it knows it's immature. The reason it's never left this house is that it's basically a frightened child. It wants only to go home. Send it back, Professor, while I try to keep it calm.

Another flash and another swirl of energy. "It's too frightened," I said anxiously. "I'm having trouble. It wants to go home more than anything, but you'll have to force it. It's irrational with fear. It's been here only a moment by its time scale."

Ann left to get the others to the cars, away from the house. I waited until they were at a safe distance.

"Now. Force it, Professor."

Energy whirled around us like a tornado. The walls, the ceilings, the floors, the furniture, all were burning fiercely, except for the bubble in which we stood.

Weatherly opened a path through the inferno, a path from us to the door. "Go with the others, Ben," he said. I started to protest, but he shut me up. "You can do just as much from outside as you can in here. And I can do more if I don't have you to worry about."

He was right. I had no protection from the thing's physical energy, energy which I suspected was manifesting itself physically because it was *here*, not where it came from. I ran through the tunnel he opened and turned at the door. The tunnel closed and I couldn't see him anymore.

I hurried down the hill to the others, still in contact with the professor's monster. The just-risen sun gleamed on the still-damp house, turning the weathered gray to copper, but flames poured from the parlor windows. Smoke billowed from other openings, the gray clouds also gilded by the sun. Flames suddenly spurted from under the eaves. The fire had gotten upstairs. Energy popped like lightning bolts.

All this I saw with my eyes and heard with my ears. What I saw and heard with my mind was different.

I caught a thought from the professor's mother but shut it out quickly, unable to bear it. The monster threshed in the professor's grip, frightened out of its mind, screaming pitifully.

I watched Professor Weatherly in the parlor but not with my eyes. He stood in a clear island surrounded by raging flames and energy. It began. The inferno cycloned away on one side of him and a tunnel opened, an endless, gleaming tunnel. He stood still, hunched in concentration.

I knew, suddenly, what was about to happen, but the professor was caught completely by surprise. There was nothing I could do to help him. I slammed shields around Ann. She jerked out of her trance and looked wildly about. She screamed at me, "No! Ben! Don't block me out!"

More energy popped. Everyone's clothing clung to their skin. I could feel my hair standing up, charged with static electricity. Helplessly I watched the professor force his monster into the tunnel.

He hadn't moved. He stood before the tunnel, surrounded by an inferno, hunched in concentration. Then, gradually, slowly, his body smudged outward, toward the tunnel. He felt it. He looked up. He strained away from the tunnel, held out his arms, warding it away. The distortion, the stretching outward, continued. His arms were caught in it, extending to half again their former length, blurring toward the tunnel.

Then a particle of his little finger broke away and streamed down the tunnel like a shooting star. More particles broke free. The tunnel was filled with shooting stars, streaking to infinity.

I threw up my shield. Weatherly's terror was too great. But, in that last split-second, I saw a comet roar away down the tunnel, and he was gone. The tunnel was closing.

I was aware of physical sensations only. I stood swaying, trying to keep from toppling over. Ann threw her arms around me. Dad put his hand on the back of my neck, not saying anything. I dropped the shields. Ann and I were one again.

"He did it," I said on an exhaustion high. "It's gone home. He sent it back. But it dragged him back with it. I was with him for a moment."

The energy was gone but the fire wasn't. The old wood of the house burned ferociously. Dad propelled us away, to the bottom of the hill, where the others waited numbly. We stood for a long time, saying nothing, watching the house burn.

Tannie had come to me and stood watching the house with her arm clutching my thigh. I had my arm on her shoulder. "What about you, Ann?" Dad asked.

"With me," I said.

"Yes." She smiled.

Tannie peeked around me, staring at Ann. Ann smiled at her and winked the same way I would. Tannie grinned like a supernova. She launched herself at Ann and hugged her.

The sheriff's car pulled up as we were about to leave. He was a nice person named Robin Walker. We told him a simplified version of what happened, a version he would believe. Ann and I made sure he believed it.

Dad backed the station wagon out of the ditch. I got in the yellow VW with Ann, and we went on to Wichita.

FREE DIRT

CHARLES BEAUMONT

Charles Beaumont is the pseudonym of story and script-writer Charles Nutt (1929–1967), who produced a prodigious number of science fiction and horror short stories during his career in addition to scripting such films as *The Seven Faces of Dr. Lao* (1964). A great many of his stories appeared in *F & SF* originally, and from 1955–1956 he collaborated with Chad Oliver to produce the Claude Adams series for *F & SF*. His stories often combined humor with horror, a recipe that left his readers laughing nervously while glancing over their shoulders. "Free Dirt" is one such story. It is the tale of Mr. Aorta, a man who never learned that there's "no such thing as a free lunch."

No fowl had ever looked so post-humous. Its bones lay stacked to one side of the plate like kindling: white, dry, and naked in the soft light of the restaurant. Bones only, with every shard and filament of meat stripped methodically off. Otherwise, the plate was a vast glistening plain.

The other, smaller dishes and bowls were equally virginal. They shone fiercely against one another. And all a pale cream color fixed upon the snowy white of a tablecloth unstained by gravies and unspotted by coffee and free from the stigmata of bread crumbs, cigarette ash, and fingernail lint.

Only the dead fowl's bones and the stippled traceries of hardened red gelatin clinging timidly to the bottom of a dessert cup gave evidence that these ruins had once been a magnificent six-course dinner.

Mr. Aorta, not a small man, permitted a mild belch, folded the newspaper he had found on the chair, inspected his vest for food leavings, and then made his way briskly to the cashier.

The old woman glanced at his check.

"Yes, sir," she said.

"All righty," Mr. Aorta said, and removed from his hip pocket a large black wallet. He opened it casually, whistling "The Seven Joys of Mary" through the space provided by his two front teeth.

The melody stopped abruptly. Mr. Aorta looked concerned. He peered into his wallet, then began removing things; presently its entire contents was spread out.

He frowned.

"What seems to be the difficulty, sir?"

"Oh, no difficulty," the fat man said, "exactly." Though the wallet was manifestly empty, he flapped its sides apart, held it upside down, and continued to shake it, suggesting the picture of a hydrophobic bat suddenly seized in midair.

Mr. Aorta smiled a weak, harassed smile and proceeded to empty all of his fourteen separate pockets. In time the counter was piled high with miscellany.

"Well!" he said impatiently. "What nonsense! What bother! Do you know what's happened? My wife's gone off and forgotten to leave me any change! Heigh-ho, well, ah—my name is James Brockelhurst: I'm with the Pliofilm Corporation: I generally don't eat out, and–here, no, I insist. This is embarrassing for you as well as for myself. I *insist* upon leaving my card. If you will retain it, I shall return tomorrow evening at this time and reimburse you."

Mr. Aorta shoved the pasteboard into the cashier's hands, shook his head, shoveled the residue back into his pockets, and, plucking a toothpick from a box, left the restaurant.

He was quite pleased with himself—an invariable reaction to the acquisition of something for nothing in return. It had all gone smoothly, and what a delightful meal!

He strolled in the direction of the streetcar stop, casting occasional licentious glances at undressed mannequins in department store windows.

The prolonged fumbling for his car token worked as efficiently as ever. (Get in the middle of the crowd, look bewildered, inconspicuous, search your pockets earnestly, the while edging from the vision of the conductor—then, take a far seat and read a newspaper.) In four years' traveling time, Mr. Aorta computed he had saved a total of $211.20.

The electric's ancient list did not jar his warm feeling of serenity. He studied the amusements briefly, then went to work on the current puzzle, whose prize ran into the thousands. Thousands of dollars, actually for nothing. Something for nothing. Mr. Aorta loved puzzles.

But the fine print made reading impossible.

Mr. Aorta glanced at the elderly woman standing near his seat; then, because the woman's eyes were full of tired pleading and insinuation, he refocused out the wire cross-hatch windows.

What he saw caused his heart to throb. The section of town was one he passed every day, so it was a wonder he'd not noticed it before— though generally there was little provocation to sight-see on what was irreverently called Death Row—a dreary round of mortuaries, columbariums, crematories, and the like, all crowded into a five-block area.

He yanked the stop signal, hurried to the rear of the streetcar, and depressed the exit plate. In a few moments he had walked to what he'd seen.

It was a sign, artlessly lettered though spelled correctly enough. It was not new, for the white paint had swollen and cracked and the rusted nails had dripped trails of dirty orange over the face of it.

The sign read:

> FREE DIRT
> APPLY WITHIN
> LILYVALE CEMETERY

and was posted upon the moldering green of a woodboard wall.

Now Mr. Aorta felt a familiar sensation come over him. It happened whenever he encountered the word "free"—a magic word that did strange and wonderful things to his metabolism.

Free. What is the meaning, the *essence* of free? Why, something for nothing. And, as has been pointed out, to get something for nothing was Mr. Aorta's chiefest pleasure in this mortal life.

The fact that it was dirt which was being offered *free* did not oppress him. He seldom gave more than fleeting thought to these things; for, he reasoned, nothing is without its use.

The other, subtler circumstances surrounding the sign scarcely occurred to him: why the dirt was being offered, where free dirt in a cemetery would logically come from, et cetera. In this connection he considered only the probable richness of the soil.

Mr. Aorta's solitary hesitation encircled such problems as: Was this offer an honest one, without strings whereby he would have to buy something? Was there a limit on how much he could take home? If not, what would be the best method of transporting it?

Petty problems: all solvable.

Mr. Aorta did something inwardly that resembled a smile, looked about, and finally located the entrance to the Lilyvale Cemetery.

These desolate grounds, which had accommodated in turn a twine factory, an upholstering firm, and an outlet for ladies' shoes, now lay swathed in a miasmic vapor—accreditable, in the absence of nearby bogs, to a profusion of windward smokestacks. The blistered hummocks, peaked with crosses, slabs, and stones, loomed gray and sad in the gloaming: withal, a place purely delightful to describe, and a pity it cannot be— for how it looked there that evening had little to do with the fat man and what was eventually to become of him.

Important only that it was a place full of dead people on their backs underground, moldering and moldered.

Mr. Aorta hurried because he despised to waste, along with everything else, time. It was not long before he had encountered the proper party and had this conversation:

"I understand you're offering free dirt."

"Yes."

"How much may one have?"

"Much as you want."

"On what days?"

"Any days—and there'll always be some fresh."

Mr. Aorta sighed in the manner of one who has just acquired a lifetime inheritance or a measured checking account. He then made an appointment for the following Saturday and went home to ruminate agreeable ruminations.

At a quarter past nine that night he hit upon an excellent use to which the dirt might be put.

His backyard, an ocher waste, lay chunked and dry, a barren stretch repulsive to all but the grossest weeds. A tree had once flourished there, in better days, a haven for suburbanite birds; but then the birds disappeared for no good reason except that this is when Mr. Aorta moved into the house, and the tree became an ugly naked thing.

No children played in this yard.

Mr. Aorta was intrigued. Who could say, perhaps something might be made to grow! He had long ago written an enterprising firm for free samples of seeds and received enough to feed an army. But the first experiments had shriveled into hard useless pips, and seized by lassitude, Mr. Aorta had shelved the project. Now . . .

A neighbor named Joseph William Santucci permitted himself to be intimidated. He lent his old Reo truck, and after a few hours the first load of dirt had arrived and been shoveled into a tidy mound. It looked beautiful to Mr. Aorta, whose passion overcompensated for his weariness with the task. The second load followed, and the third, and the fourth, and it was dark as a coalbin out when the very last was dumped.

Mr. Aorta returned the truck and fell into an exhausted, though not unpleasant sleep.

The next day was heralded by the distant clangor of church bells and the *chink-chink* of Mr. Aorta's spade, leveling the displaced graveyard soil, distributing it and grinding it in with the crusty earth. It had a continental look, this new dirt: swarthy, it seemed, black and saturnine —not at all dry, though the sun was already quite hot.

Soon the greater portion of the yard was covered, and Mr. Aorta returned to his sitting room.

He turned on the radio in time to identify a popular song, marked his discovery on a postcard, and mailed this away, confident that he would receive either a toaster or a set of nylon hose for his trouble.

Then he wrapped four bundles containing, respectively, a can of vitamin capsules, half of them gone; a half-tin of coffee; a half-full bottle of spot remover; and a box of soap flakes with most of the soap flakes missing. These he mailed, each with a note curtly expressing his total dissatisfaction, to the companies that had offered them to him on a money-back guarantee.

Now it was dinnertime, and Mr. Aorta beamed in anticipation. He sat down to a meal of sundry delicacies such as anchovies, sardines, mushrooms, caviar, olives, and pearl onions. It was not, however, that he enjoyed this type of food for any esthetic reasons, only that it had all come in packages small enough to be slipped into one's pocket without attracting the attention of busy grocers.

Mr. Aorta cleaned his plates so thoroughly, no cat would care to lick them; the empty tins also looked new and bright: even their lids gleamed iridescently.

Mr. Aorta glanced at his checkbook balance, grinned indecently, and went to look out the back window. (He was not married, so he felt no urge to lie down after dinner.)

The moon was cold upon the yard. Its rays passed over the high fence Mr. Aorta had constructed from free rocks and splashed moodily onto the now-black earth.

Mr. Aorta thought a bit, put away his checkbook, and got out the boxes containing the garden seeds.

They were good as new.

Joseph William Santucci's truck was in use every Saturday thereafter for five weeks. This good man watched curiously as his neighbor returned each time with more dirt and yet more, and he made several remarks to his wife about the oddness of it all, but she could not bear even to talk about Mr. Aorta.

"He's robbed us blind!" she said. "Look! He wears your old clothes, he uses my sugar and spices, and borrows everything else he can think of! Borrows, did I say? I mean steals. For years! I have not seen the man pay for a thing yet! Where does he work, he makes so little money?"

Neither Mr. nor Mrs. Santucci knew that Mr. Aorta's daily labors involved sitting on the sidewalk downtown, with dark glasses on and a battered tin cup in front of him. They'd both passed him several times, though, and given him pennies, both unable to penetrate the clever disguise. It was all kept, the disguise, in a free locker at the railroad terminal.

"Here he comes again, that loony!" Mrs. Santucci wailed.

Soon it was time to plant the seeds, and Mr. Aorta went about this with ponderous precision, after having consulted numerous books at the library. Neat rows of summer squash were sown in the richly dark soil; and peas, corn, beans, onions, beets, rhubarb, asparagus, watercress, and much more, actually. When the rows were filled and Mr. Aorta was stuck with extra packs, he smiled and dispersed strawberry seeds and watermelon seeds and seeds without clear description. Shortly the paper packages were all empty.

A few days passed and it was getting time to go to the cemetery again for a fresh load, when Mr. Aorta noticed an odd thing.

The dark ground had begun to yield to tiny eruptions. Closer inspection revealed that things had begun to grow in the soil.

Now, Mr. Aorta knew very little about gardening, when you got right down to it. He thought it strange, of course, but he was not alarmed. He saw things growing; that was the important point. Things that would become food.

Praising his weltanschauung, he hurried to Lilyvale, and there received a singular disappointment: Not many people had died lately. There was scant dirt to be had, hardly one truckful.

Ah, well, he thought, things are bound to pick up over the holidays; and he took home what there was.

Its addition marked the improvement of the garden's growth. Shoots and buds came higher, and the expanse was far less bleak.

He could not contain himself until the next Saturday, for obviously this dirt was acting as some sort of fertilizer on his plants—the free food called out for more.

But the next Saturday came a cropper. Not even a shovel's load. And the garden was beginning to desiccate. . . .

Mr. Aorta's startling decision came as a result of trying all kinds of new dirt and fertilizers of every imaginable description. Nothing worked. His garden, which had promised a full bounty of edibles, had sunk to new lows: It was almost back to its original state. And this Mr. Aorta could not abide, for he had put in considerable labor on the project and this labor must not be wasted. It had deeply affected his other enterprises.

So, with the caution born of desperation, he entered the quiet gray place with the tombstones one night, located freshly dug but unoccupied graves, and added to their six-foot depth yet another foot. It was not noticeable to anyone who was not looking for such a discrepancy.

No need to mention the many trips involved: It is enough to say that in time Mr. Santucci's truck, parked a block away, was a quarter filled.

The following morning saw a rebirth in the garden.

And so it went. When dirt was to be had, Mr. Aorta was obliged; when it was not, well, it wasn't missed. And the garden kept growing and growing, until—

As if overnight, everything opened up! Where so short a time past had been a parched little prairie was now a multifloral, multivegetable paradise. Corn bulged yellow from its spiny green husks; peas were brilliant green in their half-split pods, and all the other wonderful foodstuffs glowed full rich with life and showcase vigor. Rows and rows of them.

Mr. Aorta was almost felled by enthusiasm.

A liver for the moment and an idiot in the art of canning, he knew what he had to do.

It took a·while to systematically gather up the morsels; but with patience, he at last had the garden stripped clean of all but weeds and leaves and other unedibles.

He cleaned. He peeled. He stringed. He cooked. He boiled. He took all the good free food and piled it geometrically on tables and chairs and continued with this until it was all ready to be eaten.

Then he began. Starting with the asparagus—he had decided to do it in alphabetical order—he ate and ate clear through beets and celery and parsley and rhubarb, paused there for a drink of water, and went on eating, being careful not to waste a jot, until he came to watercress. By this time his stomach was twisting painfully, but it was a sweet pain, so he took a deep breath and, by chewing slowly, did away with the final vestigal bit of food.

The plates sparkled white, like a series of bloated snowflakes. It was all gone.

Mr. Aorta felt an almost sexual satisfaction, by which is meant he had had enough for now. He couldn't even belch.

Happy thoughts assailed his mind, as follows: His two greatest passions had been fulfilled: life's meaning acted out symbolically like a condensed Everyman. These two things only are what this man thought of.

He chanced to look out the window.

What he saw was a speck of bright in the middle of blackness. Small, somewhere at the end of the garden—faint yet distinct.

With the effort of a brontosaurus emerging from a tar pit Mr. Aorta rose from his chair, walked to the door, and went out into his emasculated garden. He lumbered past dangling grotesqueries formed by shucks and husks and vines.

The speck seemed to have disappeared, and he looked carefully in all directions, slitting his eyes, trying to get accustomed to the moonlight.

Then he saw it. A white-fronded thing, a plant, perhaps only a flower; but there, certainly, and all that was left.

Mr. Aorta was surprised to see that it was located at the bottom of a shallow declivity very near the dead tree. He couldn't remember how a hole could have got dug in his garden, but there were always neighborhood kids and their pranks. A lucky thing he'd grabbed the food when he did!

Mr. Aorta leaned over the edge of the small pit and reached down his hand toward the shining plant. It resisted his touch somehow. He leaned farther over and yet a little farther, and still he couldn't lay fingers on the thing.

Mr. Aorta was not an agile man. However, with the intensity of a painter trying to cover one last tiny spot awkwardly placed, he leaned just a mite farther and *plosh!* he'd toppled over the edge and landed with a peculiarly subaqueous thud. A ridiculous damned bother—now he'd have to make a fool of himself clambering out again. But, the plant . . .

He searched the floor of the pit, and searched it, and no plant could be found. Then he looked up and was appalled by two things: Number one, the pit had been deeper than he'd thought; Number two, the plant was waving in the wind above him, on the rim he had so recently occupied.

The pains in Mr. Aorta's stomach got progressively worse. Movement increased the pains. He began to feel an overwhelming pressure in his ribs.

It was at the moment of his discovery that the top of the hole was up beyond his reach that he saw the white plant in full moonglow. It looked rather like a hand, a big human hand, waxy and stiff and attached to the earth. The wind hit it, and it moved slightly, causing a rain of dirt pellets to fall upon Mr. Aorta's face.

He thought a moment, judged the whole situation, and began to climb. But the pains were too much and he fell, writhing a bit.

The wind came again and more dirt was scattered down into the hole: Soon the strange plant was being pushed to and fro against the soil, and the dirt fell more and more heavily. More and more. More heavily and more heavily.

Mr. Aorta, who had never up to this point found occasion to scream, screamed. It was quite successful, despite the fact that no one heard it.

Mr. and Mrs. Joseph William Santucci found Mr. Aorta. He was lying on the floor in front of several tables. On the tables were many plates. The plates on the tables were clean and shining.

His stomach was distended past burst belt buckle, popped buttons, and forced zipper. It was not unlike the image of a great white whale rising from placid forlorn waters.

"Ate hisself to death," Mrs. Santucci said in the manner of the concluding line of a complex joke.

Mr. Santucci reached down and plucked a tiny ball of soil from the fat man's dead lips. He studied it. And an idea came to him. . . .

He tried to get rid of the idea, but when the doctors found Mr. Aorta's stomach to contain many pounds of dirt—and nothing else—Mr. Santucci slept badly for almost a week.

They carried Mr. Aorta's body through the weedy but otherwise empty and desolate backyard, past the mournful dead tree and the rock fence.

And then they laid him to rest in a place with a moldering green woodboard wall: The wall had a little sign nailed to it, artlessly lettered though spelled correctly enough.

And the wind blew absolutely Free.

RISING WATERS

PATRICIA FERRARA

"Rising Waters" was Patricia Ferrara's first fantasy publication, in the July 1987 issue of *F & SF,* and rarely do we
encounter such polish and elegance in a first story. Ms.
Ferrara was born in Attleboro, Massachusetts, within spitting distance of H. P. Lovecraft's grave. After taking a doc-
toral degree in literature at Yale, she moved to Atlanta,
where she now teaches English and film at Georgia State
University. "Rising Waters" is a ghostly tale about strange
doings on a southern river. It is also the reason, Ms. Ferrara
informed us, that she swims only in very small pools which
have lifeguards on duty.

And eventually what had been
the flood plain of the river became part of the river itself, as age changed
the Ohana from a thin, angry sluice into a flat ribbon that rippled in the
sunlight, still as a lake. But Rory had not yet been born when his grandparents had deserted their house by the old riverbank and moved far up
into the gentle hills to a broad swell of land safe from the runoff of a
hundred snowy winters. To him, the river existed with the same reliable
constancy as the school bus. Every morning in the summer he woke up

to the river; and every night he slept beside it, thinking it of only average interest.

Mostly he wondered how he could get a ride into town to play the video games at the supermarket. Space Invaders had been his favorite, and he was startled when, in rapid succession, a Pac-Man game displaced it, and then a Millipede game. The constant change was irritating, because his quarter bought more time on a familiar game. His wrist had never gotten the trick of slipping the gobbling button around the corners, and then the bouncy spiders had proved more than he could handle. The two quarters Grandma allotted per trip bought maybe five minutes of Millipede. Grandma took him to the supermarket only once a week to help with the groceries, unless she forgot something; and since she never forgot anything, he never got any better at the games. Once they had to go back because the milk was sour, and he had to stand with her at the manager's high window while she talked bitterly about out-of-state milk and a sweet-tempered cow that had been dead and gone for fifty years. She'd held on to his arm tightly, grasping at something other than her grandson. Afterward she wouldn't let him play even one game, although he'd come all that way with her. She wanted to go straight home, and she drove there silently, her lips forming a mushy rosebud as she pouted and trembled.

Then the great boiling heat of August came, and the water of the river retreated from its banks, leaving several feet of unpleasantly sharp stones embedded in dank clay between the clipped grass and the flood. Then he was glad to be near the river. It was something to do to go down to the riverbank with his lunch in a box and spend the day cooling off in the water and getting hot in the sun. The process tired him out pretty much if he stayed until dinnertime, and the sweltering heat kept it from being boring.

He was lying on the bank one day in August, with a whiff of evening breeze reminding him that it was almost time to go in for dinner. And while he was lying there, thinking about nothing in particular, a peculiar noise drew his attention to the river. The river had never made a noise like that before. He looked west, his hands cupped over his eyes against the sun, and saw that a dark triangular streak lay motionless far out on the waves, jutting hard-edged above the line of the water, but blurry where it merged into the shining ripples. He stood up to get a closer look, but it remained a sharp outline, its details lost in the backlight of the round red sun directly behind it. He stared at it until the setting sun made his eyes water and slit closed; in the meantime, he lost track of the vitally important timing that would land him at the dinner table just as the food came onto it. His grandma was angry with him when he finally came home, and he ate his dinner lukewarm and alone.

The thing was gone when he came back the next day. Yet it had been so odd, not like a log, but geometric, like something someone had made. He let it pass until, a few days later, he flopped down on his towel, fairly winded from a swim, and breathed in great whooshes of air for a few minutes before turning over. As he sighed and vainly rolled west against the glare of the sun, the dark streak reemerged so suddenly that he jumped. The sun was just past meridian, and he could see the object clearly. It was not a triangle at all, but a quadrangle that sort of tilted in the water, and out of it thrust another flat geometric form at an angle to the first. He brooded on the puzzle for a bit until he noticed two pillars or posts propping up the second plane from beneath. The object was a roof, then, sloping down to the overhang of a porch. He debated the probability of this guess being true. He had seen pictures of houses in floods, but the river was bone-dry. He looked down to check his facts. The water stood limpid and still, and three feet back from its banks. And the roof wasn't moving, not even rocking on the water. After a bit of brooding he concluded that if it couldn't have floated down the river, then the river must have uncovered it. The physics of the matter troubled him, but he dismissed the improbabilities. After all, the thing was there.

He watched it from the bank for a while longer, wondering what house it was, when he remembered Grandma's often-repeated story of the old house, and how they had had to desert it after the last flood had wrecked it, when the federal government had made one last payment and refused to insure the place again. No one had ever heard such a thing, Grandma said. That was always the last line of her house chant. He had heard it so often, and he had paid so little attention that the upshot was he defined insurance vaguely as something no one had ever heard of. But the appearance of the house in the river made the story interesting, and he pieced odd bits of the tale together from memory and rolled it over in his mind while he looked. This might be the house. He wondered whether he should tell Grandma. But that would mean having to leave it behind while he ran up the hill, and the last time he left the thing alone, it had gone under.

After a while he struck on the idea that he might swim out to it. It was a long way out, over half a mile maybe, but the porch roof was flat enough to serve as a pier. He could rest once he was out there, and with a safe haven halfway in the round trip, it was no farther than he had swum before. And so he plunged in.

The water seemed cooler than it should have been this time of day;

after he'd gotten over the shock of the first swim of the morning, the river should feel like bathwater. But this was an adventure, and adventures always made things seem different. He pushed on through the clear water, stopping now and again to look up and correct his course. The house seemed to get no nearer, not for a long time, and he did not look back to see that nonetheless the shore was getting smaller behind him.

He was far out when his efforts were finally repaid by a better look at the house. As he paused and trod water, he could see the weathered shingles making a shaggy web of the roof, and only a great ragged gap in the grid remained inpenetrably black in the distance. This encouragement had to last him a good while longer, for his neck was aching too much for him to keep on looking as he swam. His breathing was getting uncoordinated, too, and occasionally he choked and snorted out an inadvertent gulp of water. But there was nothing to do; he had to keep on paddling to the resting place on top of the porch. When the water suddenly turned tan and thick with churned-up mud from the river bottom, he stopped and looked up again for the first time in a long time. The house rose up less than twenty feet from where he swam. It seemed to stand higher out of the water now, and he could see the top of a third pillar holding up the porch roof, and the pediment over a doorway that gaped empty beneath.

He swam through the dirty water to grasp the post closest to him, but it was slick with moss, and his hands slipped. His heart thumped fearfully in his ears. He might be too tired to climb up. His enervated fingers scratched at the rotting wood, but it flaked and splintered in his hands. He pushed his feet up around the pillar, and shimmied and hopped and scrambled until his belly creased up over the edge of the roof. And there he lay for a moment, exhausted, until a creak and a slight tilt indicated the house was listing, and he pushed himself frantically, spread-eagle, out onto the smooth grid of shingles. The creaking stopped, and he tried to rest. But his heart pounded and his nerves sang, and he could not rest.

He was not familiar with the stink of things long buried coming into the air again. It was not a comfortable smell, and as soon as he could catch his breath, he lifted his head up away from the reeking shingles, slick with mud and fungus. His body was covered with patches of the stuff in front. He tried wiping the smears off his face, away from his nose. But he only complicated the stink with a perpetual itch of red clay that clung to him from the water, and the stink and the itch together exasperated him. If he scratched or wriggled, the house creaked and moved; and when he scraped a foot on the roof to ease the itch, down he stepped, dangling into the attic. He pulled his leg back with the frantic delicacy necessary on thin ice, flattening his body out belly-up on the slimy shingles. The warmth of the sun encouraged the foul odor of the house to spread itself around and made black spots flicker in front of his eyes. He closed the lids over his eyes tightly, but the sun shone through each individual cell, and he risked lifting up a forearm over the sockets. This brought the itch to his eyes, but he kept the cool forearm aloft anyway until the red fire died down behind his eyelids and he could breathe regularly.

When he cautiously removed the arm and blinked, he saw that the sun had gone far west of the meridian. He raised himself up slowly, and eased away from the hole he'd made in the roof. He'd have to start swimming back pretty soon. It was getting late. But the tan pool spread out widely, and he felt a certain revulsion toward jumping through its opaque surface.

His cautious movements again irritated the delicate balance of the house, and he lay back down quickly to soothe it. From inside came a slight scuffling sound and then a thump that made the thin membrane of the roof quiver. The noise was startling, for Rory had assumed the house had been washed clean by the current of the river. But, of course, something could have drifted in through an empty windowframe and rattled around like a fly trying to find its way back out through a screen. The house kept shifting restively despite his stillness as he thought, and he crept carefully over to the end opposite the tilt to appease it.

This maneuver left him only inches from the original hole in the roof, and he could hear quite clearly the rattle and bump as the contents of the house wove from wall to wall. But there was no splashing noise involved, and that was odd. He looked down into the hole, something of his original curiosity rekindling. A sort of drier smell came up, equally as foul as the wet smell outside. He leaned in farther, and still nothing was visible, for little light came in through the two holes in the roof. It looked like some sort of attic or loft.

But he had leaned over too far, and with a faint whoosh the rotten shingles collapsed feebly inward and dropped him gently on the floor. He grabbed immediately upward at the sky-hanging light above him. But after his first lunges failed, he realized that his leaps brought on a chorus of angry squeaks from the house, and he stopped dead until they subsided. It was cold in there, even if he stood in the patches of light, and his teeth chattered as he stood rigidly still from his ankles to his earlobes, and his toes did a little terrified dance on the dry floor. It was dangerous inside, however low the river might be. Something rolled at him from a dark corner, and he jumped, heedless of his movement's effect on the creaking house. As the thing flashed into the sunlight, he recognized it rolling green and white in front of him, and he picked it up. It was a can of peas. It was a new can of peas, with the label dry, the tin ends still shiny. A green giant grinned at him above a heap of perfect green dots. The can was a good bit dented, and the rims were mucky from rolling on soft, rotten wood, but it was only an ordinary can of peas.

His teeth had stopped chattering, although shudders kept seizing his shoulders. He held the can of peas in his hand tightly, for he needed to grip on to something as he struggled to formulate options. The house was teetering constantly now whether he moved or not. He decided that it would be best to go to the lowest part of the sloped roof and poke through the brittle shingles with his hands; and then he would clamber onto the roof and jump off as soon as ever he could, and swim toward shore. His shoulders still ached from the swim out, but it didn't matter; he would make it back. He could float if he had to for a while, and then swim some more. But he had to get started right away. And so he slid his right foot forward like a skater across the floor toward the end of the roof. The floor leaned to follow. Then his left foot slid forward, and a slow, mushy sound squished behind him. He looked back.

There was something else in the corner where the peas came from. The sun threw one great, slanting shaft of light through the biggest hole in the roof, and he could just see a kind of gray mass standing out from the dark wall behind him. But he had no time to explore. He turned to his task again, sliding his feet forward. The gray thing scraped on the planking as the floor tipped under him. The house had bent forward far enough so that he could see the clay water through the gap in the shingles now. He leaned his body toward the opening, keeping his feet still, and one hand clutched at a rafter while the other batted the can of peas at bits of shingles and river ooze. After he'd cleared a hole big enough to jump through, his fingers curled around the rafter gently, and he pulled. It held firm, strong enough to bear his weight. He readied himself to jump. But as he closed his eyes, a vision seized him: he jumped up beautifully, up, out into the water, and the house tumbled in the air and dived after him, turning upside down over him like an empty basket. He forced his mind away from this, opened his eyes, and tossed the can of peas into the river, then clutched at the rafter with both hands. He tried to push the thoughts away, and jerked himself forward to jump; then he pulled back again from the vision of the capsized house, and his little dance of indecision shook the house more, making the gray mass behind him rock and tumble down and then up the floor, down and then up again until the lumpen mass flipped cozily around his legs and came to rest. He froze his fingers onto the rafter and pointed his tightly shut eyes straight up to the sky. His ears rang a bit, and he could hear himself panting. The tangle around his legs was heavy. He tried to move his left leg. It was stuck. He would have to look down to see how to free himself.

The sunlight hit the mass full on as he swiveled one eye down and sideways. A few details confirmed that the thing was human. He swallowed once and said, "He-hello?" There was no answer. He had expected none. He shifted his right foot gently and pushed. The body wobbled, but his left foot was still trapped. He kicked hard, and an arm rolled free from his foot, and for one strangled moment he saw the face before it shot him screaming up through the roof hole.

After the first fit of screams he descended into a whimper. He wanted to jump into the clear water and swim, but the clay pool stretched out for yards in front of him, and the body beneath still entangled him, pulling his legs under the water in his thoughts. He crawled away from the hole to the far end of the porch, away from the sound of her tumbling in the attic.

The face stood between him and his own eyelids if he shut his eyes, between him and the sun and the water if he dared open them. It was a woman's face, smashed in by great round black marks that made swollen crescents all over it. And he laughed hysterically, mixed up a little with wailing, to think she'd got her head smashed in with a can of peas.

He'd have to yell for help; there was nothing else to do, and he bellowed as loud as he could. But his voice was small and cramped with fear, and the yells didn't carry. The shore was very far away, and he could see that his grandparents' house was beginning to be covered with the shadows of the aspen trees in front. He looked up sharply. The sun had slid almost to the horizon while he was inside the attic. It was still bright on the river, but dark would come quickly once the sun was down; the river would soon be a great mirrored sheen by the darkened shore, and then the river itself would grow dark. His grandma must be looking for him. It was past dinnertime, and she knew he was down by the river. His towel would still be there on the bank. He waved his arms, hoping that she could see him backlit by the sun; he cried out a few times more. He couldn't see anyone, just the faint glow of the white house, and the vivid yellow-green of the trees and grass where the sun hit, and the shadows growing more purple behind them.

But there were police. They had motorboats; even in the dark he would be able to hear them, see their lights. Yet the shifting house might not wait. It creaked constantly now, no matter what. He tried to think of swimming again; but he couldn't, he just couldn't. He might swim round and round in circles in the dark, unable to see the shore, with the body drifting after him, waiting to ensnare his legs with its dead arms.

Soon the sun was a thin red rim glowing behind the hills, and the river was opaque and shining. He looked around for the last time, he knew, for a long time. And in the distance he saw something: a boat perhaps, for it was moving. He yelled at it, his voice hoarse from the water and the stink. It was coming swiftly, purposefully downriver toward the house, more swiftly than the current would carry it. He yelled again and waved his arms. There was more than one. Five or six specks emerged; they were boats, surely. He stopped yelling for a moment, thinking he would hear a reply; but there was no response, not even a cry muffled by the wind, nor any sound of motors or paddles lapping in the water. The boats came silently toward him, closer and closer, and his voice died in his throat. They carried no flashlights. And as they grew larger, a faint glimmer of light showed that the shallow boats streaked forward in their own widening pool of clay-colored water, and the breeze brought him the penetrating sour smell of something long buried as the house gently shifted, and knelt into the water like a trained horse bowing to its rider.

THE NIGHT OF THE TIGER

STEPHEN KING

A native of Maine, Stephen King is currently the world's best-selling author, and could be thought of as the heavyweight champion of the modern horror story. He skillfully spars with conventional horror motifs and figures and also explores more science-fictional topics such as telekinesis and telepathy. His stories, novels, and movies are gripping, mordant masterpieces with very real, very believable characters. In many of his tales—including "The Night of the Tiger"—Stephen King realistically portrays "down-home" folks suddenly confronted with situations that turn and twist to show their darker sides. "The Night of the Tiger" tells of such a dark time; it is a haunting tale of what happened at Farnum and Williams' All-American 3-Ring Circus and Side Show one stormy night.

I first saw Mr. Legere when the circus swung through Steubenville, but I'd been with the show for only two weeks; he might have been making his irregular visits indefinitely. No one much wanted to talk about Mr. Legere, not even that last night when it seemed that the world was coming to an end—the night that Mr. Indrasil disappeared.

But if I'm going to tell it to you from the beginning, I should start by saying that I'm Eddie Johnston, and I was born and raised in Sauk City. Went to school there, had my first girl there, and worked in Mr. Lillie's five-and-dime there for a while after I graduated from high school. That was a few years back . . . more than I like to count, sometimes. Not that Sauk City's such a bad place; hot, lazy summer nights sitting on the front porch is all right for some folks, but it just seemed to *itch* me, like sitting in the same chair too long. So I quit the five-and-dime and joined Farnum & Williams' All-American 3-Ring Circus and Side Show. I did it in a moment of giddiness when the calliope music kind of fogged my judgment, I guess.

So I became a roustabout, helping put up tents and take them down, spreading sawdust, cleaning cages, and sometimes selling cotton candy when the regular salesman had to go away and bark for Chips Baily, who had malaria and sometimes had to go someplace far away and holler. Mostly things that kids do for free passes—things I used to do when I was a kid. But times change. They don't seem to come around like they used to.

We swung through Illinois and Indiana that hot summer, and the crowds were good and everyone was happy. Everyone except Mr. Indrasil. Mr. Indrasil was never happy. He was the lion tamer, and he looked like old pictures I've seen of Rudolph Valentino. He was tall, with handsome, arrogant features and a shock of wild black hair. And strange, mad eyes—the maddest eyes I've ever seen. He was silent most of the time; two syllables from Mr. Indrasil was a sermon. All the circus people kept a mental as well as a physical distance, because his rages were legend. There was a whispered story about coffee spilled on his hands after a particularly difficult performance and a murder that was almost done to a young roustabout before Mr. Indrasil could be hauled off him. I don't know about that. I do know that I grew to fear him worse than I had cold-eyed Mr. Edmont, my high school principal, Mr. Lillie, or even my father, who was capable of cold dressing-downs that would leave the recipient quivering with shame and dismay.

When I cleaned the big cats' cages, they were always spotless. The memory of the few times I had the vituperative wrath of Mr. Indrasil called down on me still have the power to turn my knees watery in retrospect.

Mostly it was his eyes—large and dark and totally blank. The eyes, and the feeling that a man capable of controlling seven watchful cats in a small cage must be part savage himself.

And the only two things he was afraid of were Mr. Legere and the circus's one tiger, a huge beast called Green Terror.

As I said, I first saw Mr. Legere in Steubenville, and he was staring into Green Terror's cage as if the tiger knew all the secrets of life and death.

He was lean, dark, quiet. His deep, recessed eyes held an expression of pain and brooding violence in their green-flecked depths, and his hands were always crossed behind his back as he stared moodily in at the tiger.

Green Terror was a beast to be stared at. He was a huge, beautiful specimen with a flawless striped coat, emerald eyes, and heavy fangs like ivory spikes. His roars usually filled the circus grounds—fierce, angry, and utterly savage. He seemed to scream defiance and frustration at the whole world.

Chips Baily, who had been with Farnum & Williams since Lord knew when, told me that Mr. Indrasil used to use Green Terror in his act, until one night when the tiger leapt suddenly from its perch and almost ripped his head from his shoulders before he could get out of the cage. I noticed that Mr. Indrasil always wore his hair long down the back of his neck.

I can still remember the tableau that day in Steubenville. It was hot, sweatingly hot, and we had a shirt-sleeve crowd. That was why Mr. Legere and Mr. Indrasil stood out. Mr. Legere, standing silently by the tiger cage, was fully dressed in a suit and vest, his face unmarked by perspiration. And Mr. Indrasil, clad in one of his beautiful silk shirts and white whipcord breeches, was staring at them both, his face dead-white, his eyes bulging in lunatic anger, hate, and fear. He was carrying a currycomb and brush, and his hands were trembling as they clenched on them spasmodically.

Suddenly he saw me, and his anger found vent. "You!" He shouted. "Johnston!"

"Yes, sir?" I felt a crawling in the pit of my stomach. I knew I was about to have the Wrath of Indrasil vented on me, and the thought turned me weak with fear. I like to think I'm as brave as the next, and if it had been anyone else, I think I would have been fully determined to stand up for myself. But it wasn't anyone else. It was Mr. Indrasil, and his eyes were mad.

"These cages, Johnston. Are they supposed to be clean?" He pointed a finger, and I followed it. I saw four errant wisps of straw and an incriminating puddle of hose water in the far corner of one.

"Y-yes, sir," I said, and what was intended to be firmness became palsied bravado.

Silence, like the electric pause before a downpour. People were beginning to look, and I was dimly aware that Mr. Legere was staring at us with his bottomless eyes.

"Yes, sir?" Mr. Indrasil thundered suddenly. "Yes, sir? Yes, sir? Don't insult my intelligence, boy! Don't you think I can see? *Smell?* Did you use the disinfectant?"

"I used disinfectant yest—"

"Don't answer me back!" He screeched, and then the sudden drop in his voice made my skin crawl. "Don't you *dare* answer me back." Everyone was staring now. I wanted to retch, to die. "Now you get the hell into that toolshed, and you get that disinfectant and swab out those cages," he whispered, measuring every word. One hand suddenly shot out, grasping my shoulder. "And don't you ever, ever speak back to me again."

I don't know where the words came from, but they were suddenly there, spilling off my lips. "I didn't speak back to you, Mr. Indrasil, and I don't like you saying I did. I—I resent it. Now let me go."

His face went suddenly red, then white, then almost saffron with rage. His eyes were blazing doorways to hell.

Right then I thought I was going to die.

He made an inarticulate gagging sound, and the grip on my shoulder became excruciating. His right hand went up . . . up . . . up, and then descended with unbelievable speed.

If that hand had connected with my face, it would have knocked me senseless at best. At worst, it would have broken my neck.

It did not connect.

Another hand materialized magically out of space, right in front of me. The two straining limbs came together with a flat smacking sound. It was Mr. Legere.

"Leave the boy alone," he said emotionlessly.

Mr. Indrasil stared at him for a long second, and I think there was nothing so unpleasant in the whole business as watching the fear of Mr. Legere and the mad lust to hurt (or to kill!) mix in those terrible eyes.

Then he turned and stalked away.

I turned to look at Mr. Legere. "Thank you," I said.

"Don't thank me." And it wasn't a "don't thank *me*," but a "*don't* thank me." Not a gesture of modesty, but a literal command. In a sudden flash of intuition—empathy, if you will—I understood exactly what he meant by that comment. I was a pawn in what must have been a long combat between the two of them. I had been captured by Mr. Legere rather than Mr. Indrasil. He had stopped the lion tamer not because he felt for me, but because it gained him an advantage, however slight, in their private war.

"What's your name?" I asked, not at all offended by what I had inferred. He had, after all, been honest with me.

"Legere," he said briefly. He turned to go.

"Are you with a circus?" I asked, not wanting to let him go so easily. "You seemed to know—him."

A faint smile touched his thin lips, and warmth kindled in his eyes for a moment. "No. You might call me a policeman." And before I could reply, he had disappeared into the surging throng passing by.

The next day we picked up stakes and moved on.

I saw Mr. Legere again in Danville and, two weeks later, in Chicago. In the time between I tried to avoid Mr. Indrasil as much as possible and kept the cat cages spotlessly clean. On the day before we pulled out for St. Louis, I asked Chips Baily and Sally O'Hara, the redheaded wire walker, if Mr. Legere and Mr. Indrasil knew each other. I was pretty sure they did, because Mr. Legere was hardly following the circus to eat our fabulous lime ice.

Sally and Chips looked at each other over their coffee cups. "No one knows much about what's between those two," she said. "But it's been going on for a long time—maybe twenty years. Ever since Mr. Indrasil came over from Ringling Brothers, and maybe before that."

Chips nodded. "This Legere guy picks up the circus almost every year when we swing through the Midwest and stays with us until we catch the train for Florida in Little Rock. Makes old Leopard Man touchy as one of his cats."

"He told me he was a policeman," I said. "What do you suppose he looks for around here? You don't suppose Mr. Indrasil—?"

Chips and Sally looked at each other strangely, and both just about broke their backs getting up. "Got to see those weights and counterweights get stored right," Sally said, and Chips muttered something not too convincing about checking on the rear axle of his U-Haul.

And that's about the way any conversation concerning Mr. Indrasil or Mr. Legere usually broke up—hurriedly, with many hard-forced excuses.

We said farewell to Illinois and comfort at the same time. A killing hot spell came on, seemingly at the very instant we crossed the border, and it stayed with us for the next month and a half, as we moved slowly across Missouri and into Kansas. Everyone grew short of temper, including the animals. And that, of course, included the cats, which were Mr. Indrasil's responsibility. He rode the roustabouts unmercifully, and myself in particular. I grinned and tried to bear it, even though I had my own case of prickly heat. You just don't argue with a crazy man, and I'd pretty well decided that was what Mr. Indrasil was.

No one was getting any sleep, and that is the curse of all circus performers. Loss of sleep slows up reflexes, and slow reflexes make for danger. In Independence, Sally O'Hara fell seventy-five feet into the nylon netting and fractured her shoulder. Andrea Solienni, our bareback rider, fell off one of her horses during rehearsal and was knocked unconscious by a flying hoof. Chips Baily suffered silently with the fever that was always with him, his face a waxen mask, with cold perspiration clustered at each temple.

And in many ways, Mr. Indrasil had the roughest row to hoe of all. The cats were nervous and short-tempered, and every time he stepped into the Demon Cat Cage, as it was billed, he took his life in his hands. He was feeding the lions inordinate amounts of raw meat right before he went on, something that lion tamers rarely do, contrary to popular belief. His face grew drawn and haggard, and his eyes were wild.

Mr. Legere was almost always there, by Green Terror's cage, watching him. And that, of course, added to Mr. Indrasil's load. The circus began eyeing the silk-shirted figure nervously as he passed, and I knew they were all thinking the same thing I was: *He's going to crack wide open, and when he does—*

When he did, God alone knew what would happen.

The hot spell went on, and temperatures were climbing well into the nineties every day. It seemed as if the rain gods were mocking us. Every town we left would receive the showers of blessing. Every town we entered was hot, parched, sizzling.

And one night, on the road between Kansas City and Green Bluff, I saw something that upset me more than anything else.

It was hot—abominably hot. It was no good even trying to sleep. I rolled about on my cot like a man in a fever delirium, chasing the sandman but never quite catching him. Finally I got up, pulled on my pants, and went outside.

We had pulled off into a small field and drawn into a circle. Myself and two other roustabouts had unloaded the cats so they could catch whatever breeze there might be. The cages were there now, painted dull silver by the swollen Kansas moon, and a tall figure in white whipcord breeches was standing by the biggest of them. Mr. Indrasil.

He was baiting Green Terror with a long, pointed pike. The big cat was padding silently around the cage, trying to avoid the sharp tip. And the frightening thing was, when the staff did punch into the tiger's flesh, it did not roar in pain and anger as it should have. It maintained an ominous silence, more terrifying to the person who knows cats than the loudest of roars.

It had gotten to Mr. Indrasil too. "Quiet bastard, aren't you?" He grunted. Powerful arms flexed, and the iron shaft slid forward. Green Terror flinched, and his eyes rolled horribly. But he did not make a sound. "Yowl!" Mr. Indrasil hissed. "Go ahead and yowl, you monster! Yowl!" And he drove his spear deep into the tiger's flank.

Then I saw something odd. It seemed that a shadow moved in the darkness under one of the far wagons, and the moonlight seemed to glint on staring eyes—green eyes.

A cool wind passed silently through the clearing, lifting dust and rumpling my hair.

Mr. Indrasil looked up, and there was a queer listening expression on his face. Suddenly he dropped the bar, turned, and strode back to his trailer.

I stared again at the far wagon, but the shadow was gone. Green Tiger stood motionlessly at the bars of his cage, staring at Mr. Indrasil's trailer. And the thought came to me that it hated Mr. Indrasil not because he was cruel or vicious, for the tiger respects these qualities in its own animalistic way, but rather because he was a deviate from even the tiger's savage norm. He was a rogue. That's the only way I can put it. Mr. Indrasil was not only a human tiger, but a rogue tiger as well.

The thought jelled inside me, disquieting and a little scary. I went back inside, but still I could not sleep.

The heat went on.

Every day we fried, every night we tossed and turned, sweating and sleepless. Everyone was painted red with sunburn, and there were fistfights over trifling affairs. Everyone was reaching the point of explosion.

Mr. Legere remained with us, a silent watcher, emotionless on the surface, but, I sensed, with deep-running currents of—what? Hate? Fear? Vengeance? I could not place it. But he was potentially dangerous, I was sure of that. Perhaps more so than Mr. Indrasil was, if anyone ever lit his particular fuse.

He was at the circus at every performance, always dressed in his nattily creased brown suit, despite the killing temperatures. He stood silently by Green Terror's cage, seeming to commune deeply with the tiger, who was always quiet when he was around.

From Kansas to Oklahoma, with no letup in the temperature. A day without a heat prostration case was a rare day indeed. Crowds were beginning to drop off; who wanted to sit under a stifling canvas tent when there was an air-conditioned movie just around the block?

We were all as jumpy as cats, to coin a particularly applicable phrase. And as we set down stakes in Wildwood Green, Oklahoma, I think we all knew a climax of some sort was close at hand. And most of us knew it would involve Mr. Indrasil. A bizzare occurrence had taken place just prior to our first Wildwood performance. Mr. Indrasil had been in the Demon Cat Cage, putting the ill-tempered lions through their paces. One of them missed its balance on its pedestal, tottered, and almost regained it. Then, at that precise moment, Green Terror let out a terrible ear-splitting roar.

The lion fell, landed heavily, and suddenly launched itself with rifle-bullet accuracy at Mr. Indrasil. With a frightened curse he heaved his chair at the cat's feet, tangling up the driving legs. He darted out just as the lion smashed against the bars.

As he shakily collected himself preparatory to reentering the cage, Green Terror let out another roar—but this one monstrously like a huge, disdainful chuckle.

Mr. Indrasil stared at the beast, white-faced, then turned and walked away. He did not come out of his trailer all afternoon.

That afternoon wore on interminably. But as the temperature climbed, we all began looking hopefully toward the west, where huge banks of thunderclouds were forming.

"Rain, maybe," I told Chips, stopping by his barking platform in front of the sideshow.

But he didn't respond to my hopeful grin. "Don't like it," he said. "No wind. Too hot. Hail or tornadoes." His face grew grim. "It ain't no picnic, ridin' out a tornado with a pack of crazy-wild animals all over the place, Eddie. I've thanked God more'n once when we've gone through the tornado belt that we don't have no elephants.

"Yeah," he added gloomily, "you better hope them clouds stay right on the horizon."

But they didn't. They moved slowly toward us, cyclopean pillars in the sky, purple at the bases and awesome blue-black through the cumulonimbus. All air movement ceased, and the heat lay on us like a woolen winding-shroud. Every now and again thunder would clear its throat farther west.

About four, Mr. Farnum himself, ringmaster and half owner of the circus, appeared and told us there would be no evening performance; just batten down and find a convenient hole to crawl into in case of trouble. There had been corkscrew funnels spotted in several places between Wildwood and Oklahoma City, some within forty miles of us.

There was only a small crowd when the announcement came, apathetically wandering through the sideshow exhibits or ogling the animals. But Mr. Legere had not been present all day; the only person at Green Terror's cage was a sweaty high school boy with a clutch of books. When Mr. Farnum announced the U.S. Weather Bureau tornado warning that had been issued, he hurried quickly away.

I and the other two roustabouts spent the rest of the afternoon working our tails off, securing tents, loading animals back into their wagons, and making generally sure that everything was nailed down.

Finally only the cat cages were left, and there was a special arrangement for those. Each cage had a special mesh "breezeway" accordioned up against it, which, when extended completely, connected with the Demon Cat Cage. When the smaller cages had to be moved, the felines could be herded into the big cage while they were loaded up. The big cage itself rolled on gigantic casters and could be muscled around to a position where each cat could be let back into its original cage. It sounds complicated, and it was, but it was just the only way.

We did the lions first, then Ebony Velvet, the docile black panther that had set the circus back almost one season's receipts. It was a tricky business coaxing them up and then back through the breezeways, but all of us preferred it to calling Mr. Indrasil to help.

By the time we were ready for Green Terror, twilight had come—a queer, yellow twilight that hung humidly around us. The sky above had taken on a flat, shiny aspect that I had never seen and which I didn't like in the least.

"Better hurry," Mr. Farnum said as we laboriously trundled the Demon Cat Cage back to where we could hook it to the back of Green Terror's show cage. "Barometer's falling off fast." He shook his head worriedly. "Looks bad, boys. Bad." He hurried on, still shaking his head.

We got Green Terror's breezeway hooked up and opened the back of his cage. "In you go," I said encouragingly.

Green Terror looked at me menacingly and didn't move.

Thunder rumbled again, louder, closer, sharper. The sky had gone jaundice, the ugliest color I have ever seen. Wind-devils began to pick jerkily at our clothes and whirl away the flattened candy wrappers and cotton-candy cones that littered the area.

"Come on, come on," I urged, and poked him easily with the blunt-tipped rods we were given to herd them with.

Green Terror roared ear-splittingly, and one paw lashed out with blinding speed. The hardwood pole was jerked from my hands and splintered as if it had been a greenwood twig. The tiger was on his feet now, and there was murder in his eyes.

"Look," I said shakily. "One of you will have to go get Mr. Indrasil, that's all. We can't wait around."

As if to punctuate my words, thunder cracked louder, the clapping of mammoth hands.

Kelly Nixon and Mike McGregor flipped for it; I was excluded because of my previous run-in with Mr. Indrasil. Kelly drew the task, threw us a wordless glance that said he would prefer facing the storm, and then started off.

He was gone almost ten minutes. The wind was picking up velocity now, and twilight was darkening into a weird six o'clock night. I was scared, and am not afraid to admit it. That rushing, featureless sky, the deserted circus grounds, the sharp, tugging wind-vortices—all that makes a memory that will stay with me always, undimmed.

And Green Terror would not budge into his breezeway.

Kelly Nixon came rushing back, his eyes wide. "I pounded on his door for 'most five minutes!" He gasped. "Couldn't raise him!"

We looked at each other, at a loss. Green Terror was a big investment for the circus. He couldn't just be left in the open. I turned bewilderedly, looking for Chips, Mr. Farnum, or anybody who could tell me what to do. But everyone was gone. The tiger was our responsibility. I considered trying to load the cage bodily into the trailer, but I wasn't going to get my fingers in that cage.

"Well, we've just got to go and get him," I said. "The three of us. Come on." And we ran toward Mr. Indrasil's trailer through the gloom of coming night.

We pounded on his door until he must have thought all the demons of hell were after him. Thankfully, it finally jerked open. Mr. Indrasil swayed and stared down at us, his mad eyes rimmed and oversheened with drink. He smelled like a distillery.

"Damn you, leave me alone," he snarled.

"Mr. Indrasil—" I had to shout over the rising whine of the wind. It was like no storm I had ever heard of or read about, out there. It was like the end of the world.

"You," he gritted softly. He reached down and gathered my shirt up in a knot. "I'm going to teach you a lesson you'll never forget." He glared at Kelly and Mike, cowering back in the moving storm shadows. "Get out!"

They ran. I didn't blame them; I've told you—Mr. Indrasil was crazy. And not just ordinary crazy—he was like a crazy animal, like one of his own cats gone bad.

"All right," he muttered, staring down at me, his eyes like hurricane lamps. "No juju to protect you now. No grisgris." His lips twitched in a wild, horrible smile. "He isn't here now, is he? We're two of a kind, him and me. Maybe the only two left. My nemesis—and I'm his." He was rambling, and I didn't try to stop him. At least his mind was off me.

"Turned that cat against me, back in 'fifty-eight. Always had the power more'n me. Fool could make a million—the two of us could make a million if he wasn't so damned high and mighty . . . what's that?"

It was Green Terror, and he had begun to roar ear-splittingly.

"Haven't you got that damned tiger in?" he screamed, almost falsetto. He shook me like a rag doll.

"He won't go!" I found myself yelling back. "You've got to—"

But he flung me away. I stumbled over the fold-up steps in front of his trailer and crashed into a bone-shaking heap at the bottom. With something between a sob and a curse, Mr. Indrasil strode past me, face mottled with anger and fear.

I got up, drawn after him as if hypnotized. Some intuitive part of me realized I was about to see the last act played out.

Once clear of the shelter of Mr. Indrasil's trailer, the power of the wind was appalling. It screamed like a runaway freight train. I was an ant, a speck, an unprotected molecule before that thundering cosmic force.

And Mr. Legere was standing by Green Terror's cage.

It was like a tableau from Dante. The near-empty cage clearing inside the circle of trailers; the two men, facing each other silently, their clothes and hair rippled by the shrieking gale; the boiling sky above; the twisting wheatfields in the background, like damned souls bending to the whip of Lucifer.

"It's time, Jason," Mr. Legere said, his words flayed across the clearing by the wind.

Mr. Indrasil's wildly whipping hair lifted around the livid scar across the back of his neck. His fists clenched, but he said nothing. I could almost feel him gathering his will, his life force, his id. It gathered around him like an unholy nimbus.

And then I saw with sudden horror that Mr. Legere was unhooking Green Terror's breezeway—and the back of the cage was open!

I cried out, but the wind ripped my words away.

The great tiger leapt out and almost flowed past Mr. Legere. Mr. Indrasil swayed, but did not run. He bent his head and stared down at the tiger.

And Green Terror stopped.

He swung his huge head back to Mr. Legere, almost turned, and then slowly turned back to Mr. Indrasil again. There was a terrifyingly palpable sensation of directed force in the air, a mesh of conflicting wills centered around the tiger. And the wills were evenly matched.

I think, in the end, it was Green Terror's own will—his hate of Mr. Indrasil—that tipped the scales.

The cat began to advance, his eyes hellish, flaring beacons. And something strange began to happen to Mr. Indrasil. He seemed to be folding in on himself, shriveling, accordioning. The silk shirt lost shape, the dark, whipping hair became a hideous toadstool around his collar.

Mr. Legere called something across to him, and, simultaneously, Green Terror leapt.

I never saw the outcome. The next moment I was slammed flat on my back, and the breath seemed to be sucked from my body. I caught one crazily tilted glimpse of a huge, towering cyclone funnel, and then the darkness descended.

When I awoke, I was in my cot just aft of the grainery bins in the all-purpose storage trailer we carried. My body felt as if it had been beaten with padded Indian clubs.

Chips Baily appeared, his face lined and pale. He saw my eyes were open and grinned relievedly. "Didn't know as you were ever gonna wake up. How you feel?"

"Dislocated," I said. "What happened? How'd I get here?"

"We found you piled up against Mr. Indrasil's trailer. The tornado almost carried you away for a souvenir, m'boy."

At the mention of Mr. Indrasil, all the ghastly memories came flooding back. "Where is Mr. Indrasil? And Mr. Legere?"

His eyes went murky, and he started to make some kind of an evasive answer.

"Straight talk," I said, struggling up on one elbow. "I have to know, Chips. I *have* to."

Something in my face must have decided him. "Okay. But this isn't exactly what we told the cops—in fact we hardly told the cops any of it. No sense havin' people think we're crazy. Anyhow, Indrasil's gone. I didn't even know that Legere guy was around."

"And Green Tiger?"

Chips's eyes were unreadable again. "He and the other tiger fought to death."

"*Other* tiger? There's no other—"

"Yeah, but they found two of 'em, lying in each other's blood. Hell of a mess. Ripped each other's throats out."

"What—where—"

"Who knows? We just told the cops we had two tigers. Simpler that way." And before I could say another word, he was gone.

And that's the end of my story—except for two little items. The words Mr. Legere shouted just before the tornado hit: "*When a man and an animal live in the same shell, Indrasil, the instincts determine the mold!*"

The other thing is what keeps me awake nights. Chips told me later, offering it only for what it might be worth. What he told me was that the strange tiger had a long scar on the back of its neck.

POOR LITTLE WARRIOR!

BRIAN W. ALDISS

Britisher Brian Aldiss is a novelist, editor, poet, and critic
whose work has received wide acclaim. His role in the field
of science fiction has been one of pathfinder; in his early
works he routinely broke with the conventions of sf and
tried new approaches to traditional sf ideas, emphasizing
imagery and style over "hardware," and writing with un-
beatable zest. Although "Poor Little Warrior!" is primarily
a science fiction tale, its culmination will shudder the shoes
off you. In this story Claude Ford travels to the past to hunt
big big game . . . only to find that it isn't as easy as he had
thought.

Claude Ford knew exactly how it
was to hunt a brontosaurus. You crawled heedlessly through the mud
among the willows, through the little primitive flowers with petals as
green and brown as a football field, through the beauty-lotion mud. You
peered out at the creature sprawling among the reeds, its body as graceful
as a sock full of sand. There it lay, letting the gravity cuddle it nappy-
damp to the marsh, running its big rabbit-hole nostrils a foot above the
grass in a sweeping semicircle, in a snoring search for more sausage reeds.
It was beautiful: here horror had reached its limits, come full circle and

finally disappeared up its own sphincter. Its eyes gleamed with the live-liness of a week-dead corpse's big toe, and its compost breath and the fur in its crude aural cavities were particularly to be recommended to anyone who might otherwise have felt inclined to speak lovingly of the work of Mother Nature.

But as you, little mammal with opposed digit and .65 self-loading, semi-automatic, dual-barreled, digitally computed, telescopically sighted, rustless, high-powered rifle gripped in your otherwise defenseless paws, slide along under the bygone willows, what primarily attracts you is the thunder lizard's hide. It gives off a smell as deeply resonant as the bass note of a piano. It makes the elephant's epidermis look like a sheet of crinkled lavatory paper. It is gray as the Viking seas, daft-deep as cathedral foundations. What contact possible to bone could allay the fever of that flesh? Over it scamper—you can see them from here!—the little brown lice that live in those gray walls and canyons, gay as ghosts, cruel as crabs. If one of them jumped on you, it would very likely break your back. And when one of those parasites stops to cock its leg against one of the bronto's vertebrae, you can see it carries in its turn its own crop of easy livers, each as big as a lobster, for you're near now, oh, so near that you can hear the monster's primitive heart organ knocking, as the ventricle keeps miraculous time with the auricle.

Time for listening to the oracle is past: you're beyond the stage for omens, you're now headed in for the kill, yours or his; superstition has had its little day for today, from now on only this windy nerve of yours, this shaky conglomeration of muscle entangled untraceably beneath the sweat-shiny carapace of skin, this bloody little urge to slay the dragon, is going to answer all your orisons.

You could shoot now. Just wait till that tiny steam-shovel head pauses once again to gulp down a quarryload of bulrushes, and with one inex-pressibly vulgar bang you can show the whole indifferent Jurassic world that it's standing looking down the business end of evolution's sex shooter. You know why you pause, even as you pretend not to know why you pause; that old worm conscience, long as a baseball pitch, long-lived as a tortoise, is at work; through every sense it slides, more monstrous than the serpent. Through the passions: saying here is a sitting duck, O Eng-lishman! Through the intelligence: whispering that boredom, the kite-hawk who never feeds, will settle again when the task is done. Through the nerves: sneering that when the adrenaline currents cease to flow the vomiting begins. Through the maestro behind the retina: plausibly forcing the beauty of the view upon you.

Spare us that poor old slipper-slopper of a word, *beauty*; holy mom, is this a travelogue, nor are we out of it? *"Perched now on this titanic creature's back, we see a round dozen—and, folks, let me stress that round—of gaudily plumaged birds, exhibiting between them all the color you might expect to find on lovely, fabled Copacabaña Beach. They're so round because they feed from the droppings that fall from the rich man's table. Watch this lovely shot now! See the bronto's tail lift. . . . Oh, lovely, yep, a couple of hayricks-full at least emerging from his nether end. That sure was a beauty, folks, delivered straight from consumer to consumer. The birds are fighting over it now. Hey, you, there's enough to go round, and anyhow, you're round enough already. . . . And nothing to do now but hop back up onto the old rump steak and wait for the next round. And now as the sun sinks in the Jurassic West, we say 'Farewell on that diet' . . ."*

No, you're procrastinating, and that's a life work. Shoot the beast and put it out of your agony. Taking your courage in your hands, you raise it to shoulder level and squint down its sights. There is a terrible report; you are half stunned. Shakily, you look about you. The monster still munches, relieved to have broken enough wind to unbecalm the Ancient Mariner.

Angered (or is it some subtler emotion?), you now burst from the bushes and confront it, and this exposed condition is typical of the straits into which your consideration for yourself and others continually pitches you. Consideration? Or again something subtler? Why should you be confused just because you come from a confused civilization? But that's a point to deal with later, if there is a later, as these two hog-wallow eyes pupiling you all over from spitting distance tend to dispute. Let it not be by jaws alone, O monster, but also by huge hooves and, if convenient to yourself, by mountainous rollings upon me! Let death be a saga, sagacious, Beowulfate.

Quarter of a mile distant is the sound of a dozen hippos springing boisterously in gymslips from the ancestral mud, and next second a walloping great tail as long as Sunday and as thick as Saturday night comes slicing over your head. You duck as duck you must, but the beast missed you anyway because it so happens that its coordination is no better than yours would be if you had to wave the Woolworth Building at a tarsier. This done, it seems to feel it has done its duty by itself. It forgets you. You just wish you could forget yourself as easily; that was, after all, the reason you had to come the long way here. *Get Away from It All*, said the time travel brochure, which meant for you getting away from Claude Ford, a husbandman as futile as his name with a terrible wife called Maude. Maude and Claude Ford. Who could not adjust to themselves, to each other, or to the world they were born in. It was the best reason in the as-it-is-at-present-constituted world for coming back here to shoot giant saurians—if you were fool enough to think that one hundred and fifty million years either way made an ounce of difference to the muddle of thoughts in a man's cerebral vortex.

You try to stop your silly, slobbering thoughts, but they have never really stopped since the coca-collaborating days of your growing up; God, if adolescence did not exist, it would be unnecessary to invent it! Slightly, it steadies you to look again on the enormous bulk of this tyrant vegetarian into whose presence you charged with such a mixed death-life wish, charged with all the emotion the human orga(ni)sm is capable of. This time the bogeyman is real, Claude, just as you wanted it to be, and this time you really have to face up to it before it turns and faces you again. And so again you lift Ole Equalizer, waiting till you can spot the vulnerable spot.

The bright birds sway, the lice scamper like dogs, the marsh groans, as bronto sways over and sends his little cranium snaking down under the bile-bright water in a forage for roughage. You watch this; you have never been so jittery before in all your jittered life, and you are counting on this catharsis wringing the last drop of acid fear out of your system forever. OK, you keep saying to yourself insanely over and over, your million-dollar twenty-second-century education going for nothing, OK, OK. And as you say it for the umpteenth time, the crazy head comes back out of the water like a renegade express and gazes in your direction.

Grazes in your direction. For as the champing jaw with its big blunt molars like concrete posts works up and down, you see the swamp water course out over rimless lips, lipless rims, splashing your feet and sousing the ground. Reed and root, stalk and stem, leaf and loam, all are intermittently visible in that masticating maw and, struggling, straggling, or tossed among them, minnows, tiny crustaceans, frogs—all destined in that awful, jaw-full movement to turn into bowel movement. And as the glump-glump-glumping takes place, above it the slime-resistant eyes again survey you.

These beasts live up to two hundred years, says the time travel brochure, and this beast has obviously tried to live up to that, for its gaze is centuries old, full of decades upon decades of wallowing in its heavyweight thoughtlessness until it has grown wise on twitterpatedness. For you it is like looking into a disturbing misty pool; it gives you a psychic shock, you fire off both barrels at your own reflection. Bang-bang, the dum-dums, big as paw-paws, go.

With no indecision, those century-old lights, dim and sacred, go out.

These cloisters are closed till Judgment Day. Your reflection is torn and bloodied from them forever. Over their ravaged panes nictitating membranes slide slowly upward, like dirty sheets covering a cadaver. The jaw continues to munch slowly, as slowly the head sinks down. Slowly, a squeeze of cold reptile blood toothpastes down the wrinkled flank of one cheek. Everything is slow, a creepy Secondary Era slowness like the drip of water, and you know that if you had been in charge of creation, you would have found some medium less heartbreaking than Time to stage it all in.

Never mind! Quaff down your beakers, lords, Claude Ford has slain a harmless creature. Long live Claude the Clawed!

You watch breathless as the head touches the ground, the long laugh of neck touches the ground, the jaws close for good. You watch and wait for something else to happen, but nothing ever does. Nothing ever would. You could stand here watching for an hundred and fifty million years, Lord Claude, and nothing would ever happen here again. Gradually your bronto's mighty carcass, picked loving clean by predators, would sink into the slime, carried by its own weight deeper; then the waters would rise, and old Conqueror Sea come in with the leisurely air of a cardsharp dealing the boys a bad hand. Silt and sediment would filter down over the mighty grave, a slow rain with centuries to rain in. Old bronto's bed might be raised up and then down again perhaps half a dozen times, gently enough not to disturb him, although by now the sedimentary rocks would be forming thick around him. Finally, when he was wrapped in a tomb finer than any Indian rajah ever boasted, the powers of the Earth would raise him high on their shoulders until, sleeping still, bronto would lie in a brow of the Rockies high above the waters of the Pacific. But little any of that would count with you, Claude the Sword; once the midget maggot of life is dead in the creature's skull, the rest is no concern of yours.

You have no emotion now. You are just faintly put out. You expected dramatic thrashing of the ground, or bellowing; on the other hand, you are glad the thing did not appear to suffer. You are like all cruel men, sentimental; you are like all sentimental men, squeamish. You tuck the gun under your arm and walk round the dinosaur to view your victory.

You prowl past the ungainly hooves, round the septic white of the cliff of belly, beyond the glistening and how-thought-provoking cavern of the cloaca, finally posing beneath the switch-back sweep of tail-to-rump. Now your disappointment is as crisp and obvious as a visiting card: the giant is not half as big as you thought it was. It is not one half as large, for example, as the image of you and Maude is in your mind. Poor little warrior, science will never invent anything to assist the titanic death you want in the contraterrene caverns of your fee-fi-fo fumblingly fearful id!

Nothing is left to you now but to slink back to your timemobile with a belly full of anticlimax. See, the bright dung-consuming birds have already cottoned on to the true state of affairs; one by one they gather up their hunched wings and fly disconsolately off across the swamp to other hosts. They know when a good thing turns bad, and do not wait for the vultures to drive them off; all hope abandon, ye who entrail here. You also turn away.

You turn, but you pause. Nothing is left but to go back, no, but A.D. 2181 is not just the home date; it is Maude. It is Claude. It is the whole awful, hopeless, endless business of trying to adjust to an overcomplex environment, of trying to turn yourself into a cog. Your escape from it into *the Grand Simplicities of the Jurassic*, to quote the brochure again, was only a partial escape, now over.

So you pause, and as you pause something lands socko on your back, pitching your face forward into tasty mud. You struggle and scream as lobster claws tear at your neck and throat. You try to pick up the rifle but cannot, so in agony you roll over, and next second the crab-thing is greedying it on your chest. You wrench at its shell, but it giggles and pecks your fingers off. You forgot when you killed the bronto that its parasites would leave it, and that to a little shrimp like you they would be a deal more dangerous than their host.

You do your best, kicking for at least three minutes. By the end of that time there is a whole pack of the creatures on you. Already they are picking your carcass loving clean. You're going to like it up there on top of the Rockies; you won't feel a thing.

NINA

ROBERT BLOCH

Although he has been writing since 1934, the name of Robert Bloch instantly conjures up images of that modern masterpiece of horror, *Psycho* (1959), from which Alfred Hitchcock made the classic film. Bloch is a witty and polished writer, and one easily able to manipulate his readers' nerve-endings to heights of terror. Horror stories often employ the device of introducing things or people who are not actually what they appear to be. In "Nina," Robert Bloch takes this idea, transplants it to the steamy jungle of South America, and proceeds to scare us to death with what is and what is not.

fter the lovemaking Nolan needed another drink.

He fumbled for the bottle beside the bed, gripping it with a sweaty hand. His entire body was wet and clammy, and his fingers shook as they unscrewed the cap. For a moment Nolan wondered if he was coming down with another bout of fever. Then, as the harsh heat of the sun scalded his stomach, he realized the truth.

Nina had done this to him.

Nolan turned and glanced at the girl who lay beside him. She stared up through the shadows with slitted eyes unblinking above high cheek-bones, her thin brown body relaxed and immobile. Hard to believe that only moments ago this same body had been a writhing, wriggling coil of insatiable appetite, gripping and enfolding him until he was drained and spent.

He held the bottle out to her. "Have a drink?"

She shook her head, eyes hooded and expressionless, and then Nolan remembered that she didn't speak English. He raised the bottle and drank again, cursing himself for his mistake.

It had been a mistake, he realized that now, but Darlene would never understand. Sitting there safe and snug in the apartment in Trenton, she couldn't begin to know what he'd gone through for her sake—hers and little Robbie's. Robert Emmett Nolan II, nine weeks old now, his son, whom he'd never seen. That's why he'd taken the job, signed on with the company for a year. The money was good, enough to keep Darlene in comfort and tide them over after he got back. She couldn't have come with him, not while she was carrying the kid, so he came alone, figuring no sweat.

No sweat. That was a laugh. All he'd done since he got here was sweat. Patrolling the plantation at sunup, loading cargo all day for the boats that went downriver, squinting over paperwork while night closed down on the bungalow to imprison him behind a wall of jungle darkness. And at night the noises came—the hum of insect hordes, the bellow of cai-mans, the snorting snuffle of peccary, the ceaseless chatter of monkeys intermingled with the screeching of a million mindless birds.

So he'd started to drink. First the good bourbon from the company's stock, then the halfway-decent trade gin, and now the cheap rum.

As Nolan set the empty bottle down he heard the noise he'd come to dread worst of all—the endless echo of drums from the huts huddled beside the riverbank below. Miserable wretches were at it again. No wonder he had to drive them daily to fulfil the company's quota. The wonder was that they did anything at all after spending every night wailing to those damned drums.

Of course it was Moises who did the actual driving; Nolan couldn't even chew them out properly because they were too damned dumb to understand plain English.

Like Nina, here.

Again Nolan looked down at the girl who lay curled beside him on the bed, silent and sated. She wasn't sweating; her skin was curiously cool to the touch, and in her eyes was a mystery.

It was the mystery that Nolan had sensed the first time he saw her staring at him across the village compound three days ago. At first he thought she was one of the company people—somebody's wife, daughter, sister. That afternoon, when he returned to the bungalow, he caught her staring at him again at the edge of the clearing. So he asked Moises who she was, and Moises didn't know. Apparently she'd just arrived a day or two before, paddling a crude catamaran downriver from somewhere out of the denser jungle stretching a thousand miles beyond. She had no English, and according to Moises, she didn't speak Spanish or Portuguese either. Not that she'd made any attempts to communicate; she kept to herself, sleeping in the catamaran moored beside the bank across the river and not even venturing into the company store by day to purchase food.

"*Indio*," Moises said, pronouncing the word with all the contempt of one in whose veins ran a ten percent admixture of the proud blood of the *conquistadores*. "Who are we to know the way of savages?" He shrugged.

Nolan had shrugged, too, and dismissed her from his mind. But that night as he lay on his bed, listening to the pounding of the drums, he thought of her again and felt a stirring in his loins.

She came to him then, almost as though the stirring had been a silent summons, came like a brown shadow gliding out of the night. Soundlessly she entered, and swiftly she shed her single garment as she moved across the room to stand staring down at him on the bed. Then, as she sank upon his nakedness and encircled his thighs, the stirring in his loins became a throbbing and the pounding in his head drowned out the drums.

In the morning she was gone, but on the following night she returned. It was then that he'd called her Nina—it wasn't her name, but he felt a need to somehow identify this wide-mouthed, pink-tongued stranger who slaked herself upon him, slaked his own urgency again and again as her hissing breath rasped in his ears.

Once more she vanished while he slept, and he hadn't seen her all day. But at times he'd been conscious of her secret stare, a coldness falling upon him like an unglimpsed shadow, and he'd known that tonight she'd come again.

Now, as the drums sounded in the distance, Nina slept. Unmindful of the din, heedless of his presence, her eyes hooded and she lay somnolent in animal repletion.

Nolan shuddered. That's what she was; an animal. In repose, the lithe brown body was grotesquely elongated, the wide mouth accentuating the ugliness of her face. How could he have coupled with this creature? Nolan grimaced in self-disgust as he turned away.

Well, no matter—it was ended now, over once and for all. Today the message had arrived from Belem: Darlene and Robbie were on the ship, ready for the flight to Manaos. Tomorrow morning he'd start downriver to meet them, escort them here. He'd had his qualms about their coming; they'd have to face three months in this hellhole before the year was up, but Darlene had insisted.

And she was right. Nolan knew it now. At least they'd be together and that would help see him through. He wouldn't need the bottle anymore, and he wouldn't need Nina.

Nolan lay back and waited for sleep to come, shutting out the sound of the drums, the sight of the shadowy shape beside him. Only a few hours until morning, he told himself. And in the morning the nightmare would be over.

The trip to Manaos was an ordeal, but it ended in Darlene's arms. She was blonder and more beautiful than he'd remembered, more loving and tender than he'd ever known her to be, and in the union that was their reunion Nolan found fulfillment. Of course there was none of the avid hunger of Nina's coiling caresses, none of the mindless thrashing to final frenzy. But it didn't matter; the two of them were together at last. The two of them, and Robbie.

Robbie was a revelation.

Nolan hadn't anticipated the intensity of his own reaction. But now, after the long trip back in the wheezing launch, he stood beside the crib in the spare bedroom and gazed down at his son with an overwhelming surge of pride.

"Isn't he adorable?" Darlene said. "He looks just like you."

"You're prejudiced." Nolan grinned, but he was flattered. And when the tiny pink starshell of a hand reached forth to meet his fingers, he tingled at the touch.

Then Darlene gasped.

Nolan glanced up quickly. "What's the matter?" he said.

"Nothing." Darlene was staring past him. "I thought I saw someone outside the window."

Nolan followed her gaze. "No one out there." He moved to the window, peered at the clearing beyond. "Not a soul."

Darlene passed a hand before her eyes. "I guess I'm just overtired," she said. "The long trip—"

Nolan put his arm around her. "Why don't you go lie down? Mama Dolores can look after Robbie."

Darlene hesitated. "Are you sure she knows what to do?"

"Look who's talking!" Nolan laughed. "They don't call her Mama for nothing—she's had ten kids of her own. She's in the kitchen right now, fixing Robbie's formula. I'll go get her."

So Darlene went down the hall to their bedroom for a siesta, and Mama Dolores took over Robbie's schedule while Nolan made his daily rounds in the fields.

The heat was stifling, worse than anything he could remember. Even Moises was gasping for air as he gunned the jeep over the rutted roadway, peering into the shimmering haze.

Nolan wiped his forehead. Maybe he'd been too hasty, bringing Darlene and the baby here. But a man was entitled to see his own son, and in a few months they'd be out of this miserable sweatbox forever. No sense getting uptight; everything was going to be all right.

But at dusk, when he returned to the bungalow, Mama Dolores greeted him at the door with a troubled face.

"What is it?" Nolan said. "Something wrong with Robbie?"

Mama shook her head. "He sleeps like an angel," she murmured. "But the *señora*—"

In their room Darlene lay shivering on the bed, eyes closed. Her head moved ceaselessly on the pillows even when Nolan pressed his palm against her brow.

"Fever." Nolan gestured to Mama Dolores, and the old woman held Darlene still while he forced the thermometer between her lips.

The red column inched upward. "One hundred and four." Nolan straightened quickly. "Go fetch Moises. Tell him I want the launch ready, *pronto*. We'll have to get her to the doctor at Manaos."

Darlene's eyes fluttered open; she'd heard.

"No, you can't! The baby—"

"Do not trouble yourself. I will look after the little one." Mama's voice was soothing. "Now you must rest."

"No, please . . ."

Darlene's voice trailed off into an incoherent babbling, and she sank back. Nolan kept his hand on her forehead; the heat was like an oven. "Now just relax, darling. It's all right. I'm going with you."

And he did.

If the first trip had been an ordeal, this one was an agony: a frantic thrust through the sultry night on the steaming river, Moises sweating over the throttle as Nolan held Darlene's shuddering shoulders against the straw mattress in the stern of the vibrating launch. They made Manaos by dawn and roused Dr. Robales from slumber at his house near the plaza.

Then came the examination, the removal to the hospital, the tests, and the verdict. A simple matter, Dr. Robales said, and no need for alarm. With proper treatment and rest she would recover. A week here in the hospital—

"A week?" Nolan's voice rose. "I've got to get back for the loading. I can't stay here that long!"

"There is no need for you to stay, *señor*. She shall have my personal attention, I assure you."

It was small comfort, but Nolan had no choice. And he was too tired to protest, too tired to worry. Once aboard the launch and heading back, he stretched out on the straw mattress in a sleep that was like death itself.

Nolan awakened to the sound of drums. He jerked upright with a startled cry, then realized that night had come and they were once again at anchor beside the dock. Moises grinned at him in weary triumph.

"Almost we do not make it," he said. "The motor is bad. No matter, it is good to be home again."

Nolan nodded, flexing his cramped limbs. He stepped out onto the dock, then hurried up the path across the clearing. The darkness boomed.

Home? This corner of hell, where the drums dinned and the shadows leapt and capered before flickering fires?

All but one, that is. For as Nolan moved forward, another shadow glided out from the deeper darkness beside the bungalow.

It was Nina.

Nolan blinked as he recognized her standing there and staring up at him. There was no mistaking the look on her face or its urgency, but he had no time to waste in words. Brushing past her, he hastened to the doorway and she melted back into the night.

Mama Dolores was waiting for him inside, nodding her greeting.

"Robbie—is he all right?"

"*Sí, señor*. I take good care. *Por favor*, I sleep in his room."

"Good." Nolan turned and started for the hall, then hesitated as Mama Dolores frowned. "What is it?" he said.

The old woman hesitated. "You will not be offended if I speak?"

"Of course not."

Mama's voice sank to a murmur. "It concerns the one outside."

"Nina?"

"That is not her name, but no matter." Mama shook her head. "For two days she has waited there. I see you with her now when you return. And I see you with her before—"

"That's none of your business!" Nolan reddened. "Besides, it's all over now."

"Does she believe that?" Mama's gaze was grave. "You must tell her to go."

"I've tried. But the girl comes from the mountains; she doesn't speak English—"

"I know." Mama nodded. "She is one of the snake people."

Nolan stared at her. "They worship snakes up there?"

"No, not worship."

"Then what do you mean?"

"These people—they *are* snakes."

Nolan scowled. "What is this?"

"The truth, *señor*. This one you call Nina—this girl—is not a girl. She is of the ancient race from the high peaks, where the great serpents dwell. Your workers here, even Moises, know only the jungle, but I come from the great valley beneath the mountains, and as a child I learned to fear those who lurk above. We do not go there, but sometimes the snake people come to us. In the spring, when they awaken, they shed their skins, and for a time they are fresh and clean before the scales grow again. It is then that they come to mate with men."

She went on like that, whispering about creatures half serpent and half human, with bodies cold to the touch, limbs that could writhe in boneless contortion to squeeze the breath from a man and crush him like the coils of a giant constrictor. She spoke of forked tongues, of voices hissing forth from mouths yawning incredibly wide on movable jawbones. And she might have gone on, but Nolan stopped her now; his head was throbbing with weariness.

"That's enough," he said. "I thank you for your concern."

"But you do not believe me."

"I didn't say that." Tired as he was, Nolan still remembered the basic rule—never contradict these people or make fun of their superstitions. And he couldn't afford to alienate Mama now. "I shall take precautions," he told her gravely. "Right now I've got to rest. And I want to see Robbie."

Mama Dolores put her hand to her mouth. "I forget—the little one, he is alone—"

She turned and padded hastily down the hallway, Nolan behind her. Together they entered the nursery.

"Ah!" Mama exhaled a sigh of relief. "The *pobrecito* sleeps."

Robbie lay in his crib, a shaft of moonlight from the window bathing his tiny face. From his rosebud mouth issued a gentle snore.

Nolan smiled at the sound, then nodded at Mama. "I'm going to turn in now. You take good care of him."

"I will not leave." Mama settled herself in a rocker beside the crib. As

Nolan turned to go, she called after him softly. "Remember what I have told you, *señor*. If she comes again—"

Nolan moved down the hall to his bedroom at the far end. He hadn't trusted himself to answer her. After all, she meant well; it was just that he was too damned tired to put up with any more nonsense from the old woman.

In his bedroom something rustled.

Nolan flinched, then halted as the shadow-shape glided forth from the darkened corner beside the open window.

Nina stood before him and she was stark naked. Stark naked, her arms opening in invitation.

He retreated a step. "No," he said.

She came forward, smiling.

"Go away—get out of here."

He gestured her back. Nina's smile faded and she made a sound in her throat, a little gasp of entreaty. Her hands reached out—

"Dammit, leave me alone!"

Nolan struck her on the cheek. It wasn't more than a slap, and she couldn't have been hurt. But suddenly Nina's face contorted as she launched herself at him, her fingers splayed and aiming at his eyes. This time he hit her hard—hard enough to send her reeling back.

"Out!" he said. He forced her to the open window, raising his hand threateningly as she spewed and spit her rage, then snatched her garment and clambered over the sill into the darkness beyond.

Nolan stood by the window watching as Nina moved away across the clearing. For a moment she turned in a path of moonlight and looked back at him—only a moment, but long enough for Nolan to see the livid fury blazing in her eyes.

Then she was gone, gliding off into the night, where the drums thudded in distant darkness.

She was gone, but the hate remained. Nolan felt its force as he stretched out upon the bed. Ought to undress, but he was too tired. The throbbing in his head was worse, pulsing to the beat of the drums. And the hate was in his head too. God, that ugly face! Like the thing in mythology —what was it?—the Medusa. One look turned men to stone. Her locks of hair were live serpents.

But that was legend, like Mama Dolores's stories about the snake people. Strange—did every race have its belief in such creatures? Could there be some grotesque, distorted element of truth behind all these old wives' tales?

He didn't want to think about it now; he didn't want to think of anything. Not Nina, not Darlene, not even Robbie. Darlene would be all right, Robbie was fine, and Nina was gone. That left him, alone here with the drums. Damned pounding. Had to stop, had to stop so he could sleep—

It was the silence that awakened him. He sat up with a start, realizing he must have slept for hours, because the shadows outside the window were dappled with the grayish pink of dawn.

Nolan rose, stretching, then stepped out into the hall. The shadows were darker here and everything was still.

He went down the hallway to the other bedroom. The door was ajar and he moved past it, calling softly. "Mama Dolores—"

Nolan's tongue froze to the roof of his mouth. Time itself was frozen as he stared down at the crushed and pulpy thing sprawled shapelessly beside the rocker, its sightless eyes bulging from the swollen purple face.

No use calling her name again; she'd never hear it. And Robbie—

Nolan turned in the frozen silence, his eyes searching the shadows at the far side of the room.

The crib was empty.

Then he found his voice and cried out, cried out again as he saw the open window and the gray vacancy of the clearing beyond.

Suddenly he was at the window, climbing out and dropping to the matted sward below. He ran across the clearing, through the trees, and into the open space before the riverbank.

Moises was in the launch, working on the engine. He looked up as Nolan ran toward him, shouting.

"What are you doing here?"

"There is the problem of the motor. It requires attention. I come early, before the heat of the day—"

"Did you see her?"

"Who, señor?"

"The girl—Nina—"

"Ah, yes. The *Indio.*" Moises nodded. "She is gone, in her catamaran, up the river. Two, maybe three hours ago, just as I arrive."

"Why didn't you stop her?"

"For what reason?"

Nolan gestured quickly. "Get that engine started—we're going after her."

Moises frowned. "As I told you, there is the matter of the repairs. Perhaps this afternoon—"

"We'll never catch her then!" Nolan gripped Moises's shoulder. "Don't you understand? She's taken Robbie!"

"Calm yourself, *señor*. With my own eyes I saw her go to the boat and she was alone, I swear it. She does not have the little one."

Nolan thought of the hatred in Nina's eyes, and he shuddered. "Then what did she do with him?"

Moises shook his head. "This I do not know. But I am sure she has no need of another infant."

"What are you talking about?"

"I notice her condition when she walked to the boat." Moises shrugged, but even before the words came, Nolan knew.

"Why do you look at me like that, *señor?* Is it not natural for a woman to bulge when she carries a baby in her belly?"

WEREWIND

J. MICHAEL REAVES

California is a place of dichotomies. On the one hand is the glamour and glitter of the movie industry, the sun and fun and lure of the beaches; on the other there is the blood darkness of Charlie Manson, the Zebra murders, the ominous undercurrent of strange cults and ideas. In "Werewind," J. Michael Reaves captures both faces of California, and in so doing crafts a suspenseful thriller about an out-of-work actor, a series of bizarre Hollywood murders, and a persistent Santa Ana windstorm that mysteriously coincides with the killings.

"**W** . . . arning everyone to stay off the streets if possible, particularly in the coastal and canyon areas. The winds have been clocked at forty-five miles an hour, and the Tujunga and Beverly Glen fires are still out of control. Travelers' advisories are posted for all freeways, Angeles Crest and the Grapevine. I repeat, please do not drive unless absolutely necessary.

"In other news, the Hollywood Scalper's fifth victim has been identified as Karen Lacey, a twenty-two-year-old actress. The pattern of mutilation murders connected with show business thus continues. . . ."

Simon Drake turned the car radio's volume down when he heard a sudden grating sound in the old Chrysler's engine. Holding his breath, he turned off Hollywood Boulevard onto a side street, and a moment later the engine quit, and the car coasted to a stop near an empty parking lot.

"Oh, *Christ!*" Simon twisted the key several times, but the only result was the ominous grinding noise. He slumped back against the hot plastic seat cover and watched the palm trees near Sunset slowly shredding in the wind. "That's it," he muttered. "I've lost the part." He grimaced in disgust, then winced as his chapped lips cracked.

He was thirty-three years old and had ninety-one dollars in the bank. His rent was overdue, and his boss at the Cahuenga Liquor Store had told him not to bother coming back when he had left for his latest interview. And now he was going to miss that interview, and probably a role he wanted more than anything, because of engine trouble.

Simon slammed his hands against the steering wheel. Sweat blurred his vision. The car's interior was stifling; he had the windows up despite the ninety-degree weather. It was impossible to drive otherwise during a Santa Ana windstorm; the hot dry gusts struck like solid blows. Simon looked about. There was no one on this street and only a few people crossing the intersection at Hollywood Boulevard. The wind kept most people indoors. A newspaper was slashed in half by his car's aerial. The wind howled. It hadn't stopped in six days; it wasn't going to stop now just because he had to walk to a phone.

He sighed and opened the door, pushing with all of his hundred and fifty pounds against the wind. His eyes began to water behind his sunglasses. The gusts tore at the permanent his agent had suggested. The air smelled of smoke; sepia clouds from the canyon fires covered most of the sky. The baleful sunlight was appropriate lighting for his life, Simon thought as he walked toward the boulevard, leaning into the wind. He looked at his watch and realized he could not reach Marathon Studios on time now.

He stifled a yawn as he walked; he had gotten little sleep the night before, due to a neighbor's Doberman. The dog had barked all night at the wind. He watched the cars creeping cautiously along. A Dodge van cut in front of a Mercedes, and the little old lady driving the latter hit the horn and shouted a curse. Simon, watching her, stepped on a wad of chewing gum and kicked his foot free with the same curse. The wind fanned anger like it fanned the canyon fires. Even so, Simon felt that he had much to be angry about. He had come to L.A. from New York five years before, a graduate of a good acting school, with several commercials and plays to his credit. His fascination was horror movies; his ambition, to be the next Boris Karloff. But so far he had barely been able to stay alive with a few bit parts on Saturday morning TV shows and a role in a low-budget vampire spoof. He had expected it to be hard. He had expected to struggle. But for five years?

Near a hot dog stand he saw a pay phone. As he reached for it, a spark he could see in the sunlight arced from his finger to the metal casing, painfully. He was too tired even to curse. He put his last dime in and dialed.

The greasy smell from the hot dog stand reminded him that he had had no breakfast or lunch. For the last month he had been living mostly on money from his part-time job, which was not nearly enough for the rent plus photographs and résumé copies. So he had not bought groceries for two weeks.

During those same two weeks, however, Simon's agent had convinced Martin Knox, who was producing a horror picture, to consider Simon for the lead. Knox had been dubious, but after several tests Simon was still in the running. Or had been . . . Martin Knox's temper was legendary in the industry, and he did not like to be kept waiting.

Simon wanted the part, and not only for economic reasons. He was sure that he could do things with the character that would win an Oscar, the first for a horror picture lead since Fredric March in the 1931 *Dr. Jekyll and Mr. Hyde.* He watched the tourists and locals as he waited for the studio switchboard to put him through. The Hollywood freaks would not be out in force until after dark, but some had already braved the heat and the wind. Krishna folk with tambourines and Jesus freaks with tracts eyed each other warily. Aging hippies, long hair beginning to gray, shuffled by. And, of course, there were the few too strange for any description. The Hollywood Scalper, Simon was sure, would look tame in a lineup with some of these. He saw Trapper Jake approaching: an old man, but still tall and burly, with long braided hair, a Bowie knife and pouch, and hand-stitched buckskin clothes. Despite appearances, he was an amiable sort; once, while Simon and a date had waited in a movie line, he had regaled them with a story of being raised by bears in Yosemite. Simon turned and huddled against the phone stall. He wanted no tales from Trapper Jake today.

Martin Knox answered the phone. "Hello, Simon." His voice was barely audible over the wind. "Why aren't you here?" He sounded annoyed.

"Car trouble, Mr. Knox. I was hoping we could reschedule—?"

"I see." Silence for a moment. Simon could picture Knox vividly, sitting owllike behind his desk, eyes hooded. "Well, I'm afraid it won't be necessary, Simon. I think we'll be going with another actor. Your tests make you look too short for the part."

Simon tightened his fingers around the receiver. "I'm five-eleven," he said.

"You're also late." The phone clicked, and a dial tone began.

Simon hung up carefully, not allowing himself to slam the receiver onto the hook, not allowing himself any feelings at all. Not thinking about how much he had wanted this part, about what he could have done with it. So you want to be in pictures, he said to himself.

He dug into his pocket and came up with a lone nickel. He stared at it, realizing that he couldn't even call a tow truck. He closed his hand over the nickel suddenly, digging fingernails into his palm.

A gust of wind hit the phone stall hard enough to shake the phone; it gurgled and dropped his dime into the return bin. Simon fished it out and looked at it, stifling a sudden strong urge to laugh. Christ, he thought. My SAG dues are coming up too.

He called a tow truck, then stood staring across Hollywood Boulevard, wishing he knew someone he could call and talk to. In five years he had made few friends here. Usually he was too busy to feel the lack of companionship; hustling parts and working took up all of his time. But occasionally the loneliness would hit him hard.

The heat waves from the street, when not scattered by the wind, gave the scene a wavering, dreamlike appearance. Sometimes it seemed to him as if all Los Angeles was a mirage, populated by ghosts. The very ground was insubstantial, prone to earthquakes, and the city's main product was fantasy. Simon stood there, overwhelmed by loneliness and a sense of unreality. Then a sudden loud noise—an empty soft-drink can, propelled by the wind—made him jump nervously backward. He collided with someone and felt himself seized in a powerful grip and spun roughly about. "You watch who the *hell* you're knocking around!" a voice shouted, and he was pushed violently into the hot dog stand; the sharp edge of the counter dug into his back. Half stunned by surprise and pain, Simon saw that it was amiable Trapper Jake who had pushed him. The giant old man, resembling in beard and buckskin the bear he claimed had raised him, came toward Simon. His face was choleric with rage and both fists were raised. Passersby stopped to watch with interest.

Simon ran past the phone stall toward the edge of the building. Jake changed course to intercept him, but at that moment a particularly strong burst of wind upset an overflowing wire trash bin, scattering garbage across the star-inlaid sidewalk. Jake slipped on a paper plate greased with chili and sprawled headlong through the trash, to the vast amusement of the stand's patrons. Simon did not wait to see what would happen next; he turned the corner and ran. The wind seemed almost to help him, lifting him in great lunar leaps down the deserted side street. He ran, full of panic, elbows pumping, lungs sucking in the crackling air. The fear combined with his hunger to exhaust him quickly. He reached the empty parking lot by his car, stumbled across the low chain at its edge, and collapsed. The hot blacktop, dusted with light ash from the fires, scorched his cheek and arms. With a groan of pain he rolled into the shade of a nearby brick building.

He lay there for a few minutes, sobbing with pain and anger. He pounded both scraped hands painfully against the rough asphalt. There had to be an end to this run of bad luck—he would make an end to it, somehow! Someway, he promised himself, aware of the last-reel triteness of it and not caring, he would make of this moment a turning point. He wanted to act, and to eat three times a day; he wanted his name, eventually, on a sidewalk star. And he wanted that role more than he wanted breath in his lungs. He wanted it, and he intended to have it.

The wind was still blowing; harder now, it seemed. Simon looked about him. There was no one in the lot's kiosk. Against the adjoining wall was a large trash bin; a department store mannikin with a broken head grinned, one-eyed, at him. The sun, like a spotlight with a red gel, cast crimson light over the scene. Simon felt again a dreamlike quality suffusing everything. He could hear the wind, but it seemed somehow distant. The feeling was that of loneliness and waiting.

The wind howled.

A dust devil blew into the parking lot, a skittering whirl of hot dry air, picking up litter and dust and the fine white ash from the fires and spinning it all about. But instead of coming apart after a moment, it kept spinning, faster and faster. It began to shrink. The debris that had defined it before was flung from it. There was only dust and ash now, and then not even that; just a silvery spinning of air, growing denser.

It was assuming a human shape.

The wind was still blowing, but it did not disturb the whirling shape. There was a breathless tension to the air around Simon. The shape coalesced, solidified. . . .

It became a woman.

She seemed younger than Simon, with silver hair and pale skin. She was naked. Though she looked solid, she seemed also insubstantial, as though she would blur or become transparent if viewed from another angle. Her face was beautiful, but somehow he could not make out her features clearly. Her eyes were wide and blank, like unminted silver coins.

She smiled at him. The smile would have been touching had it not been for the blank eyes; they made it hideous. It was a smile full of yearning, full of gratitude, of waiting at last fulfilled. She took two steps toward Simon. He drew back against the wall, making a high, thin sound in his throat. She hesitated—and then a gust seized her, spun her around like a ballerina, faster and faster, until her hair was a thinning silver stain in the air, and the lines of her body ran like pale paint.

Then she was gone, and Simon was alone in the lot, save for the cry of the wind.

It had been a hallucination, of course. That was the only possible explanation. Considering the stress he had been under, it was a wonder he had not seen the beast from 20,000 fathoms in that parking lot. So Simon told himself, starting as he stumbled out of the lot and continuing for the rest of the day. By evening he had almost convinced himself of it.

Hallucination or not, he had made a promise to himself, there in the parking lot. He did not intend to let the part in Knox's picture escape him. He had been invited to a party the following evening, and he knew that Martin Knox would be there. Perhaps Simon could persuade him to reconsider.

He arrived late at the small house deep in the maze of Laurel Canyon. He had almost changed his mind about coming; the thought of confronting Knox did unpleasant things to his stomach. But he had to make the effort. Also, he did not receive invitations to many parties.

Jon Shea, the host, handed him a drink at the door. He was also an actor, tall and well-built—he and Simon were members of the same gym. "How've you been, Simon?" Jon asked. "You're looking a bit wasted."

"Haven't been getting much sleep," Simon said. "Neighbor's dog keeps me up all night." He always felt slightly uncomfortable around Jon— any criticism, no matter how minor, from him always produced in Simon a need to explain and justify. Jon Shea was only a year older than Simon, but he had done much better as an immigrant New York actor: three movies and currently featured player in a TV series. Simon resented him for it, and disliked himself for feeling that way.

"This damn wind keeps me awake," Jon said. "My grandma says— she's from the old country, you know"—Simon recalled that Jon's name had been longer and full of consonants before his agency suggested a change—"anyway, she says a wind like this is a devil wind, an evil spirit—hey, are you okay?"

Simon had stopped in the hallway and leaned against the redwood wall. "Fine. Drink's a little strong . . . what did your grandmother say about the wind?"

"Oh, she's got a lot of old stories like that." He looked past Simon into the living room, where people circulated. "Gotta go play host. Lots of ladies around. Find yourself one." Then he was gone, before Simon could stop him.

Simon walked slowly through the small, cozy house, edging his way around groups of people, still feeling the coldness that had gripped his gut when Jon had mentioned his grandmother's theory about the wind. He thought about the apparition in the parking lot. Coincidence, he said to himself, sounding the word out syllable by syllable, chanting it as he might a mantra. Coincidence. A comforting word to know.

Disco accompanied his nervous heartbeat. The windows rattling in the wind sounded occasionally above the music. Simon rubbed the cool glass he held against one check as he paused in the doorway of the game room. An overhead light and ceiling fan hung over the pool table, where Knox was sinking the last ball. Several onlookers applauded as the cushion shot hit the pocket. The only one not watching was a woman with short dark hair, playing a Pachenko machine in a far corner.

Knox raised his glass to the applause and started out of the room. A large man in a dark suit followed him. Simon took a deep breath and stepped forward as Knox was about to pass him. "Mr. Knox," he said, smiling. That was as far as he got before a large hand encircled his arm, fingers meeting thumb easily. Simon looked up at the man accompanying Knox. He was very large; his face was battered and slightly bored. A pair of black horn-rimmed glasses looked startlingly incongruous on him.

"It's all right, Daniel," Knox said. Simon's arm was released. He recalled that many people in the industry had hired bodyguards in the past week, since the scalper killings began. "Thank you," Simon said to Knox, somehow keeping the smile in place. "I just wanted to talk to you a bit more about the lead in your picture."

Knox's face was expressionless. "What exactly did you want to say?"

Simon dropped the smile for a serious look. The thought crossed his mind that he was acting harder now than he ever had in his life. "Frankly, I hope to talk you into reconsidering. I feel I'm right for the part."

Knox's face was as motionless as a freeze frame. "I'm afraid it's too late for that. Terrence Froseth is set for the part. I've already talked with his agent—"

Simon did not know who Terrence Froseth was, and did not care. Realizing that pressing the issue was bad form, he nevertheless plunged ahead. "It's never too late," he said intensely. "After all, Gable wasn't the first choice for *Gone With the Wind*. Karloff wasn't the first choice for the monster in *Frankenstein*."

"You put yourself in good company," Knox said dryly. "I must say your persistence is admirable, though you need to learn some manners . . . if Froseth cannot take the part for any reason, perhaps we shall talk further. That's all I'll say on the matter." He walked down the hallway. Daniel looked coolly at Simon and followed.

Someone in the room turned on a small television set, and a news anchorman's voice filled the air. "As of this evening the latest fire in Topanga is under control. To repeat, the wind has increased slightly since yesterday, and driving is still hazardous.

"Police have not released the identity of the latest victim of the Hollywood Scalper, but they do confirm that he was a film director. This is the sixth scalper victim in as many days. . . ."

The conversation had stopped, and the room's occupants were gathered intently around the set as Simon walked down the hall. He stood before a window and watched the trees, ghastly in orange and green lawn lights, thrashing in the wind. It had been blowing for a solid week. It suddenly occurred to him that the Hollywood Scalper's spree had started the day after the Santa Anas had begun to blow. The wind makes people crazy, he thought, remembering Trapper Jake.

The Hollywood Scalper was yet another item of worry: a psychotic who killed only show business people, knifing them and then cutting a small scalplock from them, which he presumably kept. But all the victims to date had been people more advanced in their careers than Simon was. Surely he was beneath the scalper's notice.

He was still staring out the window, when there suddenly appeared before him a pale, transparent face floating in the night. He turned with a gasp—someone was standing behind him. Simon sighed in relief. For an instant, the shape of her face and the effect of the reflection had made him think—

The dark-haired woman from the game room stepped back a pace. "I didn't mean to startle you."

Simon smiled. "No problem. I—thought you were someone else."

She smiled as well. "My name's Molly Harren—and you're Simon Drake. I saw you in that movie—"

"Oh, God, no," he said, hiding his head in mock despair. "Don't tell me you saw *Disco Dracula*!"

"You were good," she said, laughing, as did he. "The movie was abysmal, of course, but you were good." Simon grinned at her. Her black hair framed a fascinating face, with large, dark liquid eyes. Though she was laughing at the moment, he could see that her normal expression was studious, almost intense. She wore a sleeveless evening dress, and it showed her to be in very good shape—not merely sleek and well-fed like most of the people there, but lean, with graceful curves of musculature. She obviously kept herself in shape with more than the obligatory morning jog. And her name sounded familiar. . . . "Are you an actress?"

"No. A writer."

It hit him then, and his jaw dropped. "You wrote *Blackout!*"

She nodded. "But that wasn't my title. I called it *The Dark Side of Town.*"

He had been about to compliment her on the screenplay—it had been one of his favorite recent suspense films, about a psychotic terrorizing a town during a power failure. Instead, he said, "That's a much better title."

She nodded, pursing her lips in disgust. "The studios are all into one-word titles now. 'Easier audience understanding.' They're talking a sequel, and of course they want to call it *Blackout II*. So imaginative." Then she shook her head and smiled. "Sorry. I—well, I overheard your conversation with Knox. I just wanted you to know that I understand how you feel. It isn't easy dealing with them sometimes."

Conversation came easily after that. They discussed her screenplay and his career, and the common interest they shared in horror and suspense films. Simon forgot about the disappointment of losing the Marathon part, at least momentarily. It had been quite some time since he had met a woman he could talk with so easily, one with whom he shared so many interests. He was aware once again of how lonely he had been, because now, for a time, he was not.

It was almost two A.M. when they noticed people leaving. "I'd better be going," Molly said. "It was very nice meeting you, Simon."

They were sitting on a rattan couch under a framed one-sheet poster of one of Jon Shea's three movies. Simon glanced at it as they stood and only realized later that he did not feel the usual pang of jealously. He considered and discarded several clever come-on lines, and instead said simply, "I'd like to follow you home, Molly."

She smiled slightly, almost wistfully. "I think I'd like you to—but not tonight, I'm afraid. Why don't we get together for lunch—say, Wednesday?"

Wednesday was fine with him. He offered to walk her to her car. When they stepped outside, the wind struck at them savagely. Simon leaned into it, his shirt collar whipping at his neck as he watched her drive away in a pale Fiat. The wind was strong enough to buffet the small car over the white line several times—he hoped she reached home safely.

His own car was still in the shop, and so he walked home, down Laurel Canyon to Hollywood, up Highland to Franklin. It was a long, nervous walk. Black and white patrol cars, spectral under the mercury lamps, cruised the streets. He was two blocks from his apartment when one stopped him and, after checking his ID, gave him a ride the rest of the way. It was after three when he wearily climbed the steps to his second-story apartment in the hills above Cahuenga. The building was one of the older Spanish-style constructions, with pantiles and archways and a small open court filled with cactus and jacaranda. Simon could smell the heavy scent of the flowers, now strong, now faint, as the wind gusted. He could hear the power lines above the building humming, and he could also hear the Doberman in the yard next door barking. He saw it, a black shape restlessly prowling the driveway beyond the Cyclone fence. It would be another sleepless night.

The street's acoustics made the wind sound sometimes like wolves howling, sometimes like babies screaming. Something flickered in the corner of Simon's vision as he stepped onto his porch; he heard a sharp *crack!* like a whip. He turned quickly and saw that a TV antenna line had come loose and was flapping against a wall across the street. All the way home he had felt like a character in a Val Lewton film, sure that someone or something had been following him, constantly looking behind him at the skirling leaves and clattering debris that the wind hurled about. He stared down at the deserted street, leached of color by the moon. The wind now sounded like the wailing of lost souls. He could not have felt more alone if he were the last man on Earth; he wished desperately that Molly had said yes.

Despite the night sounds, he managed to fall asleep, but not for long. He dreamed that someone was sinking in a black lake, calling to him, stretching long white arms out to him. He awoke with a start, still hearing his name being called.

The water bed rocked him gently as he rubbed his eyes. His body and shorts were damp with sweat. He looked at the luminous face of his watch: four-thirty. The wind still blew outside, but the dog had stopped barking. He felt more tired than ever. Understandable, with nightmares of someone drowning and calling his name. . . .

He heard the call again.

Simon lay quite still. Over the ceaseless rise and fall of the wind he had heard his name—a long, wailing cry, faint, breathless, like the cry of a woman drowning. He lay and listened with his entire body. And it came again: *Simonnn . . .* drawn out and whispered, almost as though the wind itself had cried to him.

It *was* the wind! He heard it again, the rising whistle outside shaping itself into his name. He stared at the ceiling, not daring to turn his head, afraid to look at the silvered square of the window, knowing he would have to when the call came again.

Simonnn. . . .

He turned his head toward the window.

Limned in the moonlight, hair like streamers of fog, she stared at him with eyes cold as stars.

Simon rolled over and out of the bed with a cry and ran down the hall. The light of the full moon, coming through the living room window, spotlighted a large poster of Lon Chaney, Jr., as the wolf man. It seemed to be coming out of the poster toward him, jaws opening wide; Simon gasped, turned, and stumbled into a hanging planter. The leaves scratched his face like spiders' legs. He clawed open the front door, lunging outside into the hot, moving air, not thinking, simply running. He looked down from the porch at the street—shadows crawled in the wind. Then something—a blown leaf, his hair, or *her hand*—brushed his cheek. With a shriek he leapt down the tiled steps, tripped and fell, scrambled to his feet, turned—

She stood before him.

She was not more than three feet away. As before, she appeared corporeal and yet ghostly. Her hair floated behind her like a gossamer web. Her eyes were still silver wells, looking at him but not seeing him. Her expression was that of ineffable loneliness and longing.

She reached for him.

Simonnn. . . .

He did not see her lips move; the wind seemed to whisper his name. Frozen with fear, he saw the approaching hands very clearly: they were as pale and smooth as blown snow, no trace of fingerprints or veining. Her lips parted in a smiling rictus, and behind them was only darkness. . . .

Simon shut his eyes and flung himself backward, hands flailing the air before him. He felt one pass through coldness, and then he had turned and was plunging through a flower bed, not feeling the cactus rake his bare legs, fingers hooking into the links of the Cyclone fence, the wind tearing, shrieking at him. He pulled himself up and over the fence, fell against cool concrete and heard a low growl nearby. He realized then where he had fled.

The Doberman leapt, a shadow with gleaming teeth. Simon lurched to his feet and ran, knowing it was useless. Then, above the wind's howling, he heard a crackling sound. He ran against a wall, knocking the breath from his lungs and falling. He turned over and saw that one of the high-tension lines from the power pole overhead had come loose. Like a sparkling whip it fell, lashing the charging dog squarely across the back. The dog's growl changed to an agonized yelp—the force of the shock hurled it across the driveway to land, quivering, against the fence. The broken power line danced and scattered sparks across the concrete.

Simon looked about him quickly, but there was no sign of her anywhere. The only sounds were the wind and the hissing of the power line. Oddly enough, all the noise had not aroused the neighbors. He looked at the dog—it had stopped quivering.

The wind brought the smell of burned flesh to him, and he turned away to be sick.

Hey, Simon," Jon Shea said. "You're just in time to applaud. I'm going for two-seventy-five today."

Simon had just entered the workout area of the Golden West Health Spa. The large room, walled with mirrors, was filled with men working body-building equipment. An AM rock station played over the members' grunts and groans. Jon lay prone on a bench press, seized the bar, and raised it over his chest, straining as he lifted a stack of weights six times. He rose slowly, skin shining with sweat, and looked at Simon. "You don't look good. Maybe you shouldn't work out."

"I—didn't get much sleep last night," Simon replied. He was pale, and he leaned against a rack of barbells. His legs still smarted from the cactus and the fall onto the driveway. "I just came in to ask you a question," he continued.

"Sure. Shoot."

Simon stared through the floor-to-ceiling window at the jogging track outside. No one was jogging, despite the rarity of a smog-free day. The wind vibrated the glass before him and he stepped back hastily.

"Your grandmother called this a demon wind, you said. What did she mean?"

Jon blinked in surprise. "Oh, it's just legends, you know. They had stories about werewinds, that were supposed to take human shape—you better sit down, you look awful."

Simon did so. "Go on, please," he said faintly.

Jon scratched his head. "I don't remember that much about it . . . they're not evil so much as just lonely, sort of lost souls, I guess. You know how the wind is always described as sounding lonely? Well, the werewind is drawn to lonely people." He peered closely at Simon, who was staring out the window at the wind-shook spires of the Chinese Theatre. "Why the interest?"

"Oh . . . I had an idea it might make a good horror movie."

Jon snorted. "Everybody's a writer. But I think you're too late on that one. Molly Harren asked me about it days ago."

Simon asked, "How do you stop a werewind?"

"That's what Molly asked. I'll tell you what I told her—look in the library. I don't remember. It's all bullshit anyway."

"Yeah," Simon said, standing. "Right." He opened the door to leave, but at that moment the music piped into the spa stopped, and a voice said: "This is a news bulletin from KCCO. Yet another Hollywood Scalper victim has been found, this one in West Los Angeles. The body has been identified as that of Terrence Froseth, a young actor. This is the seventh scalper victim in seven days . . ."

Simon saw Jon go pale beneath his tan. Across the floor another actor released his grip on a pulley and a stack of weights crashed down.

Simon leaned against the door, feeling quite weak. He felt a number of other emotions as well: horror and sympathy were among them. But the dominant feeling was a hideous sense of relief. And unbidden into his mind came a thought that disgusted him: I'm back in the running again.

Outside, the wind howled.

Simon left the gym and took a bus down to Mannie's Auto Repair on Melrose. He gave Mannie a check, wondering vaguely how he would cover it, then drove downtown to the main branch of the Los Angeles Library. There he spent several hours under the high, carved ceilings leafing through books of legends and superstitions.

He found several spells to make the wind blow, and a few references to various kinds of wind demons and manifestations both malign and benign. At last he discovered a passing reference to the legend of the werewind. According to the paragraph, the werewind could be bound by tying knots in a length of hair. The stronger the wind, the more knots were required, and it would not abate until the last knot had been tied. The passage cited an in-depth work on the subject in *The Omnibus of the Occult*, but when he looked for that book, he found that it had already been checked out.

Simon stood before the card catalogue files and pressed the heels of his hands against his eyes until green patterns spun in the darkness. He was not quite sure what to do next. He told himself that he should be out job-hunting, or looking through the trades and nagging his agent. But he did not move. He stood quietly, wishing he could stop the thoughts that whirled like dust devils through his head.

Such an apparition simply could not be—at least not as he stood there with the sun streaming through the latticed windows. And so, Simon thought, I am probably having a nervous breakdown. He clasped his hands together to stop their trembling. Was any career worth this? But on the other hand, what else could he do? At thirty-three, with only odd jobs behind him, how could he hope to make a decent living even if he was interested in anything other than acting? He had been through worse times. He had lived in a Greenwich Village loft without heat during the winter while auditioning for plays. Things had gotten better since then. They would get better still, he told himself. Persistence, determination; those were the keys, even more than talent. Knox had indicated that he would reconsider if Froseth could not take the part. And Froseth certainly could not take the part now. He was dead.

And did the Hollywood Scalper or someone like him lie in wait for the next lead as well? Who knew—who could decipher the motivations of a sociopath? The wind seemed to encourage such psychotics—he had heard that there had already been one copycat killing similar to the scalper's work. If Simon came into the limelight, might he not be the next victim?

He shook his head. He could not let fear rule him. Acting was his life—it had to be worth risking his life for. He wanted the lead in that picture more than he had ever wanted any role. He would wait a day or so, out of respect to the dead, and then call Knox again.

The library would be closing soon; he turned toward the exit. It was rush hour now. Usually he tried to avoid the bumper-to-bumper crawl of freeway traffic, but he knew that today he would feel safer driving in that sluggish flow, surrounded by cars and people. In the wind.

"We repeat, Los Angeles police have taken into custody twenty-seven-year-old Greg Corey. He is charged with the Hollywood Scalper murders that have terrorized Los Angeles for the past eight days. . . ."

Simon heard the news while driving down La Cienega toward a health food restaurant where he was to meet Molly for lunch. He almost cheered out loud. Things at last seemed to be looking up! According to the report, it was a virtual certainty that the suspect was the scalper—he had been caught in an attack on a producer and had admitted to the other slayings. Thank God, Simon thought. At least I don't have to worry about that anymore.

He found Molly sitting at a corner table, all but hidden by a large potted fern. The corner was dark save for a candle's glow; after the merciless sunlight, Simon could see little except dazzle. "I hope you don't mind," she said. "I like seclusion when I eat." She looked different; he realized her hair was longer. She was wearing a fall.

They ordered. "Did you hear the news?" he asked. "The Hollywood Scalper's been caught."

She nodded and smiled. "But not before your competition was removed."

Simon blinked, somewhat nonplused and secretly uncomfortable because of his similar thoughts. "Well, of course, I don't look at it that way—"

"I understand," she said. "It is a terrible thing, but you mustn't let that stop you from taking advantage of it." She frowned at his expression. "Does that sound ruthless? I guess I am rather ruthless—you have to be in this town if you care about your art at all. If you have to work with people who think that having money gives them the right to dictate creativity."

Simon felt vaguely uncomfortable at her intensity. "Well, I haven't been in a position to argue with them too much. And I'm under no delusions about the artistic quality of my work so far."

"Everyone has to start somewhere. You were good in that cheap film; you don't have to worry. But the frustration applies more to me than to you, because I'm a writer. The film *starts* with me. No matter how good the actor, the director, the effects, without a good script the film is nothing. And so when a good script is written and they ruin it, it's a crime. More—it's a sin. You see?"

He saw that this was obviously her holy crusade, and so he merely nodded, though privately he felt that an actor's interpretation of a script was just as important as the script. Their lunch arrived and they spoke of other things. "I've raised the money to produce my latest script," she said. "That way, no idiot can ruin my work—if it fails it will be my fault. But this damned Santa Ana weather is delaying production. I'm losing money each day the wind blows. Not to mention nearly losing my house in Topanga to the fire."

Simon agreed with considerable feeling that the wind must stop soon. The subject changed, and he told her how much he wanted the lead in Knox's picture.

Molly nodded. "Martin Knox is one of the few good producers. Be careful of him, though; he has a temper, and money to back it up."

Simon looked stubborn. "I *know* I'm right for that part."

"Then you will probably get it, now that Froseth is dead. The show must go on—people have to have their fix of cinematic fantasy." She sounded slightly bitter. "The hell of it is, movies and TV are what's real to the rest of the world. Not us—not the ones responsible. We're just ghosts."

Her use of the word startled him. They split the check and left the cool interior for the wind and the sun.

The wind struck them both with a hard, dry gust as they descended the brick steps to the parking lot—Molly missed her footing and almost fell. Simon grabbed her arm, steadying her. "Thanks!" she shouted over the howling. "I really think this goddamn wind is out to get me."

Again her innocent words jarred him; he looked quickly, fearfully, around the parking lot, but there was no sign of the werewind. They walked over to her car and hesitated in the inevitable awkward moment of good-bye, Simon realized that he was very much afraid of her leaving him today—afraid to be alone again. "Molly," he said, "I'd like to invite you back to my place. I—it's not a come-on, really." The truth surprised him. He was not thinking of sex at all. He simply wanted to be with her; almost as big a fear as the werewind was the fear of his loneliness.

She looked away from him at the distant Hollywood Hills, clear and sharp in the dry air. The wind tore at her long dark fall; he wondered fleetingly why she wore it on such a day. At last she said, "I'm tempted." She chuckled as though surprised at herself. "You don't know what it takes to admit even that much; we Hollywood ghosts shy away from emotional commitments." She looked at him, then took his face in her hands and kissed him lightly on the mouth. The wind staggered them, almost ruined the moment. "I appreciate the offer very much, but . . . no. I have work that must be done."

"I understand, but—" The wind pushed them against the car. "God-dammit!" Simon shouted, losing his temper and striking futilely at the air.

"Relax. You can't stop it that way," she said. "You've more important things to think about, like talking to Martin Knox. Let me know how that turns out, okay?"

He nodded. Then she was in the car and backing out of the lot. He saw a smile thrown his way, and then she was gone. The sound of the engine was quickly lost in the wind's roar.

Too late, he thought of asking her what she knew about the werewind.

Jon had told him she was possibly thinking about a script based on it. Simon shuddered. He would not want to be in it.

The streets were almost deserted. The news station said that the wind in the canyons at times reached near-hurricane force. Simon drove carefully. On his way back to his apartment he saw one lone pedestrian—a tall woman with silver hair, standing on a corner of Santa Monica Boulevard. His heartbeat shook him for an instant before he realized that it was one of the few hookers still braving the wind. She looked at him with flat curiosity. He drove on.

At home the mail contained a notice from his answering service that he was being dropped for nonpayment. Simon hurled the notice at the wall. The fact that it was too light to strike with any degree of force and instead only drifted to the floor increased his anger. He seized the telephone, tempted to throw it; instead, he sat down and pressed the number of Marathon Studios. He had intended to wait a day or so, but he had been waiting too long, he told himself.

There was a long wait after he gave the secretary his name, during which time Simon breathed deeply to relax. I will not sound eager or get angry, he told himself. I will offer my condolences and then ask about the part. After all, as Molly had said, the show must go on.

"Yes, Simon."

"I just wanted to say I was sorry to hear about Froseth, Mr. Knox."

"Yes, it is a tragedy." Knox's voice was emotionless.

"A pity they couldn't have caught the scalper before this." Simon hesitated; Knox said nothing. "Have you given any thought to a replacement? I know this is rather quick, but . . ."

He trailed off. Knox said, "I'm sorry, Simon, but after further thought, I still don't think you'd be right for the part."

Simon heard someone say, "Am I still too short, Mr. Knox? I could wear stacked heels, you know."

"It's not exactly—"

"Or am I 'too' something else?" Simon realized that he was saying these words to Knox; he listened, faintly embarrassed, as if he were a bystander eavesdropping on a quarrel. "Am I too tall now? Too fat maybe? Too thin?"

"We have your résumé on file," Knox said distantly. "Good-bye, Simon."

Simon sat listening numbly to the dial tone. It's over, he thought. I've done it now.

He hung up and stared out the window at the waving trees. He listened to the wind—the omnipresent, maddening wind. That was the cause of it all, he thought. He had been doing okay until the wind had started, so long ago. The future had not looked particularly bright, but he had been able to handle the pressure. Now he had ruined everything because of that damned wind. . . .

The dial tone gave way to a siren; he depressed the cradle button, then began to punch his agent's number. He stopped before hitting the last digit. What would he say? Well, Sid, I went a little crazy, started yelling at Martin Knox, so I'll be about as welcome at Marathon now as the scalper would be at Disneyland. He hung up again, then looked at the clock. It was after six—Knox would have left the studio by now. If I could talk to him again, Simon thought, face-to-face. Apologize. Explain about the wind, how it had sawed away at his nerves . . . it was understandable, surely. . . .

It took several phone calls to learn Knox's home address; he finally got it from Jon Shea. Simon told Jon part of what had happened, and Jon tried to counsel a different course: "Let it lie for a while, Simon. Give him a call in a few days; maybe the wind'll die down by then, everybody'll be back to normal. We've all been under stress—he understands that. But don't push it now. He's got a temper too. . . ."

He did not listen. That evening he drove west on Sunset, toward the ocean. As usual, there were few cars out; even on the Strip the lanes were clear. The wind hammered at the Chrysler. As the evening grew darker, Simon had to restrain himself from driving faster. Near Beverly Glen the boulevard was blocked off—he had to detour around UCLA. Ashes from the canyon fire fell like dirty snowflakes; at one point he had to turn on his wipers.

It was almost dark when he reached Knox's house in Pacific Palisades. The day's end washed the ocean in neon-red and orange. Knox's house was on a cliff overlooking the Pacific Coast Highway. Simon parked at one end of the long, curved driveway, next to a lawn mower and a trash can full of shrubbery clippings left by a gardener.

He had given no thought to what he would say—he had not thought at all during the long drive. He pressed the doorbell and stood before the massive carved door. It opened; Martin Knox stared at him in disbelief.

"What the hell do you want?"

"To apologize," Simon said.

"This is absurd." Knox began to close the door.

"Wait, please," Simon said; then, as the door continued to close, he suddenly shouted "I said *wait!*" and grabbed it. The burst of anger had struck like a wind gust and vanished as quickly, but it had done its harm—it had aroused Knox's temper. "That does it," the producer said in a low voice. He turned and shouted, "Daniel!"

Simon stepped off the porch into the wind. "Mr. Knox, I came only to apologize . . . it's the wind, don't you see? It's making everyone crazy. . . ."

Knox opened the door again, and Daniel stood beside him. "Throw him off the property," Knox said. "Don't be too gentle."

Simon backed up as Daniel came toward him. The wind whirled about them. Daniel approached quickly, looking bored. Simon turned and ran toward his car, fumbling his keys from his pocket. He had parked near the edge of the bluff. He stabbed the keys at the door lock; living in Hollywood had habituated him to locking the car. Daniel came around the front of the car and reached for him.

As he did, a blast of wind knocked Simon off balance; he fell backward, away from the huge bodyguard. The same gust knocked the gardener's can over. The wind seized the leaves and grass trimmings and spun them in a green flurry across the lawn. As Daniel bent to seize Simon's shirt, the cloud of leaves and grass struck them like confetti, swirling around them, blinding them. Daniel waved his arms, staggered to one side— and slipped, falling over the bluff.

Simon screamed. He crawled to the edge, looking down. It was not a sheer drop to the highway below, but it was close enough. He saw Daniel's motionless dark form sprawled on the steep slope.

He stood carefully, holding on to the car. He looked back toward the house and saw Knox standing in the doorway, staring at him. He knew it appeared as if he had pushed Daniel over the cliff. Knox slammed the door. He's calling the police, Simon thought.

But another thought came to him, far more terrifying than that. There was a pattern to these events: when the wind struck, *she* appeared.

The Chrysler spun out of the driveway and down the winding road toward Sunset. Simon had no idea where he was going. He merely wanted to get away, to escape what he knew would surely come to him—the soulless, smiling werewind. He breathed raggedly, looking about frantically for any sign of her. There was none. He began to wonder where he could go.

Not back to his apartment, surely. He needed someone he could trust, someone he could tell what had happened. Molly. It had to be Molly.

She had said she lived in Topanga, in an A-frame on Grandview Drive. He did not have her number with him, did not know if she was home, but he started north on the Pacific Coast Highway nonetheless. She *had* to be home!

Soon he was driving recklessly up the winding road between sheer cliffs, toward Fernwood. Black skeletal trees, remnants of the recent fire, surrounded him. The wind between the close canyon walls was like a shotgun blast. He found the street and the house, high on a hillside. Parked in the gravel driveway was her Fiat.

As he stepped out of his car, the wind knocked him off balance again; he sprawled in an untended bed of ivy beside the ramshackle porch. Scrambling to his feet, teeth clenched against screaming, he pounded on the door. Beyond the flimsy shelter of porch and bushes it seemed that demons shrieked and tore at the earth.

The yellow porch light went on above him and he saw her silhouette behind the door window. After a moment, the door opened a crack.

"Simon?" She sounded tired and confused. "What is it? What are you doing here?"

"Let me in, please, Molly," he pleaded. "Please. I'm in trouble."

"I can't, Simon." Half of her face was visible against the crack, swallow in the porch light. "I'm working on something very important—"

"*Please!*" The wind screamed about him, tugging at his hair like fingers, *her* fingers. . . .

Molly looked torn with indecision. At last she said, "All right, if you're in trouble. But it can be only a moment. Then you'll have to go." She opened the door and Simon entered quickly.

They stood in a small living room. A picture window in the far wall looked out on the lights of Topanga. Simon noticed distractedly that the place was a mess—dead plants in pots, clothing strewn everywhere, books and records stacked haphazardly on old, worn furniture. Far in the back of his mind he was surprised and slightly disappointed—he had thought she would be neater.

A television was on in one corner, inaudible due to the wind outside.

Molly faced him, wearing jeans and a dark T-shirt. He noticed she was not wearing her fall this time. "Well?" she said. "What's wrong?"

"I don't know where to start," he said wearily. Even inside, the wind forced him to speak loudly. The whole house shook with its force. The lights dimmed, then returned. Molly looked at them in concern.

"Simon, I don't want to turn you out if you're in trouble, but you have to hurry! The wind is getting worse!"

"I know!" he said. "Jon Shea was right! It's a werewind—I've seen it!"

Her eyes went wide and her face paled. She seized his arms in a surprisingly strong grip. "*What?*"

"We've got to try the hair," he said, aware that he was babbling and not caring. "The spell, tying knots in the hair—"

"How did you know about that?" She was shaking him, her gaze burning with sudden rage. For an instant Simon was more afraid of her than of the werewind.

And then a blast of air hit the house and the picture window exploded into the room. Simon saw it but had no time to dodge. He felt flying splinters of glass sting his cheeks, miraculously missing his eyes. And he saw the rage in Molly's face turn to shock as a score of cuts and lacerations stitched the length of her back. She sagged into his arms and he felt blood running over his hands. He looked at her back, pulled strips of her shirt, cut by the glass, away from the wounds. None appeared to be serious. He looked about for something to serve as bandages—

—and saw who stood in the shattered window, framed by the night and the jagged glass.

Simon backed up, letting Molly fall to her knees. The gales still boomed and battered outside, but did not enter the house. The werewind approached him as he retreated in terror. Behind him a narrow flight of stairs led up to darkness; Simon turned and fled up them. They opened onto a narrow loft lit by a single dim bulb. A door at the far end led out onto a porch. On the walls hung several varying lengths of dark, knotted rope; on the table was an open book. The title at the top of the page was *The Omnibus of the Occult*. Also on the table was another length of rope—then he realized it was hair, Molly's dark fall, with knots tied in half its length.

Simonnn. . . .

Simon grabbed the fall, hands sweaty with terror. Simultaneously the wind struck the house again, shaking it to its foundations with a sound like thunder as she appeared at the head of the stairs, facing him.

Sobbing, Simon tied another knot in the fall. Her mouth opened in a silent scream, revealing darkness; arms extended, she came toward him. Simon backed up, whimpering, somehow managing to fumble yet another knot together. Then he turned and flung himself against the porch door as she came around the table.

He stumbled out onto the porch, into the wind.

It struck him like a giant fist, hurling him, half stunned, against the railing. It tore at the length of hair in his hand, but somehow he managed to retain it. She followed him onto the porch, unaffected by the wind. Simon hooked one arm around the railing as the wind buffeted him, and she came closer, closer. . . .

Hanging there over darkness, half paralyzed with fear, he managed to twist the final knot in the length of hair as the werewind touched him with her cold hands.

The howling rose to a scream. A final blast struck him, almost hurling him from the porch—and seized her as well, tearing at her, streaming her away like mist. Simon thought he heard a single, long-drawn-out cry. . . .

And the wind stopped.

Suddenly there was silence, louder than the wind, and stillness. Simon sagged to his knees, hearing his blood pounding. Hardly daring to believe it, he pulled himself to his feet. The air was motionless. For the first time in over a week the wind had stopped.

He began to laugh as he looked out at the night and the still trees. He did not laugh long—his throat was too dry. Welcome tears moistened his eyes and cheeks. It was over. He had won! He and Molly were safe!

Then he turned toward the house with a gasp. "Jesus. Molly!" he shouted, running back into the loft. He staggered down the stairs into the living room.

She was not there.

The TV set droned quietly in the corner, broadcasting the news.

"I repeat, the winds seem to have stopped everywhere.

"Recapping our top story, police have admitted that Greg Corey, arrested earlier today, is not the Hollywood Scalper. New evidence shows him to be a copycat killer who imitated the scalper's crimes. The real scalper is still at large. . . ."

"Molly?"

He looked closely for the first time at the fall he still held. It was not a fall. He could see very clearly the knot of flesh on one end of it, dark with dried blood. He remembered the other knotted lengths he had thought were ropes, hanging on the loft wall. He knew now that they were not ropes.

It occurred to him then that the werewind had never harmed him, had in fact saved him from Trapper Jake and the Doberman and Daniel.

Simon heard a noise behind him and turned.

Light glinted on a knife blade.

"I'm sorry, Simon," Molly said. "I did like you. . . ."

DRESS OF WHITE SILK

RICHARD MATHESON

In the early years of *F & SF*, editors Anthony Boucher and J. Francis McComas accepted a story, "Born of Man and Woman," (1950) from one Richard Matheson. "As we read the manuscript," they wrote, "we assumed that it was by some well-established professional, indulging in an off-trail literary exercise under a pseudonym. We hastily accepted that story and asked Mr. Matheson for some personal information . . . to learn to our happy astonishment that this was the first story he had ever sold!" Richard Matheson has since gone on to become the professional Messrs. McComas and Boucher assumed him to be in 1950, writing numerous stories and novels and working extensively in films and television, most recently with Steven Spielberg. "Dress of White Silk," first published in *F & SF* in October 1951, is typical of his style. It is a terrifying, moving, and beautifully written story of a mere . . . child.

Quiet is here and all in me.

Granma locked me in my room and wont let me out. Because its happened she says. I guess I was bad. Only it was the dress. Mommas dress I mean. She is gone away forever. Granma says your momma is in heaven. I don't know how. Can she go in heaven if shes dead?

Now I hear granma. She is in mommas room. She is putting mommas dress down the box. Why does she always? And locks it too. I wish she didnt. Its a pretty dress and smells sweet so. And warm. I love to touch it against my cheek. But I cant never again. I guess that is why granma is mad at me.

But I amnt sure. All day it was only like everyday. Mary Jane came over to my house. She lives across the street. Every day she comes to my house and play. Today she was.

I have seven dolls and a fire truck. Today granma said play with your dolls and it. Dont you go inside your mommas room now she said. She always says it. She just means not mess up I think. Because she says it all the time. Dont go in your mommas room. Like that.

But its nice in mommas room. When it rains I go there. Or when granma is doing her nap I do. I dont make noise. I just sit on the bed and touch the white cover. Like when I was only small. The room smells like sweet.

I make believe momma is dressing and I am allowed in. I smell her white silk dress. Her going out for night dress. She called it that I dont remember when.

I hear it moving if I listen hard. I make believe to see her sitting at the dressing table. Like touching on perfume or something I mean. And see her dark eyes. I can remember.

Its so nice if it rains and I see eyes on the window. The rain sounds like a big giant outside. He says shushshush so everyone will be quiet. I like to make believe that in mommas room.

What I like almost best is sit at mommas dressing table. It is like pink and big and smells sweet too. The seat in front has a pillow sewed in it. There are bottles and bottles with bumps and have colored perfume in them. And you can see almost your whole self in the mirror.

When I sit there I make believe to be momma. I say be quiet mother I am going out and you cannot stop me. Its something I say I dont know why like hear it in me. And oh stop your sobbing mother they will not catch me I have my magic dress.

When I pretend I brush my hair long. But I only use my own brush from my room. I didnt never use mommas brush. I dont think granma is mad at me for that because I never use mommas brush. I wouldnt never.

Sometimes I did open the box up. Because I know where granma puts the key. I saw her once when she wouldnt know I saw her. She puts the key on the hook in mommas closet. Behind the door I mean.

I could open the box lots of times. Thats because I like to look at mommas dress. I like best to look at it. It is so pretty and feels soft and like silky. I could touch it for a million years.

I kneel on the rug with roses on it. I hold the dress in my arms and like breathe from it. I touch it against my cheek. I wish I could take it to sleep with me and hold it. I like to. Now I cant. Because granma says. And she says I should burn it up but I loved her so. And she cries about the dress.

I wasnt never bad with it. I put it back neat like it was never touched. Granma never knew. I laughed that she never knew before. But she knows now I did it I guess. And shell punish me. What did it hurt her? Wasnt it my mommas dress?

What I like the real best in mommas room is look at the picture of momma. It has a gold thing around it. Frame is what granma says. It is on the wall on top of the bureau.

Momma is pretty. Your momma was pretty granma says. Why does she? I see momma there smiling on me and she *is* pretty. For always.

Her hair is black. Like mine. Her eyes are even pretty like black. Her mouth is red so red. I like the dress and its the white one. It is all down on her shoulders. Her skin is white almost white like the dress. And so too are her hands. She is so pretty. I love her even if she is gone away forever I love her so much.

I guess I think thats what made me bad. I mean to Mary Jane.

Mary Jane came from lunch like she does. Granma went to do her nap. She said dont forget now no going in your mommas room. I told her no granma. And I was saying the truth but then Mary Jane and I was playing fire truck. Mary Jane said I bet you havent no mother I bet you made up it all she said.

I got mad at her. I have a momma I know. She made me mad at her to say I made up it all. She said Im a liar. I mean about the bed and the dressing table and the picture and the dress even and everything.

I said well Ill show you smarty.

I looked into granmas room. She was doing her nap still. I went down and said to Mary Jane to come on because granma wont know.

She wasnt so smart after then. She giggled like she does. Even she made a scaredy noise when she hit into the table in the hall upstairs. I said youre a scaredy cat to her. She said back well *my* house isnt so dark like this. Like that was so much.

We went in mommas room. It was more dark than you could see. So I took back the curtains. Just a little so Mary Jane could see. I said this is my mommas room I suppose I made up it all.

She was by the door and she wasnt smart then either. She didnt say any word. She looked around the room. She jumped when I got her arm. Well come on I said.

I sat on the bed and said this is my mommas bed see how soft it is. She didnt say nothing. Scaredy cat I said. Am not she said like she does.

I said to sit down how can you tell if its soft if you dont sit down. She sat down by me. I said feel how soft it is. Smell how like sweet it is.

I closed my eyes but funny it wasnt like always. Because Mary Jane was there. I told her to stop feeling the cover. You said to she said. Well stop it I said.

See I said and I pulled her up. Thats the dressing table. I took her and brought her there. She said let go. It was so quiet and like always. I started to feel bad. Because Mary Jane was there. Because it was in my mommas room and momma wouldnt like Mary Jane there.

But I had to show her the things because. I showed her the mirror. We looked at each other in it. She looked white. Mary Jane is a scaredy cat I said. Am not am not she said anyway nobodys house is so quiet and dark inside. Anyway she said it smells.

I got mad at her. No it doesnt smell I said. Does so she said you said it did. I got madder too. It smells like sugar she said. It smells like sick people in your mommas room.

Dont say my mommas room is like sick people I said to her.

Well you didnt show me no dress and youre lying she said there isnt no dress. I felt all warm inside so I pulled her hair. Ill show you I said and dont never say Im a liar again.

She said Im going home and tell my mother on you. You are not I said youre going to see my mommas dress and youll better not call me a liar.

I made her stand still and I got the key off the hook. I kneeled down. I opened the box with the key.

Mary Jane said pew that smells like garbage.

I put my nails in her and she pulled away and got mad. Dont you pinch me she said and she was all red. Im telling my mother on you she said. And anyway its not a white dress its dirty and ugly she said.

Its not dirty I said. I said it so loud I wonder why granma didnt hear. I pulled out the dress from the box. I held it up to show her how its white. It fell open like the rain whispering and the bottom touched the rug.

It is too white I said all white and clean and silky.

No she said she was so mad and red it has a hole in it. I got more madder. If my momma was here shed show you I said. You got no momma she said all ugly. I hate her.

I have. I said it way loud. I pointed my finger to mommas picture. Well who can see in this stupid dark room she said. I pushed her hard and she hit against the bureau. See then I said mean look at the picture. Thats my momma and shes the most beautiful lady in the whole world.

Shes ugly she has funny hands Mary Jane said. She hasnt I said shes the most beautiful lady in the world!

Not not she said *she has buck teeth*.

I dont remember then. I think like the dress moved in my arms. Mary Jane screamed. I dont remember what. It got dark and the curtains were closed I think. I couldnt see anyway. I couldnt hear nothing except buck teeth funny hands buck teeth funny hands even when no one was saying it.

There was something else because I think I heard some one call *dont let her say that!* I couldnt hold to the dress. And I had it on me I cant remember. Because I was like grown up strong. But I was a little girl still I think. I mean outside.

I think I was terrible bad then.

Granma took me away from there I guess. I dont know. She was screaming god help us its happened its happened. Over and over. I dont know why. She pulled me all the way here to my room and locked me in. She wont let me out. Well Im not so scared. Who cares if she locks me in a million billion years? She doesnt have to even give me supper. Im not hungry anyway.

Im full.

GLADYS'S GREGORY

JOHN ANTHONY WEST

"Gladys's Gregory" is a tale that could perhaps be cate-
gorized more as black humor or satire than as traditional
horror—yet the events it depicts are more than gruesome
(it's one of our favorite stories). First published in *F & SF*
in February 1963, it has been anthologized many times—
perhaps because its topic is always current and one that
concerns us all—yet, because of its merit, we have included
it again in this volume. In "Gladys's Gregory," John Anthony West shows us an entire community that is preoccupied with weight, and each member of the community
has in fact—one might say—a "steak" in the outcome.

Ladies, members of the club, I am
honored to be here today, to tell you about this year's contest in our
community, and this year's contest winner, Gladys's Gregory. And I want
to thank you all for your interest and for your kind attention.

I begin with statistics from the medical record. Gladys's Gregory upon
his arrival at our community.

HEIGHT:	6'5½"
WEIGHT:	242
CHEST:	49"

WAIST:	36"
NECK:	18½"

I anticipate your admiration, ladies. Therefore, let me present the dark side of the coin immediately. Gregory, upon arriving, was 28 years old, yet his weight had scarcely changed since his college days when he was an all-American football player. He had been married three *full* years. Club members! Please jump to no hasty conclusions. Hear me out before you heap blame on Gladys. Bear in mind that here, true, we have Gregory; 242 pounds of raw material. But this figure had not changed for *eight* years.

Unfortunately, I admit, the women of our community did not view the situation objectively either. "Gladys's fault," they shouted, and indignation ran rampant.

We thought of Beth Shaefer, who had brought her Milton from a gangling 164 to 313 pounds in less than three years; Sally O'Leary with three strikes against her at the onset, her Jamie an ex-jockey, fighting gamely nevertheless and bringing him out finally at 245; Joan Granz, who nursed her Marvin to 437 and a second prize despite his dangerous cardiac condition. Certainly, all of you can appreciate our feelings.

Now, Gladys's Gregory was a football coach, and one day, driving past the stadium, the first clue to a nasty situation revealed itself. Gladys's Gregory was participating in the *actual* physical exercise.

I saw him hurl himself repeatedly at a stuffed dummy; saw him lead five minutes of strenuous calisthenics, then, undaunted, lead his team in a race around the track. The bitterest among Gladys's enemies would be forced to admit that perhaps it wasn't her fault entirely. To this day I see the flesh-building calories dripping from his pores in perspiration.

The next morning I paid a call on Gladys. She was a sweet young thing, far from the malicious vixen rumor had painted her. I recounted the stadium scene, and poor Gladys knew it all too well. She had even stranger tales to tell. He mowed the lawn with a *hand* mower, played handball off season, ran the two miles from the school to his home in a track suit. The girl was desolate.

We discussed his diet, and I was shocked beyond words. Red meat! She fed him red meat, and fish, and eggs, and green vegetables. . . .

"Eclairs!" I shouted at her. "Potatoes! Chocolate layer cake! Beer! Butter!"

But no. Gregory hated these things. Wouldn't touch them.

"He doesn't love you," I said.

"But he does," Gladys moaned, her voice cracking, "in his own way he does."

I suggested the strategy that was so often effective when contests had not yet gained their present popularity and opposition was stronger.

As we all know, we have more sexual stamina than our mates. A wife, subtly camouflaging her motives under the attractive cover of passion, can reduce a husband to a state of sexual fatigue in a matter of weeks. And a sexually sated husband is ripe for intelligent handling. Evening after evening he sits quietly. Eating. He marshals his energies for the night ahead and gradually he puts on weight. At a certain point his obesity interferes with his virility, and at this point the intelligent wife begins to demand less. The husband, by this time swathed in comfortable flesh, is only too happy to be let alone. Now the wife decreases her demands to nothing, and the husband, carrying no burden of calorie-consuming anxiety, prepares for the contest.

With Gladys's Gregory, this method proved futile. After a month's trial Gladys was but a shadow of her former self, while Gregory was seen everywhere, with his squad, mowing the lawn, his unsightly muscles bulging, a smug grin on his face.

At a special community meeting an ingenious plan was devised. We would make Gladys and Gregory the most socially prominent couple in the community. They soon found their social calendar booked solid: dinners, breakfasts, buffets, picnics. . . . Gregory found himself seated down to tables groaning with carbohydrates. He was under constant surveillance. No sooner had he wiped the whipped cream from his lips, before a plate, mountain-high in ice cream, bristling with macaroons, was thrust before him. His mug of beer never reached the halfway mark before some vigilant wife refilled it for him.

At this time, ladies, I must point out that Gregory was in no way a conscious rebel, nor was he malicious or subversive. We must set aside his foolish notions of physical culture and regard him as he was—a charming man and an ideal husband: affable, reticent, and quite unintelligent. The militant fury of our community women soon gave way to a genuine solicitousness. And a beaming Gladys reported that he was wearing his belt out two notches.

A carefully coached Gladys waged psychological warfare. Magazines were left open about the house, all of them turned to calorie-rich advertisements. At parties she flirted openly with the heftiest husbands still allowed free.

By spring Gregory weighed an estimated 290. Bewildered, he still clung to his old notions. "Gotta get in shape for spring training," he would mumble, his mouth filled with chocolate mousse.

At 310 our cooperative spirit dwindled. The women, all at once, realized what they had wrought and were horrified by the prospect.

Meanwhile Gladys, grown confident, moved swiftly and with brilliant technical strategy. She consulted a fortune-teller, who hinted to her that, given the chance, her Gregory would founder himself on brazil nuts. She bought a trial pound, and they were gone in five minutes.

Well, ladies, brazil nuts! It was the last straw. Calorie-filled brazil nuts. Community spirit turned to a hostile chill and then to virulent envy. He couldn't stop eating brazil nuts! Anxious eyes searched hopefully for the telltale signs of arrested development, the tight skin and fishy-eyed expression that signifies that a husband is nearing peak despite his apparent potential. We looked for hints of unsightly bloating. But at 325 Gregory was barely filling out. On his own he developed a taste for sweets.

The contest of that year was pure anticlimax. Jenny Schultz's Peter took a first at 423, but the prodigious Gregory was on the minds of all.

Shortly after, Gladys, contrary to expectation, put her Gregory into seclusion. It was the cause of hope. Certainly Gladys had overplayed her hand and had sacrificed strategy for youthful impetuosity. But her self-confidence incensed the ladies of our community.

For the first time in history our women banded together in an effort to counteract Gregory's impending victory. Surely the emotions that prompted this action were not entirely commendable, but, ladies, put yourself in our place. Would you be willing to undergo the heartache, the effort, even the expense of preparing a husband for a contest whose outcome was obvious in advance?

How long would it take her to prepare her Gregory? This was the burning question. The average husband takes three or four years, as we all know. Certainly Gregory was a special case. Four years for him would mean excess flab. Three years seemed most logical, but with Gregory two years did not seem impossible, and Gladys had already displayed eagerness and impatience. It was the studied opinion of our community that Gladys would enter Gregory in two years. Therefore, it was but a simple matter for the rest to hold their husbands for a different year. Should Gregory be the only entry, his would be a hollow victory.

Our solution was bold but strong. The women made an agreement to enter their husbands the following year despite the fact that many would not have reached peak. It was felt that should a three-year plan misfire (as it might through a slip of the tongue, chicanery, a thousand reasons), four or five years of seclusion would be unbearable for all wives concerned and of course with husbands, decline is most rapid after peak has been attained. Women whose husbands had been in seclusion under a year were permitted to breach the contract.

A period of curious tension ensued. Gladys's arrogance was hidden beneath a cover of interest in community affairs while the other women masked their complicity and hatred under the guise of camaraderie in the face of healthy competition.

Gladys took to having provisions delivered: quarter kegs of beer, bushels of potatoes, sacks of flour. Oh, yes! She would set a record in two years, but it would be a wasted triumph.

And then she could outdo herself. We all remembered Elizabeth Bent's Darius who, several years earlier, having had almost the potential of a Gregory, and eager to set a record, had allowed himself to be pushed too hard. He died six weeks before the contest; a sensational but disqualified 621.

With the contest a month away, Gregory was forgotten. True, this year's contest lacked the element of surprise. Everyone (but Gladys) knew which other husbands would be shown. The probable winner could be guessed with reasonable accuracy . . . but still, a contest is a contest, and the air was charged with the familiar bitter rivalry.

Contest day dawned hot and bright, and an excited crowd gathered at the stadium. This year, of course, there was little of that intense speculation: Who was entered by surprise; who was staying another year in seclusion?

But five minutes before the procession one question rippled through the audience. Has anyone seen Gladys? An expectant audience became a feverish one. Necks craned. Sharp eyes searched the crowd. She was not to be seen. A murmur of anger swept the stands. Could she have prepared her Gregory in a single year? No! No! It could not be done.

The band struck up, and slowly the gaily painted, bunting-draped trucks passed before the stand. Twenty-six in all. How many women had entered the agreement to show their husbands. Twenty-five? Twenty-six? No one remembered.

The trucks circled the field. Attention was divided between the parade and the entrance to catch Gladys's expected tardy arrival among the spectators.

The fanfare rose brassy and shrill, and the trucks halted. The wives debouched from the cabs and stood before their vehicles. We all know the tension of this moment, as the audience takes in the line of wives at a glance, sees two dozen or more women dressed in their best, tries at the same time to remember those who might have been there and are not. That tense moment when years of planning, hoping, working, scheming, unfold too quickly . . . But in this split-second all eyes focused on one person, and one person alone. Gladys.

She stood before her truck, stunning in white organdy, fresh as a daisy, showing nothing of what must have been a tense and lonely ordeal, not a single wrinkle was visible, not a strand of hair astray. I could feel hatred gathering in a storm.

The other wives in the contest glared helplessly at Gladys. The trumpet sounded, and the wives released the covers of their trucks. It was the breathless instant when the husbands stood revealed. But this time every eye focused on truck seventeen: Gladys's Gregory.

There was no applause, none of the usual wild cheering, nothing but an awed silence. In that single moment every wife present knew that her own small hopes were forever extinguished. They that never, never in their maddest daydreams had conceived of a Gregory.

He stood as though rooted to the back of the truck: monolithic. His face missed that bloated look usually found on the truly elephantine husbands; his brow was furrowed in thick folds of flesh; his cheeks, neither flabby nor swollen, hung in rich jowls like steaks. His neck was a squat cone leading unbroken into shoulders so gigantic that instead of easing into the inevitable paunch he seemed to drop sheer. He was perfect. A pillar, a block, a mountain, solid and immobile. He turned slowly, proudly. Front face, profile, rear view, front face. His weight was incalculable. He was bigger, heavier, more immense, more beautiful than anything we had ever witnessed. Hatred in the audience turned to despair. Our granddaughter might beg to hear about Gladys's Gregory, but *we* had seen him. For us there would be no more contests. Not a woman among us thought of Gladys's original torments; her years of social ostracism. But how could they?

The weighing began, and the audience cursed and fretted. Sixteen before Gregory. The winches lifted the husbands to the weighing platform and the results were announced: 345, 376, 268 (someone laughed), 417, 430 (someone clapped—a relative no doubt), 386, 344. Not a flurry of interest. The dismayed wives who had worked and schemed for years for this opportunity, who asked only for fair competition, wept openly. Then 403, 313. The wait seemed endless.

Gregory was next, but Gladys had a surprise in store. As the men went to adjust the slings on Gregory, Gladys waved them off. She attached a strong pipe ladder to the truck, and, ponderously, but without hesitation, Gregory descended.

He was still able to walk!

Shoulders thrown back to balance his magnificent bulk, he swayed and lurched toward the stairs that led to the platform. He tested the frail banister, and it sundered. Using a section of the rail as a cane, he veered up the stairs while a breathless crowd waited for the sound of breaking planks. The stairs groaned but held, and Gregory made his own way to the scale.

Well, ladies, what difference does the actual figure make? It was all over. After seeing Gregory, cold statistics were irrelevant. The figure, however, was 743 pounds.

Gregory turned slowly, proudly, on the scale and smiled. There was no applause but, first singly, then in groups, then en masse the audience stood. Even jealousy and hatred were powerless in the presence of the contestant who would stand as a monument to Gladys and our community, and as an inspiration to the world.

Now, ladies, I wish, I only wish that I could finish this report on the note that such a performance deserves. Unfortunately, one incident marred the perfection of Gladys's Gregory's victory.

Our club, like all others, has always adhered to the tacit but traditional practice: *The contest winner is permitted to choose the manner in which he would like to be served.*

Gladys's Gregory, however, out of sheer spite (the argument still rages on this point), or hearkening back to some primitive instinct, demanded to be served raw.

Having no precedent to act upon, and fearing to break so time-honored a custom, we complied reluctantly with the request, creating acute physical discomfort for many and an acute physical revulsion in all. A motion is now under discussion in our community which will, in the future, relieve the contest winner of this responsibility. In view of our unfortunate experience, ladies, it is part of my mission here today to urge you and your club, and all other clubs to pass a similar amendment at your earliest convenience.

I thank you for bearing with me, ladies.

BY THE RIVER, FONTAINEBLEAU

STEPHEN GALLAGHER

Stephen Gallagher's first credits in writing were for British radio and television. He then turned to fiction writing full-time; his first novel, *Chimera*, was published in the United States in 1982 by St. Martin's Press. *F & SF* has been fortunate enough to publish a number of his eerie and excellent short stories, among which we feel "By the River, Fontainebleau" is his best to date, and that means it is *very* good indeed. In it, Stephen Gallagher shares with us a horrific vision of infatuation. This surrealistic tale is perhaps the most frightening of the entire collection. It all depends, shall we say, on how you *look* at it.

We sheltered under the great oak for more than an hour, watching as the rain came down in sheets. The sky was as dark as old lead, and when the thunder came it seemed to shake the very soil of the forest. Even Antoine couldn't pretend that this was nothing more than a brief spring shower, and so we sat together in a bleak silence with our packs at our feet and our oilskin coats over our heads. It was then, I suppose, that I really came to my decision.

When the rain finally stopped, we shouldered our baggage and walked on. The lane had now mostly turned to mud, and a weak sun showed through the trees and raised a mist from the sodden ground. I wasn't in much of a mood to appreciate it, but after a while Antoine started to whistle. Ten minutes or so later we came to a shallow, fast-running river where the lane disappeared and reemerged over on the far side, and so wet and miserable was I by this time that I waded in to make the crossing without hesitation or complaint. Every step was taking me nearer to home, and this was all that I cared for.

But it soon became obvious that the track would take us no farther than the farm that stood on the opposite bank, as it led straight into a yard that had no exit. It was a mean-looking place, charmless and squalid even in the late afternoon sunlight, and my immediate impulse was to turn around and walk away. But Antoine, ever an optimist, said, "You think they'll take pity and feed us?"

"They're more likely to hit us over the head and rob us," I told him. "You stay here and look after the gear. I'll ask the way."

I left him and went on into the yard, looking for some sign of life. A few hens were picking over the barren ground close to where four scrawny goats stood in a makeshift pen, and a dog was barking somewhere over beyond the barn. The corner of the yard to my left was shaded by a large chestnut tree, and it was on the dry beaten earth in the shelter of this that I saw a terrible sight.

It was an underweight pig, trussed and made ready for slaughter; this was obviously the farm's regular spot for killing, because hooks had been fixed to the tree's lower branches for carcasses to be hung as they bled. What made the sight so terrible was the way in which the pig had been prepared. Each of its feet had been cut at the knuckle, sliced right back so that the bone showed bloodless and white. Those bound-together limbs were almost severed, but still the pig squirmed as it tried to stand.

I turned my head aside, and went on by. It was out in the open on the far side of the barn that I finally found the people that I was looking for; and an unwashed, surly crowd they turned out to be, a father and four brothers with narrow faces and dark, piercing stares. They were hauling logs for cutting, but all work stopped when they saw me. As I addressed myself to the older man, the others simply stood and watched, their mouths open and their hands hanging by their sides whilst a dim spark of intelligence burned in each pair of eyes. It went badly until I realized that money was the key that would unlock their patient and persistent misunderstanding, and then at the end of the process I learned nothing more than that the only way to regain the Paris road would be to return along the track by which we'd arrived. I thanked the farmer—feeling defeated and foolish because really I ought to have been cursing him—and trudged back to Antoine.

Antoine was where I'd left him. The packs with our easels and our brushes and our sketchbooks were at his feet, and he was leaning on the wall with a distant, thoughtful expression on his face. He was looking toward the chestnut tree. This was something that I'd avoided doing on my way back, but now I had to turn and see what it was that was affecting him so; and it was then that I realized that the trussed pig had been taken away at some time during my short absence, and that a different scene was now before him.

"I'm staying, Marcel," he said.

I didn't understand. "Staying where?"

"Right here. They must have a room or a loft or a barn, and they're not going to turn down good money. And it's late, and I'm tired. . . ."

"Any other reason?" I said, and I gave a pointed glance across to where, under the chestnut tree, a young girl was now standing and unselfconsciously brushing her hair. She was looking into a broken old mirror that she'd hung from one of the butchery hooks, and she didn't seem to be aware of us at all. She was barefoot, and in a cotton shift so damp and clinging that it was plain she wore nothing underneath. To my eyes she was nothing more than an ordinary farm girl, too heavy for grace and probably too dull for conversation . . . but who could say what she was to Antoine? I'd already learned, during the weeks of our walking tour, that his eyes and mine often seemed to see by a different light. Now, in answer to my question, he was smiling and saying nothing more.

"Then," I said, "you stay alone, Antoine."

This surprised him. "Are we going to argue over this?"

"No," I said, leaning on the wall beside him, "Not an argument. I simply don't want to get in your way. It's over for me, Antoine, and there's no point in me pretending otherwise. I've had enough of walking and sketching and being face-to-face with nature. I've yawned through sunrises and I've shivered through the rain, and if I died without ever seeing another tree or village or field of wheat, I'd be dying happy. What I'm trying to say is that I'm not an artist, Antoine. If these past few weeks have been the test, then I'm admitting that I've failed. I'm footsore and I'm aching, and I've got nothing left to prove. I'm going back to Paris tonight."

This had been my decision, back in the forest and under the oak. The excursion that had seemed so appealing to two young would-be painters

had turned into a drudgery of patchy weather and drafty inns and a
yearning for home; I'd carried on sketching only as a kind of dogged duty,
something that I wouldn't have bothered with if Antoine hadn't been
there. I hadn't looked back through the pages, and didn't care to. My
artistic talent, I'd realized, wasn't strong enough to survive outside of the
most pampered of drawing room conditions—which, I suppose, meant
that it wasn't a real talent at all. A useful way of persuading young women
to undress for me, perhaps, but not art.

"Oh, Marcel," Antoine said with sympathy. "Has it really been hell
for you?"

"I'm going to be a dull citizen, Antoine," I told him. "I was *born* to
be a dull citizen. It took a trip like this to make me realize how much
I'd been looking forward to it."

He glanced across the yard again, to where the plain farm girl stood
beneath the chestnut tree. For a moment it seemed that her eyes strayed
from the mirror and met his, but her face betrayed nothing at all.

"I can't come with you," he said.

"I understand that."

I told him where to find the farmer, and while he was gone I transferred
all of the pastels and the paints and the charcoal sticks from my luggage
into his own. It was a strange feeling, the feeling of letting go of a dream.
It was relief and regret, inextricably mixed. I also gave him my two
untouched canvases in their carrying frame, and my fixing atomizer.
When Antoine returned, he told me of the terms that the farmer had
fixed for him to stay on; put simply, they were giving him two weeks in
their barn with whatever meals the family could spare, in return for every
franc that he carried. I was horrified, but Antoine was unruffled. He
made me promise that I would go to his father and collect his monthly
allowance, and that before the two weeks expired I would return with
the money. Although I wouldn't have cared if I never saw the forest of
Fontainebleau again, I was uneasy at the notion of leaving Antoine
completely at the mercy of his new obsession. This way, at least, I'd be
able to check on him.

He walked with me back to the river. There was little more than an
hour of daylight left, and I had some way to go. Before I set out across
the ford, I said, "What shall I tell your father?"

"Whatever you like," he said. "Whatever you think he needs to hear.
But do it for me, Marcel."

I'd have said more, but he was already casting a longing look back
toward the yard. A half hour's familiarity made it seem no less squalid

to me than it had been at first sight . . . but, as I said, Antoine often seemed to see things with a different eye. An artist's eye, perhaps. My test had come and gone; and the next two weeks would be his.

I stayed that night in Barbizon, and made it back to Paris by the next evening. I entered the family home by the back door, partly because I was ashamed of what I saw as my failure, but mostly because I was aware that I looked like a tramp. The next few days saw the beginning of the process of my absorption into the family's business dealings, a strange world of ledger entries and manifests that somehow bore a relation to real ships that sailed somewhere out on real oceans. I was given a position as an apprentice clerk in order that I should be able to learn from the most fundamental of basic principles.

Even though I'd known what to expect, the long hours and the rigid timekeeping came as something of a shock to me. I'd sent out a note to Antoine's parents assuring them of his safety as soon as I'd arrived home, but it wasn't until the Friday that I was able to go and see them in the evening with his request.

The news was not good. My own father, to his credit, had been willing to let my preoccupations run themselves out; it was as if he'd foreseen the result and quietly made his preparations for when that time came around. Antoine's father had no such patience. All that he gave me was a message: There would be no allowance until Antoine abandoned his games and returned home.

Saturday was a half day, and as soon as my work was finished I set out for the railway station. It was late in the afternoon before I finally came into sight of the farm again. The place was much as I remembered it, although I dare say that I had changed in its eyes; I now wore my one decent suit and overcoat, and came prepared for the shallow river crossing.

It was a warm day. Spring was slipping toward summer, and the breeze no longer cut. The broken looking glass was still hanging under the chestnut tree, and it swung lightly back and forth as I stood in the doorway to the barn and called Antoine's name. He'd been sleeping *here*? Half of the place was taken up with hay, all the way to the upper loft, and there was nothing in the way of furniture. The slatted walls were badly fitted, and some of the gaps in the planking were a hand's width. But this was his lodging, all right, because over on the clear part of the floor I saw his easel and a stool and some of his materials laid out. Antoine's possessions, but no Antoine. I set out to search.

I finally found him in a clearing no more than two hundred meters from the barn. The girl, as I'd half expected, was with him. She was sitting on the ground with her hands clasped around her knees as Antoine sketched her, but on seeing me, with a cry of "Marcel!" he threw aside his pad and jumped up to greet me.

I'll confess that I was shocked, although I hid it well. In the space of less than a week he'd deteriorated like a man in the grip of a serious illness. He seemed thinner, and there were dark rings round his eyes that made them seem sunken and staring; but his manner was lively enough, and he seemed pleased to see me . . . although how much of this was genuine eagerness and how much of it was due to the money that he assumed I'd brought with me, I couldn't say.

They had a basket with them, and together we dined on cheese and rough wine and bread that had the texture of damp thatch. Antoine introduced the girl as Lise, short for Anneliese; I knew within a moment of hearing her speak that she was no native French girl, although her accent was one that I couldn't place. She seemed shy and ate nothing, and took only a little of the wine.

Antoine gave me his sketchbook to look through, just as we'd done at the end of each of our days together. As I'd expected, he'd been spending all of his time on the girl, switching between head studies and full-length portrayals, some of them hardly more than a few swift lines depicting the essence of some moment of motion. Although I didn't show it, I was disappointed. I was hoping that there would be some sign here, some showing-through of the vision that had motivated him, but each drawing seemed little more than a technical exercise. Perhaps there was nothing to envy here after all, I thought. Nothing other than a casual infatuation made practical by the artist-model relationship—a situation that I, at least, could understand, although I was strangely disappointed that I found nothing more.

Lise asked if Antoine was finished with his sketching for the day, and then excused herself. I noted a certain pain in Antoine's eyes as he watched her go.

"Who is she?" I said as soon as she was decently out of earshot.

"I don't know. She's an orphan, I think. The family just ignores her."

"Does she work on the farm?"

"I don't think so," he said, his face reflecting some of his uncertainty as if it were a question that he'd thought over a number of times in the past few days. "I can't be sure. She disappears for hours at a time, but . . . it's not important anyway. Did you speak to my father?"

I had no choice then but to give him the hard news. I saw his face fall, and the air of vague contentment that had offset the wasting of his features was replaced by a kind of desperation.

"Then I don't know what to do," he said. "They won't let me stay here without money. They've bled me white already. You don't understand these people."

"Not half as well as they seem to understand you," I told him. "It *is* because of the girl, isn't it?"

He looked down, and didn't answer.

"Then," I went on, "why don't you simply take her away?"

But he was dismissing the idea even before I'd finished suggesting it. "That's not possible," he said. "It pains her to walk any distance." And then, going on as if this minor quibble had been enough to put an end to the entire argument, he was getting to his feet and saying, "I can see only one way out. You'd better come with me."

He said nothing more as he led the way back toward the barn. Over by another of the outbuildings I saw one of the four sons watching us as we passed. He made no sign toward us, and Antoine didn't even glance his way.

Lise wasn't there when we arrived, nor did Antoine seem to expect her to be. He went over to the easel, and I followed; and then I waited as he hesitated for a moment before drawing away the paint-splashed cloth that had been draped to protect the canvas.

It was a painting, in full oils. I stood amazed. It was wonderful.

It showed that vision of the first moment in which Antoine had seen Lise under the chestnut tree. It was every detail that I'd seen, but transformed; I now realized that I'd been so preoccupied with my own discomfort that I'd been aware of almost nothing, nothing at all. Lise stood, hairbrush in hand, dappled in late afternoon sunlight with soft blue shadows behind her. In her plain features was a kind of quiet beauty as she studied her image in the glass; I knew instinctively that it was a sad picture, a celebration of the brevity of all experience and of life itself.

And as I looked, I felt something within me die. I thought of my own pretty, nondescript Fontainebleau landscapes and finally knew for sure that my decision had been a right one. My technique was as good as Antoine's, if not slightly better, but technique was only half the story. To paint, one first had to see. And I didn't, until led to it.

"You have to take it to Paris for me," he said. "Sell it for whatever you can get."

I nodded slowly. There was no question about it now, I would help him however I could. "I'm envious, you know," I said.

"Don't be," he said, staring at his own canvas as if it disturbed him somehow. "The things we want most aren't always the things that make us happy."

I gave him most of the money that I had with me, including what I had set aside for a night's lodging before returning to the town. I sensed a certain reluctance in Antoine as we climbed a ladder and he showed me the upper loft where I could sleep, but I took it as a natural aversion to charity between friends. I didn't see it that way; if I was going to be a bourgeois, I thought ruefully, I might as well go the whole hog and become a patron of the arts.

A blanket in the hay was not my idea of comfort, but it was all that was available. I was warm enough, but the hay stuck at me through the thin wool from every angle; and though my overcoat, rolled, made a reasonable pillow, I couldn't help wondering what it would look like when I came to shake it out in the morning. No wonder Antoine was looking such a wreck, I thought, after a week of this.

I don't know what time it was when I awoke, but it must have been somewhere around two or three o'clock. I lay uneasy, looking at where the cloudy moonlit sky showed through the spaces in the walls, and I heard voices from below. They were whispering, but the night was so still that it was impossible not to hear.

"I remember leaving you and your friend," Lise was saying. "I was so tired after sitting for you this morning. But I don't remember where I went."

"You went where you always go," I heard Antoine say. "To the big stack of straw behind the house. You made yourself a space and you burrowed down inside."

"But the next thing that I knew, it was dark and I was standing out under the tree again. I was exhausted, and it was as if I'd been running. What had I been *doing*?"

"You were sleeping, that's all. Like you always do."

But Lise seemed scared, unable to accept so simple an explanation. "But you know this?" she said insistently. "You've seen me?"

There was a long silence from Antoine. And then he said, "Yes."

I heard her moving slightly, making the hay rustle. She said, "I sometimes feel as if you're the only one who really sees me. As I am, I mean. As if, when you close your eyes, I no longer exist . . . because I didn't, in a way, before you came along."

Antoine said, "That's just foolish talk."

Her next question was one that I wouldn't have expected. She said, "Who am I, Antoine?" And she sounded lost and miserable, as if the answer would never be known.

"Sleep, now," he told her.

It was a good suggestion, and one that I wished I could follow; but further sleep seemed to elude me, and all that I could do was to squirm miserably in that itchy byre. Antoine's breathing became deep and noisy, which was of no help. And after a while I heard the sound below of somebody rising and making their way toward the door of the barn.

Moving as silently as I could, I crawled over to the trap by which I'd entered the loft, and peered down. Lise was at the doorway, framed in moonlight, and she was looking back at Antoine. I could not make out her expression, but her general attitude suggested a regretful leave-taking. Of Antoine himself I could see little more than the creamy blur of his shirt in the darkness. Then she turned and walked out into the yard.

A board creaked as I moved across to the unglazed window from where I'd be able to see down into the yard, but Antoine didn't stir. She was moving quickly now, a faint shape in a simple dress, and she was heading toward the back of thé house as Antoine had said; and then as I watched, I saw another form rise from the shadows to meet her. This was, I guessed from his brutish outline, either the farmer or one of his four sons, and he seemed to have been waiting; I saw him raise a rod or a switch of some kind, and to swipe at the air with it as if to speed her in the direction in which she was already going. He followed her through the gap between the buildings, and then bent to something that I couldn't see; but then I heard the scrape of a wooden gate across the rutted dirt, and the bang of it falling shut.

When they were gone from sight, Lise being casually driven ahead like some common farm animal, I returned to my blanket. It was obvious that she'd been expected, up and away the moment that Antoine was fully asleep, like a sheep being called to the fold at the end of the day. And having seen the way in which she'd been treated, I could only reflect that perhaps she'd been right: Antoine's vision of her differed so much from theirs that it was almost as if he'd actually created her beauty out of some more basic stuff, to which she could revert only when Antoine's attention moved elsewhere, as in sleep.

And sleep, unexpectedly, was what these idle and speculative thoughts led me to.

Breakfast was left outside for us in the morning. It was meager but decent. Antoine carefully packed the picture, wary of the paint that was still soft in the patches; he called it *La Jeune Fille au Miroir*, The Looking-Glass Girl. Lise sat aside and watched us; she'd returned to the barn some time before I'd woken, I didn't know when. She said little, and ate nothing. I now found it difficult to imagine how I could ever have thought her plain.

I suppose that to develop my fanciful thought from the night before, I now saw her as through Antoine's eyes. My own first impression now counted for nothing; it was not that I had simply changed an opinion to acquiesce to the views of another, but more that I'd found the actual fabric of my world transformed by the intensity of his vision. But it was an intensity that was draining him, I could see; he looked no better physically now than he had when I'd arrived, and seemed perhaps even a little worse. I wondered if a taste of success from the sale of the painting might nourish him.

I was on my way before ten, knowing that I had a long walk and a carriage drive ahead of me before I'd even reach the railway. My toughest boots had leaked a little during the river crossing the previous day, but they'd dried out overnight and Antoine went out to negotiate a ride of some kind so that I wouldn't be restarting the journey with a squelch. I didn't hear what was said or what was promised, but after ten minutes a dilapidated trap pulled by an even more dilapidated pony came rattling into the yard.

The morning sun struck a shimmering light from the river as we waved our good-byes and my transport jarred its way into the rutted crossing. My driver was one of the four brothers that I'd seen on my first visit to the farm, and I wondered if he might have been the one who had waited in the yard for Lise in the moonlight. I thought about asking . . . but he hadn't said one word to me so far, and seemed unlikely to. He sat with his shoulders hunched, and his eyes apparently fixed on the horse's rear end. I was half expecting to be set down on the opposite bank, but it soon became clear that Antoine's bargaining would take me farther as we continued, wheels dripping, down the lane. I turned for one last wave to Antoine's solitary figure, and then I faced front with *La Jeune Fille au Miroir* held protectively by my side.

I had a strange feeling of loss, as if I'd left a world that I might never be sure of reentering. The river was its boundary, the banks its borderland.

Ten minutes later, as we came into sight of the main crossroads, my coachman spoke.

"We've told your friend," he said suddenly and without any preamble, "we can't eat his pictures. When his money's gone, so's he."

It was a moment before I could be certain that I was the one being addressed; he hadn't lifted his eyes from the mare's backside. But when I was sure, I said, "Would you consider letting Lise come away with him?"

I watched for a reaction but saw none. He simply said, "Why?"

"She doesn't work for you, she isn't one of you . . . there's no future for her here. Antoine's family is very rich. He could set her up in apartments of her own and give her an income. She could send you money."

It was my boldest stroke, but it was having little effect; he was shaking his head slowly, and this angered me.

"It's rather late to start considering her moral welfare, isn't it?" I demanded. "Since you see fit to send her out to sleep in a barn with strangers."

"That doesn't matter," he said, reining the nag in so that we came to a halt at the empty crossroads. "She can't leave, that's all."

Such were my initial efforts on Antoine's behalf; and I now have to report that I had little more success in my new role as artist's agent. I gave my choice of dealer a lot of thought, and settled on one whom I believed would be sympathetic to the picture's fresh and quite modern approach to its subject; he had, I knew, recently made a buying trip to England and returned with several works of Constable that were considered to be almost revolutionary in their treatment of nature. I left the painting in his hands for several days, and then called on him to check on progress.

He'd found a buyer. But when I heard the sum on offer, my initial excitement died and went cold within me.

"So little?" I said. "But . . ."

"You might get more if you let it hang in the gallery for a few weeks, but I doubt it," he said. "And I wouldn't want to get a reputation for handling this kind of material." But then he conceded, "I'm not saying it isn't good."

"But if it's good, it *must* bring more."

"Not so. Good isn't what sells . . . fashionable is what sells. We're talking about classical characters in idealized landscapes. Nature rearranged in the studio. Now, you tell me. How do I sell this little farm girl in a market like that?"

It was a good piece of work, I *knew* it; knew it with a greater confidence than I had ever brought to any work of my own. I said, "Are you telling me that this painting is at fault because there's too much of the truth in it?"

He shrugged delicately. "If you like. For what it's worth, I think your friend's very brave. But I can't sell his nerve, either . . . I just sell pictures."

What could I do? Antoine's tenure at the farm would last only as long as his ability to pay matched the greed of his landlords. The sum I'd been offered wouldn't buy him more than a few days grace at current rates, but any effort to find a better price for the picture would take time. Even then, there were no guarantees of any greater success. With a sense of defeat, I accepted the offer.

There had to come a point, I'd decided, where Antoine would have to get his obsession into some kind of perspective. He'd found himself in a situation that had made a conceptual breakthrough possible, but now it was time to give some consideration to the strategy of his new career. After all, hadn't he already made his first commercial sale? And if I was beginning to sound like his father in this way of thinking, I didn't dwell on the fact long enough for it to bother me.

I went out again on the following Sunday. Antoine was waiting for me, on the wrong side of the river.

He was sitting on a rock by the crossing, staring into the fast-running current. If I'd been shocked by his appearance before, I was horrified now. He was filthy and wretched, his skin gray with ill health under its ingrained surface of dirt; his hair was like old straw, and his entire body was hunched and bent. I saw what looked like dried wounds on his hands, and when he looked up at my approach, it was with the eyes of the starving.

For a moment I was unable to speak. To see a friend reduced so far, so fast! His bags, easel, and paints were beside him; they lay as if thrown there, the easel broken and the paints scattered and trampled into the riverside mud.

"Antoine!" I finally managed to say. "What happened here?"

"The money was gone, so they threw me out," he said simply. His voice was rough and weak. "I've been here for two days. When I tried to go back in, they set the dogs on me."

This, I assumed, would explain the wounds on his hands. "That's outrageous," I said. "I'm going to speak to them. Let them set the dogs on *me*, if they dare."

I stormed across the ford, not caring how much noise I made or how much spray I created. Antoine, after rising unsteadily from his rock, hesitated for a while and then began to follow me at a distance.

The yard was in silence, and to me seemed just as grim as it had on that first day. Lise's mirror no longer hung under the chestnut tree, and from the dark stains on the ground I'd have guessed that the butchery hooks had been put to recent use. With Antoine still trailing along behind, I took a look in the barn; some of the hay had been carted out, but there was no sign of anyone around.

"We're too late," Antoine said, but I paid him no attention and went out through the back doors of the barn. Out here, at least, I found a sign of life in the form of the remains of a recent fire; it was smoking still, and as I drew closer I saw that the smoke actually came from a scattering of almost-extinct coals in the bottom of a shallow pit. They lay on a bed of deep ash, and there was more ash and hay mingled in with the earth that had been spaded out onto the ground beside the excavation. Even without extending my hand, I could feel the heat.

I was not to be stopped. Antoine started to speak again, but I didn't wait to listen; I was already on my way toward the stone house with its steeply pitched roof and its inch-thick doors, as stolid and as resistant to inquiry as I knew the people inside it to be. I strode across a kitchen garden, where almost nothing grew, and hesitated at the side entrance; I could hear noises from inside, the sounds of a number of people together, and so without knocking I threw back the unbolted door before me and stepped through.

The noise ended as I entered, as sharply as if it had been cut by a blade. I saw a plain whitewashed room with a broad table down its center, around which at least a dozen people sat; it seemed that the same face turned toward me in twelve or thirteen slightly differing forms, from a child of three to a woman so old and pale that she seemed bloodless. One of them, a man of around thirty years, was bibbed like a baby and being fed with a spoon. All of their eyes save his were on me; he continued to look eagerly at his plate.

I'd interrupted a feast, and a strange feast it was; on the table stood nothing but meat and dishes of liquid fat, and more of this in one spread than such a family might normally expect to see in a year. I saw joints and ribs and bones already picked clean, and at the far end of the table a plate piled high with roasted offal. This, I didn't doubt, was all the product of the cooking pit that I'd seen behind the barn. The sight and the smell made me queasy at the excess on display; the faces that now studied me blankly were bloated and smeared with grease.

Nobody spoke. But in my mind I heard that voice from days before: *Tell your friend, we can't eat his pictures.*

And then came something that terrified me, as if the hooks that held the backcloth of my world had suddenly slipped in their holes and allowed a corner to fall, revealing the dark machinery that usually stood concealed. It happened as my gaze came to rest on one of the smaller serving dishes, runny with juices and melted fat. The joint that lay on it was charred around the edges, the skin scored and crisp; but for no more than a second it was recognizable, nails and all, as a human hand. I blinked and stared, and even as I did so, the joint seemed to shimmer and to change, becoming indistinct for a moment before being restored to my sight in a less obvious form. I might have called it an illusion, but I knew that it was not; it was, I am certain, the final demise of Antoine's vision, crushed by the presence of the same poverty and ignorance and need that had given it birth.

The retarded thirty-year-old began to wail and to drum on the table with his fists, and I took three halting steps back and grabbed at the door handle to pull it closed on that terrible scene.

Antoine hadn't followed me to the house. He'd stayed back, and now waited at some distance. He seemed to be hugging himself, his left arm holding his right as if he were nursing some half-healed bruise. I went across to him and turned him and began to usher him out of the yard, and he complied without protest. On the other side of the river we gathered up such of his things as were worth taking away; I gave him a few small pieces to carry, but the heaviest baggage I carried myself.

It was in this way that we walked down the lane, myself well laden and Antoine allowing himself to be hastened along. I couldn't take him onto the railway, not in a public compartment in his present state and condition, but there was enough money from the sale of the painting to be able to afford a horse and carriage to take us all the way back to Paris. We would arrive late and in darkness, but that would be no disadvantage.

I spoke on the subject only once as we left Corbeil after a half hour's rest. Antoine was huddled by the window, looking like a bundle of miserable sticks.

I said, "When you slept. Do you know where she went to?"

Antoine slowly turned his head so that his bleak eyes met mine. "I never wondered," he said.

And although I knew that he lied, I never asked him again.

PRIDE

CHARLES L. GRANT

Charles Grant is a congenial man with a deep, dark imagination, a force to be reckoned with in the field of horror. He first began publishing in the fields of science fiction and horror with his story. "The House of Evil," which appeared in *F & SF* in 1968. Since that time he has developed an entire town, Oxrun Station, in which many of his stories—including "Pride"—are set. It is an ordinary small town with a predilection for certain "strange" happenings. "Pride" tells of one such event—the chance meeting of a man and a woman—the resultant love that occurs—and something else.

It was the middle of August when the nights changed in Oxrun Station. Some blamed it on the anticipation of a hurricane battering its way up the coast, its vanguard of ghost-clouds muting the stars; others blamed the two-week heat wave that had softened the tarmac, singed tempers and lawns; and still others accused the dying that robbed the evenings of their softness, filed edges on laughter, made walking the streets an exercise in silence.

As happened to me the night I left the Chancellor Inn and noted with a frown the empty porches, empty sidewalks. Usually there were strollers, creaking rockers, quiet whispers; usually the cars didn't move quite so fast. And usually I didn't have to listen to my heels on the pavement—flat, without echoes, as if I weren't there at all. The only sign of my passing were the shadows at my feet, darting ahead, sweeping back, teasing forward once again. I tried not to watch them, set reins on imagination, but I couldn't help jumping when a cat wailed behind a hedge.

A self-conscious grin as my left hand massaged the back of my neck while my right sought a trouser pocket. Nerves, I told myself; even the Lone Ranger would recheck his guns tonight. Nerves. It happened every time I fell into brooding, which today I suspected was working overtime.

First there'd been the letter from my former wife, Carole. After expressing her customary, and sometimes genuine concern for my welfare, she proceeded to extoll the therapeutic value of remarriage, in her case to a diplomat apparently drowning in money. I doubted the jibe was intended with malice, just as I'd doubted any of them over the years had been aimed at the jugular—but one can bleed to death by drops as well as gashes, and neither of us was weeping when the final papers were signed.

Then there was the slow and inexplicable erosion of my clients, and an unpleasant case which would be completed in the morning, a case that some had hoped would be the end of all the killing.

Late in April the first body had been discovered just outside of Harley, twenty minutes from the Station. A young man, horribly mutilated, dismembered, partially devoured. Four more were uncovered at three- and four-week intervals, each one somewhat nearer. Then, last week, Syd Foster had been arrested, charged with all five brutal murders, and that of his nephew, right here in the village. It was shocking, it was scandal, and virtually no one believed it. The arrest had been a reflex, an unthinking reaction to the outcry for safety, and Syd was my client and I was going to set him free.

That did not make me the most popular man in some parts of the county, but for a change the unobserved technicalities were a pleasure to behold. Syd was fifty, a postman and a loner, and I'd known him for years. He was no more a cannibal than I was a Darrow.

So I walked, and I pondered, and I almost missed the woman.

She was leaning against a red maple between sidewalk and curb, one arm around the bole and her head slightly inclined as if sharing a lover's whisper. Not overwhelmingly beautiful, but certainly attractive enough: gold-brown hair that sifted down and away from a face of gentle curves, eyes wide-set and dark, thin lips, peaked chin, the rest of her willow slender in a print blouse and snug jeans.

She was humming.

I stopped, then, and I stared, finally cleared my throat falsely and found some faint courage. "Excuse me," I said in my best Samaritan voice, "but are you lost or something? Can I help you?"

She smiled, almost shyly. "No. I'm perfectly here, thanks."

I smiled back awkwardly and waited for inspiration to unleash the charm. But I could have waited all night for the silence I suffered. So I put a finger to my brow in a see-you salute and moved on. As far as the corner, where I stopped and glanced back. She was watching me, still smiling, finally pulling back her hair, away from her eyes, behind her ears. A hesitation, a quick look to either side, and she walked toward me, hands clasped behind her back, shoes silent on the pavement.

"Jean," she told me, "and to tell you the truth, yes, I do think I'm lost."

"Brian Farrell," I said, wondering about her perfume, rather odd and oddly compelling. "Where are you headed?"

She gave me an address on Woodland Avenue, three blocks to our right and four blocks up. I started to point, then drew back my arm. "If you like, I'll walk you," I said. "It's on my way, and I wouldn't mind, really." I grinned, feeling foolish.

"Well, I wouldn't mind either," she said, put a hand to my elbow, and allowed me to lead her.

And as we walked she questioned me about the dark houses, the lack of pedestrian traffic, and I told her about the dying—and the inevitable conclusion that if Syd Foster was innocent, the killer was still free. She shuddered and hugged my arm; I straightened, and tried not to smile.

"That's really . . . horrid," she said as we came to her street. "You sound like you know an awful lot about it, though. I mean, more than what you read in the *Herald*."

"I should," I said, after debating the answer. "I'm Syd Foster's lawyer."

There was no response. Instead, she scratched idly the back of my hand until we reached her front gate, set in a privet hedge that surrounded her home. Then, before I could say anything, she thanked me graciously for the escort, shook my hand, and left me standing alone, in front of a bulky gray Victorian caged by willow and beech, with a station wagon in the driveway and a yellow light on the porch. I blinked when the front door closed, blinked when the light died, stood for a long moment thinking I'd said something wrong. A shrug, then, and I walked away, turned around, and walked back to double-check the address with a squint and a nod. What I would do with it I didn't know, but the fancies that came with it took my mind off Foster as I moved on home.

To dreams. Swirling, red-coated dreams I'd been having for weeks. Tangled sheets, a lost pillow, and several times waking to wonder why I'd wakened. Oversleeping at last and rushing late to the office to learn that Foster's hearing had been postponed to Friday. I was annoyed, and felt reprieved, and the relief on my face not soon enough hidden.

"You still go in two days," my partner told me stiffly.

Chester Frazier and I had been affiliated for just four years that month, an association instigated by Carole, who had ambitions I didn't, and who'd hoped some of Chet's drive would somehow rub off. Unfortunately for her (and I'm not sure about me), he had come to resent strongly my less than wholehearted devotion to the concept of the flamboyant. Not that there was all that much opportunity for it in Oxrun, but by the nature of the village there was a great deal of money and lots of connections to be made. He dogged them avidly. I ducked them quietly, preferring instead the relatively uncomplicated. For me, that meant wills and small suits and handling the estates of the far-from-wealthy. Chet called it charity work; I figured somebody had to do it, and it might as well be me. To save me from myself, then—and because he liked me, really cared—it was he who'd talked the judge into appointing me Foster's counsel. Small wonder he was put off when I wasn't enraged at the delay.

"No big deal," I said when he finally stopped his grousing. "All it means, for crying out loud, is two more nights in a cell. And if you believe him, he doesn't want to leave anyway."

"He could be out on bail, you know."

"He doesn't want it, Chet," I said patiently, marching over familiar ground. "Whoever, whatever's out there doing this has scared him to death. He thinks he's safer behind bars than in his own home."

"Brian, there are times . . ."

He stopped and shook his head in weary resignation, left my office for the deserted reception area out front. I watched him from my desk, rose, and stood at the door. Frowned. He was a large man, girth and height, with curled blond hair and hand-tailored suits, and generally he moved like a man with a mission. Today, however, he almost shambled across the carpet.

"You look tired," I said.

He turned away from the plate-glass window overlooking Centre Street and made his slow way back to me, leaned against the wall that separated our rooms. "I am," he confessed. "Elizabeth needs braces, Amy's heart murmur isn't clearing, and for the past three days Alice has had me up four or five times a night to check on prowlers she keeps hearing in the yard." His smile was one-sided. "It's amazing," he said, "how the mundane can kill you."

I would have tried wit to lighten his mood, but he'd inadvertently taken one of Carole's favorite lines. So I tried to change the subject.

"I met a girl last night. Lives over on Woodland. Nice girl. Pretty." I grinned. "I think I'm in lust."

"Oh, great, Brian, just great. Your practice is seeping away through the baseboard, and you say you're in love."

"Lust," I corrected him. "I don't know her that well."

He didn't appreciate the joke. Instead, he grunted sourly and ducked into his office. It was just as well. At that moment my phone rang—another client moving out, thanks for all this killing going on. It was an old woman with seven cats and little money, and I didn't bother to argue because I knew she wouldn't handle the shadows stalking their homes—but I wished it would happen to Chet for a change. I was getting tired of it, just as I'd grown tired of Carole not understanding that comfort to me didn't have to mean rich.

When that ended, however, I had only been relieved; the call I'd just taken was making me scared.

Worse. At the end of the day Chet hinted rather strongly he was seriously considering finally going it alone. He had expenses, he told me, and he couldn't carry me much longer unless I got off the mark.

It was a long walk home, then, and a tasteless short dinner. I couldn't read, couldn't watch television, couldn't find the nerve to walk over to Jean's. The way things were going, she'd probably not know me.

The porch was the best place I'd discovered for self-pity, watching the neighbors enjoying their lives, watching the children enjoying their living. A good dose of maudlin now and then, I thought, was good for the soul, but that, too, was deined me the moment I stepped out.

The humidity had turned to fog, the air touched with ice, and some blocks away I heard a police siren screaming. It was the wrong sound for the night, the wrong sound for the times. I shuddered and went in, would have gone straight to bed but the telephone rang.

"Brian? Brian Farrell?"

I gasped, and I grinned, and since the telephone table was right in the hallway, I sat at the bottom of the staircase and aimed my feet toward the door. "Jean? Is that you, Jean?" Brilliant, I thought; you should write for the theater.

"Am I bothering you?"

A bitter laugh. "Anything but."

She paused, and I heard a faint rustling on the line. "I hope you're not mad, but when I heard that siren I thought about what you told me last night and . . ." She laughed, sounded breathless. "Well, I scared myself is what I did. I needed a friendly voice."

"At your disposal," I said gallantly, and hoped Carole's ears were smarting.

We talked for almost an hour, most of it, I realized later, about my own problems, not hers, and when I rang off with a promise for dinner, I was virtually whistling.

But the dreams came again, not over till dawn.

And when I got to the office, Chet wasn't there.

Puzzled, but not worried, I left a message on his desk and went to see Foster. He wasn't talking, however, and I was gone in ten minutes. He bothered me, I supposed, more than he should have, a concern not helped by the change in the weather—the clouds had thickened, had grayed, and a drizzle started falling. Strong enough to streak dust on windows and darken the curbs, but not enough to wash them or to warrant a coat. Dismal, I decided, was the perfect word for the day.

When I returned from lunch, Chet was waiting. Impatiently, close to anger. His hair was unkempt and his shirtfront was wrinkled.

"Jesus," I said. "Chet, did something happen to—"

He shut me off with a slash of his hand, turned, and went into my office, where he poured himself a whiskey from my bottle on the sideboard. His hands were trembling, and just at his temple a tic pulled at his eye.

"I've been to the police," he said. "I talked to Fred Borg."

I didn't know what to say. So I said nothing. Just sat.

"Last night—"

"The siren," I said quickly.

He nodded after a moment, after draining his glass. "I was walking around the house from the garage after taking out the garbage. Bunch of kids had been cutting through the yard, I think I mentioned it yesterday. Alice's prowler. Anyway, I heard something, so I went back to have a look. Intrepid husband stalks wily teenager, or an alley cat, you know?" His smile was grotesque. "It was something, but I don't know what the hell it was. It stayed under the trees, growling at me." He poured another drink. "When I tried to get to the back door, it came after me."

"My God," I said softly, more stunned by his look than by what he was saying—it was almost as if he were ready to cry.

"I don't know what made me do it," he continued, "but I grabbed my lighter from my pocket and lit it. I wanted to see what it was, but I scared it off instead. But it was big, Brian. Christ, it was big."

"Well, what did they find? Some kind of dog?"

His look turned to disgust. "Nothing. Not a goddamned thing. I could tell Borg thought I was drinking or something. If it hadn't been for the, uh . . . any other time he probably would've made me blow up the balloon. As it is, he told me about a dozen other calls he gets every night. Trying to make me feel better. A member of the loony club." Then he looked at his glass and tried a weak smile. "Alice is having a fit. She wants me to sell the place today and move to New York. That's why I came in, to get a few papers and do some work at home. She . . . well, if anybody calls . . ."

"Sure, of course," I said quickly.

He nodded as he set his glass down. "And you're ready for Foster this afternoon?"

"Chet, for God's sake, give me some credit, all right?"

It was the wrong thing to say, an against-the-grain stroking of his already frayed temper.

"Credit? You want credit? For what, Brian? For pissing away a great chance to set yourself up as a damned fine lawyer? For fucking up a perfectly good marriage? For screwing around with some woman while your life goes down the tubes?" He shoved a trembling hand back through his hair, raised a fist, and dropped it. "I don't understand people like you, Brian." An apology of sorts. "I swear to God, I don't understand."

He left before I could respond, but by the time the front door slammed shut, I realized I had nothing to say. The language we spoke was English, but somewhere along the line all the communications broke down and what came to our ears was little more than gibberish.

Nevertheless, I was angry. So much so that by the time I reached Judge Ford's chambers in the courthouse, my manner had become brusque, my words clipped, my presentation aimed not only at freeing Syd but flaying the prosecution and police as cold-bloodedly as I could. No histrionics here, just a marching out of statements placing Syd miles away from each of the first four killings, a few tart reminders about Constitutional law and Miranda, and not a few acid comments about damages done to my client's reputation.

When I was through, the prosecution folded—as he would have done if I'd only smiled and told him his case was full of shit. But he was also perspiring, and Judge Ford couldn't help the admiration in his voice as he dismissed the case, sent us home, and gave me a look that wondered what the hell kind of pills I'd been taking since I'd seen him last.

It was, admittedly, an excellent job, one Chet would have been proud of had he seen it. Syd, on the other hand, only thanked me curtly and left me standing on the courthouse steps, trying hard not to run as he headed for home. I returned to the empty office and filed all the papers, straightened up my desk, wandered about for nearly an hour before realizing I was pacing. I should have been pleased with myself, and in a way I was. But it was a desperate, cold, emotionless sort of pleasure, a combination of the residue of ash my anger had left me and the understanding that, unlike Chet, I could never become addicted to something like this.

I ate at the Chancellor Inn.

I drank at the Chancellor Inn.

I wondered what was wrong with me that I couldn't exult over my victory. After all, an innocent man was free, and the police were free to find the real killer.

I wanted to call Jean, and I didn't know her last name.

I stepped outside, and it was dark. Cool. The wind working at the trees and the drizzle hardening to rain. I lifted my collar and shoved my hands into my pockets, thinking I'd stop by Chet's and see how he was doing. Instead, I found myself outside Foster's house, blinking water from my eyelids as I tried to form the question that would get Syd to tell me just what it was, specifically, that had frightened him so much.

The front door was locked, no response to my knocking. I stepped off the porch and made my way around back, noting as I went that all the lights were on, top floor and bottom.

As I reached the corner, I heard someone grunting.

I stopped, ignoring the dampness that crawled down my back and clung to my cheeks. I listened, knowing I'd heard that sound somewhere before. Then the grunting was replaced by a snarling, the snarling by feet running across wet grass. A single stride, and I was in the tiny backyard, staring through the soft glare of the kitchen lights reaching out to the dark. I could see nothing, though something told me there was movement out there. A swirling, receding movement that had me moving after it until I saw the open back door.

My hesitation stalled me, swerved me, had me on the concrete stoop and inside, one hand up to shade my eyes from the overhead light.

Syd was lying partway beneath a small table, the chairs shoved back against the cabinets, two of them on their sides. There was red all over the tiled floor, bright red, running red, most of it pooled by the stumps where Syd's arms and legs used to be.

It was a fever dream then: the air filled with black motes, and all motion was studied. I fell into a calm and called the police, then fell into the yard and vomited my dinner. Blue lights, and flashlights, and a hand on my shoulder, an arm around my waist. Chet materializing and sitting with me in the station while I told my story and swallowed back the tears. He offered me a ride home. I declined; I needed to walk. I needed to breathe. I needed to drive that grunting from my head—like the softly deep sound of a contented animal feeding.

It never occurred to me that I might be in danger.

Nor did I head for anyplace in particular until I found myself on Woodland Avenue and nearly ran to Jean's gate, pulled it open, and raced to the front door. She answered my knocking in moments, saw my face, and pulled me slowly into the living room, murmuring and stroking until I was seated on a couch, knees together and hands clasped in my lap. When she left I almost stood, but there was no strength left in my legs; when she returned I must have looked at her like a lost puppy finally found by its mistress. She smiled, knelt beside me, and pushed me back. A towel to my hair, my face; she took off my shoes and socks and dried my feet, until, at her urging, I told her what had happened, what I'd found.

She said nothing, and I kept on talking. She kissed my cheek, and I closed my eyes. And kept on talking.

She stripped off my jacket and shirt, dried my chest and back. And I kept on talking. Taking in the touch of her, the smell of her, feeling her breath against my ear as she whispered sympathies and soothings and a number of other things I did not hear because I finally told her how afraid I was—not of the nightcreature stalking the Station, but of the glass partitions that had been slamming down around me one by one, cutting me off from wife, work, and the last of my friends.

"As if," I said as I stared at the ceiling, "I'm turning into a ghost. Life goes on, but not around me. I'm not there anymore."

"No," she said gently, tracing a sharp nail along my jaw. "No, but you're here."

I smiled, grateful, and looked around the room at the furniture heavy and heavily padded, at the fringed floor lamps, at the floral carpet, the floral wallpaper. Not cluttered, not spare.

"You live here alone." Not really a question.

"For the time being," she said. She gestured at the room and at the rooms beyond. "Mother left it to us, me and my sisters. I came to see if it was all right, worth keeping or worth selling." She sighed lightly and lay her cheek against my shoulder, reminding me it was bare. "It's big, though."

I shifted slightly. "It's late."

She said, "Stay."

I neither grinned like a rake nor silently thanked my lucky stars; I merely followed her upstairs, where she made love to me, slept beside me, fixed me breakfast in the morning, and pushed me out laughing, sending me home for some fresh clothes for the weekend. I very nearly ran, almost didn't answer the phone as I was leaving with my suitcase.

It was Chet, come to a decision.

"Don't say it," I told him, not really caring, thinking about Jean, the way she looked at me, the way she listened. "And you don't have to explain, either. I understand."

"You always understand," he said wearily. "I think that's part of your problem, Brian. You understand so goddamned well . . . ah, the hell with it. Look, there'll be formalities and things—I'll call you later and we can—"

"I'll be at Jean's," I said. "Don't bother to call, I'll talk to you on Monday."

"Jean," he said flatly. I could almost see him shaking his head. "You never learn, do you."

"About what? Christ, Chet, you haven't even met her."

"I don't have to, pal. Unless she's into submission, she'll eat you alive." A pause. "Just don't be stupid, Brian," he said more softly, more concerned. "You've had a hell of a week."

I rang off without saying good-bye, locked the door behind me, and just did beat the next spate of rainfall to Jean's porch. When I burst inside, however, all grinning and foolish, the house was empty. I called, felt cold, hurried from room to room praying aloud I hadn't been wrong. Then I heard her calling my name, found a partially open door in the kitchen and went through to the garage, where she was working under the hood of the station wagon.

"Damned thing's gone again," she said, straightening and wiping her hands on a greasy rag. "She has a zillion miles on her, but I was hoping she'd last at least until fall." She grinned and slammed the hood down, punched at it and mimed a wince.

"How long has it been giving you trouble?" I tried to sound knowledgeable, though it sounded pompous.

"Since I got here, in April."

I nodded and returned to the kitchen, stood at the back door and watched the rain slant in on the back of the wind. A cold wind now that flayed the trees and churned puddles in the grass. It was dusk at noon, and felt like midnight.

She was moving about the garage, shifting things, heavy and awkward.

April, she'd said—yet she'd told me she hadn't known about the killings, or my involvement with Syd, or my profession at all.

April, she'd said—when I'd first started fading.

The rain and Syd Foster's and something running through the dark; the kitchen and the blood and—

She grunted softly as she came into the room, and suddenly there was ice lodged deep in my throat.

When I turned she was standing in the doorway, the living room behind her. No lights had been turned on, and her face and figure were in shadow, pale shadows that had me squinting to keep her form from shifting. The wind keened in the eaves and across the mouth of the chimney; a gust, and the panes rattled. I looked to the floor and saw my shadow framed by the door window behind me, dark serpents and worms writhing down toward my shoulders.

Then she spoke my name lovingly and I moved around the room because I couldn't stand still; she began to talk quietly and I tried through the wind and the cold and the images of blood to listen and understand, without having to scream: about how people thought of this animal and that, how cats were female and dogs were male, women were feline and men were bestial, and with roles these days so swiftly blurring—

I opened the refrigerator; it was empty.

—wouldn't it be fascinating to think about what new mythic creatures would have to conform to new dreams, what extraordinary night-things would have to fill in the void; but it wasn't all that bad because people wouldn't believe any more than they used to, and with violence still growing—

The cupboards, the cabinets, the drawers were all empty.

—who'd know the difference between two types of nightmare, as long as there was care taken in the hunting.

I leaned over the sink and thought of Chet's warning.

"Who are you?" I said, and wished I'd been drinking.

"Jean," she said simply.

"What . . . what are you?" I said, and wished I were dreaming.

"Your lover, a friend—"

"You know what I mean," I said harshly, spun around, and she was still standing there, in the doorway, in the shadow. I wanted to be afraid, the most natural reaction, but first there was the anger of what I thought was betrayal.

"Someone," she said, "who's been looking for someone like you. Not weak in the old sense, but not always strong enough to fight his own battles. A wonderful streak of feminine sensitivity, plus a little masculine posturing he knows is a sham. A man, Brian, who was more alone than he knew."

"You drove them away," I said weakly.

"There are times, like now, when vulnerability breeds belief."

I should have argued, but I couldn't. The wind was too noisy, and I couldn't focus my anger, and when she started to move toward me, I was too frightened to run.

"We have needs too," she said when she reached me, tilting her head and looking up at me sideways. "Physical"—her hands on my hips— "emotional"—that smile she first gave me—"and the practical, Brian. In the smaller towns we like I think they still call it respectability, a lot easier to get with a solid man in the house. Like a lawyer, for instance. A low-keyed man who never rocks the boat."

"You drove them away."

"You do what you have to."

Then a word caught me, and echoed. "You said . . . we?"

"Why, my sisters," she said, and her expression turned bemused. "A small lie. There's no mother. I came here looking, and one day I found you."

The house trembled at a blow, and rain crashed against the windows.

Her bemusement grew. "Why . . . why don't you think of yourself as something like the king of beasts, Brian, with five lovely mates to choose from, who'll keep you warm, make you content, keep the world from intruding and making you sad. You'll work, of course, because a man like you has to. But so will we, until it's time to move on." She touched my chin with a finger. "Think about it, darling, don't be rash. I know what you're thinking, you know, what you'd like to do now."

I shook my head, once.

"Of course you want to run," she said sternly. "You wouldn't be human if you didn't. And you're wondering how you could ever live with my sisters and me." She shrugged. "Well, sometimes it works and sometimes it doesn't."

I watched and said nothing when she started to leave me. It was too much, and it wasn't enough, and she had all my feelings pegged down to the last. And worse—she knew I almost believed and, in almost believing, was tempted.

I followed her into the front hall. She opened the front door and helped me into my coat. Then she smiled warmly, and sadly. "Go ahead," she said. "It's all right, believe me: But as a favor to me, please stay on the porch."

I nodded dumbly, shivering at the wind that clutched wildly at my jacket and my hair, crossed the threshold with my arms folded tightly over my chest. But before I could even begin to wonder about madness and nightmares and the perfect reality of the storm in spite of its fury, she whispered my name as she closed the door behind me. I turned and she was shadow, she was shimmering, she was Jean and she was smiling.

"Two things to consider," she said, "just to help you out. The most important is this: you'll never, ever, have to be alone again. We'll give you more pride than any man's ever had."

Oh, Jesus, I thought; for God's sake, stop smiling!

She did. Abruptly. Expressionless now.

"The other thing is . . ." and she glanced to the street, to the storm, back to me. "They won't believe you if you decide you have to run."

And she left me alone as she closed the door, grunting.

LONGTOOTH

EDGAR PANGBORN

Edgar Pangborn (1909–1976) will be remembered by long-time readers of science fiction and fantasy for his fine stories about Davy, which showed the triumph of art and scholarship against religious oppression; these were combined into a novel, *Davy,* published in 1964. Although Edgar Pangborn was best known for his science fiction stories, he also was the creator of such taut, literate tales of horror as "Longtooth." "Longtooth" takes place in rural Maine, and concerns something frightening that is born, lives— and kills—briefly in the peaceful forest.

My word is good. How can I prove it? Born in Darkfield, wasn't I? Stayed away thirty more years after college, but when I returned I was still Ben Dane, one of the Darkfield Danes, Judge Marcus Dane's eldest. And they knew my word was good. My wife died and I sickened of all cities; then my bachelor brother Sam died, too, who'd lived all his life here in Darkfield, running his one-man law office over in Lohman—our nearest metropolis, pop. 6437. A fast coronary at fifty; I had loved him. Helen gone, then Sam—I wound up my unimportances and came home, inheriting Sam's housekeeper Adelaide Simmons, her grim stability and celestial cooking. Nostalgia for Maine is a serious matter, late in life: I had to yield. I expected a gradual drift into my childless old age playing correspondence chess, translating a few of the classics. I thought I could take for granted the continued respect of my neighbors. I say my word is good.

I will remember again that middle of March a few years ago, the snow skimming out of an afternoon sky as dirty as the bottom of an old aluminum pot. Harp Ryder's back road had been plowed since the last snowfall; I supposed Bolt-Bucket could make the mile and a half in to his farm and out again before we got caught. Harp had asked me to get him a book if I was making a trip to Boston, any goddamn book that told about Eskimos, and I had one for him, De Poncins's *Kabloona*. I saw the midget devils of white running crazy down a huge slope of wind, and recalled hearing at the Darkfield News Bureau, otherwise Cleve's General Store, somebody mentioning a forecast of the worst blizzard in forty years. Joe Cleve, who won't permit a radio in the store because it pesters his ulcers, inquired of his Grand Inquisitor who dwells ten yards behind your right shoulder: "Why's it always got to be the worst in so-and-so many years, that going to help anybody?" The bureau was still analyzing this difficult inquiry when I left, with my cigarettes and as much as I could remember of Adelaide's grocery list after leaving it on the dining table. It wasn't yet three when I turned in on Harp's back road, and a gust slammed at Bolt-Bucket like death with a shovel.

I tried to win momentum for the rise to the high ground, swerved to avoid an idiot rabbit and hit instead a patch of snow-hidden melt-and-freeze, skidding to a full stop from which nothing would extract me but a tow.

I was fifty-seven that year, my wind bad from too much smoking and my heart (I now know) no stronger than Sam's. I quit cursing—gradually, to avoid sudden actions—and tucked *Kabloona* under my parka. I would walk the remaining mile to Ryder's, stay just to leave the book, say hello, and phone for a tow; then, since Harp never owned a car and never would, I could walk back and meet the truck.

If Leda Ryder knew how to drive, it didn't matter much after she married Harp. They farmed it, back in there, in almost the manner of Harp's ancestors of Jefferson's time. Harp did keep his two hundred laying hens by methods that were considered modern before the poor wretches got condemned to batteries, but his other enterprises came closer to antiquity. In his big kitchen garden he let one small patch of weeds fool themselves for an inch or two, so he'd have it to work at; they survived nowhere else. A few cows, a team, four acres for market crops, and a small dog Droopy, whose grandmother had made it somehow with a dachshund. Droopy's only menace in obese old age was a wheezing bark. The Ryders must have grown nearly all vital necessities except chewing tobacco and once in a while a new dress for Leda. Harp could snub the twentieth century, and I doubt if Leda was consulted about it in spite of his obsessive devotion for her. She was almost thirty years younger, and yes, he should not have married her. Other side up just as scratchy; she should not have married him, but she did.

Harp was a dinosaur perhaps, but I grew up with him, he a year the younger. We swam, fished, helled around together. And when I returned to Darkfield growing old, he was one of the few who acted glad to see me, so far as you can trust what you read in a face like a granite promontory. Maybe twice a week Harp Ryder smiled.

I pushed on up the ridge, and noticed a going-and-coming set of wide tire tracks already blurred with snow. That would be the egg truck I had passed a quarter hour since on the main road. Whenever the west wind at my back lulled, I could swing around and enjoy one of my favorite prospects of birch and hemlock lowland. From Ryder's Ridge there's no sign of Darkfield two miles southwest except one church spire. On clear days you glimpse Bald Mountain and his two big brothers, more than twenty miles west of us.

The snow was thickening. It brought relief and pleasure to see the black shingles of Harp's barn and the roof of his Cape Codder. Foreshortened, so that it looked snug against the barn; actually house and barn were connected by a two-story shed fifteen feet wide and forty feet long—woodshed below, hen loft above. The Ryders' sunrise-facing bedroom window was set only three feet above the eaves of that shed roof. They truly went to bed with the chickens. I shouted, for Harp was about to close the big shed door. He held it for me. I ran, and the storm ran after me. The west wind was bouncing off the barn; eddies howled at us. The temperature had tumbled ten degrees since I left Darkfield. The thermometer by the shed door read fifteen degrees, and I knew I'd been a damn fool. As I helped Harp fight the shed door closed, I thought I heard Leda, crying.

A swift confused impression. The wind was exploring new ranges of passion, the big door squawked, and Harp was asking: "Ca' break down?" I do still think I heard Leda wail. If so, it ended as we got the door latched and Harp drew a newly fitted two-by-four bar across it. I couldn't understand that: the old latch was surely proof against any wind short of a hurricane.

"Bolt-Bucket never breaks down. Ought to get one, Harp—lots of company. All she did was go in the ditch."

"You might see her again come spring." His hens were scratching overhead, not yet scared by the storm. Harp's eyes were small gray glitters of trouble. "Ben, you figure a man's getting old at fifty-six?"

"No." My bones (getting old) ached for the warmth of his kitchen-dining-living-everything room, not for sad philosophy. "Use your phone, okay?"

"If the wires ain't down," he said, not moving, a man beaten on by other storms. "Them loafers didn't cut none of the overhang branches all summer. I told 'em of course, I told 'em how it would be . . . I meant, Ben, old enough to get dumb fancies?" My face may have told him I thought he was brooding about himself with a young wife. He frowned, annoyed that I hadn't taken his meaning. "I meant, *seeing* things. Things that can't be so, but—"

"We can all do some of that at any age, Harp."

That remark was a stupid brushoff, a stone for bread, because I was cold, impatient, wanted in. Harp had always a tense one-way sensitivity. His face chilled. "Well, come in, warm up. Leda ain't feeling too good. Getting a cold or something."

When she came downstairs and made me welcome, her eyes were reddened. I don't think the wind made that noise. Droopy waddled from her basket behind the stove to snuff my feet and give me my usual low passing mark.

Leda never had it easy there, young and passionate with scant mental resources. She was twenty-eight that year, looking tall because she carried her firm body handsomely. Some of the sullenness in her big mouth and lucid gray eyes was sexual challenge, some pure discontent. I liked Leda; her nature was not one for animosity or meanness. Before her marriage the Darkfield News Bureau used to declare with its customary scrupulous fairness that Leda had been covered by every goddamn thing in pants within thirty miles. For once the bureau may have spoken a grain of truth in the malice, for Leda did have the smoldering power that draws men without word or gesture. After her abrupt marriage to Harp—Sam told me all this; I wasn't living in Darkfield then and hadn't met her— the garbage-gossip went hastily underground: enraging Harp Ryder was never healthy.

The phone wires weren't down, yet. While I waited for the garage to answer, Harp said, "Ben, I can't let you walk back in that. Stay over, huh?"

I didn't want to. It meant extra work and inconvenience for Leda, and

I was ancient enough to crave my known safe burrow. But I felt Harp wanted me to stay for his own sake. I asked Jim Short at the garage to go ahead with Bolt-Bucket if I wasn't there to meet him. Jim roared: "Know what it's doing right now?"

"Little spit of snow, looks like."

"Jesus!" He covered the mouthpiece imperfectly. I heard his enthusiastic voice ring through cold-iron echoes: "Hey, old Ben's got that thing into the ditch again! Ain't that something . . . ? Listen, Ben, I can't make no promises. Got both tow trucks out already. You better stop over and praise the Lord you got that far."

"Okay," I said. "It wasn't much of a ditch."

Leda fed us coffee. She kept glancing toward the landing at the foot of the stairs where a night-darkness already prevailed. A closed-in stairway slanted down at a never-used front door; beyond that landing was the other ground floor room-parlor, spare, guestroom—where I would sleep. I don't know what Leda expected to encounter in that shadow. Once when a chunk of firewood made an odd noise in the range, her lips clamped shut on a scream.

The coffee warmed me. By that time the weather left no loophole for argument. Not yet 3:30, but west and north were lost in furious black. Through the hissing white flood I could just see the front of the barn forty feet away. "Nobody's going no place into that," Harp said. His little house shuddered, enforcing the words. "Leda, you don't look too brisk. Get you some rest."

"I better see to the spare room for Ben."

Neither spoke with much tenderness, but it glowed openly in him when she turned her back. Then some other need bent his granite face out of its normal seams. His whole gaunt body leaning forward tried to help him talk. "You wouldn't figure me for a man'd go off his rocker?" he asked.

"Of course not. What's biting, Harp?"

"There's something in the woods, got no right to be there." To me that came as a letdown of relief: I would not have to listen to another's marriage problems. "I wish, b' Jesus Christ, it would hit somebody else once, so I could say what I know and not be laughed at all to hell. I *ain't* one for dumb fancies."

You walked on eggs, with Harp. He might decide any minute that *I* was laughing. "Tell me," I said. "If anything's out there now, it must feel a mite chilly."

"Ayah." He went to the north window, looking out where we knew the road lay under white confusion. Harp's land sloped down the other side of the road to the edge of mighty evergreen forest. Katahdin stands more than fifty miles north and a little east of us. We live in a withering shrink-world, but you could still set out from Harp's farm and, except for the occasional country road and the rivers—not many large ones— you could stay in deep forest all the way to the tundra, or Alaska. Harp said, "This kind of weather is when it comes."

He sank into his beat-up kitchen armchair and reached for *Kabloona*. He had barely glanced at the book while Leda was with us. "Funny name."

"Kabloona's an Eskimo word for white man."

"He done these pictures . . . ? Be they good, Ben?"

"I like 'em. Photographs in the back."

"Oh." He turned the pages hastily for those, but studied only the ones that showed the strong Eskimo faces, and his interest faded. Whatever he wanted was not here. "These people, be they—civilized?"

"In their own way, sure."

"Ayah, this guy looks like he could find his way in the woods."

"Likely the one thing he couldn't do, Harp. They never see a tree unless they come south, and they hate to do that. Anything below the Arctic is too warm."

"That a fact . . . ? Well, it's a nice book. How much was it?" I'd found it second-hand; he paid me to the exact penny. "I'll be glad to read it." He never would. It would end up on the shelf in the parlor with the Bible, an old almanac, a Longfellow, until someday this place went up for auction and nobody remembered Harp's way of living.

"What's this all about, Harp?"

"Oh . . . I was hearing things in the woods, back last summer. I'd think, fox, then I'd know it wasn't. Make your hair stand right on end. Lost a cow, last August, from the north pasture acrosst the rud. Section of board fence tore out. I mean, Ben, the two top boards was *pulled out from the nail holes*. No hammer marks."

"Bear?"

"Only track I found looked like bear except too small. You know a bear wouldn't *pull* it out, Ben."

"Cow slamming into it, panicked by something?"

He remained patient with me. "Ben, would I build a cow-pasture fence nailing the crosspieces from the outside? Cow hit it with all her weight she might bust it, sure. And kill herself doing it, be blood and hair all over the split boards, and she'd be there, not a mile and a half away into the woods. Happened during a big thunderstorm. I figured it had to be somebody with a spite ag'inst me, maybe some son of a bitch wanting the prop'ty, trying to scare me off that's lived here all my life and my family before me. But that don't make sense. I found the cow a week later, what was left. Way into the woods. The head and the bones. Hide tore up and flang around. Any *person* dressing off a beef, he'll cut whatever he wants and take off with it. He don't sit down and chaw the meat off the *bones*, b'Jesus Christ. He don't tear the thighbone out of the joint. . . . All right, maybe bear. But no bear did that job on that fence and then driv old Nell a mile and a half into the woods to kill her. Nice little Jersey, clever's a kitten. Leda used to make over her, like she don't usually do with the stock. . . . I've looked plenty in the woods since then, never turned up anything. Once and again I did smell something. Fishy, like bear-smell but—*different*."

"But Harp, with snow on the ground—"

"Now you'll really call me crazy. When the weather is clear, I ain't once found his prints. I hear him then, at night, but I go out by daylight where I think the sound was, there's no trail. Just the usual snow tracks. I know. He lives in the trees and don't come down except when it's storming, I got to believe that? Because then he does come, Ben, when the weather's like now, like right now. And old Ned and Jerry out in the stable go wild, and sometimes we hear his noise under the window. I shine my flashlight through the glass—never catch sight of him. I go out with the ten gauge if there's any light to see by, and there's prints around the house—holes filling up with snow. By morning there'll be maybe some marks left, and they'll lead off to the north woods, but under the trees you won't find it. So he gets up in the branches and travels thataway? . . . Just once I have seen him, Ben. Last October. I better tell you one other thing first. A day or so after I found what was left of old Nell, I lost six roaster chickens. I made over a couple box stalls, maybe you remember, so the birds could be out on range and roost in the barn at night. Good doors, and I always locked 'em. Two in the morning, Ned and Jerry go crazy. I got out through the barn into the stable, and they was spooked, Ned trying to kick his way out. I got 'em quiet, looked all over the stable—loft, harness room, everywhere. Not a thing. Dead quiet night, no moon. It had to be something the horses smelled. I come back into the barn, and found one of the chicken-pen doors open—*tore* out from the lock. Chicken thief would bring along something to pry with—wouldn't he be a Christly idjut if he didn't . . . ? Took six birds, six nice eight-pound roasters, and left the heads on the floor—bitten off."

"Harp—some lunatic. People *can* go insane that way. There are old stories—"

"Been trying to believe that. Would a man live the winter out there? Twenty below zero?"

"Maybe a cave—animal skins."

"I've boarded up the whole back of the barn. Done the same with the hen-loft windows—two-by-fours with four-inch spikes driv slantwise. They be twelve feet off the ground, and he ain't come for 'em, not yet. . . . So after that happened I sent for Sheriff Robart. Son of a bitch happens to live in Darkfield, you'd think he might've took an interest."

"Do any good?"

Harp laughed. He did that by holding my stare, making no sound, moving no muscle except a disturbance at the eye corners. A New England art; maybe it came over on the *Mayflower*. "Robart he come by, after a while. I showed him that door. I showed him them chicken heads. Told him how I'd been spending my nights out there on my ass, with the ten gauge." Harp rose to unload tobacco juice into the range fire; he has a theory it purifies the air. "Ben, I might've showed him them chicken heads a shade close to his nose. By the time he got here, see, they wasn't all that fresh. He made out he'd look around and let me know. Mid-September. Ain't seen him since."

"Might've figured he wouldn't be welcome?"

"Why, he'd be welcome as shit on a tablecloth."

"You spoke of—seeing it, Harp?"

"Could call it seeing . . . All right. It was during them Indian summer days—remember? Like June except them pretty colors, smell of windfalls—God, I like that, I like October. I'd gone down to the slope acrosst the rud where I mended my fence after losing old Nell. Just leaning there, guess I was tired. Late afternoon, sky pinking up. You know how the fence cuts acrosst the slope to my east wood lot. I've let the bushes grow free—lot of elder, other stuff the birds come for. I was looking down toward that little break between the north woods and my wood lot, where a bit of old growed-up pasture shows through. Pretty spot. Painter fella come by a few years ago and done a picture of it, said the place looked like a coro, dunno what the hell that is, he didn't say."

I pushed at his brown study. "You saw it there?"

"No. Off to my right in them elder bushes. Fifty feet from me, I guess. By God, I didn't turn my head. I got it with the tail of my eye and turned the other way as if I meant to walk back to the rud. Made like busy with something in the grass, come wandering back to the fence some nearer. He stayed for me, a brownish patch in them bushes by the big yellow birch. Near the height of a man. No gun with me, not even a stick . . . Big shoulders, couldn't see his goddamn feet. He don't stand more'n five feet tall. His hands, if he's got real ones, hung out of my sight in a tangle of elder bushes. He's got brown fur, Ben, reddy-brown fur all over him. His face, too, his head, his big thick neck. There's a shine to fur in sunlight, you can't be mistook. So—I did look at him direct. Tried to act like I still didn't see him, but he knowed. He melted back and got the birch between him and me. Not a sound." And then Harp was listening for Leda upstairs. He went on softly: "Ayah, I ran back for a gun, and searched the woods, for all the good it did me. You'll want to know about his face. I ain't told Leda all this part. See, she's scared, I don't want to make it no worse, I just said it was some animal that snuck off before I could see it good. A big face, Ben. Head real human except it sticks out too much around the jaw. Not much nose—open spots in the fur. Ben, the—the *teeth!* I seen his mouth drop open and he pulled up one side of his lip to show me them stabbing things. I've seen as big as that on a full-growed bear. That's what I'll hear, I ever try to tell this. They'll say I seen a bear. Now, I shot my first bear when I was sixteen and Pa took me over toward Jackman. I've got me one maybe every other year since then. I know 'em, all their ways. But that's what I'll hear if I tell the story."

I am a frustrated naturalist, loaded with assorted facts. I know there aren't any monkeys or apes that could stand our winters except maybe the harmless Himalayan langur. No such beast as Harp described lived anywhere on the planet. It didn't help. Harp was honest; he was rational; he wanted a reasonable explanation as much as I did. Harp wasn't the village atheist for nothing. I said, "I guess you will, Harp. People mostly won't take the—unusual."

"Maybe you'll hear him tonight, Ben."

Leda came downstairs, and heard part of that. "He's been telling you, Ben. What do you think?"

"I don't know what to think."

"Led', I thought, if I imitate that noise for him—"

"No!" She had brought some mending and was about to sit down with it, but froze as if threatened by attack. "I couldn't stand it, Harp. And —it might bring them."

"Them?" Harp chuckled uneasily. "I don't guess I could do it that good he'd come for it."

"Don't *do* it, Harp!"

"All right, hon." Her eyes were closed, her head drooping back. "Don't git nerved up so."

I started wondering whether a man still seeming sane could dream up such a horror for the unconscious purpose of tormenting a woman too young for him, a woman he could never imagine he owned. If he told her a fox bark wasn't right for a fox, she'd believe him. I said. "We shouldn't talk about it if it upsets her."

He glanced at me like a man floating up from underwater. Leda said in a small, aching voice: "I wish to God we could move to Boston."

The granite face closed in defensiveness. "Led', we been over all that. Nothing is going to drive me off of my land. I got no time for the city at my age. What the Jesus would I do? Night watchman? Sweep out somebody's back room, b'Jesus Christ? Savings'd be gone in no time. We been all over it. We ain't moving nowhere."

"I could find work." For Harp, of course, that was the worst thing she could have said. She probably knew it from his stricken silence. She said clumsily, "I forgot something upstairs." She snatched up her mending and she was gone.

We talked no more of it the rest of the day. I followed through the milking and other chores, lending a hand where I could, and we made everything as secure as we could against storm and other enemies. The long-toothed furry thing was the spectral guest at dinner, but we cut him, on Leda's account, or so we pretended. Supper would have been awkward anyway. They weren't in the habit of putting up guests, and Leda was a rather deadly cook because she cared nothing about it. A Darkfield girl, I suppose she had the usual twentieth-century mishmash of television dreams until some impulse or maybe false signs of pregnancy tricked her into marrying a man out of the nineteenth. We had venison treated like beef and overdone vegetables. I don't like venison even when it's treated right.

At six Harp turned on his battery radio and sat stone-faced through the day's bad news and the weather forecast—"a blizzard which may prove the worst in forty-two years. Since three P.M., eighteen inches have fallen at Bangor, twenty-one at Boston. Precipitation is not expected to end until tomorrow. Winds will increase during the night with gusts up to seventy miles per hour." Harp shut it off, with finality. On other evenings I had spent there he let Leda play it after supper only kind of soft, so there had been a continuous muted bleat and blatter all evening. Tonight Harp meant to listen for other sounds. Leda washed the dishes, said an early good night, and fled upstairs.

Harp didn't talk, except as politeness obliged him to answer some blah of mine. We sat and listened to the snow and the lunatic wind. An hour of it was enough for me; I said I was beat and wanted to turn in early. Harp saw me to my bed in the parlor and placed a new chunk of rock maple in the pot-bellied stove. He produced a difficult granite smile, maybe using up his allowance for the week, and pulled out a bottle from a cabinet that had stood for many years below a parlor print—George Washington, I think, concluding a treaty with some offbeat sufferer from hepatitis who may have been General Cornwallis if the latter had two left feet. The bottle contained a brand of rye that Harp sincerely believed to be drinkable, having charred his gullet forty-odd years trying to prove it. While my throat healed, Harp said, "Shouldn't've bothered you with all this crap, Ben. Hope it ain't going to spoil your sleep." He got me his spare flashlight, then let me be, and closed the door.

I heard him drop back into his kitchen armchair. Under too many covers, lamp out, I heard the cruel whisper of the snow. The stove muttered, a friend, making me a cocoon of living heat in a waste of outer cold. Later I heard Leda at the head of the stairs, her voice timid, tired, and sweet with invitation: "You comin' up to bed, Harp?" The stairs creaked under him. Their door closed; presently she cried out in that desired pain that is brief release from trouble.

I remembered something Adelaide Simmons had told me about this house, where I had not gone upstairs since Harp and I were boys. Adelaide, one of the very few women in Darkfield who never spoke unkindly of Leda, said that the tiny west room across from Harp and Leda's bedroom was fixed up for a nursery, and Harp wouldn't allow anything in there but baby furniture. Had been so since they were married seven years before.

Another hour dragged on, in my exasperations of sleeplessness.

Then I heard Longtooth.

The noise came from the west side, beyond the snow-hidden vegetable garden. When it snatched me from the edge of sleep, I tried to think it was a fox barking, the ringing, metallic shriek the little red beast can belch dragonlike from his throat. But wide awake, I knew it had been much deeper, chestier. Horned owl?—no. A sound that belonged to ancient times when men relied on chipped stone weapons and had full reason to fear the dark.

The cracks in the stove gave me firelight for groping back into my clothes. The wind had not calmed at all. I stumbled to the west window, buttoning up, and found it a white blank. Snow had drifted above the lower sash. On tiptoe I could just see over it. A light appeared, dimly illuminating the snowfield beyond. That would be coming from a lamp in the Ryders' bedroom, shining through the nursery room and so out, weak and diffused, into the blizzard chaos.

Yaaarrhh!

Now it had drawn horribly near. From the north windows of the parlor I saw black nothing. Harp squeaked down to my door.

" 'Wake, Ben?"

"Yes. Come look at the west window."

He had left no night-light burning in the kitchen, and only a scant glow came down to the landing from the bedroom. He murmured behind me, "Ayah, snow's up some. Must be over three foot on the level by now."

Yaaarrhh!

The voice had shouted on the south side, the blinder side of the house, overlooked only by one kitchen window and a small one in the pantry where the hand pump stood. The view from the pantry window was mostly blocked by a great maple that overtopped the house. I heard the wind shrilling across the tree's winter bones.

"Ben, you want to git your boots on? Up to you—can't ask it. I might have to go out." Harp spoke in an undertone as if the beast might understand him through the tight walls.

"Of course." I got into my knee boots and caught up my parka as I followed him into the kitchen. A .30-caliber rifle and his heavy shotgun hung on deerhorn over the door to the woodshed. He found them in the dark.

What courage I possessed that night came from being shamed into action, from fearing to show a poor face to an old friend in trouble. I went through the Normandy invasion. I have camped out alone, when I was younger and healthier, and slept nicely. But that noise of Longtooth stole courage. It ached along the channel of the spine.

I had the spare flashlight, but knew Harp didn't want me to use it here. I could make out the furniture, and Harp reaching for the gun rack. He already had on his boots, fur cap, and mackinaw. "You take this'n," he said, and put the ten gauge in my hands. "Both barrels loaded. Ain't my way to do that, ain't right, but since this thing started—"

Yaaarrhh!

" Where's he got to now?" Harp was by the south window. "Round this side?"

"I thought so. . . . Where's Droopy?"

Harp chuckled thinly. "Poor little shit! She come upstairs at the first sound of him and went under the bed. I told Led' to stay upstairs. She'd want a light down here. Wouldn't make sense."

Then, apparently from the east side of the hen loft and high, booming off some resonating surface: *Yaaarrhh!*

"He can't! Jesus, that's twelve foot off the ground!" But Harp plunged out into the shed, and I followed. "Keep your light on the floor, Ben." He ran up the narrow stairway. "Don't shine it on the birds, they'll act up."

So far the chickens, stupid and virtually blind in the dark, were making only a peevish tut-tutting of alarm. But something was clinging to the outside of the barricaded east window, snarling, chattering teeth, pounding on the two-by-fours. With a fist?—it sounded like nothing else. Harp snapped, "Get your light on the window!" And he fired through the glass.

We heard no outcry. Any noise outside was covered by the storm and the squawks of the hens scandalized by the shot. The glass was dirty from their continual disturbance of the litter; I couldn't see through it. The bullet had drilled the pane without shattering it, and passed between the two-by-fours, but the beast could have dropped before he fired. "I got to go out there. You stay, Ben." Back in the kitchen he exchanged rifle for shotgun. "Might not have no chance to aim. You remember this piece, don't y'?—eight in the clip."

"I remember it."

"Good. Keep your ears open." Harp ran out through the door that gave on a small paved area by the woodshed. To get around under the east loft window he would have to push through the snow behind the barn, since he had blocked all the rear openings. He could have circled the house instead, but only by bucking the west wind and fighting deeper drifts. I saw his big shadow melt out of sight.

Leda's voice quavered down to me: "He—get it?"

"Don't know. He's gone to see. Sit tight. . . ."

I heard that infernal bark once again before Harp returned, and again it sounded high off the ground; it must have come from the big maple. And then moments later—I was still trying to pierce the dark, watching for Harp—a vast smash of broken glass and wood, and the violent bang of the door upstairs. One small wheezing shriek cut short, and one scream such as no human being should ever hear. I can still hear it.

I think I lost some seconds in shock. Then I was groping up the narrow stairway, clumsy with the rifle and flashlight. Wind roared at the opening of the kitchen door, and Harp was crowding past me, thrusting me aside. But I was close behind him when he flung the bedroom door open. The blast from the broken window that had slammed the door had also blown out the lamp. But our flashlights said at once that Leda was not there. Nothing was, nothing living.

Droopy lay in a mess of glass splinters and broken window sash, dead from a crushed neck—something had stamped on her. The bedspread had been pulled almost to the window—maybe Leda's hand had clenched on it. I saw blood on some of the glass fragments, and on the splintered sash, a patch of reddish fur.

Harp ran back downstairs. I lingered a few seconds. The arrow of fear was deep in me, but at the moment it made me numb. My light touched up an ugly photograph on the wall, Harp's mother at fifty or so, petrified and acid-faced before the camera, a puritan deity with shallow, haunted eyes. I remembered her.

Harp had kicked over the traces when his father died, and quit going to church. Mrs. Ryder "disowned" him. The farm was his; she left him with it and went to live with a widowed sister in Lohman, and died soon, unreconciled. Harp lived on as a bachelor, crank, recluse, until his strange marriage in his fifties. Now here was Ma still watchful, pucker-faced, unforgiving. In my dullness of shock I thought: Oh, they probably always made love with the lights out.

But now Leda wasn't there.

I hurried after Harp, who had left the kitchen door to bang in the wind. I got out there with rifle and flashlight, and over across the road I saw his torch. No other light, just his small gleam and mine.

I knew as soon as I had forced myself beyond the corner of the house and into the fantastic embrace of the storm that I could never make it. The west wind ground needles into my face. The snow was up beyond the middle of my thighs. With weak lungs and maybe an imperfect heart I could do nothing out here except die quickly to no purpose. In a moment Harp would be starting down the slope of the woods. His trail was already disappearing under my beam. I drove myself a little farther, and an instant's lull in the storm allowed me to shout: "Harp! I can't follow!"

He heard. He cupped his mouth and yelled back: "Don't try! Git back to the house! Telephone!" I waved to acknowledge the message and struggled back.

I only just made it. Inside the kitchen doorway I fell flat, gun and flashlight clattering off somewhere, and there I stayed until I won back enough breath to keep myself living. My face and hands were ice blocks, then fires. While I worked at the task of getting air into my body, one thought continued, an inner necessity: *There must be a rational cause. I do not abandon the rational cause.* At length I hauled myself up and stumbled to the telephone. The line was dead.

I found the flashlight and reeled upstairs with it. I stepped past poor Droopy's body and over the broken glass to look through the window

space. I could see that snow had been pushed off the shed roof near the
bedroom window; the house sheltered that area from the full drive of the
west wind, so some evidence remained. I guessed that whatever came
must have jumped to the house roof from the maple, then down to the
shed roof and then hurled itself through the closed window without regard
for it as an obstacle. Losing a little blood and a little fur.

I glanced around and could not find that fur now. Wind must have
pushed it out of sight. I forced the door shut. Downstairs, I lit the table
lamps in kitchen and parlor. Harp might need those beacons—if he came
back. I refreshed the fires, and gave myself a dose of Harp's horrible
whiskey. It was nearly one in the morning. If he never came back?

It might be days before they could plow out the road. When the storm
let up I could use Harp's snowshoes, maybe . . .

Harp came back at 1:20, bent and staggering. He let me support him
to the armchair. When he could speak he said, "No trail. No trail." He
took the bottle from my hands and pulled on it. "Christ Jesus! What can
I do? Ben . . . ? I got to go to the village, get help. If they got any help
to give."

"Do you have an extra pair of snowshoes?"

He stared toward me, battling confusion. "Hah? No, I ain't. Better
you stay anyhow. I'll bring yours from your house if you want, if I can
git there." He drank again and slammed in the cork with the heel of his
hand. "I'll leave you the ten guage."

He got his snowshoes from a closet. I persuaded him to wait for coffee.
Haste could accomplish nothing now; we could not say to each other
that we knew Leda was dead. When he was ready to go, I stepped outside
with him into the mad wind. "Anything you want me to do before you
get back?" He tried to think about it.

"I guess not, Ben . . . God, ain't I *lived* right? No, that don't make
sense? God? That's a laugh." He swung away. Two or three great strides
and the storm took him.

That was about two o'clock. For four hours I was alone in the house.
Warmth returned, with the bedroom door closed and fires working hard.
I carried the kitchen lamp into the parlor, and then huddled in the nearly
total dark of the kitchen with my back to the wall, watching all the
windows, the ten gauge near my hand, but I did not expect a return of
the beast, and there was none.

The night grew quieter, perhaps because the house was so drifted
in that snow muted the sounds. I was cut off from the battle, buried
alive.

Harp would get back. The seasons would follow their natural way, and somehow we would learn what had happened to Leda. I supposed the beast would have to be something in the human pattern—mad, deformed, gone wild, but still human.

After a time I wondered why we had heard no excitement in the stable. I forced myself to take up gun and flashlight and go look. I groped through the woodshed, big with the jumping shadows of Harp's cordwood, and into the barn. The cows were peacefully drowsing. In the center alley I dared to send my weak beam swooping and glimmering through the ghastly distances of the hayloft. Quiet, just quiet; natural rustling of mice. Then to the stable, where Ned whickered and let me rub his brown cheek, and Jerry rolled a humorous eye. I suppose no smell had reached them to touch off panic, and perhaps they had heard the barking often enough so that it no longer disturbed them. I went back to my post, and the hours crawled along a ridge between the pits of terror and exhaustion. Maybe I slept.

No color of sunrise that day, but I felt paleness and change; even a blizzard will not hide the fact of dayshine somewhere. I breakfasted on bacon and eggs, fed the hens, forked down hay, and carried water for the cows and horses. The one cow in milk, a jumpy Ayrshire, refused to concede that I meant to be useful. I'd done no milking since I was a boy, the knack was gone from my hands, and relief seemed less important to her than kicking over the pail; she was getting more amusement than discomfort out of it, so for the moment I let it go. I made myself busy work shoveling a clear space by the kitchen door. The wind was down, the snowfall persistent but almost peaceful. I pushed out beyond the house and learned that the stuff was up over my hips.

Out of that, as I turned back, came Harp in his long, snowshoe stride, and down the road three others. I recognized Sheriff Robart, overfed but powerful; and Bill Hastings, wry and ageless, a cousin of Harp's and one of his few friends; and last, Curt Davidson, perhaps a friend to Sheriff Robart but certainly not to Harp.

I'd known Curt as a thickwitted loudmouth when he was a kid; growing to man's years hadn't done much for him. And when I saw him I thought, irrationally perhaps: Not good for our side. A kind of absurdity, and yet Harp and I were joined against the world simply because we had experienced together what others were going to call impossible, were going to interpret in harsh, even damnable ways; and no help for it.

I saw the white thin blur of the sun, the strength of it growing. Nowhere in all the white expanse had the wind and the new snow allowed us any mark of the visitation of the night.

•

The men reached my cleared space and shook off snow. I opened the woodshed. Harp gave me one hopeless glance of inquiry and I shook my head.

"Having a little trouble?" That was Robart, taking off his snowshoes.

Harp ignored him. "I got to look after my chores." I told him I'd done it except for that damn cow. "Oh, Bess, ayah, she's nervy. I'll see to her." He gave me my snowshoes that he had strapped to his back. "Adelaide, she wanted to know about your groceries. Said I figured they was in the ca'."

"Good as an icebox," says Robart, real friendly.

Curt had to have his pleasures too. "Ben, you sure you got hold of old Bess by the right end, where the tits was?" Curt giggles at his own jokes, so nobody else is obliged to. Bill Hastings spat in the snow.

"Okay if I go in?" Robart asked. It wasn't a simple inquiry: He was present officially and meant to have it known. Harp looked him up and down.

"Nobody stopping you. Didn't bring you here to stand around, I suppose."

"Harp," said Robart pleasantly enough, "don't give me a hard time. You come tell me certain things has happened, I got to look into it is all." But Harp was already striding down the woodshed to the barn entrance. The others came into the house with me, and I put on water for fresh coffee. "Must be your ca' down the rud a piece, Ben? Heard you kind of went into a ditch. All's you can see now is a hump in the snow. Deep freeze might be good for her, likely you've tried everything else." But I wasn't feeling comic, and never had been on those terms with Robart. I grunted, and his face shed mirth as one slips off a sweater. "Okay, what's the score? Harp's gone and told me a story I couldn't feed to the dogs, so what about it? Where's Mrs. Ryder?"

Davidson giggled again. It's a nasty little sound to come out of all that beef. I don't think Robart had much enthusiasm for him either, but it seems he had sworn in the fellow as a deputy before they set out. "Yes, sir," said Curt, "that was *really* a story, that was."

"Where's Mrs. Ryder?"

"Not here," I told him. "We think she's dead."

He glowered, rubbing cold out of his hands. "Seen that window. Looks like the frame is smashed."

"Yes, from the outside. When Harp gets back you'd better look. I closed the door on that room and haven't opened it. There'll be more snow, but you'll see about what we saw when we got up there."

"Let's look right now," said Curt.

Bill Hastings said, "Curt, ain't you a mite busy for a dep'ty? Mr. Dane said when Harp gets back." Bill and I are friends; normally he wouldn't mister me. I think he was trying to give me some flavor of authority.

I acknowledged the alliance by asking: "You a deputy too, Bill?" Giving him an opportunity to spit in the stove, replace the lid gently, and reply: "Shit no."

Harp returned and carried the milk pail to the pantry. Then he was looking us over. "Bill, I got to try the woods again. You want to come along?"

"Sure, Harp. I didn't bring no gun."

"Take my ten gauge."

"Curt here'll go along," said Robart. "Real good man on snowshoes. Interested in wild life."

Harp said, "That's funny, Robart. I guess that's the funniest thing I heard since Cutler's little girl fell under the tractor. You joining us too?"

"Fact is, Harp, I kind of pulled a muscle in my back coming up here. Not getting no younger neither. I believe I'll just look around here a little. Trust you got no objection? To me looking around a little?"

"Coffee's dripped," I said.

"Thing of it is, if I'd've thought you had any objection, I'd've been obliged to get me a warrant."

"Thanks, Ben." Harp gulped the coffee scalding. "Why, if looking around the house is the best you can do, Sher'f, I got no objection. Ben, I shouldn't be keeping you away from your affairs, but would you stay? Kind of keep him company? Not that I got much in the house, but still—you know—"

"I'll stay." I wished I could tell him to drop that manner; it only got him deeper in the mud.

Robart handed Davidson his gun belt and holster. "Better have it, Curt, so to be in style."

Harp and Bill were outside getting on their snowshoes; I half heard some remark of Harp's about the sheriff's aching back. They took off. The snow had almost ceased. They passed out of sight down the slope to the north, and Curt went plowing after them. Behind me Robart said, "You'd think Harp believed it himself."

"That's how it's to be? You make us both liars before you've even done any looking?"

"I got to try to make sense of it is all." I followed him up to the bedroom. It was cruelly cold. He touched Droopy's stiff corpse with his foot. "Hard to figure a man killing his own dog."

"We get nowhere with that kind of idea."

"Ben, you got to see this thing like it looks to other people. And keep out of my hair."

"That's what scares me, Jack. Something unreasonable did happen, and Harp and I were the only ones to experience it—except Mrs. Ryder."

"You claim you saw this—animal?"

"I didn't say that. I heard her scream. When we got upstairs this room was the way you see it." I looked around, and again couldn't find that scrap of fur, but I spoke of it, and I give Robart credit for searching. He shook out the bedspread and blankets, examined the floor and the closet. He studied the window space, leaned out for a look at the house wall and the shed roof. His big feet avoided the broken glass, and he squatted for a long gaze at the pieces of window sash. Then he bore down on me, all policeman personified, a massive, rather intelligent, conventionally honest man with no patience for imagination, no time for any fact not already in the books. "Piece of fur, huh?" He made it sound as if I'd described a Jabberwock with eyes of flame. "Okay, we're done up here." He motioned me downstairs—all policemen who'd ever faced a crowd's dangerous stupidity with their own.

As I retreated I said, "Hope you won't be too busy to have a chemist test the blood on that sash."

"We'll do that." He made move-along motions with his slab hands. "Going to be a pleasure to do that little thing for you and your friend."

Then he searched the entire house, shed, barn, and stable. I had never before watched anyone on police business; I had to admire his zeal. I got involved in the farce of holding the flashlight for him while he rooted in the cellar. In the shed I suggested that if he wanted to restack twenty-odd cords of wood he'd better wait till Harp could help him; he wasn't amused. He wasn't happy in the barn loft either. Shifting tons of hay to find a hypothetical corpse was not a one-man job. I knew he was capable of returning with a crew and machinery to do exactly that. And by his lights it was what he ought to do. Then we were back in the kitchen, Robart giving himself a manicure with his jackknife, and I down to my last cigarette, almost the last of my endurance.

Robart was not unsubtle. I answered his questions as temperately as I could—even, for instance: "Wasn't you a mite sweet on Leda yourself?" I didn't answer any of them with flat silence; to do that right you need an accompanying act like spitting in the stove, and I'm not a chewer. From the north window he said: "Comin' back. It figures." They had been out a little over an hour.

Harp stood by the stove with me to warm his hands. He spoke as if alone with me: "No trail, Ben." What followed came in an undertone: "Ben, you told me about a friend of yours, scientist or something, professor—"

"Professor Malcolm?" I remembered mentioning him to Harp a long while before; I was astonished at his recalling it. Johnny Malcolm is a professor of biology who has avoided too much specialization. Not a really close friend. Harp was watching me out of a granite despair as if he had asked me to appeal to some higher court. I thought of another acquaintance in Boston, too, whom I might consult—Dr. Kahn, a psychiatrist who had once seen my wife, Helen, through a difficult time. . . .

"Harp," said Robart, "I got to ask you a couple, three things. I sent word to Dick Hammond to get that goddamned plow of his into this road as quick as he can. Believe he'll try. Whiles we wait on him, we might's well talk. You know I don't like to get tough."

"Talk away," said Harp, "only Ben here he's got to get home without waiting on no Dick Hammond."

"That a fact, Ben?"

"Yes. I'll keep in touch."

"Do that," said Robart, dismissing me. As I left he was beginning a fresh manicure, and Harp waited rigidly for the ordeal to continue. I felt morbidly that I was abandoning him.

Still—corpus delicti—nothing much more would happen until Leda Ryder was found. Then if her body were found dead by violence, with no acceptable evidence of Longtooth's existence—well, what then?

I don't think Robart would have let me go if he'd known my first act would be to call Short's brother Mike and ask him to drive me into Lohman, where I could get a bus for Boston.

Johnny Malcolm said, "I can see this is distressing you, and you wouldn't lie to me. But, Ben, as biology it won't do. Ain't no such animile. You know that."

He wasn't being stuffy. We were having dinner at a quiet restaurant, and I had, of course, enjoyed the roast duckling too much. Johnny is a rock-ribbed beanpole who can eat like a walking famine with no regrets. "Suppose," I said, "just for argument and because it's not biologically inconceivable, that there's a basis for the yeti legend."

"Not inconceivable. I'll give you that. So long as any poorly known corners of the world are left—the Himalayan uplands, jungles, tropic swamps, the tundra—legends will persist and some of them will have little gleams of truth. You know what I think about moon flights and all that?" He smiled; privately I was hearing Leda scream. "One of our strongest reasons for them, and for the biggest flights we'll make if we don't kill civilization first, is a hunt for new legends. We've used up our best ones, and that's dangerous."

"Why don't we look at the countries inside us?" But Johnny wasn't listening much.

"Men can't stand it not to have closed doors and a chance to push at them. Oh, about your yeti—he might exist. Shaggy anthropoid able to endure severe cold, so rare and clever the explorers haven't tripped over him yet. Wouldn't have to be a carnivore to have big ugly canines— look at the baboons. But if he was active in a Himalayan winter, he'd have to be able to use meat, I think. Mind you, I don't believe any of this, but you can have it as a biological not-impossible. How'd he get to Maine?"

"Strayed? Tibet—Mongolia—Arctic ice."

"Maybe." Johnny had begun to enjoy the hypothesis as something to play with during dinner. Soon he was helping along the brute's passage across the continents, and having fun till I grumbled something about alternatives, extraterrestrials. He wouldn't buy that, and got cross. Still hearing Leda scream, I assured him I wasn't watching for little green men.

"Ben, how much do you know about this—Harp?"

"We grew up along different lines, but he's a friend. Dinosaur, if you like, but a friend."

"Hardshell Maine bachelor picks up dizzy young wife—"

"She's not dizzy. Wasn't. Sexy, but not dizzy."

"All right. Bachelor stewing in his own juices for years. Sure he didn't get up on that roof himself?"

"Nuts. Unless all my senses were more paralyzed than I think, there wasn't time."

"Unless they were more paralyzed than you think."

"Come off it! I'm not senile yet. . . . What's he supposed to have done with her? Tossed her into the snow?"

"Mph," said Johnny, and finished his coffee. "All right. Some human freak with abnormal strength and the endurance to fossick around in a Maine blizzard stealing women. I liked the yeti better. You say you suggested a madman to Ryder yourself. Pity if you had to come all the way here just so I could repeat your own guesswork. To make amends, want to take in a bawdy movie?"

"Love it."

The following day Dr. Kahn made time to see me at the end of the afternoon, so polite and patient that I felt certain I was keeping him from his dinner. He seemed undecided whether to be concerned with the traumas of Harp Ryder's history or those of mine. Mine were already somewhat known to him. "I wish you had time to talk all this out to me. You've given me a nice summary of what the physical events appear to have been, but—"

"Doctor," I said, "it *happened*. I heard the animal. The window *was* smashed—ask the sheriff. Leda Ryder did scream, and when Harp and I got up there together, the dog had been killed and Leda was gone."

"And yet, if it was all as clear as that, I wonder why you thought of consulting me at all, Ben. I wasn't there. I'm just a headshrinker."

"I wanted . . . Is there any way a delusion could take hold of Harp *and* me, disturb our senses in the same way? Oh, just saying it makes it ridiculous."

Dr. Kahn smiled. "Let's say, difficult."

"Is it possible Harp could have killed her, thrown her out through the window of the *west* bedroom—the snow must have drifted six feet or higher on that side—and then my mind distorted my time sense? So I might've stood there in the dark kitchen all the time it went on, a matter of minutes instead of seconds? Then he jumped down by the shed roof, came back into the house the normal way while I was stumbling upstairs? Oh, hell."

Dr. Kahn had drawn a diagram of the house from my description, and peered at it with placid interest. "Benign" was a word Helen had used for him. He said, "Such a distortion of the time sense would be—unusual. . . . Are you feeling guilty about anything?"

"About standing there and doing nothing? I can't seriously believe it was more than a few seconds. Anyway, that would make Harp a monster out of a detective story. He's not that. How could he count on me to freeze in panic? Absurd. I'd've heard the struggle, steps, the window of the west room going up. Could he have killed her and I known all about it at the time, even witnessed it, and then suffered amnesia for that one event?"

He still looked so patient, I wished I hadn't come. "I won't say any trick of the mind is impossible, but I might call that one highly improbable. Academically, however, considering your emotional involvement—"

"I'm not emotionally involved!" I yelled that. He smiled, looking much more interested. I laughed at myself. That was better than poking him in the eye. "I'm upset, Doctor, because the whole thing goes against reason. If you start out knowing nobody's going to believe you, it's all messed up before you open your mouth."

He nodded kindly. He's a good joe. I think he'd stopped listening for what I didn't say long enough to hear a little of what I did say. "You're not unstable, Ben. Don't worry about amnesia. The explanation, perhaps some human intruder, will turn out to be within the human norm. The norm of possibility does include such things as lycanthropic delusions, maniacal behavior, and so on. Your police up there will carry on a good search for the poor woman. They won't overlook that snowdrift. Don't underestimate them, and don't worry about your own mind, Ben."

"Ever seen our Maine woods?"

"No, I go away to the Cape."

"Try it sometime. Take a patch of it, say about fifty miles by fifty, that's twenty-five hundred square miles. Drop some eager policemen into it, tell 'em to hunt for something they never saw before and don't want to see, that doesn't want to be found."

"But if your beast is human, human beings leave traces. Bodies aren't easy to hide, Ben."

"In those woods? A body taken by a carnivorous animal? Why not?" Well, our minds didn't touch. I thanked him for his patience and got up. "The maniac responsible," I said. "But whatever we call him, Doctor, he was *there*."

Mike Short picked me up at the Lohman bus station and told me something of a ferment in Darkfield. I shouldn't have been surprised. "They're all scared, Mr. Dane. They want to hurt somebody." Mike is Jim Short's younger brother. He scrapes up a living with his taxi service and occasional odd jobs at the garage. There's a droop in his shaggy ringlets, and I believe thirty is staring him in the face. "Like old Harp, he wants to tell it like it happened and nobody buys. That's sad, man. You been away what, three days? The fuzz was pissed off. You better connect with Mr. Sheriff Robart like soon. He climbed all over my ass just for driving you to the bus that day, like I should've known you shouldn't."

"I'll pacify him. They haven't found Mrs. Ryder?"

Mike spat out the car window, which was rolled down for the mild air. "Old Harp he never got such a job of snow-shoveling done in all his days. By the c'munity, for free. No, they won't find her." In that there was plenty of I-want-to-be-asked, and something more, a hint of the mythology of Mike's generation.

"So what's your opinion, Mike?"

He maneuvered a fresh cigarette against the stub of the last and drove on through tiresome silence. The road was winding between ridged mountains of plowed, rotting snow. I had the window down on my side, too, for the genial afternoon sun, and imagined a tang of spring. At last Mike said, "You prob'ly don't go along . . . Jim got your ca' out, by the way. It's at your place. . . . Well, you'll hear 'em talking it all to pieces. Some claim Harp's telling the truth. Some say he killed her himself. They don't say how he made her disappear. Ain't heard any talk against you, Mr. Dane, nothing that counts. The sheriff's peeved, but that's just on account you took off without asking." His vague, large eyes watched the melting landscape, the ambiguous messages of spring. "Well, I think, like, a demon took her, Mr. Dane. She was one of his own, see? You got to remember, I knew that chick. Okay, you can say it ain't scientific, only there is a science to these things, I read a book about it. You can laugh if you want."

I wasn't laughing. It wasn't my first glimpse of the contemporary medievalism and won't be my last if I survive another year or two. I wasn't laughing, and I said nothing. Mike sat smoking, expertly driving his twentieth-century artifact while I suppose his thoughts were in the seventeenth, sniffing after the wonders of the invisible world, and I recalled what Johnny Malcolm had said about the need for legends. Mike and I had no more talk.

Adelaide Simmons was dourly glad to see me. From her I learned that the sheriff and state police had swarmed all over Harp's place and the surrounding countryside, and were still at it. Result, zero. Harp had repeatedly told our story and was refusing to tell it anymore. "Does the chores and sets there drinking," she said, "or staring off. Was up to see him yesterday, Mr. Dane—felt I should. Couple days they didn't let him alone a minute, maybe now they've eased off some. He asked me real sharp, was you back yet. Well, I redd up his place, made some bread, least I could do."

When I told her I was going there, she prepared a basket while I sat in the kitchen and listened. "Some say she busted that window herself, jumped down, and run off in the snow, out of her mind. Any sense in that?"

"Nope."

"And some claim she deserted him. Earlier. Which'd make you a liar. And they say whichever way it was, Harp's made up this crazy story because he can't stand the truth." Her clever hands slapped sandwiches into shape. "They claim Harp got you to go along with it, they don't say how."

"Hypnotized me, likely. Adelaide, it all happened the way Harp told it. I heard the thing too. If Harp is ready for the squirrels, so am I."

She stared hard, and sighed. She likes to talk, but her mill often shuts off suddenly, because of a quality of hers which I find good as well as rare: I mean that when she has no more to say she doesn't go on talking.

I got up to Ryder's Ridge about suppertime. Bill Hastings was there. The road was plowed slick between the snow ridges, and I wondered how much of the litter of tracks and crumpled paper and spent cigarette packages had been left by sight-seers. Ground frost had not yet yielded to the mud season, which would soon make normal driving impossible for a few weeks. Bill let me in, with the look people wear for serious illness. But Harp heaved himself out of that armchair, not sick in body at least. "Ben, I heard him last night. Late."

"What direction?"

"North."

"You hear it, Bill?" I set down the basket.

My pint-size friend shook his head. "Wasn't here." I couldn't guess how much Bill accepted of the tale.

Harp said, "What's the basket?—oh. Obliged. Adelaide's a nice woman." But his mind was remote. "It was north, Ben, a long way, but I think I know about where it would be. I wouldn't've heard it except the night was so still, like everything had quieted for me. You know, they been a-deviling me night and day. Robart, state cops, mess of smart little buggers from the papers. I couldn't sleep, I stepped outside like I was called. Why, he might've been the other side of the stars, the sky so full of 'em and nothing stirring. Cold . . . You went to Boston, Ben?"

"Yes. Waste of time. They want it to be something human—anyhow, something that fits the books."

Whittling, Bill said neutrally, "Always a man for the books yourself, wasn't you, Ben?"

I had to agree. Harp asked, "Hadn't no ideas?"

"Just gave me back my own thoughts in their language. We have to find it, Harp. Of course some wouldn't take it for true even if you had photographs."

Harp said, "Photographs be goddamned."

"I guess you got to go," said Bill Hastings. "We been talking about it, Ben. Maybe I'd feel the same if it was me. . . . I better be on my way or supper'll be cold and the old woman raising hellfire." He tossed his stick back in the woodbox.

"Bill," said Harp, "you won't mind feeding the stock couple, three days?"

"I don't mind. Be up tomorrow."

"Do the same for you sometime. I wouldn't want it mentioned any-place."

"Harp, you know me better'n that. See you, Ben."

"Snow's going fast," said Harp when Bill had driven off. "Be in the woods a long time yet, though."

"You wouldn't start this late."

He was at the window, his lean bulk shutting off much light from the time-seasoned kitchen where most of his indoor life had been passed. "Morning, early. Tonight I got to listen."

"Be needing sleep, I'd think."

"I don't always get what I need," said Harp.

"I'll bring my snowshoes. About six? And my carbine—I'm best with a gun I know."

He stared at me awhile. "All right, Ben. You understand, though, you might have to come back alone. I ain't coming back till I get him, Ben. Not this time."

At sunup I found him with Ned and Jerry in the stable. He had lived eight or ten years with that team. He gave Ned's neck a final pat as he turned to me and took up our conversation as if night had not intervened. "Not till I get him. Ben, I don't want you drug into this ag'inst your inclination."

"Did you hear it again last night?"

"I heard it. North."

The sun was at the point of rising when we left on our snowshoes, like morning ghosts ourselves. Harp strode ahead down the slope to the woods without haste, perhaps with some reluctance. Near the trees he halted, gazing to his right, where a red blaze was burning the edge of the sky curtain; I scolded myself for thinking that he was saying good-bye to the sun.

The snow was crusted, sometimes slippery even for our web feet. We entered the woods along a tangle of tracks, including the fat tire marks of a snow scooter. "Guy from Lohman," said Harp. "Hired the goddamn thing out to the state cops and hisself with it. Goes pootin' around all over hell, fit to scare everything inside eight, ten miles." He cut himself a fresh plug to last the morning. "I b'lieve the thing is a mite farther off than that. They'll be messing around again today." His fingers dug into my arm. "See how it is, don't y'? They ain't looking for what we are. Looking for a dead body to hang on to my neck. And if they was to find her the way I found—the way I found—"

"Harp, you needn't borrow trouble."

"I know how they think," he said. "Was I to walk down the road beyond Darkfield, they'd pick me up. They ain't got me in shackles because they got no—no body, Ben. Nobody needs to tell me about the law. They got to have a body. Only reason they didn't leave a man here overnight, they figure I can't go nowhere. They think a man couldn't travel in three, four foot of snow. . . . Ben, I mean to find that thing and shoot it down. . . . We better slant off thisaway."

He set out at a wide angle from those tracks, and we soon had them out of sight. On the firm crust our snowshoes left no mark. After a while we heard a grumble of motors far back, on the road. Harp chuckled viciously. "Bright and early like yesterday." He stared back the way we had come. "They'll never pick that up without dogs. That son of a bitch Robart did talk about borrying a hound somewhere, to sniff Leda's clothes. More likely give 'em a sniff of mine, now."

We had already come so far that I didn't know the way back. Harp would know it. He could never be lost in any woods, but I have no mental compass such as his. So I followed him blindly, not trying to memorize our trail. It was a region of uniform old growth, mostly hemlock, no recent lumbering, few landmarks. The monotony wore down native patience to a numbness, and our snowshoes left no more impression than our thoughts.

An hour passed, or more; after that sound of motors faded. Now and then I heard the wind move peacefully overhead. Few bird calls, for most of our singers had not yet returned. "Been in this part before, Harp?"

"Not with snow on the ground, not lately." His voice was hushed and careful. "Summers. About a mile now, and the trees thin out some. Stretch of slash where they were taking out pine four, five years back and left everything a christly pile of shit like they always do."

No, Harp wouldn't get lost here, but I was well lost, tired, sorry I had come. Would he turn back if I collapsed? I didn't think he could, now, for any reason. My pack with blanket roll and provisions had become infernal. He had said we ought to have enough for three or four days. Only a few years earlier I had carried heavier camping loads than this without trouble, but now I was blown, a stitch beginning in my side. My wristwatch said only nine o'clock.

The trees thinned out as he had promised, and here the land rose in a long slope to the north. I looked up across a tract of eight or ten acres, where the devastation of stupid lumbering might be healed if the hurt region could be let alone for sixty years. The deep snow, blinding out here where only scrub growth interfered with the sunlight, covered the worst of the wreckage. "Good place for wild ras'berries," Harp said quietly.

"Been time for 'em to grow back. Guess it was nearer seven years ago when they cut here and left this mess. Last summer I couldn't hardly find their logging road. Off to the left—"

He stopped, pointing with a slow arm to a blurred gray line that wandered up from the left to disappear over the rise of ground. The nearest part of that gray curve must have been four hundred feet away, and to my eyes it might have been a shadow cast by an irregularity of the snow surface; Harp knew better. Something had passed there, heavy enough to break the crust. "You want to rest a mite, Ben? Once over that rise I might not want to stop again."

I let myself down on the butt of an old log that lay tilted toward us, cut because it had happened to be in the way, left to rot because they happened to be taking pine. "Can you really make anything out of that?"

"Not enough," said Harp. "But it could be him." He did not sit by me but stood relaxed with his load, snowshoes spaced so he could spit between them. "About half a mile over that rise," he said, "there's a kind of gorge. Must've been a good brook, former times, still a stream along the bottom in summer. Tangle of elders and stuff. Couple, three caves in the bank at one spot. I guess it's three summers since I been there. Gloomy goddamn place. There was foxes into one of them caves. Natural caves, I b'lieve. I didn't go too near, not then."

I sat in the warming light, wondering whether there was any way I could talk to Harp about the beast—if it existed, if we weren't merely a pair of aging men with disordered minds. Any way to tell him the creature was important to the world outside our dim little village? That it ought somehow to be kept alive, not just shot down and shoveled aside? How could I say this to a man without science, who had lost his wife and also the trust of his fellow men?

Take away that trust and you take away the world.

Could I ask him to shoot it in the legs, get it back alive? Why, to my own self, irrationally, that appeared wrong, horrible, as well as beyond our powers. Better if he shot to kill. Of if I did. So in the end I said nothing, but shrugged my pack into place and told him I was ready to go on.

With the crust uncertain under that stronger sunshine, we picked our way slowly up the rise, and when we came at length to that line of tracks, Harp said matter-of-factly, "Now you've seen his mark. It's him."

Sun and overnight freezing had worked on the trail. Harp estimated it had been made early the day before. But wherever the weight of Longtooth had broken through, the shape of his foot showed clearly down there in its pocket of snow, a foot the size of a man's but broader, shorter. The prints were spaced for the stride of a short-legged person. The arch of the foot was low, but the beast was not actually flat-footed. Beast or man. I said, "This is a man's print, Harp. Isn't it?"

He spoke without heat. "No. You're forgetting, Ben. I seen him."

"Anyhow, there's only one."

He said slowly, "Only one set of tracks."

"What d'you mean?"

Harp shrugged. "It's heavy. He could've been carrying something. Keep your voice down. That crust yesterday, it would've held me without no web feet, but he went through, and he ain't as big as me." Harp checked his rifle and released the safety. "Half a mile to them caves. B'lieve that's where he is, Ben. Don't talk unless you got to, and take it slow."

I followed him. We topped the rise, encountering more of that lumberman's desolation on the other side. The trail crossed it, directly approaching a wall of undamaged trees that marked the limit of the cutting. Here forest took over once more, and where it began, Longtooth's trail ended. "Now you seen how it goes," Harp said. "Anyplace where he can travel above ground he does. He don't scramble up the trunks, seems like. Look here—he must've got aholt of that branch and swung hisself up. Knocked off some snow, but the wind knocks off so much, too, you can't tell nothing. See, Ben, he—he figures it out. He knows about trails. He'll have come down out of these trees far enough from where we are now so there ain't no chance of us seeing the place from here. Could be anywhere in a half circle, and draw it as big as you please."

"Thinking like a man."

"But he ain't a man," said Harp. "There's things he don't know. How a man feels, acts. I'm going on to them caves." From necessity, I followed him. . . .

I ought to end this quickly. Prematurely I am an old man, incapacitated by the effects of a stroke and a damaged heart. I keep improving a little—sensible diet, no smoking, Adelaide's care. I expect several years of tolerable health on the way downhill. But I find, as Harp did, that it is even more crippling to lose the trust of others. I will write here once more, and not again, that my word is good.

It was noon when we reached the gorge. In that place some melancholy part of night must always remain. Down the center of the ravine between tangles of alder, water murmured under ice and rotting snow, which here and there had fallen in to reveal the dark brilliance. Harp did not enter the gorge itself but moved slowly through tree cover along the left edge, eyes flickering for danger. I tried to imitate his caution. We went a hundred yards or more in that inching advance, maybe two hundred. I heard only the occasional wind of spring.

He turned to look at me with a sickly triumph, a grimace of disgust and of justification too. He touched his nose and then I got it also, a rankness from down ahead of us, a musky foulness with an ammoniacal tang and some smell of decay. Then on the other side of the gorge, off in the woods but not far, I heard Longtooth.

A bark, not loud. Throaty, like talk.

Harp suppressed an answering growl. He moved on until he could point down to a black cave mouth on the opposite side. The breeze blew the stench across to us. Harp whispered, "See, he's got like a path. Jumps down to that flat rock, then to the cave. We'll see him in a minute." Yes, there were sounds in the brush. "You keep back." His left palm lightly stroked the underside of his rifle barrel.

So intent was he on the opening where Longtooth would appear, I may have been first to see the other who came then to the cave mouth and stared up at us with animal eyes. Longtooth had called again, a rather gentle sound. The woman wrapped in filthy hides may have been drawn by that call or by the noise of our approach.

Then Harp saw her.

He knew her. In spite of the tangled hair, scratched face, dirt, and the shapeless deer pelt she clutched around herself against the cold, I am sure he knew her. I don't think she knew him, or me. An inner blindness, a look of a beast wholly centered on its own needs. I think human memories had drained away. She knew Longtooth was coming. I think she wanted his warmth and protection, but there were no words in the whimper she made before Harp's bullet took her between the eyes.

Longtooth shoved through the bushes. He dropped the rabbit he was carrying and jumped down to that flat rock snarling, glancing sidelong at the dead woman who was still twitching. If he understood the fact of death, he had no time for it. I saw the massive overdevelopment of thigh and leg muscles, their springy motions of preparation. The distance from the flat rock to the place where Harp stood must have been fifteen feet. One spear of sunlight touched him in that blue-green shade, touched his thick red fur and his fearful face.

Harp could have shot him. Twenty seconds for it, maybe more. But he flung his rifle aside and drew out his hunting knife, his own long tooth, and had it waiting when the enemy jumped.

So could I have shot him. No one needs to tell me I ought to have done so.

Longtooth launched himself, clawed fingers out, fangs exposed. I felt the meeting as if the impact had struck my own flesh. They tumbled roaring into the gorge, and I was cold, detached, an instrument for watching.

It ended soon. The heavy brownish teeth clenched in at the base of Harp's neck. He made no more motion except the thrust that sent his blade into Longtooth's left side. Then they were quiet in that embrace, quiet all three. I heard the water flowing under the ice.

I remember a roaring in my ears, and I was moving with slow care, one difficult step after another, along the lip of the gorge and through mighty corridors of white and green. With my hard-won detached amusement I supposed this might be the region where I had recently followed poor Harp Ryder to some destination or other, but not (I thought) one of those we talked about when we were boys. A band of iron had closed around my forehead, and breathing was an enterprise needing great effort and caution, in order not to worsen the indecent pain that clung as another band around my diaphragm. I leaned against a tree for thirty seconds or thirty minutes, I don't know where. I knew I mustn't take off my pack in spite of the pain, because it carried provisions for three days. I said once: "Ben, you are lost."

I had my carbine, a golden bough, staff of life, and I recall the shrewd management and planning that enabled me to send three shots into the air. Twice.

It seems I did not want to die, and so hung on the cliff edge of death with a mad stubbornness. They tell me it could not have been the second day that I fired the second burst, the one that was heard and answered —because they say a man can't suffer the kind of attack I was having and then survive a whole night of exposure. They say that when a search party reached me from Wyndham Village (eighteen miles from Dark-field), I made some garbled speech and fell flat on my face.

I woke immoblized, without power of speech or any motion except for a little life in my left hand, and for a long time memory was only a jarring of irrelevancies. When that cleared, I still couldn't talk for another long deadly while. I recall someone saying with exasperated admiration that with cerebral hemorrhage on top of coronary infarction, I had no damn right to be alive; this was the first sound that gave me any pleasure. I remember recognizing Adelaide and being unable to thank her for her presence. None of this matters to the story, except the fact that for months I had no bridge of communication with the world; and yet I loved the world and did not want to leave it.

One can always ask: What will happen next?

Sometime in what they said was June my memory was (I think) clear. I scrawled a little, with the nurse supporting the deadened part of my arm. But in response to what I wrote, the doctor, the nurses, Sheriff Robart, even Adelaide Simmons and Bill Hastings, looked—sympathetic. I was not believed. I am not believed now, in the most important part of what I wish I might say: that there are things in our world that we do not understand, and that this ignorance ought to generate humility. People find this obvious, bromidic—oh, they always have!—and therefore they do not listen, retaining the pride of their ignorance intact.

Remnants of the three bodies were found in late August, small thanks to my efforts, for I had no notion what compass direction we took after the cut-over area, and there are so many such areas of desolation I couldn't tell them where to look. Forest scavengers, including a pack of dogs, had found the bodies first. Water had moved them, too, for the last of the big snow melted suddenly, and for a couple of days at least there must have been a small river raging through that gorge. The head of what they are calling the "lunatic" got rolled downstream, bashed against rocks, partly buried in silt. Dogs had chewed and scattered what they speak of as "the man's fur coat."

It will remain a lunatic in a fur coat, for they won't have it any other way. So far as I know, no scientist ever got a look at the wreckage, unless you glorify the coroner by that title. I believe he was a good vet before he got the job. When my speech was more or less regained, I was already through trying to talk about it. A statement of mine was read at the inquest—that was before I could talk or leave the hospital. At this ceremony society officially decided that Harper Harrison Ryder, of this township, shot to death his wife, Leda, and an individual, male, of unknown identity, while himself temporarily of unsound mind, and died of knife injuries received in a struggle with the said individual of unknown, and so forth.

I don't talk about it because that only makes people more sorry for me, to think a man's mind should fail so, and he not yet sixty.

I cannot even ask them: "What is truth?" They would only look more saddened, and I suppose shocked, and perhaps find reasons for not coming to see me again.

They are kind. They will do anything for me, except think about it.

GLORY

RON GOULART

What would a horror anthology be without a vampire story? "Glory" *is* a vampire story, but of a very different sort than those usually seen in horror anthologies, and it's a work typical of the mordant style of Ron Goulart. He (as with many of the writers in this collection) published his first science fiction piece, "Letters to the Editor," in *F & SF* and since then, happily, has been a regular contributor. His tales often employ the traditional themes and motifs of science fiction or horror but with satiric twists that create an irresistible zaniness. "Glory" is a story of the movie industry. Film companies are continuously reviving old films; film stars of yesteryear regain popularity, and both movie houses and television indulge in an orgy of movies featuring these stars. In "Glory" one such "revival" leads to very . . . *draining* . . . consequences.

One of the most puzzling mysteries in the entire history of Hollywood was finally solved only a few weeks ago. And had things gone just a shade differently, the truth about what really happened to one of the brightest, loveliest motion picture stars of the thirties would have been revealed to the world. That didn't quite happen, though, and this is why.

Dennis Hoff had been sitting in his undersized office in the middle of the Golem Brothers Talent Agency, located just beyond walking distance of Wilshire Boulevard, on that particular hot, hazy Tuesday afternoon. He was a plump, pink man of thirty-eight with not enough hair.

"She's perfect for the part, Joel," he was saying into his phone.

"I admit, Den, she *looks* like a hooker. But when she read for me, she fluffed her lines."

"That was only in your office, Joel. On camera, trust me, Mindy can deliver. She's terrif—"

"Den, it takes a special talent to futz up a line like, 'Oof!' But I am still interested in . . . Who's the girl you sent me for *Nun with a Gun?*"

Hoff glanced toward his narrow doorway and saw a friend of his hesitating on the threshold. He nodded at him to wait a minute. "That was Lindy. Yep, she's exactly right for—"

"Why don't you give them distinctive names? Mindy, Lindy, they all sound—Got another call. Get back to you, Den."

Hanging up, Hoff grinned. "On the brink of placing two of my clients with Konheim Productions. C'mon in."

Jack Wilker was a modest-sized, dark-haired man in his early thirties. He almost always wore faded gray warm-up suits like the one he was decked out in today. Tucked up under his arm was a scruffy attaché case.

"Smoking is going to kill you."

"It's not me who smokes, you know, old buddy. It's the Golem brothers, both Nat and Larry," he said. "You look less gloomy today."

Taking a deep breath, Jack entered and sat opposite the desk. "I'm going to break out of the hack novelist ranks. No more books in the Spykiller series. . . . I can say good-bye to *Bombs in the Bahamas, Guns in Guatemala, Bazookas in Brazil.*"

The phone rang.

"Excuse me, Jack. Hello? Nothing just yet, Ernie. But, trust me, Vegas is very, very interested. The only thing that's making them a bit uneasy is the way you bill yourself. 'The Grand Old Man of Salsa,' Ernie, they think is a put-off. Remember I did tell you we might have to come up with something peppier? Okay, think about it all, and I'll get back to you. Right now I've got Boz Eager here in my office to sign his contracts for that new cable series, *Gay Cop.* So, *vaya con Dios*, old buddy."

"You're going to get struck by lightning someday," suggested Jack.

"Naw, only lies'll get rid of Ernie Caliente. Have you ever tried to book a seventy-six-year-old marimba player?"

"Not since college."

"A pain in the toke." Leaning back in his chair, he made a small, sad sound. "So why the elation?"

"Nonfiction."

Hoff watched him for a few seconds. "That gets you excited?"

Jack slapped his attaché case on his lap. "You know that Capricorn/AA is planning a twenty-five-million dollar movie about Glory Sands, the sexy blond actress who vanished without a—"

"I've been trying to interest Blummer over there in Mindy Mandrake for the past three—"

"I thought her name was Lindy?"

"That's Lindy Landfill."

Nodding absently, Jack continued, "Okay, what I've been working on is a bio of Glory Sands. Her disappearing without a trace back in 1937 is one of the most puzzling mysteries in the entire history of Hollywood." Chuckling, he opened the case. "Yet nobody's done a book on her glittering yet tragic life in years. So I figured I'd put together a proposal and sell the book for a nice five-figure advance."

"Not a bad notion. Is that what's got you so buoyed up, the notion of doing—"

"Better than that, Den." He thrust a hand into the attaché case. "No, I made a discovery late yesterday at a secondhand bookshop down in Oil Beach. Place has a whole damn wall of movie stuff and related crap. Fairly cheap." He produced a slender, weathered, leather-bound volume and held it up, hand jiggling slightly. "Do you know what this is? This is Peter Yarko's last diary."

"That's exactly what I was about to guess. Who the hell is Peter Yarko?"

Jack's head tilted back, eyebrows climbing. "You mean you're trying to get Lindy Landfill a part in *The Glory Story*, and you don't even know—"

"Mindy Mandrake."

"And you don't even know who Yarko was?"

"Hey, I live right here in the present. Only hicks from the sticks play Hollywood trivia, old buddy," said Hoff. "I have to think about current talents like Ernie Caliente, Boz Eater, Lin—"

"Peter Yarko was the director of *The Devil Is a Blonde*, *Blond Explosion*, *The Blond President*, and—"

"Ah, proving blondes do have more fun." Then Hoff snapped his fingers. "I remember now; he's the Polish gink who arrived out of nowhere with Glory Sands in tow in the early thirties. Directed her in her first few pics, got screwed by MGM and tossed out. Sure, Victor Yarko."

"Peter Yarko." Jack eased the thin, musty book open. "I don't know how this ended up in that particular bookstore. The point is, nobody's apparently read it ever, beyond the title page. *My Diary. Vol. 33/P. Yarko. 1937.*"

"How much'd you pay for that?"

"Twenty bucks."

"You consider that cheap?"

"Just hush a minute and listen to—"

"Yarko disappeared about the same time she did, didn't he? Right, the movie's going to imply he murdered her in a fit of jealousy and joined the Foreign Legion to—"

"Spanish Civil War. Yarko quit Hollywood, went to Spain to fight on the Loyalist side, and was killed within a few weeks." Jack was leafing through the foxed pages of the old diary as he spoke. "Glory Sands had disappeared without a trace three days before he took off for Spain. By the time anybody thought to question him, Yarko was long gone."

"And he left a big Hollywood-Moorish mansion up in Beverly Hills," remembered Hoff. "Sure, all his nitwit relatives fought for years over who owned it, and it's been sitting empty since the seventies."

"Listen to this final entry. 'Wednesday, March 3, 1937. They took Glory away from me, and that was wrong. Yet I now realize it was also wrong of me to have unleashed her and brought her here to America. But that's been mended, and now, thanks to Tumly, she rests under an eternal spell and the world is safe again and MGM can take a hike. The secret room beneath my wine cellar shall be her last resting place, and never again shall she rise from her coffin. . . .'"

"Tumly," muttered Hoff, stroking his pudgy pink chin, "Tumly. Sure, that must be Byers Tumly. He's still working the occult dodge. Eighty-some years old. I booked him on *Odd, Isn't It?* a couple years back when those pinhead shows were pop—"

"Den, you're missing the point." He rose up excitedly, and his attaché case plumped to the floor, spilling copies of his Spykiller novels to the thin rug. "See, I've solved the damn mystery that's baffled the world for half a century. I know where her body is, I know who put it there, and I figure I can get at least fifty thousand as an advance."

"Sit." Hoff made a lower-yourself motion with his right hand. "You have completely, old buddy, missed the real and salient point of all this."

"It's that I can now write the first complete biography of Glory Sands," said Jack, grinning. "I can become a literary lion, a Pulitzer Prize contender, and a fellow who isn't always three and a half months behind in his alimony payments to not one but two former wives. With an advance in the neighborhood of fifty thou, I can—"

"Fifty thou is jelly beans," the pudgy talent agent informed him. "We can make millions on this."

"How? Sell my book to Capricorn/AA as a source of—"

"We sell Glory Sands herself to them, schmuck."

Jack blinked. "Why would they want a corpse? The publicity value of a dead body doesn't seem to me to—"

"She ain't a corpse, ninny." Grunting, he reached out to grab the mildewed diary from his friend's grasp. "Listen attentively now. '. . . An eternal spell . . . never again shall she rise. . . .' You're supposed to have a way with words, yet you didn't tumble to the obvious and glaring nuances herein. Glory Sands *isn't* dead; she only sleeps. She's down there under that deserted manse in a state of suspended animation. Like Sleeping Beauty and other comatose ladies of lore and legend."

"I suppose you could interpret the—"

"Attend to me, lad," ordered Hoff, tapping the open pages of the Yarko diary. "This director gink had her put into a trance. Don't ask me why, but that's what the guy did. After all, there were some strange folks in Hollywood even back then. Motives don't matter. Important thing is, she can be revived."

"Who's missing nuances now? It says *eternal* spell, and that—"

"Byers Tumly," Hoff shut the book. "Byers Tumly is alive at this moment, even as we speak, and you sit there like a lunk missing the hotdamn point. Byers Tumly, a crackerjack mystic with the powers of black magic at his command, lives with his sappy granddaughter in Pasadena."

"So?"

"What Tumly can do, Tumly can undo."

"Reverse the spell?"

"Yes, indeed, old buddy, reverse the spell and bring her back to life."

Jack scratched his armpit. "In a way, that'd be great," he said finally. "What I'm saying is, she'd certainly be a good source of information for my biograph—"

"What is Blummer over at C/AA looking for, yearning for, beating the bush for? He's been turned down by Cybill Shepherd and couldn't cut a deal with Meryl Streep. He's seriously contemplating, in the vein of Selznick's hunt for a suitable Scarlett O'Hara, a nationwide search for an unknown to portray Glory Sands upon the silver screen."

"Wait now. We can't do that."

"Why not, pray tell?"

"It's too unusual and strange, for one thing. What I'm saying is, if Glory Sands does awaken from this trance, she's still going to look exactly like she did fifty years ago," said Jack. "Either that or she might be a wrinkled-up mummy who—"

"You still don't comprehend what I intend."

"And how could we explain her to people? Tell them the truth, and they'll suspect either a hoax or they'll be scared off. I don't imagine Blummer at Capricorn/AA is anxious to hire a reanimated corpse to—"

"We aren't going to let anyone know she's really Glory Sands."

"Then how can I finish the biography or—"

"You don't. Not until after we sell her to Blummer to play herself in the bio-pic." Hoff bounced in his chair as he explained this. "No, we market her as an amazing Glory Sands lookalike. A young and talented newcomer who was born—destined, if you will—to play this role. We introduce her to Blummer—hell, she's a cinch to land the role—and then he promotes her like crazy. As her managers, we get a handsome percentage of everything—her salary, the poster money, the advertising loot, the whole flapping casaba. Twenty percent of millions is going to be a lot more than a paltry advance from some Manhattan book—"

"She might not go along with the idea."

Hoff scoffed. "Hey, this is what I do for a living, amigo," he reminded Jack. "I thrive on selling half-wits inept and malformed actors and actresses that they really have no earthly use for. I can sure as heck, trust me, persuade Glory Sands to pretend to be a gifted unknown."

"And suppose, once we pry open the coffin, she's a little wizened-up mummy?"

"Then I'll get her a job with Ernie Caliente." Hoff rose up. "Let us, however, look only on the bright side. We are, old buddy, on the brink of great things."

A gust of hot night wind came rushing across the weedy back acre of the walled-in Yarko estate. It caught hold of Byers Tumly, inflated the heavy plaid overcoat the frail old mystic insisted on wearing, nudged him over a long-dead hedge, and dumped him into a dry fish pond.

"Indeed . . . hum hum," he murmured, sprawled facedown next to a broken stone cherub who was clutching a gulping dolphin. "I am . . . don't you know . . . beginning to remember. This pond, yes . . . used to be fish in it."

Jack caught the wizard's thin arm and yanked him to his feet. "I don't know much about occult ritual," he said to Hoff, who was carrying a large flashlight and a satchel full of rattling tools, "but shouldn't our mystic be sober for this?"

"He is sober."

"Hum hum . . . Peter Yarko . . . remember the night well . . . wind in the willows . . . cast a spell . . . ancient runes . . . Calabar . . . Egbo . . . Nyamba . . . indeed, indeed."

"He's tipsy." Jack guided him around a marble faun and toward the dark, sprawling mansion.

"He's merely old."

The wind came skimming across the sharply slanting tile roofs, twisting the lame weathercock, making rude, raspy sounds.

"Age doesn't smell like an old bar rag."

"Whatever was the reason for casting the spell? . . . paid me handsomely . . . hum hum . . . Sign of Solomon . . . salamander . . . Obambo."

"It'd be encouraging if he could recall why Glory Sands is sealed up in the bowels of this—"

"The diary already explained all that, old buddy. Yarko was ticked off at her, so he had our wizard here put her into a trance."

"C'mon, Den, every time you get mad at a lady, you don't call a sorcerer to—"

"I don't, true, but I don't happen to be a brooding, tormented artist like Yarko." Hoff halted in front of the boarded-up rear door of the deserted house.

". . . better off this way," muttered old Tumly, swaying as the wind whipped around him. "Make world safe for . . . democracy . . . something like that . . . Nergal . . . Astaroth . . . Moloch."

After setting his satchel carefully on the mossy ground, Hoff extracted a crowbar. "First thing to do is get rid of these boards." He started to do that.

"This is what's popularly called breaking and entering," mentioned Jack. He was clutching the ancient sorcerer, to keep him from blowing away.

"You can tell the cops it's research for your next crime novel," said Hoff, ripping away another old board. "But I really doubt they pay any attention to this pile any longer."

The nails shrieked as he pulled them free. Downhill somewhere a lone hound commenced howling forlornly.

"A bad sign," observed Tumly. "Perturbed spirits prowl."

Jack asked him, "You sure you have no idea why Glory Sands was—"

"It'll come back to me." He chuckled in a rusty way. "Yes . . . hum . . . this excitement is good for me. Gets the brain to clicking along once again. . . . Sitting in Pasadena can be . . . Do you have any idea how many game shows there are on television?"

"Must be about—"

"There," announced Hoff. "All the boards are down. Now I'll pick the lock."

"You know how to do this sort of thing?"

"Well, it ought to be relatively simple, shouldn't it? Thousands of people who never even graduated from high school become burglars." He squatted before the tarnished doorknob.

"Yes, I remember this house," said Tumly, wrapping his large plaid overcoat tighter around him and venturing along the dusty hallway. "It didn't smell so strongly of rot and decay then."

The long corridor, paneled with dark-stained wood and floored with dusky mosaic tiles, was thick with the odors of mildew and neglect.

Hoff played the beam of his light ahead, touching the carved panels, the wrought-iron wall lamps, the serpentine pattern in the tiles. "What a setting," he remarked. "This must inspire the creative writer in you, Jack."

"Inspires me to want to get clear before the cops find—"

"This way." Tumly was pointing to their left. "There's a stairway off yonder kitchen . . . hum hum . . . I'm remembering more by the minute. Yes, she lies down below."

The old wizard lurched, tottered, and caught hold of a dusty wine bottle on one of the racks that filled the damp, stone-walled room. "Hum, yes. It's coming back to—"

Jack made a grab for his sleeve. "This is not time to go guzzling—"

"I'd never touch port." Tumly caught hold of the bottle by its neck, pushed it downward. "This particular bottle happens to be a concealed lever, young man."

A rumbling started up across the shadowy wine cellar. Gravelly noises came rattling up from below. Next came an echoing, bumping thump.

"He *is* remembering rightly." Hoff turned the beam of the flash onto the twisting stairway that was showing now in the large rectangle that had opened in the floor.

The coffin was down there, a heavy thing of bronze. It rested on a low stone pedestal, gobs of scarlet sealing wax dabbed around the edges of the domed lid.

Hoff hurried across the chill stone floor and knelt next to it. "This hasn't been futzed with," he said. "Meaning Glory's still inside."

"This is going to make a great chapter in my book." Jack approached the bronze coffin. "Yeah, and I can spin off lots of articles too. Slick magazines first, then supermarket tabloids."

The old mystic shuffled over. "Things are growing ever clearer," he assured them, poking his knobby hands into the pockets of his immense overcoat.

"And Glory Sands is really inside there?" Jack asked him.

"Helped deposit the lady within it myself." Tumly had located a magnifying glass with a bit of fuzz sticking to its lens. He made a slow circuit of the coffin. "Hum hum. . . . Yes, to be sure . . . simple enough restraining spell . . . yes." From another lumpy pocket he brought forth a fat black candle. "Stick this on that shelf over there, young man, and light it."

Jack obliged, nose wrinkling at the acrid smell the sputtering candle produced. "Can you—"

"Quiet, please." Tumly had straightened up, and there was a small skin-bound volume open in his quivering hands. "Beelzebub . . . Beelzebub . . . Beelzebub."

Shivering, Jack took a few backward steps.

The old sorcerer continued on, mixing Latin with incantations in even older, deader languages.

Five long minutes passed.

Then the thick globs of crimson wax sizzled and started melting. Clotted streams of red dribbled down across the bronze sides of the heavy casket.

"Now, be quick, lift the lid free," Tumly ordered.

Hoff took the far side, Jack the other. Grunting, they managed to lift it up and away.

While they were leaning the lid against the stone wall, a satiny rustle sounded within the open casket.

A very pretty blond young woman in a white satin evening gown sat up in the casket and looked around at the three of them.

"Ah, yes," said Tumly. "I remember now why we sealed her up. She's a vampire."

Hoff, grinning broadly, came into the cottage out of the fuzzy glare of the afternoon. "Absolutely great," he announced, waving the manila envelope he held aloft in his pudgy right hand. "I picked up the contact prints of the pics we had Orlando of Hollywood shoot a couple of nights ago, and they're completely sensational. She looks, specially in that slinky satin dress she was interred in, just like Glory Sands."

"She *is* Glory Sands." Jack was sitting in his favorite, and only, armchair and gazing into his small, empty fireplace. "She was hidden away under Yarko's place because of her vampire ways. But now you've stuck me with baby-sitting a potential kill—"

"C'mon, she agreed to downplay that stuff," the agent reminded him. "Glory's as eager as we are for a new career in—"

"Also, Den, I don't see why we had to spend so damn much on those photos."

"Because, old buddy, we are going first cabin on this whole venture. We're going to sell that platinum bimbo as—"

"Not so loud," cautioned Jack in a lowered voice. "But what I'm talking about is, I have to pay rent on this place, and I've had to shelve my bio so—"

"What are you so uneasy about? She can't hear us." Hoff settled into the wicker sofa with his broad back to the view of the overgrown yard outside. "Vampires sleep by day, don't they?"

"Nertz," observed a feminine voice from the next room.

"Apparently that isn't always so." Jack nodded toward the doorway of his kitchen.

"Well, then that's even better for us. That way we won't have to con Blummer into filming *The Glory Story* entirely at night."

"You bozos really hand me a laugh." The lovely blonde, wearing one of Jack's candy-striped shirts and a brand-new pair of designer jeans, came into the parlor holding a fat bologna sandwich. "Where'd you get your facts about vampires anyhow, from some B-movie starring that dippy Hungarian hophead who went flapping around in a cape? Jeez." She perched on the arm of Jack's chair, one pretty leg swinging out and tapping the base of his old floor lamp. "Vampires have been getting a bad press for . . . Hey, are you sure dames wear this kind of slacks nowadays? They're so tight my fanny's going to sleep."

Watching her, Hoff nodded approvingly and chuckled. "Perfect, she's perfect. That sassy 1930s patina will knock Blummer and his toadies on their respective tokes."

After taking a bite of her sandwich, Glory said, "This bologna sure as heck doesn't taste like the bologna I remember."

"Fifty years," reminded Jack, "have passed since you last tasted—"

"Darn, I never figured bologna would change." Sliding off the chair arm, she crossed to the window. "Smog, huh? It sure does a swell job of mucking up the air. Don't you ever have your shrubs trimmed, Jack? I had two Japs who did—"

"How'd you like to see your pictures, Glory?" Hoff was shaking the proof sheets from the envelope. "You look great."

"Cameras love me," she explained, biting into her sandwich. "Even in Paris in the 1870s, I—"

"Whoa now," cut in Jack, "you were alive in the 1870s?"

"Why the heck do you think I became a vampire in the first place, sweetheart?" She turned to face him, wiping a speck of mayonnaise from her dimpled cheek. "Immortality. Sure, I was born in Lisbon . . . that's in Portugal . . . in 1726."

Hoff lowered the photos to his lap. "Glory, we better not mention that fact to anybody else, okay?"

"You think I'm a dope? I mean, honey, I want to start making dough again more than you guys even." She gave Jack's small forlorn parlor a disdainful look. "I sure don't want to live in this cracker box much longer."

"Exactly. And as soon as I sell you to Blummer, we'll start looking at mansions in Bel Air," promised the agent. "That's the sort of setting Gloria Sanctum needs."

"Jeez, what a dippy name." The reanimated actress lowered herself to sit on the bare hardwood floor, leaning her slim back against the built-in bookshelves. "I know I can't call myself Gloria Sands anymore, but—"

"Gloria Sanctum has a certain flair," Hoff assured her. "And preserves your initials."

"I never even much liked Glory Sands. That was Yarko's idea," she said, shaking her lovely head. "Imagine that bum having a spell put on me and dumping me in his darn basement."

"Apparently," said Jack, not quite looking at her, "he was concerned about your vampire activities and—"

"Hell, no. I think he just wanted to give MGM the finger." Finishing her sandwich, she licked her fingers. "Yarko exaggerated things, like most creative bozos."

"Are you suggesting," said Jack, "that you really weren't much of a practicing vampire?"

"Look, sweetheart, once in a while I did maybe drain some sap of his blood," she admitted, smiling attractively. "I mean, you're a vampire and that's what you do, you know? But I was discreet and I didn't do it often. Rarely with anybody in show business."

"So there's really not that much to worry about," said Hoff.

Very gracefully the blond actress stood up. "Let me see the pictures, Denny."

"To me, Glory . . . Gloria, rather. Better get used to using your new name." He handed her the sheets. "To me, Gloria, the shots of you smiling right into the camera are the best."

She studied the shots. "My left profile isn't bad either," she remarked. "Being buried for fifty years hasn't really hurt my looks any."

"Gloria, you're as lovely now as—"

"Hey!" After staring out the window, Jack hopped up and ran for the door.

"What's wrong, old buddy?"

"Somebody outside, peeking over my hedge at us."

The two men ran out into the hedged-in yard. But there was no one out there now.

"You get a look at him?" asked Hoff.

"Not really, but . . . It was a guy . . . and there was something vaguely familiar about him."

"Hey, you two," called Glory, "come on back in here and let me tell you which ones of these we're going to use."

Jack tossed another shovelful of dirt aside. "What was it you were going to tell me when you first got here, Den?"

"Huh?" Hoff was thumbing through the notebook he'd found in the pocket of the dead man sprawled on the garage floor. "Oh, yeah, good news. Blummer was very, very impressed with the glossies of Glory . . . Gloria. He wants her to come in and read on Monday. It's a sure thing, far as I can tell."

The grave was getting deeper. "Don't you think maybe this is a snag?"

"How so?" Hoff shut the notebook.

"You were paying attention when I explained to you that I found this guy out behind my cottage a couple hours ago, at sundown? What I'm saying is, he was killed by a vampire."

"Well, any half-wit can see that," said the agent. "He's got those two puncture marks in his throat, and he's been drained of his blood."

"Glory did it."

"Call her Gloria."

"Gloria. Glory. She admitted as much before she locked herself in the bedroom."

"Let her sulk for a while; that's okay."

"But she—"

"He's got only himself to blame, old buddy." Hoff slapped the notebook against his thigh. "This is Walt Downey, a free-lance writer for *The National Intruder*. He's also the very same chap you spotted prowling amongst your shrubbery a few days ago."

"A reporter? Damn, that means—"

"A *free-lance*," cut in Hoff. "Nobody knows what he was planning to write about next. Seems he was interviewing Tumly for some other article, and the old gink let slip a reference to us and Gloria."

"What sort of reference?"

"Sort of to the fact that we'd brought her back from the grave. Keep digging, will you?"

"That's splendid. Glory's resurrection's going to become a mass media event."

"Downey had only, according to his notes, begun to investigate. He wasn't yet sure if we had Glory Sands or were simply cooking up a hoax for publicity purposes," said Hoff. "Fortunately for us, she got him just in time."

"It's murder."

"Not necessarily. The fact she's a vampire would make a good defense," the agent said, watching Jack work on the reporter's grave. "Sure, she can plead she couldn't help herself. But it'll never come to that. We bury this gink and—"

"Making us accessories."

"From what I can learn out of his effects, old buddy, Downey had no near kith or kin. Even the *Intruder* won't miss him, since most free-lance writers are expendable," said Hoff. "Let's, therefore, strive to look only on the bright side. Think about what our share of her salary of, say, four hundred thousand dollars per picture is going to be. And keep digging."

Glory took another sip from her glass. "Phooey," she remarked. "This stuff sure doesn't taste like orange juice."

"Let's get back to the issue." Jack was seated across his small lopsided breakfast table from her.

" 'Made from concentrate.' Whatever the heck that might be. I mean, how dippy can you get?" She clicked the glass down. "You got fresh oranges out the kazoo all around here, and you dumbbells—"

"About Downey."

"Who?"

"The reporter you got rid of the other night. We really have to talk about—"

"Jeez, are you still squawking about that? Denny didn't think it was all that important."

"Glory, I have a small garage. If you keep on—"

"The guy was poking his nose into our business, wasn't he?"

"Having all your blood drained from your body isn't quite the punishment that fits that particular—"

"Okay, okay, swell. Don't keep nagging, okay? I'm doing the best I can," the blonde told him. "I just wish we'd get that contract signed so—"

"Blummer was favorably impressed with you when you read for him, according to Den."

"Blummer, what a twerp," she said, tangling her fingers in her silky hair. "You know what he used to be? A certified public accountant. That sure isn't my idea of a mogul. And that dippy director . . . what's his name?"

"Piet Goedewaagen."

"He's younger than I am," she said, frowning. "Younger than I'm supposed to be, I mean. He passed out cold before I even got to the second page of my dumb scene."

"Goedewaagen has a drug problem, I hear."

"He fell off his darn chair. Plunk on the rug."

"Let the producer worry about him. You—"

"Woody Van Dyke never fell off his chair. When we shot *Blonde Fever* up at Catalina in thirty-five, he—"

"How often are you likely to attack people?"

"¿Quién sabe? as they say in Tijuana." She shrugged gracefully. "It sort of depends on my mood and whether I'm bored or not. Sometimes, you know, I just get the urge."

Jack took an unenthusiastic bite of his cold toast. "Glory, could—"

"Call me Gloria. We don't want to spoil—"

"Killing people is going to spoil things a lot sooner than my calling you the wrong name," he said. "Now, when you were here before, back in the 1930s, about how often did you attack—"

"Not all that much. It fluctuated."

"Can you give me a ballpark figure? What I'm asking is, how many victims did—"

"Oh, less than a hundred."

"A hundred?" He dropped his toast.

"Less than, I said."

"Ninety?"

"Give or take."

"How'd you keep people from finding out that—"

"Yarko took care of most of that," answered Glory. "Seeing that they got buried or lost in an out-of-the-way place. And sometimes I'd go after a nobody down on Skid Row."

"You were in Hollywood from 1933 to 1937." He eased a small calculator out of his jacket pocket. "That's four years. So we divide ninety victims by four, and we get . . . oy! . . . 22.5 per year."

"That's a cute gadget. Can I see how it—"

The phone sounded out in the parlor. "You can fool with it. Here." Tossing her the pocket calculator, he sprinted into the next room. "Hello?"

"We're on the real brink now, old buddy. I just got a call," said Hoff.

"I'm not hearing you too clearly. What's that noise in the background?"

"Marimba music." The agent raised his voice. "Blummer just phoned. Wants me over at C/AA in one hour. I smell six figures in the offing."

"Listen, Den," said Jack, hand masking the mouthpiece. "If we unleash this creature on the world, we're going to be responsible for at least 22.5 deaths per year for—"

"Ernie, that's *bastante*, old amigo. I like the new act, and, trust me, I'll book you at someplace terrific. Now get the hell out of here. Adios," Hoff was saying. "Okay, Jack, you—"

"Twenty-two point five. That's the number of victims we can count on each year that she's still aboveground." Jack glanced at the kitchen doorway. "So what we have to do, we have to get Tumly and seal her up again under—"

"Can't get Tumly."

"You didn't book him off in the boondocks someplace?"

"The poor old gink passed on."

"That's . . . wait a second. How?"

"What?"

"How'd Tumly come to die?"

Hoff coughed. "Don't scream and yell when I fill you in."

"Never mind. I know. His daughter found him sprawled out someplace with all the blood missing from—"

"Grandaughter, it was, who found the poor soul."

"Yeah, and Glory was gone the night before last," he said in an intense whisper. "Wouldn't explain where she'd—"

"Let's keep looking on the bright side," said Hoff. "When I next visit your place at dusk, I have no doubt that I'll have a very nice contract close to my girlishly pounding heart."

"No, nope. You have to get another sorcerer then. He can put—"

"Where am I going to get a sorcerer?"

"You're a goddamn talent agent. Go find one. And quick. If you can find an eighty-year-old salsa player, then—"

"Calm yourself. Put Glory on the phone," requested the agent. "I'll impart to her all the good things that are in the offing, and use my considerable powers of persuasion to convince her to lay off her hobby for a while. I'll get her to promise she won't do anything to futz up her budding career."

"Vampires," said Jack, "don't keep promises."

Hoff arrived at dusk, his stride slower than usual. His pudgy body had a mournful sag. "Idiots," he said as he stepped into the parlor. "I should have remembered that this is Hollywood."

Jack was in his favorite armchair, surrounded by shadows.

"I go over to see Blummer," continued the unhappy agent. "I am ushered into his vast Capricorn/AA office. And what does that nitwit tell me?"

Jack didn't respond.

"He tells me," said Hoff, "they've decided they don't want Glory to play Glory Sands in their movie. And why? I'll tell you why. She's not right for the part."

Jack didn't respond.

Slowly Hoff crossed the dim room. "Well, don't be gloomy, old buddy. I'll come up with a new way to sell her to somebody." He reached out and clicked on the floor lamp next to the chair.

That was when he saw the marks on Jack's throat.

BUG HOUSE

LISA TUTTLE

American-born Lisa Tuttle resides in England and is both
a journalist and story writer. She was one of the early members of the Clarion Writers' Workshop and, in 1974, won
the John W. Campbell Award for best new science fiction
writer. Although she has written numerous impressive science fiction stories, Ms. Tuttle excels in the contemporary
horror tale and in her ability to terrify readers. "Bug House"
is a particularly creepy and effective chiller.

The house was a wreck, resting like
some storm-shattered ship on a weedy headland overlooking the ocean.
Ellen felt her heart sink at the sight of it.

"This it?" asked the taxi driver dubiously, squinting through his windshield and slowing the car.

"It must be," Ellen said without conviction. She couldn't believe that
her aunt—or anyone else—lived in this house.

The house had been built, after the local custom, out of wood, and
then set upon cement blocks that raised it three or four feet off the ground.

But floods seemed far less dangerous to the house now than the winds, or simply time. The house was crumbling on its blocks. The boards were weatherbeaten and scabbed with flecks of ancient gray paint. Uncurtained windows glared blankly, and one shutter hung at a crazy angle. Between the boards of the sagging second-story balcony, Ellen could see daylight.

"I'll wait for you," the driver said, pulling up at the end of an overgrown driveway. "In case there's nobody here."

"Thanks," Ellen said, getting out of the backseat and tugging her suitcase after her. She counted the fare out into his hand and glanced up at the house. No sign of life. Her shoulders slumped. "Just wait to be sure someone answers the door," she told the driver.

Trudging up the broken cement path to the front door, Ellen was startled by a glimpse of something moving beneath the house. She stopped short and peered ahead at the dark space. Had it been a dog? A child playing? Something large and dark, moving quickly—but it was gone now or in hiding. Behind her, Ellen could hear the taxi idling. For a brief moment she considered going back. Back to Danny. Back to all their problems. Back to his lies and promises.

She walked forward again, and when she reached the porch she set her knuckles against the warped gray door and rapped sharply, twice.

An old, old woman, stick-thin and obviously ailing, opened the door. Ellen and the woman gazed at each other in silence.

"Aunt May?"

The old woman's eyes cleared with recognition, and she nodded slightly. "Ellen, of course!"

But when had her aunt grown so old?

"Come in, dear." The old woman stretched out a parchment claw. At her back, Ellen felt the wind. The house creaked, and for a moment Ellen thought she felt the porch floor give beneath her feet. She stumbled forward into the house. The old woman—her aunt, she reminded herself—closed the door behind her.

"Surely you don't live here all alone," Ellen began. "If I'd known— if Dad had known—we would have . . ."

"If I'd needed help I would've asked for it," Aunt May said with a sharpness that reminded Ellen of her father.

"But this house," Ellen said. "It's too much for one person. It looks like it might fall down at any minute, and if something should happen to you here, all alone . . ."

The old woman laughed, a dry, papery rustle. "Nonsense. This house will outlast me. And appearances can be deceiving. Look around you— I'm quite cozy here."

Ellen saw the hall for the first time. A wide, high-ceilinged room with a brass chandelier and a rich Oriental carpet. The walls were painted a cream color, and the grand staircase looked in no danger of collapse.

"It does look a lot better inside," Ellen said. "It looked deserted from the road. The taxi driver couldn't believe anyone lived here."

"The inside is all that matters to me," said the old woman. "I have let it all go rather badly. The house is honeycombed with dry rot and eaten by insects, but even so it's in nowhere near as bad shape as I am. It will still be standing when I'm underground, and that's enough for me."

"But, Aunt May . . ." Ellen took hold of her aunt's bony shoulders. "Don't talk like that. You're not dying."

That laugh again. "My dear, look at me. I am. I'm long past saving. I'm all eaten up inside. There's barely enough of me left to welcome you here."

Ellen looked into her aunt's eyes, and what she saw there made her vision blur with tears.

"But doctors . . ."

"Doctors don't know everything. There comes a time, my dear, for everyone. A time to leave this life for another one. Let's go in and sit down. Would you like some lunch? You must be hungry after that long trip."

Feeling dazed, Ellen followed her aunt into the kitchen, a narrow room decorated in green and gold. She sat at the table and stared at the wallpaper, a pattern of fish and frying pans.

Her aunt was dying. It was totally unexpected. Her father's older sister—but only eight years older, Ellen remembered. And her father was a vigorously healthy man, a man still in the prime of life. She looked at her aunt, saw her moving painfully slowly from cupboard to counter to shelf, preparing a lunch.

Ellen rose. "Let me do it, Aunt May."

"No, no, dear. I know where everything is, you see. You don't. I can still get around all right."

"Does Dad know about you? When was the last time you saw him?"

"Oh, dear me, I didn't want to burden him with my problems. We haven't been close for years, you know. I suppose I last saw him—why, it was at your wedding, dear."

Ellen remembered. That had been the last time she had seen Aunt May. She could hardly believe that woman and the one speaking to her now were the same. What had happened to age her so in only three years?

May set a plate on the table before Ellen. A pile of tuna and mayonnaise was surrounded by sesame crackers.

"I don't keep much fresh food on hand," she said. "Mostly canned goods. I find it difficult to get out shopping much anymore, but then, I haven't much appetite lately either. So it doesn't much matter what I eat. Would you like some coffee? Or tea?"

"Tea, please. Aunt May, shouldn't you be in a hospital? Where someone would care for you?"

"I can care for myself right here."

"I'm sure Dad and Mom would love to have you visit . . ."

May shook her head firmly.

"In a hospital they might be able to find a cure for you."

"There's no cure for dying except death, Ellen."

The kettle began to whistle, and May poured boiling water over a teabag into a cup.

Ellen leaned back in her chair, resting the right side of her head against the wall. She could hear a tiny, persistent, crunching sound from within the wall—termites?

"Sugar in your tea?"

"Please," Ellen responded automatically. She had not yet touched her lunch and had no desire for anything to eat or drink.

"Oh, dear," sighed Aunt May. "I'm afraid you'll just have to drink it plain. It must have been a very long time since I used this—there are more ants here than sugar grains."

Ellen watched her aunt drop the whole canister into the garbage can.

"Aunt May, is money a problem? I mean, if you're staying here because you can't afford—"

"Bless you, no." May sat down at the table beside her niece. "I have some investments and enough money in the bank for my own needs. And this house is my own too. I bought it when Victor retired, but he didn't stay long enough to help me enjoy it."

In a sudden rush of sympathy, Ellen leaned over and would have taken her frail aunt in her arms, but May fluttered her hand in a go-away motion, and Ellen drew back.

"With Victor dead, some of the joy went out of fixing it up. Which is why it still looks much the same old wreck it was when I bought it. This property was a real steal, because nobody wanted the house. Nobody but me and Victor." May cocked her head suddenly and smiled. "And maybe you? What would you say if I left this house to you when I die?"

"Aunt May, please don't . . ."

"Nonsense. Who better? Unless you can't stand the sight of it, of course, but I'm telling you, the property is worth something, at least. If the house is too far gone with the bugs and the rot, you can pull it down and put up something you and Danny like better."

"It's very generous of you, Aunt May. I just don't like to hear you talk about dying."

"No? It doesn't bother me. But if it disturbs you, then we'll say no more about it. Shall I show you your room?

"I don't go upstairs anymore," May said, leading the way slowly up the staircase, leaning heavily on the banister and pausing often in her climb. "I moved my bedroom downstairs. It was too much trouble to always be climbing up and down."

The second floor smelled strongly of sea damp and mold.

"This room has a nice view of the sea," May said. "I thought you might like it." She paused in a doorway, gesturing to Ellen to follow. "There are clean linens in the hall closet."

Ellen looked into the room. It was sparely furnished with bed, dressing table, and straight-backed chair. The walls were an institutional green and without decoration. The mattress was bare, and there were no curtains at the french doors.

"Don't go out on the balcony—I'm afraid parts of it have quite rotted away," May cautioned.

"I noticed," Ellen said.

"Well, some parts go first, you know. I'll leave you alone now, dear. I'm feeling a bit tired myself. Why don't we both just nap until dinner-time?"

Ellen looked at her aunt and felt her heart twist with sorrow at the weariness on that pale, wrinkled face. The small exertion of climbing upstairs had told on her. Her arms trembled slightly, and she looked gray with weariness.

Ellen hugged her. "Oh, Aunt May," she said softly. "I'm going to be a help to you, I promise. You just take it easy. I'll look after you."

May pulled away from her niece's arms, nodding. "Yes, dear. It's very nice to have you here. We welcome you." She turned and walked away down the hall.

Alone, Ellen suddenly realized her own exhaustion. She sank down on the bare mattress and surveyed her bleak little room, her mind a jumble of problems old and new.

She had never known her Aunt May well enough to become close to her—this sudden visit was a move born of desperation. Wanting to get away from her husband for a while, wanting to punish him for a recently discovered infidelity, she had cast about for a place she could escape to

—a place she could afford, and a place where Danny would not be able to find her. Aunt May's lonely house on the coast had seemed the best possibility for a week's hiding. She had expected peace, boredom, regret—but she had never expected to find a dying woman. It was a whole new problem that almost cast her problems with Danny into insignificance.

Suddenly she felt very lonely. She wished Danny were with her, to comfort her. She wished she had not sworn to herself not to call him for at least a week.

But she would call her father, she decided. Should she warn him against telling Danny? She wasn't sure—she hated letting her parents know her marriage was in trouble. Still, if Danny tried to find her by calling them, they would know something was wrong.

She'd call her father tonight. Definitely. He'd come out here to see his sister—he'd take charge, get her to a hospital, find a doctor with a miracle cure. She was certain of it.

But right now she was suddenly paralyzingly tired. She stretched out on the bare mattress. She would get the sheets and make it up properly later, but right now she would just close her eyes, just close her eyes and rest for a moment. . . .

It was dark when Ellen woke, and she was hungry.

She sat on the edge of the bed, feeling stiff and disoriented. The room was chilly and smelled of mildew. She wondered how long she had slept.

Nothing happened when she hit the light switch on the wall. So she groped her way out of the room and along the dark hall toward the dimly perceived stairs. The steps creaked loudly beneath her feet. She could see a light at the bottom of the stairs, from the kitchen.

"Aunt May?"

The kitchen was empty, the light a fluorescent tube above the stove. Ellen had the feeling that she was not alone. Someone was watching. Yet when she turned, there was nothing behind her but the undisturbed darkness of the hall.

She listened for a moment to the creakings and moanings of the old house, and to the muffled sounds of sea and wind from outside. No human sound in all of that, yet the feeling persisted that if she listened hard enough, she would catch a voice. . . .

She could make out another dim light from the other end of the hall, behind the stairs, and she walked toward it. Her shoes clacked loudly on the bare wooden floor of the back hall.

It was a night-light that had attracted her attention, and near it she saw that a door stood ajar. She reached out and pushed it farther open. She heard May's voice, and she stepped into the room.

"I can't feel my legs at all," May said. "No pain in them, no feeling at all. But they still work for me somehow. I was afraid that once the feeling went they'd be useless to me. But it's not like that at all. But you knew that; you told me it would be like this." She coughed, and there was the sound in the dark room of a bed creaking. "Come here, there's room."

"Aunt May?"

Silence—Ellen could not even hear her aunt breathing. Finally May said, "Ellen? Is that you?"

"Yes, of course. Who did you think it was?"

"What? Oh, I expect I was dreaming." The bed creaked again.

"What was that you were saying about your legs?"

More creaking sounds. "Hmmm? What's that, dear?" The voice of a sleeper struggling to stay awake.

"Never mind," Ellen said. "I didn't realize you'd gone to bed. I'll talk to you in the morning. Good night."

"Good night, dear."

Ellen backed out of the dark, stifling bedroom, feeling confused.

Aunt May must have been talking in her sleep. Or perhaps, sick and confused, she was hallucinating. But it made no sense to think—as Ellen, despite herself, was thinking—that Aunt May had been awake and had mistaken Ellen for someone else, someone she expected a visit from, someone else in the house.

The sound of footsteps on the stairs, not far above her head, sent Ellen running forward. But the stairs were dark and empty, and straining her eyes toward the top, Ellen could see nothing. The sound must have been just another product of this dying house, she thought.

Frowning, unsatisfied with her own explanation, Ellen went back into the kitchen. She found the pantry well stocked with canned goods and made herself some soup. It was while she was eating it that she heard the footsteps again—this time seemingly from the room above her head.

Ellen stared up at the ceiling. If someone was really walking around up there, he was making no attempt to be cautious. But she couldn't believe that the sound was anything but footsteps: someone was upstairs.

Ellen set her spoon down, feeling cold. The weighty creaking continued.

Suddenly the sounds overhead stopped. The silence was unnerving, giving Ellen a vision of a man crouched down, his head pressed against the floor as he listened for some response from her.

Ellen stood up, rewarding her listener with the sound of a chair scraping across the floor. She went to the cabinet on the wall beside the telephone—and there, on a shelf with the phone book, Band-Aids and light bulbs was a flashlight—just as in her father's house.

The flashlight worked, and the steady beam of light cheered her. Remembering that the light in her room hadn't worked, Ellen also took out a light bulb before closing the cabinet and starting upstairs.

Opening each door as she came to it, Ellen found a series of unfurnished rooms, bathrooms, and closets. She heard no further footsteps and found no sign of anyone or anything that could have made them. Gradually, the tension drained out of her, and she returned to her own room after taking some sheets from the linen closet.

After installing the light bulb and finding that it worked, Ellen closed the door and turned to make up the bed. Something on the pillow drew her attention: examining it more closely, she saw that it seemed to be a small pile of sawdust. Looking up the wall, she saw that a strip of wooden molding was riddled with tiny holes, leaking the dust. She wrinkled her nose in distaste: termites. She shook the pillow vigorously and stuffed it into a case, resolving to call her father first thing in the morning. May could not go on living in a place like this.

Sun streaming through the uncurtained window woke her early. She drifted toward consciousness to the cries of sea gulls and the all-pervasive smell of the sea.

She got up, shivering from the dampness which seemed to have crept into her bones, and dressed herself quickly. She found her aunt in the kitchen, sitting at the table and sipping a cup of tea.

"There's hot water on the stove," May said by way of greeting.

Ellen poured herself a cup of tea and joined her aunt at the table.

"I've ordered some groceries," May said. "They should be here soon, and we can have toast and eggs for breakfast."

Ellen looked at her aunt and saw that a dying woman shared the room with her. In the face of that solemn, inarguable fact, she could think of nothing to say. So they sat in a silence broken only by the sipping of tea, until the doorbell rang.

"Would you let him in, dear?" May said.

Ellen rose. "Shall I pay him?"

"Oh, no. He doesn't ask for that. Just let him in."

Wondering, Ellen opened the door on a strongly built young man holding a brown paper grocery bag in his arms. She put out her arms rather hesitantly to receive the groceries, but he ignored her implied offer, walking into the house and around her to the kitchen. There he set his bag down and began to unload it. Ellen stood in the doorway watching, noticing that he knew where everything went.

He said nothing to May, who seemed scarcely aware of his presence, but when everything had been put away, he sat down at the table, taking Ellen's place. He tilted his head on one side, eyeing Ellen. "You must be her niece," he said.

Ellen said nothing. She didn't like the way he looked at her. His dark, nearly black eyes seemed to be without pupils—hard eyes, without depths. And he ran those eyes up and down her body, judging her. He smiled now at her silence and turned to May. "A quiet one," he said.

May stood up, holding her empty cup.

"Let me," Ellen said quickly, stepping forward. May handed her the cup and sat down again, still without acknowledging the young man's presence. "Would you like some breakfast?" Ellen asked.

May shook her head. "You eat what you like, dear. I don't feel much like eating . . . there doesn't seem to be much point to it."

"Aunt May, you really should eat."

"A piece of toast then."

"I'd like some eggs," said the stranger. He stretched lazily in his chair. "I haven't had my breakfast yet."

Ellen looked at May, wanting some clue as to how to treat this presumptuous stranger. Was he her friend? A hired man? She didn't want to be rude to him if May didn't wish it. But May was looking into the middle distance, indifferent.

Ellen looked at the man. "Are you waiting to be paid for the groceries?" she asked.

The stranger smiled, a hard smile that revealed a set of even teeth. "I bring food to your aunt as a favor. So she won't have to go to all the trouble of getting it for herself in her condition."

Ellen stared at him a moment longer, waiting in vain for a sign from her aunt, and then turned her back on them and went to the stove to prepare breakfast. She wondered why this man was helping her aunt— was she really not paying him? He didn't strike her as the sort for disinterested favors.

"Now that I'm here," Ellen said, getting eggs and butter from the refrigerator, "you don't have to worry about my aunt. I can run errands for her."

"I'll have two fried eggs," he said. "I like the yolks runny."

Ellen glared at him but checked herself. He wasn't likely to leave just because she refused to cook his eggs—he'd probably just cook them himself. And he *had* bought the groceries.

But—her small revenge—she overcooked the eggs and gave him the slightly scorched pieces of toast.

When she sat down at the breakfast table, Ellen looked at him challengingly. "I'm Ellen Morrow," she said.

He hesitated just long enough to make her think of asking him his name more directly; then he drawled, "You can call me Peter."

"Thanks a lot," she said sarcastically. He smiled his unpleasant smile again, and Ellen felt him watching her throughout the meal. As soon as she had finished eating, she excused herself, telling her aunt that she was going to call her father.

That drew the first response of the morning from May. She put out a detaining hand, drawing it back just shy of actually touching Ellen. "Please don't worry him about me, Ellen. There's nothing he can do for me, and I don't want him charging down here for no good reason."

"But, Aunt May, you're his only sister—I have to tell him, and of course he'll want to do something for you."

"The only thing he can do for me now is to leave me alone," May said.

Unhappily, Ellen thought that her aunt was right—still, she could not leave her to die without trying to save her. Her father had to know. In order to be able to speak freely, she walked past the kitchen telephone and went back to her aunt's bedroom, where she was sure there would be an extension.

There was, and she dialed her parents' home number. The ringing at the other end of the line went on and on, until she gave up and called her father's office. As she had already half suspected, the secretary told her that her father was on one of his fishing trips—absolutely unreachable for another day or two. But she would leave word for him to call as soon as he got in.

So it had to wait. Ellen walked back toward the kitchen, her crepe-soled shoes making almost no sound on the floor.

She heard her aunt's voice saying: "You didn't come to me last night. I waited and waited. Why didn't you come?"

Almost without thinking, Ellen stopped out of sight of the doorway and went on listening.

"You said you would stay with me," May continued. Her voice had a whine in it that made Ellen uncomfortable. "You promised you would stay and look after me until the time comes."

"The girl was in the house," Peter said. "I didn't know if I should."

"What does she matter? She doesn't matter," May said sharply. "Not while I'm here, she doesn't. This is still my house and I . . . I belong to you, don't I? Don't I, dearest?"

Then there was a silence. As quietly as she could, Ellen hurried away and left the house.

The sea air, damp and warm though it was, was a relief after the moldering closeness of the house. But Ellen, taking in deep breaths, still felt sick.

They were lovers, her dying aunt and that awful young man.

That muscular, hard-eyed, insolent stranger was sleeping with her frail, elderly aunt. The idea shocked and revolted her, but she had no doubt of it—the brief conversation, her aunt's voice, could not have been more plain.

Ellen ran down the sandy, weedy incline toward the narrow beach, wanting to lose her knowledge. She didn't know how she could face her aunt, how she could stay in a house where—

She heard Danny's voice, tired, contemptuous, yet still caring: "You're so naive about sex, Ellen. You think everything's black or white. You're such a child."

Ellen started to cry, thinking of Danny, wishing she had not run away from him. What would he say to her about this? That her aunt had a right to pleasure, too, and age was just another prejudice.

But what about *him*? Ellen wondered. What about Peter—what did he get out of it? He was using her aunt in some way, she was certain of it. Perhaps he was stealing from her—she thought of all the empty rooms upstairs and wondered.

She found a piece of Kleenex in a pocket of her jeans and wiped away the tears. So much more was explained by this, she thought. Now she knew why her aunt was so desperate not to leave this rotting hulk of a house, why she didn't want her brother to come.

"Hello, Ellen Morrow."

She raised her head, startled, and found him standing directly in her path, smiling his hard smile. She briefly met, then glanced away from his dark, ungiving eyes.

"You're not very friendly," he said. "You left us so quickly. I didn't get a chance to talk to you."

She glared at him and tried to walk around him, but he fell into step with her. "You shouldn't be so unfriendly," he said. "You should try to get to know me."

She stopped walking and faced him. "Why? I don't know who you are, or what you're doing in my aunt's house."

"I think you have some idea," he said. His cool assumption nearly took her breath away. "I look after your aunt. She was all alone here before I came, with no family or friends. She was completely unprotected. You may find it shocking, but she's grateful to me now. She wouldn't approve of your trying to send me away."

"I'm here now," Ellen said. "I'm a part of her family. And her brother will come here too. She won't be left alone—at the mercy of some stranger."

"She doesn't want me to leave—not for your family or for anyone."

Ellen was silent for a moment. Then she said, "She's a sick, lonely old woman—she needs someone. But what do you get out of it? Do you think she's going to leave you her money when she dies?"

He smiled contemptuously. "Your aunt doesn't have any money. All she has is that wreck of a house—which she plans to leave to you. I give her what she needs, and she gives me what I need—which is something a lot more basic and important than money."

Afraid that she was blushing. Not wanting him to see, Ellen turned and began striding across the sand, back toward the house. She could feel him keeping pace with her at her side, but she did not acknowledge his presence.

Until he grabbed her arm—and she let out a gasp that embarrassed her as soon as she heard it. But Peter made no sign that he had noticed. Now that he had halted her, he was directing her attention to something on the ground.

Feeling foolish, still a little frightened, she let him draw her down into a crouching position beside him. It was a battle that had drawn his attention—a fight for survival in a small sandy arena. A spider, pale as the sand, danced warily on pipe-cleaner legs. Circling it, chitinous body gleaming darkly in the sunlight, was a deadly black dart of a wasp.

There was something eerily fascinating in the way the tiny antagonists circled each other, feinting, freezing, drawing back, and darting forward. The spider on its delicate legs seemed nervous to Ellen, while the wasp was steady and single-minded. Although she liked neither spiders nor wasps, Ellen hoped that the spider would win.

Suddenly the wasp shot forward; the spider rolled over, legs clenching and kicking like fingers from a fist, and the two seemed to wrestle for a moment.

"Ah, now she's got him," murmured Ellen's companion. Ellen saw that his face was intent, and he was absorbed by the deadly battle.

Glancing down again, she saw that the spider was lying perfectly still while the wasp circled it warily.

"He killed him," Ellen said.

"Not he, she," Peter corrected her. "And the spider isn't dead. Just paralyzed. The wasp is making sure that her sting has him completely under control before going on. She'll dig a hole and pull the spider into it, then lay her egg on his body. The spider won't be able to do a thing but lie in the home of his enemy and wait for the egg to hatch and start eating him." He smiled his unpleasant smile.

Ellen stood up.

"Of course, he can't feel a thing," Peter continued. "He's alive, but only in the most superficial sense. That paralyzing poison the wasp filled him with has effectively deadened him. A more advanced creature might torment himself with fears about the future, the inevitability of his approaching death—but this is just a spider. And what does a spider know?"

Ellen walked away, saying nothing. She expected him to follow her, but when she looked back she saw that he was still on his hands and knees, watching the wasp at her deadly work.

Once inside the house, Ellen locked the front door behind her, then went around locking the other doors and checking the windows. Although she knew it was likely that her aunt had given Peter a key to the house, she didn't want to be surprised by him again. She was locking the side door, close by her aunt's room, when the feeble voice called, "Is that you, dear?"

"It's me, Aunt May," Ellen said, wondering who that "dear" was meant for. Pity warred briefly with disgust, and then she entered the bedroom.

From the bed her aunt gave a weak smile. "I tire so easily now," she said. "I think I may just spend the rest of the day in bed. What else is there for me to do except wait?"

"Aunt May, I could rent a car and take you to a doctor—or maybe we could find a doctor who'd be willing to come out here."

May turned her gray head back and forth on the pillow. "No. No. There's nothing a doctor can do, no medicine in the world that can help me now."

"Something to make you feel better . . ."

"My dear, I feel very little. No pain at all. Don't worry about me. Please."

She looks so exhausted, Ellen thought. Almost all used up. And looking down at the small figure surrounded by bedclothes, Ellen felt her eyes fill with tears. Suddenly, she flung herself down beside the bed. "Aunt May, I don't *want* you to die!"

"Now, now," the old woman said softly, making no other movement. "Now, don't you fret. I felt the same way myself, once, but I've gotten over that. I've accepted what has happened, and so must you. So must you."

"No," Ellen whispered, her face pressed against the bed. She wanted to hold her aunt, but she didn't dare—the old woman's stillness seemed to forbid it. Ellen wished her aunt would put out her hand or turn her face to be kissed: she could not make the first move herself.

At last Ellen stopped crying and raised her head. She saw that her aunt had closed her eyes and was breathing slowly and peacefully, obviously asleep. Ellen stood up and backed out of the room. She longed for her father, for someone to share this sorrow with her.

She spent the rest of the day reading and wandering aimlessly through the house, thinking now of Danny and then of her aunt and the unpleasant stranger called Peter, feeling frustrated because she could do nothing. The wind began to blow again, and the old house creaked, setting her nerves on edge. Feeling trapped in the moldering carcass of the house, Ellen walked out onto the front porch. There she leaned against the railing and stared out at the gray and white ocean. Out here she enjoyed the bite of the wind, and the creaking of the balcony above her head did not bother her.

Idly, her attention turned to the wooden railing beneath her hands, and she picked at a projecting splinter with one of her fingernails. To her surprise, more than just a splinter came away beneath her fingers: some square inches of the badly painted wood fell away, revealing an interior as soft and full of holes as a sponge. The wood seemed to be trembling, and after a moment of blankness, Ellen suddenly realized that the wood was infested with termites. With a small cry of disgust Ellen backed away, staring at the interior world she had uncovered. Then she went back into the house, locking the door behind her.

It grew dark, and Ellen began to think longingly of food and companionship. She realized she had heard nothing from her aunt's room since she had left her sleeping there that morning. After checking the kitchen to see what sort of dinner could be made, Ellen went back to wake up her aunt.

The room was dark and much too quiet. An apprehension stopped Ellen in the doorway where, listening, straining her ears for some sound, she suddenly realized the meaning of the silence: May was not breathing.

Ellen turned on the light and hurried to her aunt's bed. "Aunt May. Aunt May," she said, already hopeless. She grabbed hold of one cool hand, hoping for a pulse, and laid her head against her aunt's chest, holding her own breath to listen for the heart.

There was nothing. May was dead. Ellen drew back, crouching on her knees beside the bed, her aunt's hand still held within her own. She stared at the empty face—the eyes were closed, but the mouth hung slightly open—and felt the sorrow building slowly inside her.

At first she took it for a drop of blood. Dark and shining, it appeared on May's lower lip and slipped slowly out of the corner of her mouth. Ellen stared, stupefied, as the droplet detached itself from May's lip and moved, without leaving a trace behind, down her chin.

Then Ellen saw what it was.

It was a small, shiny black bug, no larger than the nail on her little finger. And, as Ellen watched, a second tiny insect crawled slowly out onto the shelf of May's dead lip.

Ellen scrambled away from the bed, backward, on her hands and knees. Her skin was crawling, her stomach churning, and there seemed to be a horrible smell in her nostrils. Somehow, she managed to get to her feet and out of the room without either vomiting or fainting.

In the hallway she leaned against the wall and tried to gather her thoughts.

May was dead.

Into her mind came the vision of a stream of black insects bubbling out of the dead woman's mouth.

Ellen moaned, and clamped her teeth together, and tried to think of something else. *It hadn't happened.* She wouldn't think about it.

But May was dead, and that had to be dealt with. Ellen's eyes filled with tears—then, suddenly impatient, she blinked them away. No time for that. Tears wouldn't do any good. She had to think. Should she call a funeral home? No, a doctor first, surely, even if she was truly past saving. A doctor would tell her what had to be done, who had to be notified.

She went into the kitchen and turned on the light, noticing as she did so how the darkness outside seemed to drop like a curtain against the window. In the cabinet near the phone she found the thin local phone book and looked up the listing for physicians. There were only a few of them. Ellen chose the first number and—hoping that a town this size had an answering service for its doctors—lifted the receiver.

There was no dial tone. Puzzled, she pressed the button and released it. Still nothing. Yet she didn't think the line was dead, because it wasn't completely silent. She could hear what might have been a gentle breathing on the other end of the line, as if someone somewhere else in the house had picked up the phone and was listening to her.

Jarred by the thought, Ellen slammed the receiver back into the cradle. There could be no one else in the house. But one of the other phones might be off the hook. She tried to remember if there was another phone upstairs, because she shrank at the thought of returning to her aunt's room without a doctor, someone in charge, to go with her.

But even if there were another phone upstairs, Ellen realized, she had not seen it or used it, and it was not likely to be causing the trouble. But the phone in her aunt's room could have been left off the hook by either her aunt or herself. She would have to go and check.

He was waiting for her in the hall.

The breath backed up in her throat to choke her, and she couldn't make a sound. She stepped back.

He stepped forward, closing the space between them.

Ellen managed to find her voice and, conquering for the moment her nearly instinctive fear of this man, said, "Peter, you must go get a doctor for my aunt."

"Your aunt has said she doesn't want a doctor," he said. His voice came almost as a relief after the ominous silence.

"It's not a matter of what my aunt wants anymore," Ellen said. "She's dead."

The silence buzzed around them. In the darkness of the hall Ellen could not be sure, but she thought that he smiled.

"Will you go and get a doctor?"

"No," he said.

Ellen backed away, and again he followed her.

"Why don't you go and look at her," Ellen suggested.

"If she's dead," he said, "she doesn't need a doctor. And the morning will be soon enough to have her body disposed of."

Ellen kept backing away, afraid to turn her back on him. Once in the kitchen, she could try the phone again.

But he didn't let her. Before she could reach for the receiver, his hand shot out, and he wrenched the cord out of the wall. He had a peculiar smile on his face. Then he lifted the telephone, long cord dangling, into the air above his own head, and as Ellen pulled nervously away, he threw the whole thing, with great force, at the floor. It crashed jarringly against the linoleum, inches from Ellen's feet.

Ellen stared at him in horror, unable to move or speak, trying frantically to think how to escape him. She thought of the darkness outside, and of the long, unpaved road with no one near, and the deserted beach. Then she thought of her aunt's room, which had a heavy wooden door and a telephone which might still work.

He watched her all this time, making no move. Ellen had the odd idea that he was trying to hypnotize her, to keep her from running, or perhaps he was simply waiting for her to make the first move, watching for the telltale tension in her muscles that would signal her intentions.

Finally, Ellen knew she had to do something—she could not keep waiting for him to act forever. Because he was so close to her, she didn't dare try to run past him. Instead, she feinted to the left, as if she would run around him and toward the front door, but instead she ran to the right.

He caught her in his powerful arms before she had taken three steps. She screamed, and his mouth came down on hers, swallowing the scream.

The feel of his mouth on hers terrified her more than anything else. Somehow, she had not thought of that—for all her fear of him, it had not occurred to her until now that he meant to rape her.

She struggled frantically, feeling his arms crush her more tightly, pinning her arms to her sides and pressing the breath out of her. She tried to kick him or to bring a knee up into his crotch, but she could not raise her leg far enough, and her kicks were feeble little blows against his legs.

He pulled his mouth away from hers and dragged her back into the darkness of the hall and pressed her to the floor, immobilizing her with the weight of his body. Ellen was grateful for her jeans, which were tight-fitting. To get them off—but she wouldn't let him take them off. As soon as he released her, even for a moment, she would go for his eyes, she decided.

This thought was firmly in her mind as he rose off her, but he held her wrists in a crushing grip. She began to kick as soon as her legs were free of his weight, but her legs thrashed about his legs, her kicks doing no harm.

Abruptly, he dropped her hands. She had scarcely become aware of it and hadn't had time to do more than think of going for his eyes, when he, in one smooth, deceptively casual motion, punched her hard in the stomach.

She couldn't breathe. Quite involuntarily, she half doubled over, knowing nothing but the agonizing pain. He, meanwhile, skinned her jeans and underpants down to her knees, flipped her unresisting body over as if it were some piece of furniture, and set her down on her knees.

While she trembled, dry-retched, and tried to draw a full breath of air, she was aware of his fumbling at her genitals as scarcely more than a minor distraction. Shortly thereafter she felt a new pain, dry and tearing, as he penetrated her.

It was the thing she felt. One moment of pain and helplessness, and then the numbness began. She felt—or rather, she ceased to feel—a numbing tide, like intense cold, flowing from her groin into her stomach and hips and down into her legs. Her ribs were numbed, and the blow he had given her no longer pained her. There was nothing—no pain, no messages of any kind from her abused body. She could still feel her lips, and she could open and close her eyes, but from below the chin she might as well have been dead.

And besides the loss of feeling, there was loss of control. All at once she fell like a rag doll to the floor, cracking her chin painfully.

She suspected she was still being raped, but she could not even raise her head and turn to see.

Above her own labored breathing, Ellen became aware of another sound, a low, buzzing hum. From time to time her body rocked and flopped gently, presumably in response to whatever he was still doing to it.

Ellen closed her eyes and prayed to wake. Behind her shut lids, vivid images appeared. Again she saw the insect on her aunt's dead lip, a bug as black, hard, and shiny as Peter's eyes. The wasp in the sand dune, circling the paralyzed spider. Aunt May's corpse covered with a glistening tide of insects, crawling over her, feasting on her.

And when they had finished with her aunt, would they come and find her here on the floor, paralyzed and ready for them?

She cried out at the thought, and her eyes flew open. She saw Peter's feet in front of her. So he had finished. She began to cry.

"Don't leave me like this," she mumbled, her mind still swarming with fears.

She heard his dry chuckle. "Leave? But this is my home."

And then she understood. Of course he would not leave. He would stay here with her as he had stayed with her aunt, looking after her as she grew weaker, until finally she died and spilled out the living cargo he had planted in her.

"You won't feel a thing," he said.

HAND IN GLOVE

ROBERT AICKMAN

Until his death several years ago, England's Robert Aickman was interested and active in many areas, including architecture, opera, wildlife, waterways, and psychic research. He was a film and dramatic critic, lecturer and broadcaster, but we know him best as author of numerous and superb strange tales, including "Ringing the Changes," "Pages from a Young Girl's Journal" (winner of the First World Fantasy Award for best short work), and the story you are about to read, a modern Gothic tale with a number of subtle twists. It is the story of a young woman who has had a bad love affair and asks: "What is the way to mend a broken heart?" And receives the answer: "To kill the man who has broken it . . ."

. . . that subtle gauzy haze which one only finds in Essex.
—Sir Henry Channon

When Millicent finally broke it off with Nigel and felt that the last tiny bit of meaning had ebbed from her life (apart, of course, from her job), it was natural that Winifred should suggest a picnic, combined with a visit, "not too serious," as Winifred put it, to a Great House. Millicent realized that there was no alternative to clutching at the idea and vouchsafed quite effectively the expected blend of pallor and gratitude. She was likely to see much more of Winifred in the future, provided always that Winifred did not somehow choose this precise moment to dart off in some new direction.

Everyone knew about Millicent and Nigel and took it for granted, so that now she was peacefully alotted an odd day or two off, despite the importance of what she did. After all, she had been linked with Nigel, in one way or another, for a long time; and the deceptively small gradations between the different ways were the business only of the two parties. Winifred, on the other hand, had quite a struggle to escape, but she persisted because she realized how much it must matter to Millicent. There are too many people about to make it sensible to assess most kinds of employment objectively. In one important respect, Winifred's life was simpler than Millicent's: "I have never been in love," she would say. "I really don't understand about it." Indeed, the matter arose but rarely, and less often now than ten or twelve years ago.

"What about Baddeley End?" suggested Winifred, attempting a black joke, inducing the ghost of a smile. Winifred had seldom supposed that the Nigel business would end other than as it had.

"Perfect," said Millicent, entering into the spirit, extending phantom hands in gratitude.

"I'll look on the map for a picnic spot," said Winifred. Winifred had found picnic spots for them in the Cevennes, the Apennines, the Dolomites, the Sierra de Guadarrama, even the Carpathians. Incidentally, it was exactly the kind of thing at which Nigel was rather hopeless. Encountering Nigel, one seldom forgot the bull and the gate.

"We'd better use my car," continued Winifred. "Then you'll only have to do what you want to do."

And at first, upon the face of it, things had all gone charmingly as always. Millicent could be in no doubt of that. It is difficult at these times to know which to prefer: friends who understand (up to a point) or those who do not understand at all and thus offer their own kind of momentary escape.

Winifred brought the car to a stand at the end of a long lane, perhaps even bridle path, imperfectly surfaced, at least for modern traffic, even though they were no farther from their respective flats than somewhere in Essex. She had been carrying a great part of their route in her head. Now she was envisaging the picnic site.

"It's a rather pretty spot," she said with confidence. "There's a right of way, or at least a footpath, through the churchyard and down to the river."

"What river is it?" enquired Millicent idly.

"It's only a stream. Well, perhaps a *little* more than that. It's called the Waste."

"Is it really?"

"Yes, it is. Can you please hand me out the rucksack?"

In hours of freedom, Winifred always packed things into a rucksack, where earlier generations would have prepared a luncheon basket or a cabin trunk.

"I'm sorry I've made no contribution," said Millicent, not for the first time.

"Don't be foolish," said Winifred.

"At least let me carry something?"

"All right, the half bottle and the glasses. I couldn't get them in."

"How sweet of you," said Millicent. Potation was normally eschewed in the middle of the day.

"I imagine we go through the kissing gate."

From even that accepted locution Millicent slightly shrank.

The iron kissing gate stood beside the wooden lich gate, opened only on specific occasions.

With the ancient church on their right, little, low, and lichened, they descended the track between the graves. The path had at one time been paved with bricks, but many of the bricks were now missing, and weeds grew between the others.

"It's very slippery," said Millicent. "I shouldn't like to have to hurry back up." It was appropriate that she should make a remark of some kind, should show that she was still alive.

"It can't really be slippery. It hasn't rained for weeks."

Millicent had to admit the truth of that.

"Perhaps it would be better if I were to go first?" continued Winifred. "Then you could take your time with the glasses. Sorry they're so fragile."

"*You* know where we're going," responded Millicent, falling into second place.

"We'll look inside the church before we leave."

Though ivy had begun to entangle the mossy little church like a steathily encroaching octopus, Millicent had to admit that the considerable number of apparently new graves suggested the continuing usefulness of the building. On the other hand, the plastered rectory or vicarage to their left, behind the dangerous-looking hedge, was stained and grimed, and with no visible open window on this almost ideal day.

Whatever Winifred might say, the churchyard seemed very moist. But then, much of Essex is heavy clay. Everyone in the world knows that.

At the far end was another kissing gate, very creaky and arbitrary, and, beyond, a big green sloping field. There were cows drawn together in the far upper corner: "a mixed lot of animals," as Millicent's stepfather would have put it in the old days—the very old days they seemed at that moment.

Down the emerald field ran no visible track, but Winifred, with the dotted map in the forefront of her mind, pursued a steady course. Millicent knew from experience that at the bottom of Winifred's rucksack was a spacious groundsheet. It seemed just as well.

Winifred led the way through an almost nonexistent gate to the left and along a curious muddy passage between rank hedges down to the brink of the river.

Here there were small islands of banked mud with tall plants growing on them that looked almost tropical, and, to the right, a crumbling stone bridge, with an ornament of some kind upon the central panel. Rich, heavy foliage shaded the scene, but early dragonflies glinted across vague streaks of sunlight.

"The right of way goes over the bridge," remarked Winifred, "but we might do better on this side."

Sedgy and umbrous, the picnic spot was romantic in the extreme; most unlikely of discovery even at so short a distance from the human hive, from their own north side of the park. After the repast, one might well seek the brittle bones of once-loitering knights; or one might aforetime have done that, when one had the energy and the faith. Besides, Millicent had noticed that the bridge was obstructed from end to end by rusty barbed wire, with long spikes, mostly bent.

In repose on the groundsheet, they were a handsome pair: trim, effective, still, despite everything, expectant. They wore sweaters in plain colors and stained, familiar trousers. In the symphony of Millicent's abundant hair were themes of pale gray. Winifred's stout tow was at all times sturdily neutral. A poet lingering upon the bridge might have felt sad that life had offered them no more. Few people can pick out, merely from the lines on a map, so ideal a region for a friend's grief. Few people can look so sensuous in sadness as Millicent, away from the office, momentarily oblivious to its ambiguous, paranoid satisfactions.

It had indeed been resourceful of Winifred to buy and bring the half bottle, but Millicent found that the noontide wine made no difference. How could it? How could anything? Almost anything?

But then—

"Winifred! Where have all these mushrooms come from?"

"I expect they were there when we arrived."

"I'm quite certain they were not."

"Of course they were," said Winifred. "Mushrooms grow fast but not *that* fast."

"They were not. I shouldn't have sat down if they had been. I don't like sitting among a lot of giant mushrooms."

"They're quite the normal size," said Winifred, smiling and drawing up her legs. "Would you like to go?"

"Well, we *have* finished the picnic," said Millicent. "Thanks very much, Winifred, it was lovely."

They rose: two exiled dryads, the poet on the bridge might have said. On their side on the shallow, marshy, wandering river were mushrooms as far as the eye could see, downstream and up, though it was true that in neither direction could the eye see very far along the bank, being impeded one way by the bridge and the other by the near-jungle.

"It's the damp," said Millicent. "Everything is so terribly damp."

"If it is," said Winifred, "it must be always like it, because there's been very little rain. I said that before."

Millicent felt ashamed of herself, as happened the whole time now. "It was very clever of you to find such a perfect place," she said immediately. "But you always do. Everything was absolutely for the best until the mushrooms came."

"I'm not really sure that they *are* mushrooms," said Winifred. "Perhaps merely fungi."

"Let's not put it to the test," said Millicent. "Let's go. Oh, I'm so sorry. You haven't finished repacking."

Duly, the ascent was far more laborious. "Tacky" was the word that Millicent's stepfather would have applied to the going.

"Why do all the cows stay clustered in one corner?" asked Millicent. "They haven't moved one leg since we arrived."

"It's to do with the flies," said Winifred knowledgeably.

"They're not waving their tails about. They're not tossing their heads. They're not lowing. In fact, they might be stuffed or modeled."

"I expect they're chewing the cud, Millicent."

"I don't think they are." Millicent, of course, really knew more of country matters than Winifred.

"I'm not sure they're there at all," said Millicent.

"Oh, hang on, Millicent," said Winifred, without, however, ceasing to plod and without even looking back at Millicent over her shoulder, let alone at the distant cows.

Millicent knew that people were being kind to her and that it was an unsuitable moment for her to make even the smallest fuss, except perhaps a fun fuss, flattering to the other party.

They reached the willful kissing gate at the bottom of the churchyard. It made its noise as soon as it was even touched and clanged back spitefully at Millicent when Winifred had passed safely through it.

Millicent had not remembered the gate's behavior on their outward trip. Probably one tackled things differently according to whether one was descending or ascending.

But—

"Winifred, look!"

Millicent, so carefully self-contained the entire day, had all but screamed. "None of that was there just now."

She could not raise her arm to point. Ahead of them, to the left of the ascending craggy path through the churchyard, was a pile of wreaths and sprays, harps wrought from lilies, red roses twisted into hearts, irises concoted into archangel trumpets. Commerce and the commemorative instinct could hardly collaborate further.

"You didn't notice it," replied Winifred upon the instant. She even added, as at another time that day she certainly would not have done, "Your mind was on other things." She then looked over her shoulder at Millicent and smiled.

"They weren't there," said Millicent, more sure of her facts than of herself. "There's been a funeral while we were by the river."

"I think we'd have heard something," replied Winifred, still smiling. "Besides, you don't bury people in the lunch hour."

"Well, something's happened."

"Last time you just didn't notice," replied Winifred, turning away and looking ahead of her at the weedy path. "That's all."

The challenge was too much for Millicent's resolutions of mousiness. "Well, did *you*?" she inquired.

But Winifred had prepared herself. "I'm not sure whether I did or didn't, Millicent. Does it matter?"

Winifred took several steps forward and then asked, "Would you rather give the church a miss?"

"Not at all," replied Millicent. "Inside there might be an explanation of some kind."

Millicent was glad she was in the rear, because at first she had difficulty in passing the banked-up tributes. They all looked so terribly new. The oblong mound beneath them was concealed, but one could scarcely doubt that it was there. At first, the flowers seemed to smell as if they were unforced and freshly picked, not like proper funerary flowers at all, which either smell not, or smell merely of accepted mortality. But then, on second thoughts, or at a second intake of Millicent's breath, the smell was not exactly as of garden or even of hedgerow flowers either. After a few seconds, the smell seemed as unaccountable as the sudden apparition of the flowers themselves. Certainly it was not in the least a smell that Millicent would have expected or could ever much care for.

She noticed that Winifred was stumping along, still looking at the battered bricks beneath her feet.

Millicent hesitated. "Perhaps we ought to inspect some of the cards?" she suggested.

That must have been a mischievous idea because this time Winifred just walked on in silence. And, as a matter of fact, Millicent had to admit to herself that she could in any case see no cards attached to the flowers, and whatever else might be attached to them.

Winifred walked silently ahead of Millicent right up to the church porch. As she entered it, a sudden bird flopped out just above her head and straight into Millicent's face.

"That's an owl," said Millicent. "We've woken him up."

She almost expected Winifred to say that for owls it was the wrong time of day, or the wrong weather, or the close season; but Winifred was, in fact, simply staring at the wooden church door.

"Won't it open?" inquired Millicent.

"I don't really know. I can see no handle."

The awakened owl had begun to hoot mournfully, which Millicent fancied really was a little odd of it in the early afternoon.

Millicent in turn stared at the door.

"There's nothing at all."

"Not even a keyhole that we can look through," said Winifred.

"I suppose the church has simply been closed and boarded up."

"I'm not sure," said Winifred. "It looks like the original door to me. Old as old, wouldn't you say? Built like that. With no proper admittance offered."

Gazing at the door, Millicent could certainly see what Winifred meant. There were no church notices either, no local address of the Samaritans, no lists of ladies to do things.

"Let's see if we can peep in through a window," proposed Winifred.

"I shouldn't think we could. It's usually pretty difficult."

"That's because there are usually lookers-on to cramp one's style. We may find it easier here."

When they emerged from the porch, Millicent surmised that there were now two owls hooting, two at least. However, the once-bright day was losing its luster, becoming middle-aged and overcast.

"God, it's muggy," said Millicent.

"I expect there's rain on the way. You know we could do with it."

"Yes, but not here, not now."

Winifred was squeezing the tips of her shoes and her feet into places where the mortar had fallen out of the church wall, and sometimes even whole flints. She was adhering to ledges and small projections. She was forcing herself upward in the attempt to look first through one window and then, upon failing and falling, through another. "I simply can't imagine what it can look like inside," she said.

They always did things thoroughly and properly, whatever the things were, but it was not a day in her life when Millicent felt like any kind of emulation. Moreover, she did not see how she could even give assistance to Winifred. They were no longer two schoolgirls, one able to hoist up the other as easily as Santa Claus's sack.

Unavailingly, Winifred had essayed two windows on the south side of the nave and one on the south side of the chancel, which three offered clear glass, however smudgy. In the two remaining windows on that side of the church, the glass was painted, and so it was with the east window. Winifred went round to the north side, with Millicent following. Here the sun did not fall, and it seemed to Millicent that the moping owls had eased off. En route the churchyard grasses had been rank and razory.

But here the masonry was further gone in decomposition, and Winifred could jump up quite readily at the first attempt.

For a surprisingly long time, or so it seemed, Winifred stared in through the easternmost window on the northern side of the nave, but speaking no word. Here many of the small panes were missing. Indeed, one pane fell into the church from somewhere with a small, sharp clatter even while Winifred was still gazing and Millicent still standing. The whole structure was in a state of molder.

At her own rather long last, Winifred descended stiffly.

She began trying to remove the aged, clinging rubble from the knees of her trousers, but the dust was damp, too, on this side of the church particularly damp.

"Want to have a look?" Winifred asked.

"What is there to see?"

"Nothing in particular." Winifred was rubbing away, though almost certainly making matters worse. "Really, nothing. I shouldn't bother."

"Then I won't," said Millicent. "You look like a pilgrim: more on her knees than on her back, or whatever it is."

"Most of the things have been taken away," continued Winifred informatively.

"In that case, where did the funeral happen? Where did they hold the service?"

Winifred went on fiddling with her trousers for a moment before attempting a reply. "Somewhere else, I suppose. That's quite common nowadays."

"There's something wrong," said Millicent. "There's something very wrong with almost everything."

They plowed back through the coarse grass to the brick path up to the porch. The owls seemed indeed to have retired once more to their carnivorous bothies.

"We must get on with things or we shall miss Baddeley," said Winifred. "Not that it hasn't all been well worthwhile, as I hope you will agree."

But—

On the path, straight before them, between the church porch and the other by now almost familiar path which ran across the descending graveyard, right in the center of things, lay a glove.

"That wasn't there either," said Millicent immediately.

Winifred picked up the glove and they inspected it together. It was a left-hand glove in black leather or kid, seemingly new or almost so, and really rather elegant. It would have been a remarkably small left hand that fitted it, Millicent thought. People occasionally remarked upon the smallness of her own hands, which was always something that pleased her. The tiny but expensive-looking body of the glove terminated in a wider, gauntletlike frill or extension of rougher design.

"We'd better hand it in," said Winifred.

"Where?"

"At the rectory, I suppose, if that is what the place is."

"Do you think we must?"

"Well, what else? We can't go off with it. It looks costly."

"There's someone else around the place," said Millicent. "Perhaps more than one of them." She could not quite have said why she thought there might be such a crowd.

But Winifred again remained silent and did not ask why.

"I'll carry the glove," said Millicent. Winifred was still bearing the rucksack and its remaining contents, including the empty half bottle, for which the graveyard offered no litter basket.

•

The carriage gate, which had once been painted in some kind of blue and was now falling apart, crossbar from socket, and spikework from woodwork, offered no clue as to whether the abode was, or had been, rectory or vicarage. The short drive was weedy and littered. Either the trees predated the mid-Victorian building, or they were prematurely senile.

The front-door bell rang quite sharply when Winifred pushed it, but nothing followed. After a longish, silent pause, with Millicent holding the glove to the fore, Winifred rang again. Again, nothing followed.

Millicent spoke: "I believe it's open."

She pushed and together they entered, merely a few steps. The hall within, which had originally been designed more or less in the Gothic manner, was furnished, though not abundantly, and seemed to be "lived in." Coming toward them, moreover, was a bent figure, female, hirsute, and wearing a discolored apron, depending vaguely.

"We found this in the churchyard," said Winifred in her clear voice, pointing to the glove.

"I can't hear the bell," said the figure. "That's why the door's left open. I lost my hearing. You know how."

Millicent knew that Winifred was no good with the deaf: so often a matter not of decibels, but presumably of psychology.

"We found this glove," she said, holding it up and speaking quite naturally.

"I can't hear anything," said the figure disappointingly. "You know why."

"We don't," said Millicent. "Why?"

But of course that could not be heard either. It was no good trying further.

The retainer, if such she was, saved the situation. "I'll go for madam," she said, and withdrew without inviting them to seat themselves on one of the haphazard sofas or uncertain-looking chairs.

"I suppose we shut the door," said Winifred, and did so.

They stood about for a little. There was nothing to look at apart from a single colored print of lambs in the Holy Land. At each corner of the frame, the fretwork made a cross, though one of the crosses had been partly broken off.

"Nonetheless, I don't think it's still the rectory," said Winifred. "Or the vicarage."

"You're right." A middle-aged woman had appeared, wearing a loose dress. The color of the dress lay between oatmeal and cream, and round the oblong neck and the ends of the elbow-length sleeves ran wide strips of a cherry hue. The woman's shoes were faded, and she had taken little trouble with her bird's-nest hair. "You're perfectly right," said the woman. "Hasn't been a clergyman here for years. There are some funny old rectories in this county, as you may have heard."

"Boreley, you mean," said Millicent, who had always been quite interested in such things.

"That place and a number of other places," said the woman. "Each little community has its specialty."

"This was a *rectory*," Winifred inquired in the way she often did, politely elevating her eyebrows, "not a vicarage?"

"They would have found it even more difficult to keep a vicar," said the woman in the most matter-of-fact way. Millicent could see there was no wedding ring on her hand. Indeed, there was no ring of any kind on either of her rather massive, rather unshaped hands. For that matter, there were no gems in her ears, no geegaws round her neck, no Castilian combs in her wild hair.

"Sit down," said the woman. "What can I do for you? My name's Stock. Pansy Stock. Ridiculous, isn't it? But it's a perfectly common name in Essex."

Winifred often went on in that very same way about "Essex," had indeed already done so more than once during the journey down, but Millicent had always supposed it to be one of Winifred's mild fancies, which it was up to her friends to indulge. She had never supposed it to have any objective metaphysic. Nor had she ever brought herself to address anyone as Pansy and was glad that the need was unlikely to arise now.

They sat, and because it seemed to be called for, Winifred introduced herself and then Millicent. Miss Stock sat upon the other sofa. She was wearing woolly midgreen stockings.

"It's simply about this glove," went on Winifred. "We explained to your servant, but we couldn't quite make her understand."

"Lettice has heard nothing since it happened. That was the effect it had on her."

"Since *what* happened?" asked Winifred. "If we may ask, that is."

"Since she was jilted, of course," answered Miss Stock.

"That sounds very sad," said Winifred in her affable and emolient way. Millicent, after all, had not exactly been jilted, not exactly. Technically, it was she who was the jilt. Socially, it still made a difference.

"It's the usual thing in this place. I've said that each community has its specialty. This is ours."

"How extraordinary!" said Winifred.

"It happens to all the females, and not only when they're still girls."

"I wonder they remain," responded Winifred smilingly.

"They don't remain. They come back."

"In what way?" asked Winifred.

"In what is known as spirit form," said Miss Stock.

Winifred considered. She was perfectly accustomed to claims of that kind, to the many sorts it takes to make a world.

"Like the willis in *Giselle*?" she inquired helpfully.

"I believe so," said Miss Stock. "I've never been inside a theater. I was brought up not to go, and I've never seen any good reason for breaking the rule."

"It's become so expensive too," said Winifred, if only because it was what she would have said in other, doubtless more conventional circumstances.

"This glove," interrupted Millicent, actually dropping it on the floor because she had no wish to hold it any longer. "We saw it lying by itself on the churchyard path."

"I daresay you did," said Miss Stock. "It's not the only thing that's been seen lying in and around the churchyard."

Winifred politely picked up the glove, rose, and placed it on Miss Stock's sofa. "We thought we should hand it in locally."

"That's good of you," said Miss Stock. "Though no one will claim it. There's a room half full of things like it. Trinkets, knicknacks, great gold hearts the size of oysters, souvenirs of all kinds, even a pair of riding boots. Things seem to appear and disappear just as they please. No one ever inquires again for them. That's not why the females come back. Of course it was a kind action on your part. Sometimes people benefit, I suppose. They say that if one finds something, or sees something, one will come back anyway." Miss Stock paused for half a second. Then she asked casually, "Which of you was it?"

At once Millicent replied, "It was I who saw the glove first, and several other things too."

"Then you'd better take the greatest possible care," said Miss Stock, still quite lightly. "Avoid all entanglements of the heart, or you may end like Lettice."

Winifred, who was still on her feet, said, "Millicent, we really must go, or we shall *never* get to Baddeley End."

Miss Stock said at once, "Baddeley End is closed all day on Thursdays. So wherever else you go, there's no point in going *there*."

"You're right about Thursdays, Miss Stock," said Winifred, "because

I looked it up most carefully in the book before we left. But this is Wednesday."

"It's not," said Millicent. "It's Thursday."

"Whatever else it may be," confirmed Miss Stock, "it indubitably is Thursday."

There was an embarrassing blank in time, while an angel flitted through the room, or perhaps a demon.

"I now realize that it is Thursday," said Winifred. She turned pale. "Millicent, I *am* sorry. I must be going mad."

"Of course there are many, many other places you can visit," said Miss Stock. "Endless places. Almost every little hamlet has something of its own to offer."

"Yes," said Winifred. "We must have a look round."

"What, then, *do* they come back for," asked Millicent, interrupting again, "if it's not for their property?"

"I didn't say it wasn't for their property. It depends *what* property. Not for their gloves or their rings or their little false thises and thats, but for their property, nonetheless. For what they *regard* as their property, anyway. One's broken heart, if it can be mended at all, can be mended only in one way."

"And yet at times," said Millicent, "the whole thing seems so trivial, so unreal. So absurd, even. Never really there at all. Utterly not worth the melodrama."

"Indubitably," said Miss Stock. "And the same is true of religious faith, or poetry, of a walk round a lake, of existence itself."

"I suppose so," said Millicent. "But personal feeling is quite particularly—" She could not find the word.

"Millicent," said Winifred. "Let's go." She seemed past conventions with their hostess. She looked white and upset. "We've got rid of the glove. Let's go."

"Tell me," said Millicent. "What *is* the one way to mend a broken heart? If we are to take the matter so seriously, we need to be told."

"Millicent," said Winifred, "I'll wait for you in the car. At the end of the drive, you remember."

"I'm flattered that you call it a drive," said Miss Stock.

Winifred opened the front door and walked out. The door flopped slowly back behind her.

"Tell me," said Millicent. "What is the one way to mend a broken heart?" She spoke as if in capital letters.

"You know what it is," said Miss Stock. "It is to kill the man who has broken it. Or at least to see to it that he dies."

"Yes, I imagined it was that," said Millicent. Her eyes were on the Palestinian lamblets.

"It is the sole possible test of whether the feeling is real," explained Miss Stock as if she were a senior demonstrator.

"Or *was* real?"

"There can be no *was*, if the feeling's real."

Millicent withdrew her gaze from the gamboling livestock. "And have you yourself taken the necessary steps? If you don't mind my asking, of course?"

"No. The matter has never arisen in my case. I live here and I look on."

"It doesn't seem a very jolly place to live."

"It's a very instructive place to live. Very cautionary. I profit greatly."

Millicent again paused for a moment, staring across the sparsely endowed room at Miss Stock in her alarming clothes.

"What, Miss Stock, would be your final words of guidance?"

"The matter is probably out of your hands by now, let alone of mine."

Millicent could not bring herself to leave it at that.

"Do girls—women—come here from outside the village? If there really is a village? My friend and I haven't seen one and the church appears to be disused. It seems to have been disused for a very long time."

"Of course there's a village," said Miss Stock quite fiercely. "And the church is not *entirely* disused, I assure you. And there are cows and a place where they are kept; and a river and a bridge. All the normal things, in fact, though, in each case, with a local emphasis, as is only right and proper. And, yes, females frequently come from outside the village. They find themselves here, often before they know it. Or so I take it to be."

Millicent rose.

"Thank you, Miss Stock, for bearing with us and for taking in our glove."

"Perhaps something of your own will be brought to me one day," remarked Miss Stock.

"Who knows?" replied Millicent, entering into the spirit, as she regularly tried to do.

Millicent detected a yellow collecting box on a broken table to the right of the front door. In large black letters a label proclaimed JOSEPHINE BUTLER AID FOR UNFORTUNATES. From her trousers pocket Millicent extracted a contribution. She was glad she did not have to grope ridiculously through a handbag while Miss Stock smiled and waited.

Miss Stock had risen to her feet but had not advanced to see Millicent out. She merely stood there, a little dimly.

"Good-bye, Miss Stock."

In the front door, as with many rectories and vicarages, there were two large panes of glass, frosted overall but patterned *en clair* round the edge, so that in places one could narrowly see through to the outer world. About to pull the door open, which Winifred had left unlatched, Millicent apprehended the shape of a substantial entity standing noiselessly without. It was simply one thing too many. For a second time that day, Millicent found it difficult not to scream. But Miss Stock was in the mistiness behind her, and Millicent drew the door open.

"Nigel, my God!"

Millicent managed to pull fast the door behind her. Then his arms enveloped her, as ivy was enveloping the little church.

"I'm having nothing more to do with you. How did you know I was here?"

"Winifred told me, of course."

"I don't believe you. She's sitting in her car anyway, just by the gate. I'll ask her."

"She's not," said Nigel. "She's left."

"She can't have left. She was waiting for me. Please let me go, Nigel."

"I'll let you go, and then you can see for yourself."

They walked side by side in silence down the depressing, weedy drive. Millicent wondered whether Miss Stock was watching them through the narrow, distorting streaks of machine-cut glass.

There was no Winifred and no car. Thick brown leaves were strewn over the place where the car had stood. It seemed to Millicent for a moment as if the car had been buried there.

"Never mind, my dear. If you behave yourself, I'll drive you home."

"I can't see your car either." It was a notably inadequate rejoinder, but at least spontaneous.

"Naturally not. It's hidden."

"Why is it hidden?"

"Because I don't want you careering off in it and leaving me behind. You've tried to ditch me once, and once is enough for any human being."

"I didn't *try* to ditch you, Nigel. I completed the job. You were smashing up my entire life."

"Not your life, sweet. Only your idiot career, so-called."

"*Not* only."

"Albeit, I shan't leave you to walk home."

"Not home. Only to the station. I know precisely where it is. Winifred pointed it out. She saw it on the map. She said there are still trains."

"You really can't rely on Winifred."

Millicent knew that this was a lie. Whatever had happened to Winifred, Nigel was lying. Almost everything he said was a lie, more or less. Years ago it had been among the criteria by which she had realized how deeply and truly she loved him.

"You can't always rely on maps either," said Nigel.

"What's happened to Winifred?" How absurd and schoolgirlish she always seemed in her own eyes when trying to reach anything like equal terms with Nigel! The silly words leapt to her lips without her choosing or willing them.

"She's gone. Let's do a little sightseeing before we drive home. You can tell me about the crockets and finials. It will help to calm us down."

Again he put his arm tightly round her and, despite her half-simulated resistance, pushed and pulled her through the kissing gate into the church-yard. Her resistance was half-simulated because she knew from experience how useless with Nigel was anything more. He knew all the tricks by which at school big boys pinion and compel small ones, and he had never hesitated to use them against Millicent, normally, of course, upon a more or less agreed basis of high spirits, good fun, and knowing better than she what it would be sensible for them to do next. His frequent use of real and serious physical force had been another thing that had attracted her.

He dragged her down the uneven path. "Beautiful place. Peaceful. Silent as the grave."

And, indeed, it *was* quiet now, singularly different in small ways from when Millicent had been there with Winifred. Not only the owls but all the hedgerow birds had ceased to utter. One could not even detect an approaching aircraft. The breeze had dropped, and all the long grass looked dead or painted.

"Tell me about the architecture," said Nigel. "Tell me what to look at."

"The church is shut," said Millicent. "It's been closed for years."

"Then it shouldn't be," said Nigel. "Churches aren't meant to be shut. We'll have to see."

He propelled her up the path where earlier she had first seen the glove. The hand that belonged to it must be very nearly the hand of a child: Millicent realized that now.

In the porch, Nigel sat her down upon the single battered wooden bench, perhaps at one time borrowed from the local school, when there had been a local school. "Don't move, or I'll catch you one. I'm not having you leave me again, yet a while."

Nigel set about examining the church door, but really there was little to examine. The situation could be taken in very nearly at a glance and a push.

Nigel took a couple of steps back and massed himself sideways. Wasting no time, he had decided to charge the door, to break it down. Quite possibly it was already rickety, despite appearances.

But that time Millicent really did scream.

"No!"

The noise she had made seemed all the shriller when bursting upon the remarkable quietness that surrounded them. She could almost certainly have been heard in the erstwhile rectory, even though not by poor Lettice. Millicent had quite surprised herself. She was an unpracticed screamer.

She had even deflected Nigel for a moment.

She expostulated further. "Don't! Please don't!"

"Why not, chicken?" Almost beyond doubt, his surprise was largely real.

"If you want to, climb up outside and look in through the window, first." The volume and quality of her scream had given her a momentary ascendancy over him. "The other side of the church is easier."

He was staring at her. "All right. If you say so."

They went outside without his even holding on to her.

"No need to go round to the back," said Nigel. "I can manage perfectly well here. So can you, for that matter. Let's jump up together."

"No," said Millicent.

"Please yourself," said Nigel. "I suppose you've seen the bogey already. Or is it the black mass?" He was up in a single spring and adhering to nothing visible, like an ape. His head was sunk between his shoulders as he peered, so that his red curls made him resemble a larger Quasimodo, who, Millicent recollected, was always clinging to Gothic walls and descrying.

Nigel flopped down in silence. "I see what you mean," he said upon landing. "Not in the least a sight for sore eyes. Not a sight for little girls at all. Or even for big ones." He paused for a moment, while Millicent omitted to look at him. "All right. What else is there? Show me. Where do we go next?"

He propelled her back to the path across the churchyard and they began to descend toward the river.

It was, therefore, only another moment or two before Millicent realized that the pile of wreaths was no longer there: no sprays, no harps, no hearts, no angelic trumpets; only a handful of field flowers bound with common string. For a moment Millicent merely doubted her eyes yet again, though not only her eyes.

"Don't think they use this place any longer," said Nigel. "Seems full up to me. That would explain whatever it is that's been going on in the church. What happens if we go through that gate?"

"There's a big meadow with cows in it and then a sort of passage down to the river."

"*What* sort of passage?"

"It runs between briars, and it's muddy."

"We don't mind a little mud, do we, rooster? What's the river called, anyway?"

"Winifred says it's called the Waste."

"Appropriate," said Nigel. "Though not anymore, I hasten to add, not anymore."

It was exactly as he said it that Millicent noticed the headstone. "Nigel Alsopp Ormathwaite Ticknor. Strong, Patient, and True. Called to Higher Service." And a date. No date of birth: only the one date. That day's date.

The day that she had known to be a Thursday when Winifred had not.

The stone was in gray granite, or perhaps near granite. The section of it bearing the inscription had been planed and polished. When she had been here last, Millicent had been noticing little, and on the return from the picnic the inscription would not have confronted her in any case, as was shown by its confronting her now.

"Not anymore," said Nigel a third time. "Let's make it up yet again, henny."

At least, Millicent stopped. She was staring at the inscription. Nigel's hands and arms were in no way upon or around her or particularly near her.

"I love you, chickpeas," said Nigel. "That's the trouble, isn't it? We got on better when I didn't."

Seldom had Nigel been so clear-sighted. It was eerie. Still, the time of which he spoke was another thing that had been long, long ago.

"I don't know what to say," said Millicent. What other words were possible? No longer were they children, or young people, or anything at all like that.

They went forward a few paces so that the headstone now stood behind Millicent. She did not turn to see whether there were words upon the back of it.

Nigel went through the second kissing gate ahead of her. "Don't you

bother," he said. "I expect you've been down to the river with Winifred.
I know you won't run away now. I'll just take a quick peek at the fishing."

However, there seemed by now no point in not following him, and
Millicent pushed back the gate in her turn.

"Please yourself," said Nigel.

But Millicent had become aware of a development. The animals for-
merly in the far and upper corner were now racing across the open space
toward Nigel and her, and so silently that Nigel had not so much as
noticed them: "cows," she had described them, when speaking of them
to Winifred; "stock," as her stepfather might have termed them. There
is always an element of the absurd about British domestic animals be-
having as if they were in the Wild West. Still, this time it was an element
that might be overlooked.

"Nigel!" exclaimed Millicent, and drew back through the gate, which
clanged away from her.

"Nigel!!"

He went sturdily on. We really should not be frightened of domestic
animals in fields. Moreover, so quiet were these particular fields that
Nigel still seemed unaware of anything moving other than himself.

"Nigel!!!"

The animals were upon him and leaving little doubt of their intentions,
insofar as the last word was applicable. In no time, on the grass and on
the hides, there was blood, and worse than blood. Before long, there was
completely silent but visibly most rampageous trampling. Tails were raised
now, and eyes untypically stark. But the mob of beasts, by its mere mass,
probably concealed the worst from Millicent.

Seek help. That is what one is called upon to do in these cases. At
the least, call for help. Millicent, recently so vocal, found that she could
make no noise. The grand quietness had taken her in as well.

"Oh, Nigel, love."

But soon the animals were merely nuzzling around interestedly. It was
as if they had played no part in the consummation toward which they
were sniffing and over which they were slobbering.

Millicent clung to the iron gate. Never before that day had she screamed.
Never yet in her life had she fainted.

Then she became aware that the churchyard had somehow filled with
women, or, at least, that women were dotted here and there among the
mounds and memorials, sometimes in twos, threes, and fours, though
more commonly as single spies.

These women were not like the willis in Winifred's favorite ballet.
They were bleak and commonplace and often not young at all. Millicent

could not feel herself drawn to them. But she realized that they were not merely in the churchyard but in the meadow, too, from which the tempestuous cattle seemed to have withdrawn while for a second her back had been turned. In fact, at that moment the women were just about everywhere.

Absurd, absurd. Even now Millicent could not overlook that element. The whole business simply could not be worth all this, and, in the world around her, everyone knew that it was not. Sometimes one suffered acutely, yes, but not even the suffering was ever quite real, let alone the events and experience supposedly suffered over. Life was not entirely, or even mainly, a matter of walking round a lake, if one might adopt Miss Stock's persuasive analogy.

Nonetheless, it must have been more or less at this point that Millicent somehow lost consciousness.

Winifred was looking from above into her face. Winifred was no longer pale, but nearly her usual color, and renewed in confidence.

"My dear Millicent, I should have put you to bed instead of taking you out into the country! How on earth did you come to fall asleep?"

"Where are the cows?"

Winifred looked through the ironwork of the gate into the field behind her. "Not there, as far as I can see. I expect they've gone to be milked."

"They're not really cows at all, Winifred. Not ordinary cows."

"My dear girl!" Winifred looked at her hard, then seemed more seriously concerned. "Have you been attacked? Or frightened?"

"Not *me*," said Millicent.

"Then who?"

Millicent gulped and drew herself together.

"It was a dream. Merely a dream. I'd rather not talk about it."

"Poor sweet, you must be worn out. But how did you get down here? Have you been sleepwalking?"

"I was taken. That was part of the dream."

"It was shocking, that Stock woman going on as she did. You should have closed your ears."

"And eyes," said Millicent.

"I expect so," said Winifred, smiling. "It was a hideous place. If you're fully awake now, I expect you'd like to go? I've made a mess of the whole day."

"I couldn't see the car. I was looking for it."

"I moved it. I wanted to be out of sight. You couldn't have supposed I'd driven it through the churchyard."

"Anything seems possible," said Millicent as they walked up the slope. "Anything. For example, you saw all those flowers. You saw them with your own eyes. Where are they?"

"They've been taken off to some hospital. It's what people do after funerals nowadays."

"And the mushrooms down by the river?"

"They were there from the first, as I told you."

"And Miss Stock's stories?"

"She just needs a man. Oh, I'm sorry, Millicent."

"And the inside of the church?"

"That was really rather nasty. I'm not going to talk about it, I'm not even going to think about it, and I'm certainly not going to let you look at it."

"Oughtn't whatever it is to be reported somewhere?"

"Not by me," said Winifred with finality.

As they had passed for the last time through the gate leading out of the churchyard, Winifred had said, "We're going home as quickly as possible. I'm taking you to my place, and I'm putting you to bed with a sedative. I don't really know about this kind of trouble, but I've seen what I've seen, and what you need in the first place is a good, long sleep, I'm sure of it."

Millicent herself knew that grief, especially repressed grief, was said to induce second sight, let alone second thoughts.

Nonetheless, Millicent woke up at just before half past eleven. Long ago, in the early days with Nigel, one of them had each night telephoned the other at that time, and often they had conversed until midnight, when it had been agreed that the closure be applied. Such simplicities had come to an end years and years before, but on no evening since she had given up Nigel had Millicent gone to bed before that particular hour.

There was little chance of Nigel even remembering the old, sentimental arrangement and less chance of his now having anything easeful to say to her. Still, Millicent, having looked at her watch, lay there sedated and addled, but awake; and duly the telephone rang.

An extension led to the bedside in Winifred's cozy spare room. Winifred herself could not relax in a room without a telephone.

Millicent had the receiver in her hand at the first half ping of the delicate little bell.

"Hello," said Millicent softly to the darkness. Winifred had drawn all the curtains quite tight, since that was the way Winifred liked her own room at night.

"Hello," said Millicent softly, a second time. At least it could hardly now be a call for Winifred. It was all the more important not to waken her.

On the line, or at the other end of it, something seemed to stir. There could be little doubt of it. It was not a mere reflex of the mechanism.

"Hello," repeated Millicent softly.

Third time lucky, because at last there was a reply.

"Hello, feathers," said Nigel.

In all the circumstances, Millicent could not possibly just ring off, as rationally she should have done. "Are you all right?" she asked.

"What a sight you look in Winifred's nightwear. Not your style at all, crop."

Every inch of Millicent's flesh started simultaneously to fall inward. "Nigel! Where are you?"

"I'm right outside your door, gizzard. Better come at once. But do wear your own pajamas. The scarlet ones. The proper ones."

"I'm not coming, Nigel. I've told you that. I mean it."

"I'm sure you mean it since you left me to be trodden upon by a lot of bloody heifers without doing one thing except grin. It makes no difference. Less difference than ever, in fact. I want you and I'm waiting outside your door now."

She simply couldn't speak. What could she possibly say?

"You come to me, three toes," said Nigel, "*and* wearing your own clothes. Or, make no mistake, I'm coming to you."

The receiver fell from Millicent's hand. It crashed to the bedroom floor, but the carpet in Winifred's guest bedroom was substantial, and Winifred heard nothing. In any case, Winifred herself had just passed a trying day also and needed her rest before the demands of life on the morrow, the renewed call of the wild.

A group of concerned friends, male and female, clustered round Winifred after the inquest, for which a surprising number had taken time off.

"I have never been in love," said Winifred. "I really don't understand about it."

People had to accept that and get on with things, routine and otherwise. What else could they do?

STILLBORN

MIKE CONNER

Mike Conner lives in California with his wife and four children and says he is probably the only writer of science fiction and fantasy to emerge from Hopkins, Minnesota, the raspberry capital of the world. Mr. Conner's excellent stories for *F & SF* have all examined the shadowy, hidden sides of what appear, at first glance, to be benign, although perhaps uncomfortable, situations; what emerges from those shadows, however, is malignant. "Stillborn" tells the story of Claudia Fenster, a newcomer to a southern Missouri mining town, and of her exposure to the glitter of its social life and the darkness of its caverns . . . and secrets.

"I'm afraid that dress won't do, my dear," said Mrs. Phillip Ash. "Have you an extra shawl in your carriage?"

Claudia Fenster groaned inwardly at the sharp-faced older woman's critical appraisal. It was a typically hot and oppressive August day in southern Missouri, and she had worn a dress of light poplin, never dreaming it might not be appropriate.

"No," she said. "I came in the trolley." Why hadn't her husband, who had inspected Claudia the way a captain inspected his troops before he allowed her to leave the house, warned her that the dress wasn't right?

It wasn't dark and heavy as the stuff Mrs. Ash and the other three ladies of the Wednesday Afternoon Club wore. Claudia felt the color rising to her cheeks, but another of the ladies, Mrs. Elly Corporan, smiled sympathetically.

"Don't worry, my dear, I have one for you. Olivia is concerned about your catching a chill when we go down to the caverns."

"Caverns?"

"The Crystal Caverns," Mrs. Phillip Ash snapped. "We generally have our cards there all summer, unless it is raining and not too hot here. You don't fear close quarters, do you, Mrs. Fenster?"

Claudia relaxed some. "I have entered my husband's tunnels on occasion without ill effect."

"Good. Because you would be surprised at how many women whose husbands derive their wealth from the earth swoon at the notion of being swallowed up anywhere near a hole in the ground. Ah! There's Jimbo with the carriage. Ladies."

Mrs. Ash took the front seat with the wife of the Baptist minister, Mrs. Burgess, while Claudia sat behind, between Mrs. Corporan and Mrs. Titus Blakely, for the short trip along East Street to the mouth of the Crystal Caverns. Jimbo drove them slowly, so that the common citizens could see the ladies who held the prosperity of Corinth in their grasp. The husbands of Mmes. Ash and Corporan and Blakely had many years ago formed the companies which mined zinc and sulfur and galenite and white lead from the limestone strata beneath the town. In the first days they had employed oxen; now they used steam and even electricity to sustain this town. Thirty years before, Corinth had been little more than a wagon stop on a two-rut road west toward the Oklahoma Indian country.

The sun beat through the haze fearsomely, however, and even Mrs. Ash quickly grew tired of showing herself to the few people out on the street. Jimbo snapped the reins; a few moments later he pulled them up underneath the merciful shade of some hickory trees.

"You'll want this, I promise you." Mrs. Corporan smiled, pressing a crocheted wrap into Claudia's hand as they came from the carriage. While the ladies waited to one side, Jimbo opened a circuit box on a pole and threw a switch.

"Electric lights," Mrs. Blakely said proudly. Her husband had formed the Southern Missouri Mazda Lamp Company six years before. Except for St. Louis and Springfield, Corinth led the whole of the state in numbers of electric lights and machines. All the streetcar lines were being converted from horse to electric power too.

"The path is smooth, my dear, but keep one hand on the wall of the cave. We don't descend very far—else Reverend Burgess would not allow his wife to join us!" The other ladies laughed as though Mrs. Ash had said the funniest thing in the world. Then they all proceeded on the path through the opening in the limestone bank.

At first, the way seemed to lead to absolute darkness in spite of the bright bulbs strung above the way. But then Claudia's eyes began to adjust and she could detect a faint sparkling on the opposite wall of the cave, and the dagger tips of long stalactites which hung from the roof. They had not gone very far before it became hard for Claudia to believe there was a hot Missouri town above them. This was a silent world, cool and peaceful, with a breeze of its own running through the passages like the sigh of the earth herself.

Finally they reached a place with more lights, where a table for cards had been erected and there was even a sideboard with glasses and silver for the sweets and lemonade Jimbo had brought down in a hamper. Claudia looked at it all with wonder.

"Don't you fear thieves, Mrs. Ash?"

"The sort of people who resort to thievery usually are afraid of spooks and such and won't come into a place like this even with the lights on. I had to beat Jimbo to get him to come the first time. Didn't I, Jimbo?"

"Yes'um."

"You come back the usual time. And mind you, don't go wearing down the horses!"

Mrs. Ash sat down. The other ladies took it as their signal to do likewise. Claudia could not help looking around at the wonderful formations of rock which lay half hidden in the stark shadows thrown off by the Mazda lamps. What a wonderful place this was! She could easily imagine rubies or whole diamonds the size of her fist that could be scooped from the walls with a spoon. Who had first found this place, she wondered. Some lone traveling Indian, perhaps, seeking shelter from a storm?

"I asked, dear, what sort of game you prefer?"

"I'm sorry, Mrs. Ash." Claudia felt the others were not at all interested in where they were, and thus it would be impolite to remark on the natural wonder of this parlor in the earth. "I do like hearts."

"Unfortunately, we are five. Do you know canasta?"

"A little."

"Then that is what we shall deal." As she ruffled the cards, Claudia noticed that Mrs. Ash's voice—and those of the other ladies as well—seemed louder here, ringing harshly from the walls of the cave. And in the electric light, their complexions and features seemed like line drawings—though Claudia was certain hers must look equally pallorous as well. Mrs. Ash finished dealing the hand, and the game began.

"You are from Michigan, I believe?" Mrs. Burgess asked.

"Until I was married, I lived in Saginaw. Then Mr. Fenster and I took a residence near his business in Uniontown, Pennsylvania." She smiled. "Until he made his decision to purchase the tripoli enterprise here."

"Your husband makes water filters." Mrs. Ash said. It was not a question.

"And grinds tripoli into all manner of rouge and rottenstone for use in the glass and metal polishing trade. It really is an amazing material.

"In the olden days we called it chat. There's piles of it alongside any road you take leaving town."

"Your husband is to be commended for finding a use for it," Mrs. Corporan said kindly. Claudia, meanwhile, had trouble following which cards had been played and could do nothing to organize her hand, and soon the round was won by Mrs. Burgess. She took the deal and play resumed.

"Dear Mrs. Fenster, I should warn you that we try to leave convention a little behind when we come to play here. So I hope you won't be shocked if I should try to satisfy my curiosity. It's one I have cultivated ever since Phillip made your husband's acquaintance last fall. How is it he has married a girl so young as you?"

In spite of the warning, Claudia was a little shocked. Perhaps it was the strange way voices sounded in these caverns, but in Mrs. Ash's voice there seemed a distinct accusatory tone.

"Perhaps she craves tripoli," Mrs. Blakely said, and the others laughed. Claudia waited for it to subside.

"My husband was a widower, of long acquaintance with my father. They were comrades in a Pennsylvania regiment during the Great War. Both my father and my husband learned the transport trade during their service."

"Abolitionists, were they?" Mrs. Ash asked sharply.

Claudia very carefully answered, "They worked as expediters and semaphore operators."

"Then your husband was a clerk! Mercy me, ladies, it is a comfort to know we shall all be safe in our beds. Mrs. Fenster excepted, of course!" She poured herself a tumbler of lemonade and drank. "But you still did not explain how love blossomed between you. Where were all the eager boys of Saginaw?"

Claudia felt her heart pounding. They were all looking at her, waiting for her answer. A cold draft swept through the cavern with a faint whining sound which came through a small opening in a passage that was walled off with boards.

"Mrs. Ash, my marriage was an arrangement between my father and my husband to which I gave my full consent—for both their sakes. Being long without a wife and childless, my husband naturally wished for a wife who could bear him an heir—" She halted, wishing she could take back the words. Was that glee in Mrs. Phillip Ash's face?

"Of course we were aware of your difficulty in the spring. It must be very difficult to lose a child, difficult indeed." The cave wind rose, so that the sound became like a cry. Suddenly, Claudia felt chilled to her very bones. Mrs. Ash put a cold hand upon her wrist.

"Ah, but you have youth on your side. Youth conquers all afflictions. I dare say you'll soon have an entire regiment of powder grinders running underfoot."

She knows! The thought that Mrs. Ash was being deliberately cruel sickened her, and she suddenly stood. "Ladies, I beg your pardon, but the chill is really too much. Next time I shall have to dress for this place; thank you for asking me along, Mrs. Ash." Claudia turned away from the surprised women and took the path back up to the surface. The heat met her at the mouth of the cave with the force of a blow, but, somehow, Claudia found it a blessed relief.

"And so you ran away, like some silly schoolgirl? It's beyond belief, by God!" Ulysses Fenster poured himself a bourbon and adjusted his considerable girth in the direction of his wife, who had been weeping in a chair.

"I don't like them! The only woman there with any sympathy at all was Elly Corporan, but all of them are cowed by Mrs. Ash, and I will not be."

Fenster's cheeks grew red, as they invariably did when he became angry. "I have explained to you, Claudia, that our acceptance into the so-called society of this miserable town rests entirely with that woman! I'm not asking you to embrace her, but surely you can be amusing for an hour or two and demonstrate to her that you do have some modicum of breeding and poise!"

"She mocked you, Ulysses! She practically accused you of robbing the cradle, and me of seducing a foolish old man for my own gain. Was I to smile sweetly and say, 'Of course, Mrs. Ash, how amusing you are to outline such a comedy'? She'd think me weak if I didn't rise to your defense!"

"I do not require defending!" Fenster roared. "I have thus far survived the barbs of my fellow man without your assistance, and I dare say I'll continue. By God, Claudia, if you cannot give me a child, at least help me secure a place in society!"

Claudia looked up defiantly, tears filling her eyes. "I would spare you," she said, "but Mrs. Ash knows I can have no more children and she made light of it to her friends. None of them opposed her! None . . ." She collapsed into tears. Ulysses Fenster put down his glass and, looking crestfallen, knelt beside the chair.

"Claudia . . . child, I am sorry if it's true. Even her husband will agree that his wife is difficult. But don't you see she is trying to test you, to gauge your character?"

"I will not be judged by her!"

"And you shall not be, in the end. But consider how much easier life will be once we are finally accepted here. My business will prosper— and then we shall have a fine house in Carthage with a proper staff and electric lights, perhaps even a motorcar!"

"Can Mrs. Ash bring me a child?" She saw her husband's stricken expression and immediately regretted what she had said. No one had been more considerate and kind to her than Ulysses during her convalescence following her fateful and tragically unsuccessful pregnancy. Claudia touched his face.

"I promise you I shall try again. I am worth a dozen of Mrs. Phillip Ash!"

"That's the girl!" Ulysses checked his watch. "Well, I must be off to the Eagle's Club. Shall I tell Ash his wife may expect you next week?"

"If she wants me, yes!" She kissed him, and he was gone. Claudia could not help wishing that Mrs. Ash would not want her again, ever.

But she did. This time Claudia dressed in dark blue satin, with bloomers and a camisole underneath against the chill of the caverns. She rode the trolley to her destination, with the window thrown wide open, fanning herself and resisting a comic urge to pant like a dog in the back of a wagon. By the time she reached her stop on East Street, she was very grateful for the opportunity to escape the heat, if only for an hour or two. There would be heat of a different sort waiting for her in the person of Mrs. Ash, but the intervening week since she had last played cards had given Claudia time to prepare herself. She had long since accepted the death of her child, though it pained her because of the waste of that or any life. Why then should she be bothered by Mrs. Ash's cruelty in mentioning it, as though the death were Claudia's fault? God had a reason for taking the baby's life, and it was not for Claudia or Mrs. Ash to question His wisdom. Firm in her faith, Claudia entered the Crystal Caverns confidently.

The lights had been turned on, but the caverns were empty. Claudia mopped her forehead with a handkerchief and breathed deeply of the cool, refreshing air. The cave sighed in return.

Suddenly, as she had the week before, Claudia felt a strong draft stir the folds of her skirt, and a sound like a cry that seemed to come from beyond the boarded-up passageway. Claudia listened closely, unsure of what she heard. It could have just been the natural vibration of wind passing through spaces between the boards. Yet, there was something about the pitch that gave the sound an eerie, almost human character. Fascinated, Claudia made her way carefully to the spot, putting her hands on the boards and discovering that several of them were loose. She could feel air blowing through them against her fingertips, but now she was convinced that the sound, whatever it was, originated well beyond the barrier. At the same time, she realized it was not exactly like a whistle of wind either. There was a hitch in it, as though the cavern must take its next breath.

Like the caverns are crying, she thought, pulling at one of the loose boards. Then, all at once, something was pulling on her, and she let out a scream.

Jimbo, Mrs. Ash's driver, stared at her.

"You got no business with that, Mis' Fenster."

"I'm sorry!" She laughed quickly to mask her shock. "I suppose I'm a bit early and—well, I suppose it's the child in me that insists on exploring places like this." Claudia touched the boards again. "Can you tell me why this barrier's here?"

"The pit's in there."

"The pit?"

"Some of the folks call it Indian Hell. It's a place where there ain't no bottom. You toss a rock off the ledge and you never hear it drop. Too many children lost here. Mis' Ash lost her little girl here, crawled in and fell, folks say."

"That's awful!"

"It put a change on her. Always does, something like that. When the earth swallows somethin' up, folks gotta suffer. You hear what I'm saying."

"Of course," Claudia said, wanting him to go away. She did not really think he was dangerous, but deep in this cave she felt anything could happen.

"You was right to run outa here last week, mis'."

"I don't believe that's any of your concern!" she snapped, face suddenly hot in spite of the cool draft from the passage. Jimbo hardly blinked; he might have been made of stone himself.

"You'll leave these caves again. Mind you take the right way." He turned away as Claudia was about to ask what he had meant. Just then the other ladies—with the exception of Mrs. Burgess, who had the croup and could not come—came down the path. Claudia took a place next to Elly Corporan and steeled herself against some new assault by Mrs. Ash, but that lady now seemed very cordial and even allowed Claudia to deal a game of hearts. After several hands Mrs. Ash produced a cut-glass bottle from the hamper Jimbo had brought down and poured glasses for all.

"This is brandy flavored with verbena and lemon—a concoction my husband swears is a poison! But I believe it has a beneficial effect upon the respiration. Ladies!"

Claudia sipped as the others drank. Apparently it was the habit of the wednesday Afternoon Society to indulge when Mrs. Burgess was not present, and Claudia perceived the impression that the preacher's wife had withdrawn today out of consideration for that custom. Soon laughter echoed through the caverns, and the play grew sloppier. The discussion turned to various ladies of the town and the grand Miners' Ball to be held within the fortnight at the new Connor Hotel. Claudia did her best to maintain her interest in the proceedings, though the wine had made her dizzy. Occasionally, above the sound of laughter and the slap of cards, she heard the crying noise. Each time it sounded more and more lifelike, and she could not help but think of Mrs. Ash's child and her terrible fate. To fall, tumbling, into the blackness without hope . . .

At last Mrs. Ash declared the session adjourned for the day. Claudia walked unsteadily back to the surface with a pang of regret, for today she had felt safe and comfortable—and, yes, invulnerable too. Perhaps Mrs. Ash sensed it and was wise enough to renew her challenge at another time and place, for in spite of that lady's seeming friendliness—or perhaps because of it—Claudia in no way felt she had been accepted or approved the way her husband wished.

What do they want from me, she thought, boarding the trolley. Perhaps if she could suddenly become old and dried-up and barren as they were. Surely she qualified for the last point; the other two she could do nothing about.

The heat and the sound of trolley car wheels began to make her drowsy. Almost against her will she was pulled into fitful sleep, where she saw the look of terror on Ulysses's face when her labor had begun with a gush of waters during dinner. He thought she had damaged herself somehow and had practically beaten the housemaid to death urging her to go fetch the young physician, Dr. Vincent, and then Claudia's labor had begun in earnest, hours of back spasms that no amount of pillows underneath her could relieve. Claudia had closed her eyes and tried to regulate the pressure by thinking of the baby this effort—for it was more work than pain until the end—would bring her. Ulysses, whey-faced and gasping, had valiantly held her hand until at last the handsome Dr. Vincent had arrived to take control of the delivery, telling her she had not long to go, urging her to conserve her energy, ordering the maid to bring compresses for her head and chipped ice to relieve her burning throat.

And then he said, "We're ready now, Claudia—" She remembered quite clearly, remembered smiling and how her heart soared for the final effort of pushing her child free. She watched his face as he probed with his fingers to guide the infant's head through the birth passage and give its shoulders the half twist that would free it from Claudia's body. He was intent, concentrating, a look of power and confidence on his features, until, suddenly, his mastery faltered, and Vincent became as frightened as her obese old husband.

Claudia gave a final push and felt the euphoria and relief of birth, saw, for an instant, the baby in Vincent's hands and a glimpse of dark, wet hair. "Oh, let me hold him, let me—" But Vincent gave a tight-lipped shake of his head and covered the child in a blanket after severing the cord, gave the bundle to the maid with a terse instruction that Claudia could not quite hear.

"Why can't I see the baby!" she'd screamed.

"You've got to rest. I'm giving you a powder now, to help you sleep. Afterward, I'll be back to speak with you."

Claudia struggled, kicking and screaming until at last Vincent poured ether into a handerchief and held it over her mouth, a sensation she would never forget, one of drowning, of falling utterly away from her baby, the little hands stretching toward her, trying to hold her but failing with a cry that was like the sound of wind, the last sigh of a summer storm, cold and trembling and moist.

She had never seen her child. Claudia slept for a day and a night, and when she awoke it was to Dr. Vincent again, agonized with the respon-sibility of telling her the babe had been stillborn and that she must not risk having children again because of some incompatibility between her blood and that of the child that had eventually killed the babe while it was still in the womb. The tiny casket at the funeral was sealed. Claudia had not been allowed to see the body, and yet when she tried to lift the casket top, the whole box had tilted, and it seemed so light, as though it were empty.

What had they done with her baby?

The sound of the Crystal Caverns came to her, and she realized with a shiver that she had heard that same cry the moment the doctor had put ether on her face. . . .

"Ma'am?"

She sat upright, bumping her head against the trolley window. The conductor smiled at her. "End of the line, ma'am."

"End of the line . . ." She rubbed her eyes with her fingertips. "Oh, dear, I've missed my stop. Where are we?"

"Electric Park, ma'am. Northern terminus. I'll be turning around in eight minutes if you want to ride back."

"No . . . no, thank you. I think I'll walk for a while."

"We'll be running until the park closes at ten-thirty."

Claudia thanked him again and stepped down from the car. Though it was barely past suppertime, the park was crowded with children and people looking for a few hours' recreation after a long day in the mines or factories. For, although Electric Park was regularly the subject of fiery sermons from all the church pulpits of Corinth, it was in truth more popular than the churches, with its amusement arcades that featured a ride called the Washtub—"the most terrifying attraction in all Missouri!"—its beautiful Rose Grotto, and, most famous of all, the Electric Tower, a tribute to the zinc and sulfur and lead mining that made the storage of electricity in batteries possible. The tower was two hundred feet tall and carried over 80,000 Mazda lamps which, when kindled at dusk, threw off a beacon of light that could be seen for fifty miles. Even in daylight the tower was an impressive structure. This was the first time Claudia had ever seen it, for her husband had declared Electric Park to be patronized by the lowest orders of Corinth and had refused to take her there.

At any rate, the crowds made her feel better somehow. The people seemed happy, and there was joyful music from the big steam carrousel and the smell of popcorn and frankfurter sausages. Claudia watched a young couple pushing their baby carriage, and though it pained her, her heart went out to them.

She saw the entrance to the Rose Grotto and hurried toward it, for the baby had begun to cry and it had reminded her of her awful dream and the sounds she had heard in the caverns. *I wish I were stronger,* she thought a little desperately, shaken that the recovery which seemed certain a month ago seemed to be disintegrating rapidly.

"Mrs. Fenster! Is that you?"

Claudia turned, and to her dismay recognized Dr. Vincent. He smiled affably, looking handsome in an off-white suit and straw boater. She smiled as bravely as she could.

"You're looking very well! Are you here alone?" He gazed over her shoulder, searching for her husband. There had been an ugly scene between them on that awful night, and Vincent did not relish the prospect of seeing Ulysses Fenster once more. However, she put his mind at ease.

"I'm afraid I fell asleep on the trolley and came here by accident."

"Seeing you strikes my conscience hard, Mrs. Fenster. I had intended looking in on you, but your husband . . . objected to my seeing you again professionally."

Her face clouded as she was reminded of her vivid dream. She could almost smell the ether. "Perhaps he needed to fix responsibility for what happened, Doctor. So it would make some sense to him."

Vincent nodded. They began to stroll and entered the grotto. The blooms were not as numerous as earlier in the season, but there was color enough, and lovely fragrance.

"And you, Mrs. Fenster. Did you fix blame?"

"I took it myself. It seemed the easiest thing to do."

"Mrs. Fenster, I want you to know that if I had not been removed as your physician, I would have advised you to try to have another baby. I believe chances for a successful pregnancy would be good."

"Do you rely on intuition?"

"Statistics, ma'am. Diseases of the blood sometimes show a mathematical pattern in families. We don't know why, but you and your husband may have simply been unlucky."

"Yes. But please, don't speak of it. Really, I have quite forgotten about my affliction."

"Of course. Forgive me."

She turned to him suddenly. "Dr. Vincent, was the baby well formed? I know it had dark hair, but were the eyes like mine? Did Monica—" it was the first time Claudia had ever used the child's baptismal name— "did she resemble either of her parents?"

"Mrs. Fenster, please—"

"No!" She struggled to keep her voice steady. "No, you see, Doctor, when you saw fit to . . . help me to sleep, I thought for a moment I might have heard something, a squeak, a cry from the other room where you'd taken her, and I wanted to go there!"

"It was best that you didn't see. You had suffered enough already!"

"But for what! Doctor, I had a right to see that baby! I believe that I wouldn't be so plagued now if I had been able to rest my mind, to see her face, to see her lying peacefully—"

Vincent tilted his head. "Plagued, Mrs. Fenster? How are you plagued."

The words came from the depth unbidden, with a life and force of their own that shocked Claudia as much as they surprised the doctor. "I hear my baby calling for me! Oh, God, that I should believe such a thing, but late at night I hear the voice of a child on the wind, and I know it belongs to Monica. And she wants me so badly, needs to know that I still think of her and still care, and I begin to think that she is somewhere near, just beyond a veil that I must tear down with my own hands if I am to survive. I wake up knowing that Monica is still alive!" Tears prevented her from saying more; Vincent mumbled assurances and took her shoulders to steady and comfort her. She dabbed her eyes, trying to laugh.

"Oh, you must think I'm mad!"

"Not at all," he said with absolute calm. "Let's go a little farther." They rounded a turn in the path marked by clusters of white peony. "There is a reason for what has happened to you, and it is perfectly natural; you have suffered a grievous emotional injury. Your mind, in attempting to isolate that hurt and prevent it from occurring again, conjures the illusion that the baby exists somewhere. It gives you hope and prevents you from succumbing to an otherwise devastating depression of spirit."

"But surely hallucinations are a sign of some defect working its way through me."

"Perhaps." Vincent smiled. "I am no expert, of course, but I have read the case histories of a man in Vienna, a Dr. Freud, who has traced the emotional maladies of his patients to their roots deep inside life memories which seemingly were forgotten long ago. He calls this secret inner life the 'subconscious,' and finds it to be a powerful force working in all of us. How may I explain it to you? If you'd cut your finger, say, the bleeding soon stops by itself, even if you do nothing to staunch the wound. I believe that the mind is capable of the same protective action. Now you experience the bleeding—hallucination in this case. But in a little while it will stop. All you must do is recognize what you experience for what it really is and accept the phenomena. Soon they will pass."

She thought of the sounds she heard in the caverns. How could the cries not be real? It frightened her to think that her mind could no longer discriminate between the actual world and the fancies it generated—in secret!—for itself.

"Oh, look!" Vincent said as they emerged from the grotto along the eastern border of the amusement arcade. "They're going to light the tower soon." Together they watched as a brilliant red ball slowly ascended toward the pinnacle of the structure. For the moment, activity in the park ceased as everyone waited for the thousands of electric lamps to come to life. Higher and higher the globe climbed, and Claudia felt herself being caught up in the rising excitement. Here was light, made by men to replace the fading beams of the sun.

"We have banished darkness," she heard the doctor say. Without thinking she held his arm more tightly, pulling herself close to him, then leaning her head against his shoulder. For a moment she could sense power in him, rising from the ground beneath their feet, the same power that in a few moments would cause a mere frame of lumber to blaze with an almost celestial glory. Her fears shriveled. Dr. Vincent was right; she had been foolish, and now she knew it, now the cries would vanish and she could get on with the business of living with the people of Corinth, helping her husband to gain the position in society he wanted so desperately.

And then came the sound of a voice that, if loud enough, would have shaken the tower to bits. "*Mrs. Fenster!*" At first Claudia did not realize who the pinch-faced woman in the gray temperance uniform was—until she remembered that Mrs. Phillip Ash sometimes did temperance work at this very park. She gazed at Claudia coolly. There was hatred in her eyes, and triumph too.

"And Dr. Vincent. I had believed you possessed better sense than this."

"This is a chance meeting, Mrs. Ash, nothing more."

"I wonder if her husband would think the same thing. I'm sorry to have seen this, Claudia Fenster. I was beginning to think you were a nice young woman after all." Claudia's heart sank as Mrs. Ash turned abruptly and disappeared into the crowd. Vincent took a step as if to intercept her, but people closed in, craning for a better look and blocking his path.

A moment later they were lost in the sudden, terrifying glare of 80,000 Mazda lamps. And above the excited cheering of the crowd, Claudia thought she heard Dr. Vincent say, "And now must darkness be appeased." Then he was gone.

Two days later and near the same time of evening, Claudia and her husband drove toward the Connor Hotel in the cabriolet Ulysses had hired for the occasion of the Miners' Ball. He was very angry, his arms trembling so much he had difficulty controlling the reins.

"You've ruined me!" he shouted, not caring that his voice carried far along Main Street. "It is bad enough she saw you with a man not your husband in that park, but then to go to her house, to burst in uninvited to scream at her like a disgruntled scullery maid!"

"The woman hates us! Ulysses, how in the name of heaven can you wish to earn favor she will never grant? As God is my witness, I would have torn the hair from her head if her driver hadn't come to her rescue! In a day and a half she's poisoned my good name and made you a fool, and yet you still take her side—"

"Silence!" He roared. "You have broken your promise to me, Claudia, you've failed miserably to help me gain what I want most. Do you know what Ash said to me this afternoon? 'Sorry, old man, if it was up to me, you'd be in in a minute. Only Olivia believes your wife is absolutely unsuitable for the auxiliary, and, well, one goes with the other. Maybe next year,' he says. Next year! Your cracked brain has cost me at least ten thousand dollars in new business and possibly much more."

"I'm not cracked! I'm not!"

"I've half a mind to send you home to your father, if the shame wouldn't kill him! You deserve to be a spinster—"

"Ulysses— "

"Let go of my arm, damn you!"

"Turn the coach back, please. We don't have to endure this, don't you understand, it's not me, or you, *it's they* who don't know how to behave! This is Mrs. Ash's circle, the rules are hers. Let's go home. Ulysses, I can please you if you'll just give me the chance. It was father's wish, and I have always tried—"

Without warning he slapped her with the back of his hand. "You have never tried! You made a sick man of your father with your willful behavior, and now you try to do the same with me. But I won't be so easy for you, I swear! You are coming with me down that stairway, and you will smile as they all look at you. You'll smile for the whole world!"

Furiously, he lashed at the horse until they arrived in the front of the hotel. Claudia wiped her eyes and tried desperately to compose herself. She had been foolish to go see Mrs. Ash yesterday, but she had gone only to explain how she had met Dr. Vincent at Electric Park, and then to try, somehow, to reach an understanding with the older woman. But Olivia Ash had fended off any explanation or compromise; instead, viciously, she had berated Claudia for feeling sorry for herself, for thinking herself better than everyone in Corinth simply because she had lost her baby.

"I've lost one; so had Elly Corporan, and Mrs. Blakely. All of us have made the required sacrifice, but you with your whining and moaning are interested only in showing us up. How great a tragedy you suffered, my poor, poor dear—"

It was then that the glee in her eyes had set Claudia off. Something in her, strained to the breaking point, finally snapped, and she'd flown at the other woman fully intent on throttling her. Only Jimbo's quick intervention had prevented a scratching, kicking battle between them.

"You don't know what real sorrow is, dearie," Mrs. Ash had screeched. "But you will! Soon enough you will!"

Now Ulysses, jaw set, stood outside the carriage with his arm out, ready to escort her into the ballroom. She made a final, silent plea, but he was cold and adamant; Claudia was certain he would carry her inside if she didn't come of her own free will. Together they entered the carpeted lobby, followed a stairway to a mezzanine, then passed through double doors opening onto the grand carved-rosewood stairs down to the grand ballroom. The floor was crowded with the ladies and the men of Corinth, swirling about to the latest Austrian waltzes. The orchestra had been imported from St. Louis; guests had come from that city, too, and from Columbia and Springfield, and even the cow town up north, Kansas City. Claudia's heartbeat quickened. The light was dim, and there were people enough that perhaps she could pass unnoticed onto the floor. Then she gasped, as there would be no such luck for her. Mrs. Olivia Ash headed a reception line directly at the foot of the stairs. Ulysses pulled her closer.

"You'll greet her civilly, by God!"

Claudia gathered her skirts, and they descended. Mrs. Ash's eyes were the color and sheen of raven's feathers, but the woman smiled!

"Claudia, my dear! You look lovely." Mrs. Ash took Claudia's shoulders in her cold hands and kissed her on the mouth. Her lips were very dry. "You must be proud of her, Ulysses."

Ulysses was clearly startled. "Eh? Yes. Why, yes, by God! The handsomest woman in the room, present company excluded!" Mrs. Ash laughed in a precise burst.

"Go in, go in! We'll see you both later."

"There!" Ulysses whispered as they walked across the room. "She's a perfectly reasonable woman, and a better Christian than you, offering friendship after your inexcusable behavior. Do you wish to dance?"

"No."

"I see Titus Blakely over there. Perhaps I can repair some of the damage you've caused. Look cheerful, by God!" Claudia watched him move off, then found herself a seat by the balcony doors. As she sat there, she began to realize that the orchestra was slightly off-key and that the guests, who seemed elegant from the vantage at the top of the grand staircase, looked a little ragged, their dresses and cutaways stale, perhaps from hanging the whole year in storage against this occasion. This wasn't Paris, after all, nor New York or even Chicago; this was a middling town hard by the borders of Arkansas, Kansas, and the Indian Territory. The people here were acting as they thought grand people ought to act. *They were performing*, almost as if the movement and music were part of a ritual whose purpose they did not understand. Perhaps they did not want to understand.

She searched the room for Ulysses, found she could not see him. She felt faint, and the music annoyed her; so she rose and went outside to the balcony for some air.

The doors closed behind her and produced a blessed silence. After a moment she could hear the faint sound of a far-off calliope, then distant screaming that puzzled and frightened her until she remembered the Washtub at Electric Park. The tower burned magnesium-bright, imposing-looking even seven miles away, and suddenly Claudia longed to be beneath it, feeling the joy of the people who'd come to lose themselves in the light and the color and the sounds of the arcade. That was so much better than the spectacle inside the ballroom. Claudia put her hand to her face, feeling the cold place where Olivia Ash had kissed her.

You don't know what real sorrow is, dearie!

And then the wind rose, and she heard the cry again. There was no mistaking it, for it was plaintive and cold and seemed to rise from the heart of the darkened city between this balcony and the tower to the north. She held her breath, praying desperately for the sound to be just another hallucination, but it came again, louder, shaking her to her soul. For an instant she almost fainted, but then anger tore through her fear.

"Why?" she yelled, gripping the balcony rail. "Why must I suffer this!" But there was no answer, only the cry of a child on the warm night wind. Claudia looked out and could see the tops of the hickory trees that sheltered the entrance to the Crystal Caverns no more than a hundred yards from where she stood. Dr. Vincent had told her confidently that her emotional wounds would staunch themselves. Now Claudia knew that something far more serious was happening, that she must take action or the child in her mind would live on and destroy what was left of her life.

Quickly she looked into the ballroom. There was no sign of Ulysses, or Mrs. Ash, or anyone else Claudia knew. Before the balcony doors was a long table with a display of polished miner's tools. Claudia took a brass coal-oil lamp, shook it to test for fuel, then ran outside and down the steps to the back of the hotel, trying to reassure herself as she hurried along toward the caves. *It is a rational thing I'm doing. . . . Proving to myself that this thing, this voice . . . this child! . . . does not, cannot exist. Monica was dead before she ever left my womb!*

She reached the grove, approached the switch box to turn on the cavern lights. Something grabbed her arm, and she cried out, dropping the lantern. The glass chimney broke with a sound that was almost like bells.

"Mis' Fenster." The impassive black face materialized from the darkness.

"J-Jimbo? What are you doing here?" The anger came back. "Let go of me!"

"You don't want to go down there, Mis' Fenster." His eyes glittered in the moonlight, but there was no hostility in his long, wrinkled face, only sadness. Claudia recovered a little.

"I—I must go down. I believe I may have lost something valuable when I was here Wednesday. A brooch. Have you found one?"

"No, mis'."

"Well, then, I must have a look for my—" She halted, because clear and very loud came the cry, not once, but three times and echoing within the walls of the caverns. There was no mistaking it now, for Jimbo was clearly startled. Gently, Claudia pried his fingers free of her arm.

"Your given name is James?"

"Yes."

"James what?"

"I'm James Woods, Mis' Fenster, and I'm askin' you not to go down. Your child's lost once, leave it be."

"I am going down." Her voice was terribly calm. "Wait for me here, please."

James Wood shrugged finally and threw the light switch. Claudia descended the path that led into the earth, slowing to listen when she reached the card tables. There was a murmuring—maybe only the stirring of the cave wind—but then she saw that the boards had been removed from the passageway over Indian Hell. Silently cursing her trailing gown and wishing she had not broken her lantern, Claudia stepped over the pulled-away planks into a passage dark enough to swallow her whole.

At the moment she heard the cry for the third time that night, a light sputtered on ahead of her. Claudia gathered her skirts and ran, heedless of where the ledge was, or that she might fall into the abyss. A draft rose from below, humid and smelling of the earth, and she was conscious of descending slightly into a larger space and the sound of water trickling as she skirted an outcropping of dark rock and saw them waiting for her.

Men and women held torches whose light failed in the deep crevasse beyond the ledge: men and women Claudia knew. There was Dr. Vincent, wearing traces of a smile on his face, and Elly Corporan and Mrs. Burgess. In the shadows just beyond this circle she saw Phillip Ash and Ulysses, who colored and looked away.

In the center, Olivia Ash, who held in her arms a most remarkable child that was perhaps a year old. Her skin was the color of bone china, her hair silk-fine and white as sugar or salt, while grave eyes, huge like the eyes of a deer, focused on Claudia. There was a spark of recognition, then: "Maaamaaa!"

"Come in, my dear," Mrs. Ash said, her reedy voice echoing in the darkness. "She wants you, and it's time." Claudia rushed forward, pushing through the circle and snatching the baby away, to Mrs. Ash's laughter.

"She has been well cared for, though she's never seen the sun and never shall. Jimbo's been her mother and kept her well for this."

"Monica?" The child pressed close, and Claudia felt the beating of her tiny heart. Her mouth formed the word: Why?

"We live by what we take from the earth and in return she demands something of us. I've given, so has Elly; all of us who live from the earth must offer and give in return. You must give the child now. When you do, you'll be fertile again. You'll have as many more as you want."

"No! Ulysses!" But she could not see him because of the torches. "I won't give her up! Not again."

"You will, or you'll fall too. It won't be the first time. Present the child!"

"No!"

"Doctor, perhaps you can make the decision easier." Claudia saw Vincent step from the circle with a cloth pad in hand; she caught the sharp odor of ether. "Not again! Lord God, not again!" Her baby clutched at her dress as the circle closed around her, pushing her toward the brink, Vincent smiling at her, Olivia Ash laughing louder and louder—

She held Monica tightly under both her tiny arms, then suddenly, with a burst of desperate energy, swung the child around as though she were nothing but a sack of grain. The little feet caught Olivia Ash squarely in the breast, sending her gasping back into Dr. Vincent. Monica howled with fright.

"You fool!" Mrs. Ash screamed. "You'll ruin us all! Grab her, somebody!"

"No! This is my baby, understand me, mine, mine! If you want her again, you'll have to take her. How about it?" She held Monica out at arm's length toward Mrs. Ash and moved forward, shaking the baby like a doll. "Take her from me!" Mrs. Ash opened her arms. "Take her. *Take her!*" With a sudden thrust, she used the wailing child as a weapon for the second time, holding on to her clothing with her fists as she pushed Monica forward into Mrs. Ash and lunged, pushing with her legs as hard as she could before pulling back suddenly at the brink of the pit. Mrs. Ash screamed as she went over. The scream continued for a long, long time, and while it lasted, Claudia turned and ran before the others could recover from their shock and pursue her. She ran until her lungs felt as though they'd burst, and then she saw stars and heard the wind stirring the hickory trees.

James Woods blocked her path.

"I can't let you go, Mis' Fenster. That girl don't belong to you no more."

"You raised her. You fed her, damn you! Can't you see she wants to live? Can't you? Can't you? Let me take the wagon, please!"

"Mis' Ash—"

"Is dead! Do you understand, I've killed her for what she's done to us. God Almighty, they're coming!"

James Woods shifted his weight. Shouts of rage and confusion came from the mouth of the caverns. Monica whimpered, blinking painfully as though even starlight was too much for her. And then, suddenly, James turned and yanked open the switch for the cavern lights. Both of them listened to the screams.

"They took what they wanted out of her. Now she'll take back what she wants." As he said this, he helped mother and child onto the buckboard.

BALGRUMMO'S HELL

RUSSELL KIRK

When we hear the term "horror story" we usually think Gothic effects: the crumbling, shadowy estate set in a remote locale; the supernatural influence oozing down the passageway; the denial of the rational and the triumph of intuition and superstition—the dark secrets hidden in a world we thought we knew. Russell Kirk, perhaps more than any other modern writer, captures and adapts traditional gothic elements in his fantasies to create, in his own words, "tales more of the outer darkness than of the twilight zone." Balgrummo's Lodging is truly a dark and evil place. When "Balgrummo's Hell" was first published in *F & SF,* Russell Kirk noted that "it has more than a grain of true narration at the core of it, and the setting is genuine." Russell Kirk has walked in some haunted places indeed.

The moment that Horgan had slipped through the pend, Jock Jamieson had glanced up, grunted, and run for his shotgun at the gate cottage. But Horgan, having long legs, had contrived to cosh Jock right on the threshold. Now Horgan had most of the night to lift the pictures out of Balgrummo Lodging.

Before Jock could close those rusty iron gates, Nan Stennis—in her improbable role of new night nurse to Lord Balgrummo—had stalled her car in the pend. In the rain, Jock couldn't possibly have made out Nan's face, and now Horgan pulled off the silk stocking of Nan's that he had worn over his own head. With Nan's help, he trussed and gagged Jock, the tough old nut breathing convulsively, and dragged him into a kitchen cupboard of the gate cottage, and turned the key on him. Jock's morning mate, and the morning nurse, wouldn't come to relieve him until seven o'clock. That left no one between Horgan and those paintings except Alexander Fillan Inchburn, tenth Baron Balgrummo, incredibly old, incredibly depraved, and incredibly decayed in Balgrummo Lodging, which he had not left for half a century.

In that nocturnal February drizzle, Nan shivered; perhaps she shuddered. Though there could have been no one within a quarter of a mile to hear them, she was whispering. "Rafe, can you really get through it without me? I hate to think of you going into that place all alone, darling."

Competent Rafe Horgan kissed her competently. She had left her husband for him, and she had been quite useful. He honestly meant to meet her at the Mayfair by the end of the month, and take her to the Canaries; by that time he should have disposed of the Romney portrait for a fat sum, to an assured Swiss collector with a Leeds agent, enabling Horgan to take his time in disposing of the other Balgrummo pictures. Nan could have lent him a hand inside Balgrummo Lodging, but it was important for her to establish an alibi; she would change automobiles with him now, drive into Edinburgh and show herself at a restaurant, and then take the midnight train to King's Cross. The principal trouble with operations like this was simply that too many people became involved, and some of them were given to bragging. But Nan was a close one, and Horgan had spent months planning.

The only real risk was that someone might discover his name wasn't Horgan. For that, however, a thorough investigation would be required. And who would think of investigating the past of Rafe Horgan, Esq., a South African gentleman of private means who now lived in a pleasant flat near Charlotte Square? Not Dr. Euphemia Inchburn, gray spinster who liked his smile and his talk; not T. M. Gillespie, Writer to the Signet, chairman of the trustees of Lord Balgrummo's Trust. With them he had been patient and prudent, asking questions about Balgrummo Lodging only casually, in an antiquarian way. Besides, did he look as if he would carry the cosh? No, the police would be after every gang in Fossie housing estate, which sprawled almost to the policies of Balgrummo Lodging. Horgan's expenditure of charm, and even of money, would be repaid five thousand times over. The big obstacle had been Jock's shotgun, and that was overcome now.

"His high and mighty lordship's bedridden," Horgan told Nan, kissing her again, "and blind, too, they say. I'll finish here by three o'clock, girl.

Ring me about teatime tomorrow, if you feel you must; but simply talk about the weather, Nan, when you do. You'll love Las Palmas."

He stood at the forgotten gate, watching Nan get into the car in which he had come and had parked in the shadow of the derelict linoleum works that ran cheek by jowl with the north dyke of Balgrummo Lodging. When she had gone, he started up Nan's own inconspicuous black Ford, moving it far enough for him to shut the gates. He locked those gates with the big brass padlock that Jock had removed to admit "Nurse" Nan. Then, slowly and with only his dims showing, he drove up the avenue —rhododendron jungle pressing in from either side—that led to the seventeenth-century facade of Balgrummo Lodging.

"Uncle Alec and his house have everything," Dr. Effie Ichburn had said once: "Dry rot, wet rot, woodworm, death-watch beetle." Also, among those few who remembered Lord Balgrummo and Balgrummo Lodging, the twain had a most nasty repute. It was a positive duty to take the pictures out of that foul house and convey them into the possession of collectors who, if they would keep them no less private, certainly would care for them better.

Sliding out of the car with his dispatch case of tools, Rafe Horgan stood at the dark door of Balgrummo Lodging. The front was the work of Sir William Bruce, they said, although part of the house was older. It all looked solid enough by night, however rotten the timbers and the man within. Horgan had taken Jamieson's big ring of keys from the gate cottage, but the heavy main door stood slightly ajar, anyway. No light showed anywhere. Before entering, Horgan took a brief complacent survey of the tall ashlar face of what T. M. Gillespie, that mordant stick of a solicitor, called "Balgrummo's Hell."

Living well enough by his wits, Horgan had come upon Balgrummo Lodging by good fortune, less than a month after he had found it convenient to roost in Edinburgh. In a car with false license plates, he had driven out to Fossie housing estate in search of a certain rough customer who might do a job for him. Fossie, only seven years old but already slum, was the usual complex of crescents and terraces of drab council houses. Horgan had taken a wrong turn and had found himself driving down a neglected and uninhabited old lane; behind the nasty brick wall on his right had been a derelict marshaling yard for goods wagons, declared redundant by Dr. Beeching of British Railways. On his left, he had passed the immense hulk of a disused linoleum works, empty for several years, its every windowpane smashed by the lively bairns of Fossie.

Beyond the linoleum factory he had come upon a remarkably high old stone dyke, unpleasant shards of broken glass set thick in cement all along its top. Behind the wall he had made out the limbs and trunks of limes and beeches, a forest amidst suburbia. Abruptly, a formal ancient pend or vaulted gateway had loomed up. On either side, a seventeenth-century stone beast effigy kept guard, life-size almost: a lion and a griffin, but so hacked and battered by young vandals as to be almost unrecognizable. The griffin's whole head was lacking.

So much Horgan had seen at a glance, taking it that these were the vacant policies of some demolished or ruined mansion house. He had driven on to the end of the street, hoping to circle back to the housing estate, but had found himself in a cul-de-sac, the Fettinch burn flowing through bogs beyond the brick wall at the end. This triangle of wooded policies, hemmed in by goods yards, wrecked factory, and polluted streams, must be the last scrap of some laird's estate of yesteryear, swallowed but not yet digested by the city's fringe. Probably the squalor and unhealthiness of the low site had deterred Edinburgh or Midlothian—he wasn't sure within which boundary it lay—from building on it another clutch of council houses for the Fossie scheme.

Swinging round at the lane's terminal wall, Horgan had gone slowly back past the massive pend, where the harling was dropping from the rubble. To his surprise, he had noticed a gate lodge, apparently habitable, just within the iron grill of the gates; and a little wood smoke had been spiraling up from the chimney. Could there be anything worth liberating beyond those gates? He had stopped, and had found an iron bell pull that functioned. When he had rung, a tall fellow, with the look of a retired constable, had emerged from the gate cottage and had conversed with him, taciturnly, in broad Scots, through the locked grill.

Horgan had asked for directions to a certain crescent in the housing scheme, and had got them. Then he had inquired the name of this place. "Balgrummo Lodgin', sir"—with a half defensive frown. On impulse, Horgan had suggested that he would like to see the house (which, he gathered, must be standing, for he could make out beyond the trees some high dormers and roofs).

"Na, na; Himself's no receivin', ye ken." This had been uttered with a kind of incredulity at the question being put.

Growing interested, Horgan had professed himself to be something of a connoisseur of seventeenth-century domestic architecture. Where might he apply for permission to view the exterior, at any rate? He had been given to understand, surlily, that it would do no good: but everything was in the hands of Lord Balgrummo's Trust. The trust's solicitor and chairman was a Mr. T. M. Gillespie, of Reid, Gillespie, and MacIlwraith, Hanover Street.

Thus Balgrummo Lodging had been added to Rafe Horgan's list of diverse projects. A few days later, he had scraped acquaintance with Gillespie, a dehydrated bachelor. Initially, he had not mentioned Balgrummo Lodging, but had talked in Gillespie's chambers about a hypothetical Miss Horgan in Glasgow, allegedly an aunt of his, a spinster of large means, who was thinking of a family trust. Mr. Gillespie, he had heard it said, was experienced in the devising and management of such trusts. As venture capital, a check from Horgan had even been made out to Mr. Gillespie, in payment for general advice upon getting up a conceivable Janet Horgan Estates, Ltd.

Gillespie, he had discovered, was a lonely solictor who could be cultivated, and who had a dry relish for dry sherry. After a bottle, Gillespie might talk more freely than a solicitor ought to talk. They came to dine together fairly frequently—after Horgan had learnt, from a chance remark which he affected to receive casually, that some good pictures remained at the lodging. As the weeks elapsed, they were joined for a meal, once and again, by Gillespie's old friend Dr. Euphemia Inchburn, Lord Balgrummo's niece, a superannuated gynecologist. Horgan had turned on all his charm, and Dr. Inchburn had slipped into garrulity.

Perceiving that he really might be on to a good thing, Horgan had poked into old gazeteers which might mention Balgrummo Lodging; and, as he obtained from his new friends some hint of the iniquities of the tenth Baron Balgrummo, he looked into old newspaper files. He knew a little about pictures, as he did about a number of things; and by consulting the right books and catalogues, he ascertained that on the rotting walls of Balgrummo Lodging there still must hang some highly valuable family portraits—though not family portraits only—none of them exhibited anywhere since 1913. Gillespie was interested only in Scottish portrait painters, and not passionately in them; Horgan judged it imprudent to question Dr. Effie Inchburn overmuch on the subject, lest his inquisitiveness be fixed in her memory. But he became reasonably well satisfied that Lord Balgrummo, senescent monster, must possess an Opie, a Raeburn, a Ramsay or two, perhaps even three Wilkies, a good Reynolds, possibly, and a Constable, a very good Romney, a Gainsborough, it appeared, and (happy prospect) a Hogarth, two small canvasses by William Etty, a whole row of reputed Knellers, once, and just conceivably still, a Cranach and a Holbein were to be seen at the lodging. The tenth baron's especial acquisition, about 1911, had been an enormous Fuseli, perhaps unknown to compilers of catalogues, and (judging from one of Dr. Inchburn's grimaces) probably obscene. There were more pictures —the devil knew what.

Perhaps some rare books might be found in the library, but Horgan was too little of a bibliophile to pick them out in a hurry. The silver and that sort of thing presumably were in a bank—it would have been risky to inquire. Anyone but a glutton would be content with those pictures, for one night's work.

Lethargy, and the consequences of permanent confinement to his house, naturally had made Lord Balgrummo neglect his inheritance. As the decades had slipped by, he had permitted his trustees to sell nearly everything he owned, except Balgrummo Lodging—once a residence of convenience, near Edinburgh, for the Inchburns, later a dower house —and those pictures. "After all, never going out, Alec has to look at *something,*" Dr. Inchburn had murmured.

Sufficient intelligence obtained, still Horgan faced the difficulty of entering the house without the peril and expense of a gang raid, and of getting out undetected with those pictures. An attempt had been made several years before. On that occasion, Jock Jamieson, the night porter —"warden" would have been a better style—had shot to death one burglar and wounded another while they were on a ladder. Jamieson and his day mates (one of them the constable type with whom Horgan had talked at the gate) were hard, vigilant men—and, like Lord Balgrummo's nurses, excellently paid. Time had been when it seemed at least as important to keep Lord Balgrummo in (though he had given his word never to leave the policies) as to keep predators out. Gillespie had implied that the police indulged in the peculiar porters of Balgrummo Lodging a certain readiness in the use of firearms. So Horgan's expedition had been most painstakingly plotted, and it had been necessary to wait months for the coincidence of favorable circumstances, all things being held in readiness.

The presence of a nurse in the house all round the clock was a further vexation; Horgan had not relished the prospect of pursuing a frantic nurse through that crumbling warren of a place. Should she escape through some back door . . . So when, only yesterday, Gillespie had mentioned that the night nurse had quit ("Nerves, as usual, in that house—and his lordship a disagreeable patient"), and that they had not yet found a replacement, Horgan knew his moment had arrived.

For one night, Jamieson had been required to do double duty, watching the policies and looking in on Lord Balgrummo every hour. Jock Jamieson, for all his toughness, probably liked being inside the place at night no more than did the nurses. So doubtless Jock had rejoiced when a ladi-dah feminine voice (Nan Stennis's, of course) had informed him late that evening that she was calling on behalf of Mr. Gillespie, and that a new night nurse would make her appearance, in an hour or so, in her own car.

It had gone smoothly enough. Jock had opened the gate at Nan's honk, and then it had been up to Horgan, in the shadows. Had Jock been ten years younger, and less given to beer, he might have gotten his hands on the shotgun before Horgan could have reached him. But though disliking unnecessary roughness, Horgan had coshed men before, and he coshed Jock swiftly and well. No one came down that obscure lane after dark—few, indeed, in daylight. Therefore the investment in drinks and dinners for Gillespie and the Inchburn old maid, and the expenditure of Horgan's hours now would be compensated for at an hourly rate of return beyond the dreams of avarice. Swinging his handsome dispatch case, Horgan entered Balgrummo Lodging.

Within the chilly entrance hall, the first thing Horgan noticed was the pervasive odor of dry rot. With this stench of doom, what wonder they had to pay triple wages to any nurse! Condemned to solitude, neglectful of business, and latterly penurious, Lord Balgrummo had postponed repairs until the cost of restoring the lodging would have been gigantic. Even could he have found the money without selling some of his pictures, old Balgrummo probably would not have saved the house; he had no heirs of his body, the entail had been broken long before, and his heir presumptive—Dr. Effie—never would choose to live in this desolation screened by the tumbledown linoleum works. There remained only the question as to which would first tumble into atoms—Lord Balgrummo or his prison mansion.

Horgan sent the beam of his big electric torch round the hall. It flashed across the surface of what appeared to be a vast Canaletto—a prospect of Ravenna, perhaps. Was it the real article, or only from Canaletto's school? Horgan wished he knew whether it was worth the difficulty of taking and concealing, its size considered. Well, he would leave it to the last, securing the certified goods first.

He had known there was no electric light in Balgrummo Lodging: nothing had been improved there—or much repaired—since 1913. He found, however, elaborate bronze gas brackets. After fumbling, he found also that he did not know how to light them; or perhaps the gas was turned off, here in the hall. No matter: the torch would suffice, even if the black caverns beyond its ray were distressing.

Before he went to work, he must have a glance at old Balgrummo, to be quite sure that the crazy old creature couldn't totter out to do some feeble mischief. (In this house, more than fifty years before, he had done great mischief indeed.) Where would his bedroom be? On the second story, at the front, just above the library, likely enough, judging from the plan of the lodging, at which Horgan had once managed a hasty glance in Gillespie's chambers. Hanging the torch about his neck, Horgan made his way up the broad oak staircase, at first leaning on the balustrade—but presently touching that rail only gingerly, since here and there, even though he wore gloves, it felt spongy to the touch, and trembled in its rottenness when he put too much weight upon it.

At the first floor turning of the stair, Horgan paused. Had anything scraped or shuffled down there below, down in the black well of the ground floor? Of course it couldn't have, unless it was a rat. (Balgrummo kept no dogs: "The brutes don't live long at the lodging," Gillespie had murmured in an obscure aside.) How had those night nurses endured this situation, at whatever wages? One reason that Balgrummo Lodging hadn't been pillaged before this, Horgan ruminated, was the ghastly reputation of the place, lingering over five decades. Few enterprising lads, even from Fossie housing estate, would be inclined to venture into the auld bogle nobleman's precincts. Well, that ghostly wind had blown him good. No one could be more effectively rational than Rafe Horgan, who wouldn't fret about blood spilt before the First World War. Still, indubitably this was an oppressive house—stagnant, stagnant.

"Haunted?" Dr. Effie Inchburn had replied hesitantly to Horgan's jocular inquiry. "If you mean haunted by dead ancestors, Major Horgan—why, no more than most old houses here in Scotland, I suppose. Who would be troubled, after so many generations, by old General Sir Angus Inchburn in his Covenanting jackboots? Ghostly phenomena, or so I've read, seldom linger long after a man's or a woman's death and burial. But if you ask whether there's something fey at work in the house—oh, I certainly suppose so."

Having paused to polish her spectacles, Dr. Effie continued calmly enough: "That's Uncle Alec's fault. He's not present merely in one room, you know; he fills the house, every room, every hour. Presumably I seem silly to you, Major Horgan, but my impulses won't let me visit Balgrummo more than I must, even if Alec does mean to leave everything to me. Balgrummo Lodging is like a saturated sponge, dripping with the shame and the longing of Alexander Fillan Inchburn. Can you understand that my uncle loathes what he did, and yet might do it again—even the worst of it—if there were opportunity? The horror of Balgrummo Lodging isn't Lord Balgrummo nine-tenths dead; it's Balgrummo one-tenth alive, but in torment."

The tedious old girl-doctor was nearly as cracked as her noble uncle, Horgan thought. Actually he had learned from some interesting research the general character of Lord Balgrummo's offenses so long ago—acts which would have produced the hanging of anyone but a peer, in those days. Horgan nevertheless had amused himself by endeavoring, slyly and politely, to force Dr. Effie to tell him just why Balgrummo had been given the choice of standing trial for his life (by the Lords, of course, as a peer, which might have damaged the repute of that body) or of being kept in a kind of perpetual house arrest, without sentence being passed by anyone. The latter choice would not have been offered—and accepted—even so, but for the general belief that he must be a maniac.

As he had anticipated, Dr. Euphemia had turned prude. "Poor Alec was very naughty when he was young. There were others as bad as himself, but he took the whole blame on his shoulders. He was told that if he would swear never to go out, all his life, and to receive no visitors except members of his family or his solicitors, no formal charges would be pressed against him. They required him to put everything he owned into trust; and the trustees were to engage the men to watch the policies of Balgrummo Lodging, and the servants. All the original set of trustees are dead and buried; Mr. Gillespie and I weren't much more than babies when Uncle Alec had his 'trouble.' "

From Gillespie, later, Rafe Horgan had learned more about that trouble. But what was he doing, pausing in the darkness of the second-floor corridor to reminisce? A hasty inspection by the torch showed him that the Knellers, all great noses, velvets, and bosoms, were hung on this floor. And there was the Gainsborough, a good one, though it badly needed cleaning: Margaret, Lady Ross, second daughter of the fifth Lord Balgrummo. The worm had got into the picture frame, but the canvas seemed to be in decent condition, he made out on closer examination. Well, Horgan meant to cut his pictures out of their frames, to save time and space. First, though, he must look in upon Himself.

The corridor was all dust and mildew. A single charwoman, Gillespie had mentioned, came a few hours daily, Monday through Friday, to keep Balgrummo's bedroom and small parlor neat, to clean the stairs and to wash dishes in the kitchen. Otherwise, the many rooms and passages of the lodging were unceasingly shuttered against sun and moon, and the damask might fall in tatters from the walls, the ceilings drip with cobwebs, for all old Balgrummo cared. Nearly every room was left locked, though the keys, all but a few, were in the bunch (each with its metal tag) that Horgan had taken from unconscious Jock. Even Gillespie, who waited on his client four or five times a year, never had contrived to see the chapel. Balgrummo kept the chapel key in his own pocket, Gillespie fancied—and, over coffee and brandy, had mentioned this, together with other trivia, to Horgan. "It was in the chapel, you see, Rafe, that the worst of the trouble happened."

Acquiring that chapel key was an additional reason that Horgan must pay his respects to Lord Balgrummo—though he relished that necessity less, somehow, with every minute that elapsed. Henry Fuseli's most indecorous painting might be in that chapel; for the tenth baron's liturgy and ritual, fifty years before, had been a synthesis of Benin witch rites with memories of Scots diabolism, and whatever might excite the frantic fancy had been employed—all gross images. So, at least, Horgan had surmised from what he had garnered from the old newspaper files, and what Gillespie had let drop.

Uncertain of quite where he was in the house, Horgan tried the knobs of three doors in that corridor. The first two were locked; and it was improbable that the trustees ever had gone so far, even when Balgrummo was stronger, as to have him locked into his rooms at night. But the third door opened creakingly. Flashing round his light, Horgan entered an old-fashioned parlor, with what appeared to be two bonafide Wilkie landscapes on opposite walls. Across the parlor, which was scarcely bigger than a dressing room, a mahogany door stood half open. How silent! Yet something scraped or ticked faintly—a morose death-watch beetle in the paneling, probably. Despite irrational misgivings, Horgan compelled himself to pass through the inner doorway.

The beam of his torch swept to a Queen Anne bed. In it lay, motionless and with eyes shut, an extremely old man, skin and bone under a single sheet and a single blanket. A coal fire smoldered in the grate, so the room was not altogether dark. Horgan's flesh crept perceptibly—but that would be the old rumors, and the old truths, about this enfeebled thing in the bed. "In his prime, we called him Ozymandias," Gillespie had put it. But Lord Balgrummo was past obscenities and atrocities now.

"Hello, Alec!" Horgan was loud and jocular. His right hand rested on the cosh in his coat pocket. "Alec, you old toad, I've come for your pictures." But Alexander Fillan Inchburn, the last of a line that went back to a bastard of William the Lion, did not stir or speak.

T. M. Gillespie was proud of Lord Balgrummo, as the most remarkable person whose business ever had come his way. "Our Scots Giles de Rais,"

Gillespie had chuckled aridly while enjoying a Jamaican cigar from Horgan's case, "probably would not be found insane by a board of medical examiners—not even after fifty years of restriction to his own private hell. I don't think it was from malice that the procurator-fiscal of that day recommended Balgrummo Lodging—where the capital offenses had been committed—as the place of isolated residence: it merely happened that this particular house of Lord Balgrummo's was secluded enough to keep his lordship out of the public eye (for he might have been stoned), and yet near enough to the city for police surveillance, during the earlier decades. I take it that the police have forgotten his existence, or almost forgotten, by this time: for the past three or four years, he wouldn't have been able to walk unaided so far as the gate cottage."

It was something of a relief to Horgan, finding that Lord Balgrummo was past giving coherent evidence in a court of law—and therefore need not be given the quietus. Even though they no longer hanged anybody for anything, and even though Balgrummo could have been eliminated in thirty seconds by a pillow over his face, the police pursued a homicide much more energetically than they did a picture fancier.

But was this penny-dreadful monster of fifty years ago, with his white beard now making him sham-venerable in this four-poster, still among the living? Horgan almost could see the bones through his skin; Balgrummo might have come to his end during the hour or so since Jamieson had made his rounds. To be sure, Horgan took a mirror from the dressing table and held it close to the pallid sunken face. Setting his torch on its base, he inspected the mirror's surface; yes, there was a faint moist film, so the tenth baron still breathed.

Balgrummo must be stone deaf, or in a coma. Dr. Effie had said he had gone almost blind recently. Was it true? Horgan nearly yielded to a loathsome impulse to roll back those withered eyelids, but he reminded himself that somehow he wouldn't be able to endure seeing his own image in this dying man's malign pupils.

The coshing of Jock; the nervous partial exploration of this dismal house, the sight of loathsome old Balgrummo on the edge of dissolution—these trials had told on Horgan, old hand though he was at predatory ventures. With all the hours left to him, it would do no harm to sit for a few minutes in this easy chair, almost as if he were Balgrummo's nurse—keeping watch on the bed, surely, to make certain that Balgrummo wasn't (in reason's spite) shamming in some way—and to review in his brain the pictures he ought to secure first, and the rooms in which he was likely to find them.

But it would be heartening to have more light than his torch. Never turning his back on the bed, Horgan contrived to light a gas bracket near the door; either these gas fittings were simpler than those below stairs, or he had gotten the trick of the operation. The interior shutters of this bedroom being closed, there wasn't the faintest danger of a glimmer of light being perceived by chance passersby—not that anybody conceivably could pass by Balgrummo Lodging on a rainy midnight.

Lord Balgrummo seemed no less grisly in the flood of gaslight. However much exhausted by strain, you couldn't think of going to sleep, for the briefest nap, in a chair only six feet distant from this unspeaking and unspeakable thing in the bed; not when you knew just how "very naughty," in Dr. Euphemia's phrase, Balgrummo had been. The trouble for which he had paid had been only the culmination of a series of arcane episodes, progressing from hocus-pocus to the ultimate horror.

"No, not lunatic, in any ordinary definition of the term," Gillespie had declared. "Balgrummo recognized the moral character of his acts— aye, more fully than does the average sensual man. Also he was, and is, quite rational, in the sense that he can transact some ordinary business of life when pressed. He fell into a devil of a temper when we proposed to sell some of his pictures to pay for putting the house and the policies in order; he knows his rights, and that the trustees can't dispose of his plenishings against his explicit disapproval. He's civil enough, in his mocking way, to his niece, Effie, when she calls—and to me, when I have to see him. He still reads a good deal—or did, until his sight began to fail—though only books in his own library; half the ceiling has fallen in the library, but he shuffles through the broken plaster on the shaky floor."

On the right of the bed-head there hung an indubitable Constable; on the left, a probable Etty. The two were fairly small, and Horgan could take them whenever he wished. But his throat was dry, this house being so damned dusty. A decanter stood on the dressing table, a silver brandy label round its neck, and by it two cut-glass tumblers. "Not a drop for you, °Alec?" inquired Horgan, grinning defiantly at the silent man on the bed. He seated himself in the velvet-upholstered armchair again and drank the brandy neat.

"No, one can't say," Gillespie had continued (in that last conversation which now seemed so far away and long ago) "that his lordship is wholly incompetent to take a hand in the management of his affairs. It's rather that he's *distant*—preoccupied, in more senses than one. He has to exert his will to bring his consciousness back from wherever it drifts—and one can see that the effort isn't easy for him."

"He's in a brown study, you mean, Tom?" Horgan had inquired, not much interested at that time.

"It's not the phrase I would choose, Rafe. Dr. Effie talks about the 'astral body' and such rubbish, as if she half believed in it—you've heard her. That silliness was a principal subject of Balgrummo's 'researches' for two years before the trouble, you understand; his trouble was the culmination of those experiments. But of course . . ."

"Of course he's only living in the past," Horgan had put in.

"*Living?* Who really knows what that word means?" T. M. Gillespie, W.S., devoted to the memory of David Hume, professed a contempt for rationalism as profound as his contempt for superstition. "And why say *past?* Did you never think that a man might be ossified in time? What you call Balgrummo's past, Rafe, may be Balgrummo's own present, as much as this table talk of ours is the present for you and me. The trouble is his lordship's obsessive reality. Attaining to genuine evil requires strict application to the discipline, eh? Balgrummo is not merely remembering the events of what you and I call 1913, or even 'reliving' those events. No, I suspect it's this: he's embedded in those events, like a beetle in amber. For Balgrummo, one certain night in Balgrummo Lodging continues forever.

"When Dr. Effie and I distract him by raising the trivia of current business, he has to depart from *his* reality, and gropes briefly through a vexatious little dream world in which his niece and his solicitor are insubstantial shadows. In Alexander Inchburn's consciousness, I mean, there is no remembrance and no anticipation. He's not 'living in the past,' not engaging in an exercise of retrospection; for him, time is restricted to one certain night, and space is restricted to one certain house, or perhaps one certain room. Passionate experience has chained him to a fixed point in time, so to speak. But time, as so many have said, is a human convention, not an objective reality. Can you prove that your time is more substantial than his?"

Horgan hadn't quite followed Gillespie, and said so.

"I put it this way, Rafe," Gillespie had gone on didactically. "What's the time of day in hell? Why, hell is timeless—or so my grandfather told me, and he was minister at the Tron. Hell knows no future and no past, but only the everlasting moment of damnation. Also hell is spaceless; or, conceivably, it's a locked box, damnably confining. Here we have Lord Balgrummo shut up perpetually in his box called Balgrummo Lodging, where the fire is not quenched and the worm never dieth. One bloody and atrocious act, committed in that very box, literally is his enduring *reality.* He's not recollecting; he's experiencing, here and (for him) now. All the frightful excitement of that trouble, the very act of profanation and terror, lifts him out of what we call time. Between Dr. Effie and me on the one side, and distant Balgrummo on the other, a great gulf is fixed.

"If you like, you can call that gulf time. For that gulf, I praise whatever gods there be. For if any man's or woman's consciousness should penetrate to Balgrummo's consciousness, to his time scheme, to his world beyond the world—or if, through some vortex of mind and soul, anyone were sucked into that narrow place of torment—then the intruder would end like *this*." Gillespie, tapping his cigar upon an ashtray, knocked into powder a long projection of gray ash. "Consumed, Rafe."

Scratch the canny Scot, Horgan had thought then, even the pedant of the law, and you find the bogle-dreading Pict. "I suppose you mean, really, Tom, that he's out of his head," Horgan had commented, bored with tipsy and unprofitable speculation.

"I mean precisely the contrary, Rafe. I mean that anyone who encounters Lord Balgrummo ought to be on his guard against being drawn into Balgrummo's head. In what you and I designate as 1913 (though, as I said, dates have no significance for Balgrummo), his lordship was a being of immense moral power, magnetic and seductive. I'm not being facetious. Moral power is a catalyst, and can work for good or for evil. Even now I'm acutely uneasy when I sit with Balgrummo, aware that this old man might absorb me. I shouldn't wish to stir those sleeping fires by touching his passions. That's why Balgrummo had to be confined, five decades of ours ago—but not simply because he might be *physically* dangerous. Yet I can't explain to you; you've not watched Balgrummo in what you call his 'brown study,' and you never will, happy man." Their conversation then had shifted to Miss Janet Horgan's hypothetical trust.

Yet Gillespie had been a bad prophet. Here he was, clever Rafe Horgan, man of supple talents and slippery fingers, leisurely watching Lord Balgrummo in his brown study—or in his coma, more precisely—and finishing his lordship's decanter of praiseworthy brandy. You had to remember to keep watching that cadaverous face above the sheet, though; if you let your eyes close even for a second, *his* might open, for all you could tell. After all, you were only a guest in Balgrummo's very own little hell. The host mustn't be permitted to forget his manners.

Now, where would the expiring monster keep his privy effects—the key to that chapel on the floor above, for instance? Steady, Rafe boy: keep your eyes on his face as you open his bedside drawer. Right you are, Rafe; you always were lucky; the nurse had put old Alec's three keys on a chain, along with watch and pocket comb and such effects, into this very drawer. One of these keys should let you into the chapel, Rafe. Get on with you; you've drunk all the brandy a reasonable man needs.

"Don't you mean to give me a guided tour, Alec? Stately homes of Scotia, and all that? Won't you show me your chapel, where you and your young chums played your dirty little games, and got your fingers burned? Cheerio, then; don't blame me if you can't be bothered to keep an eye on your goods and chattels."

Back away from him, toward the door, Rafe. Let him lie. How had Dr. Effie put it? "He fills the house, every room, every hour." Cheerless thought, that, fit for a scrawny old maid. The talkative Euphemia must have nearly as many screws loose as had her uncle; probably she envied him his revels.

"I really believe the others led Uncle Alec into the whole business gradually," Dr. Effie had droned on the last time he had seen her. "But once in, he took command, as natural to him. He was out in Nigeria before people called it Nigeria, you know, and in Guinea, and all up and down that coast. He began collecting materials for a monograph on African magic—raising the dead, and summoning devils, and more. Presently he was dabbling in the spells, not merely collecting them—so my father told me, forty years ago. After Uncle Alec came home, he didn't stop dabbling. Some very reputable people dabbled when I was a girl. But the ones around Uncle Alec weren't in the least reputable.

"Charlatans? Not quite; I wish they had been. They fed Balgrummo's appetite. Yet he was after knowledge, at least in the beginning; and though he may have boggled, more than once, at the steps he had to descend toward the source of that knowledge, he grew more eager as he pressed down into the dark. Or so Father guessed; Father became one of Uncle Alec's original trustees, and felt it his duty to collect some evidence of what had happened—though it sickened Father, the more he uncovered of his brother's queerness.

"Toward the end, Balgrummo may have forgotten about knowledge and have leapt into passion and power. One didn't *learn* what one had sought to apprehend; one *became* the mystery, possessing it and possessed by it.

"No, not charlatans—not altogether. They took a fortune out of Uncle Alec, one way or another; and he had to pay even more to keep people quiet in those years. They had told Balgrummo, in effect, that they could raise the devil—though they didn't put it in quite that crude way. Yet they must have been astounded by their success, when it came at last. Balgrummo had paid before, and he has paid ever since. Those others paid, too—especially the man and the woman who died. They had thought they were raising the devil *for* Lord Balgrummo. But as it turned out, they raised the devil *through* Balgrummo and *in* Balgrummo. After that, everything fell to pieces."

But to hell with recollections of Euphemia Inchburn, Rafe. Dry rot, wet rot, woodworm, death-watch beetle: the devil take them all, and Balgrummo Lodging besides. One thing the devil shouldn't have—these pictures. Get on to the chapel, Rafe, and then give Nan the glad news. Thanks for the brandy, Alec: I mightn't have got through the business without it.

Yet one dram too many, possibly? Horgan was aware of a certain giddiness, but not fully aware of how he had got up those Stygian stairs, or of what he had done with his torch. Had he turned the key in the lock of the chapel door? He couldn't recall having done so. Still, here he was in the chapel.

No need for the torch; the room, a long gallery, was lit by all those candle flames in the many-branched candlesticks. Who kept Lord Balgrummo's candles alight? The stench of decay was even stronger here than it had been down below. Under foot, the floorboards were almost oozing, and mushroom rot squashed beneath his shoes. Some of the paneling had fallen away altogether. High up in the shifting shadows, the molded plaster ceiling sagged and bulged as if the lightest touch would bring it all down in slimy little particles.

Back of the altar—the altar of the catastrophic act of Balgrummo's trouble—hung the unknown Fuseli. It was no painting, but an immense cartoon, and the most uninhibited museum director never would dare show it to the most broadminded critics of art. Those naked and contorted forms, the instruments of torment fixed upon their flesh, were the inversion of the Agony. Even Horgan could not bear to look at them long.

Look at them? All those candles were guttering. Two winked out simultaneously; others failed. As the little flames sank toward extinction, Rafe Horgan became aware that he was not alone.

It was as if presences skulked in corners or behind the broken furniture. And there could be no retreat toward the door; for something approached from that end of the gallery. As if Horgan's extremity of terror fed it, the shape took on increasing clarity of outline, substance, strength.

Tall, arrogant, implacable, mindless, it drifted toward him. The face was Balgrummo's, or what Balgrummo's must have been fifty years before, but possessed: eager, eager; eager; all appetite, passion, yearning after the abyss. In one hand glittered a long knife.

Horgan bleated and ran. He fell against the cobwebby altar. And in the final act of destruction, something strode across the great gulf of time.

THE OLD DARKNESS

PAMELA SARGENT

Pamela Sargent began publishing science fiction and fantasy with her "Landed Minority" in *F & SF* in 1970 and has developed into one of the most distinctive, if underrated voices in sf. Her most recent novel is *The Shore of Women* (1986). Her writings are typified by strong characters and by her unflinching ability to examine human relationships. As an editor, her anthologies (such as the 1975 *Women of Wonder*) include stories that boast female protagonists as well as the aforementioned qualities. "The Old Darkness" examines a small group caught in a power failure and their reactions; if you thought there was something romantic about a blackout, this story may quickly change your mind.

The kitchen window was white with light; a thousand invisible hands clapped in unison. Nina tensed. The kitchen was suddenly dark; outside, the wind howled as rain drummed against the window.

"What was that?" Andrew shouted from the living room.

"I don't know. It sounded like something hit the house."

"It had to happen now—bottom of the ninth, with a tie." She heard her husband shuffle through the hallway toward the kitchen. It was growing darker outside; evening's dim gray light was fading.

"I don't know what I'm going to do about supper," Nina said, staring at her now-useless food processor. "I was just going to chop the onions."

Andrew leaned against the refrigerator. "You used to chop them without that thing."

"I know, but it's made me lazy. I can't do anything without it." She crossed the room, crept into the hall, and opened the door, peering into the dark corridor. "Everything's out."

"Nina?"

She recognized her neighbor's voice. "Rosalie?"

"Yeah, it's me. I looked outside a second ago. I can't see a light on the whole street."

"Dammnit," Nina said. "I was fixing supper."

"Well, the gas is still on. Just be glad you don't have an electric stove."

Nina cleared her throat. The darkness was making her uneasy; the air in the hallway seemed heavy and thick. She backed into her apartment, closing the door.

Andrew was still in the kitchen, dialing a number. "Who are you calling?" she asked.

"Power company. Hello? Yeah, I wanted to ask—okay, I'll wait." He leaned against the wall. Thunder rolled overhead as Nina went to the window; the wind shrieked. The rain was a silver sheet nearly parallel to the ground, a curtain buffeted by the wind.

"Hello? Yeah, I just wanted to know—uh-huh. We're on the north side. Yeah." Andrew paused. "How soon? Uh-huh. Okay. Well, thanks." He hung up. "One of the main lines is down. They said they should have it fixed in an hour or two."

"I guess we can eat late. I can't make this dish without the Cuisinart."

"Oh, come on. You can get along without electricity."

"I can't even see what I'm doing."

"We've got candles. I'll set some up for you. We've got a flashlight." He rummaged in one drawer, pulling out a box of matches. "We can rough it for one evening."

Nina finished preparing dinner by the flickering yellow light of the candles. Andrew had set one on the stove, another on the countertop, and two more on the table, with a mirror behind them to catch the light.

She shivered. The air seemed unusually cold in spite of the oven's heat. She felt oddly vulnerable without the familiar presence of electricity, unable to prepare food without it, unable to read—she couldn't even dry her long, thick hair without a hair dryer. The artifacts of technology had made her only more incompetent; she thought of the past, imagining families going about their tasks as the sun set, reading to one another by the light of a fire, drawing close against the night.

Her grandparents, believers in progress, had always told her things were better now. Human minds had been darker when people couldn't read late at night, their prejudices greater when they had lacked television's images of other places, their work harder without the appliances many took for granted. Nina was not so sure; technical civilization had isolated people from the basics of life, and had fooled them into believing that they controlled the world.

Andrew set the table, then put a portable radio and cassette player near the candles. "This isn't so bad. Kind of romantic, actually. We should do this more often."

"They still haven't repaired the line."

"They will."

"Everything in the freezer's going to get ruined."

"Forget about the freezer. It'll keep. Just don't open the door." He uncorked a bottle of wine while she served the stuffed peppers.

As she carried the plates to the table, the thunder rumbled again. Storms had always frightened her, and the darkness beyond the lighted room was filled with threatening shadows. She sat down, facing the mirror. The smell of melting wax mingled with the odor of tomato sauce and spices.

"We've got food. We've even got music." Andrew's voice sounded hollow and distant. A dark shadow loomed behind Nina, about to cloak her in black; she stared at the mirror, afraid to move. Andrew popped a cassette into the player, and the sound of Bach filled the room.

The music was soothing. Andrew began to conduct with his fork. "Magnificat," he bellowed along with the chorus.

A fist pounded on the door. Nina started. "Who is it?"

"Rosalie."

That surprised her; Rosalie usually had a gentle, tentative knock. As Nina left the light of the kitchen, the air pressed in around her; she was once again afraid. She opened the door. "Come on in."

The words were hardly out of her mouth before her neighbor was inside. Rosalie panted, then leaned against the wall, hands over her belly. Nina took her arm and led Rosalie into the kitchen, seating her across from Andrew.

"I'm all right now," Rosalie said. "It's the dark. I guess it got to me. I really got scared."

"It's okay. Do you want a pepper?"

Rosalie shook her head but accepted a glass of wine from Andrew. "I wouldn't have come over, but I couldn't stay there alone. I was going to go over to Jeff's, but the radio said people should stay off the roads—the wind's knocking down trees."

"Where's Lisanne?"

"At her father's for the weekend." Rosalie lifted her glass; her hand was shaking. She sipped some wine. "All I've got is a flashlight, so I wasn't very prepared."

Andrew turned down the music; a shadow in the corner seemed to darken. "I felt it too," Nina said. "I got the creeps when I went to answer the door."

"You're too suggestible," Andrew said in a loud voice.

"It was cold," Rosalie said in a flat tone as the candlelight flickered on her face, adding a golden glow to her coppery hair. "I was in the living room, and I felt a cold spot, right in the center of the room. Then the O'Haras started screaming at each other—I could hear them through the floor."

"The O'Haras were fighting?" Nina said, surprised.

"You bet. I didn't know she knew that kind of language. The living room got colder. Something was breathing down my neck, and I thought I heard a sigh. Then I thought, if I don't get out of here, I'll be trapped—I won't be able to—"

"A draft." Andrew gestured with his knife. "There's always a draft in this building."

"It wasn't a draft. The air was just sitting there."

Nina tried to smile. "It's a good thing my grandparents aren't here. They'd be telling old stories by now. You know, there's a legend that the first people who settled in this valley disappeared—just vanished into the woods. And once—" Andrew was warning her with his eyes. "It's just a story. No one believed it."

"You grew up here, didn't you?" Rosalie asked.

Nina nodded. "Lived here all my life, except for college." The rest of her family had left, moving to places of warmth and light, while she had remained behind, afraid to live among strangers unilluminated by familiarity.

The Bach cantata came to an end; Andrew clicked off the cassette player.

"They *still* haven't repaired the line," Nina said.

"The storm's probably worse than they expected." Rosalie's voice echoed in the kitchen. The room was darker; the candle on the stove had gone out. The shadow in the corner was now a misshapen birdlike figure; its wingtips fluttered. "I hope," Rosalie went on, "that you've got more candles. These won't last much longer."

"There's a scented one in the living room." Andrew stood up. "I'd better go get it."

"Take the flashlight," Nina said.

"I can find my way."

Nina turned toward her neighbor as Andrew left the kitchen. She was about to speak, when she saw Rosalie's lips draw back over her teeth; the woman was a predator, her jaws ready to bite, her hands claws. "That bastard," Rosalie said softly. "Ever since our divorce, he's been making Lisanne think he's the good guy. I'll bet he's telling her right now that it was all my fault."

Nina drew back. Rosalie had always been on good terms with her ex-husband; their divorce had been notable for its lack of rancor. "He was the one who wanted it," Rosalie continued. "He manipulated me into court, and I didn't even see it. I thought he was being nice, and so I got screwed on the settlement—he knew I wouldn't fight it."

Nina felt trapped. The kitchen seemed small, the walls too close. Then she heard a thud in the front of the apartment, and a cry.

She jumped up, grabbed the flashlight from the counter, and hurried into the living room. "Andy?"

He was lying on the floor, his face pale in the flashlight's beam. "Something hit me." He picked up a thick book and put it on the coffee table.

"Are you all right?" She knelt beside him. He nodded, rubbing his head. "You'd better put up another shelf."

"I haven't had time."

"Then get rid of some of that junk." Nina's voice was sharp. "It's taking over the place. Pretty soon we'll have to get an apartment just for the books." She was shouting, longing to sweep the rows of hardcover mysteries from the shelves and hurl them into the rain. "And you never do your share of the dusting either." She took a breath, feeling light-headed; the feeling of oppression had lifted.

A candle danced in the darkness, illuminating Rosalie's face. "Anything wrong?"

Nina sighed as Andrew climbed to his feet. "Book hit me in the head, that's all."

Andrew cleared the table and put the dirty dishes into the sink, then moved their remaining candles into the living room, along with the cassette player. He lighted only the scented candle, saving the others.

"We've got about three or four hours' worth of candles," he said.

"They have to have the line repaired by then." Nina, listening to the whine of the wind, was not so sure.

Andrew turned on the cassette player. Voices singing God's praises wavered, missing a few notes. He hit the machine, then turned it off.

"Haven't you got anything else?" Rosalie asked.

"I've got Vivaldi, and Handel, and some—"

"I should have brought my tapes," Rosalie interrupted. "Unfortunately, I left them in my car." She glanced at the window. "And I'm not going out in that."

Andrew said, "I can't say I'm sorry."

Rosalie lifted her head. "What's that supposed to mean?"

"I can't stand that music you're always playing—if you can even call it music."

"And just what's wrong with it?"

"It's all screaming and percussion—a perfect example of human primitivism and banality."

"Really! I suppose you think that Tinker Toy music is better."

"Don't call it Tinker Toy music."

"It's boring," Rosalie said. "It's all the same."

"How can you say that?"

"Stop it!" Nina shouted. Rosalie sank back on the couch; Andrew, seated on the floor, draped one arm over the coffee table. "We don't have to argue about it." Nina's stomach was tight with tension; she wondered if the stuffed peppers were giving her indigestion. "It's a matter of taste."

Lightning brightened the room for an instant; Andrew's mustache was black against his face. "It's a matter of taste, all right," he said. "Good taste and bad."

Before Rosalie could respond, he had turned on the music again. Andrew shook his head. "I'm sorry, Rosalie."

"It's okay. I'm sorry too."

Nina heard footsteps on the stairs, then a knock on the door; a child squealed. "I'll get it," Andrew said.

As he made his way out of the room, Nina leaned toward Rosalie. "He didn't mean it."

"I know. I feel all right now. I just wanted to lash out at someone all of a sudden."

Andrew was speaking to their callers; Nina recognized the voices of Jill and Tony Levitas. Their daughter Melanie preceded them into the room, sat down at one end of the sofa, and began to suck her thumb. The music sounded sluggish; Nina turned off the cassette player.

"Sorry," Jill said as she sat in a chair. "We didn't want to come upstairs, but—I don't know how to put it."

"You were getting the creeps," Rosalie said. "That's why I came over."

Jill lowered her voice. "Our dining room table started to move—honest to God. Then Melanie got hysterical. She said there was something in her room, and she refused to go to bed. She's never been afraid of the dark before."

Rosalie said, "The O'Haras were fighting. Can you believe it?"

"I heard them. It sounded pretty grim."

"I brought a libation," Tony said, setting a jug of wine on the table. Andrew came in with more glasses and poured the wine, then retreated to a corner with Tony.

"We were going to go out tonight," Jill said. "Then the baby-sitter called and said she couldn't make it—a tree fell in her driveway. Not that it matters—the theater's probably blacked out too. So we're stuck."

"Steinbrenner should just leave them alone and let them play ball," Andrew was saying.

"He's paying them." Tony wrapped his arms around his long, thin legs.

"Of course, we have to have this storm on practically the first night in months we were going out," Jill said bitterly. "And it'll probably be ages before we go out again. Let that be a lesson to you, Nina." Two reflected flames fluttered on Jill's glasses. "Don't have a kid until you've done everything you want to do, because you don't get a chance later on. And don't expect your husband to help."

"I heard that," Tony said.

"It's true."

"Look, I have to work. I do my share on the weekends."

"You were the one who talked me into quitting my job."

"Because it would have cost us more for you to work."

"So what? Doesn't my peace of mind mean anything to you?"

"Jill! You *hated* that job."

"At least I was with adults. I'm regressing. The biggest intellectual effort I make now is comparing the merits of *General Hospital* with *The Young and the Restless.*"

"You wanted the kid, Jill."

"*You* wanted her!"

"You know what your trouble is?" Tony's voice was unusually high. "You never bothered to look for a job you liked, because you thought some man would take care of you. Now you're bitching because you don't like housework. Well, make up your mind."

Melanie curled up, covering her head with her hands. Nina rubbed her arms; the room felt cold. Something rustled; she heard a crack. Several books flew off the shelves, crashing to the floor; one struck her in the back.

She jumped up. Inside her a snake uncoiled, creeping up to her throat. "Dammit, Andy! Do you have to get so many books?" She was shouting again. She rarely shouted, and she had done so twice in a few minutes. She strode to the window, peering out at the storm. Lights twinkled on a distant hill, reminding her of stars; at least the South Side still had power.

Five men, barely visible, were on the sidewalk below. They were drinking, ignoring the rain that drenched them. Water streamed from their jackets and hair, making them look as though they were melting. One man held his beer bottle by its top, then pitched it over the fence into the front yard.

"Shit," Nina muttered. "Somebody just threw a bottle into the yard."

Andrew was at her side. He pushed up the window, then opened the storm window behind it. Rain sprayed Nina's face.

"Hey!" Andrew shouted above the wind as he shone his flashlight on the litterers. "Pick up your bottle!" The men were still. "Don't throw your crap in our yard."

Another man drew his arm back; a bottle flew, smashing against the side of the building. A second bottle followed it, landing in the branches of the pine tree.

Nina closed the storm window hastily. "Call the police."

"You can't," Tony responded. "The phones are out now. I tried to call you before we came upstairs."

Andrew turned off the flashlight. "I've seen those guys before. They never acted like that."

Melanie whimpered and began to cry. "Hush," Jill said. Melanie wailed. "Be quiet!"

Rosalie reached for the child, trying to soothe her. "Leave her alone."

"There's something to be said for divorce," Jill said. "At least you get to unload Lisanne once in a while. How's that sound, Tony? I'll even give you custody."

"Shut up, Jill."

"I'll even pay child support."

Tony lumbered across the room. "Shut up, dammit."

"I don't know what you're complaining about," Rosalie cried. "I wish I had more time with my kid. That goddamned Elliott made sure he had someone else lined up before he told me he wanted a divorce."

Nina leaned against the windowsill. The bitter voices seemed far away, the harsh words dim. The room was warmer, as if her friends' anger had driven away the cold. She gazed at the fluttering shadows near the couch, surprised that the placid Jill and the cheerful Rosalie had such strong feelings.

Andrew gulped down his wine, reached for the jug, and poured another glass. A breath of air tickled Nina's ear. "He's had enough to drink." The voice was so low she could barely hear it; she looked around quickly. "He can't handle it. He never could hold his liquor." Before she could see where the voice was coming from, rage had taken hold of her; she clenched her fists.

Andrew knelt, hitting the cassette player. "Damn battery's dead. Go get some more."

Nina said, "There aren't any more."

"You mean you didn't pick any up?"

"I was going to get some tomorrow." She screamed the words. "You expect me to remember everything."

Andrew poured himself more wine. Nina reached for the bottle; he pulled it away.

"You've had enough, Andy."

"Get off my case." He gulped the wine defiantly.

"Andy, stop it. You know you can't drink that much."

"I'll do what I please. I don't need your permission."

"He'll be a drunk, just like his father," the voice sighed.

"You'll be like your father," Nina said. "You'll drink yourself right into the hospital."

"It's only wine, for Christ's sake." Andrew stood up. "I can't tell you how many times I've wanted to tie one on, and how many times I resisted. You and your nagging. Leave me alone. You'd like to see me drunk, wouldn't you, just to prove your point."

Nina heard a slap. "You son of a bitch!" Jill shouted. "Now you're turning into a wife beater. Go ahead, hit me again."

Tony said, "I'll give you more than a slap next time."

Nina wanted to scream. The voice was whispering again. "Jill always has her television set on too loud. And Tony forgets to mow the lawn. And Melanie leaves her toys on the stairs." She covered her ears, but could still hear the voice. "Admit it," the voice said. "You hate them."

"No!" Nina cried. Melanie had stopped weeping; the racking sobs she heard now were Rosalie's. "We've got to stop this." She felt a sharp pain in her chest, and gasped for air. The room was darker; the walls creaked as the wind outside gusted. "We've never had arguments before—what's the matter with us?" The pain was worse; she sat down, clutching her abdomen. She hated everyone in the room, and the only way she could get rid of the hate was to let it out.

"She's right," Tony said; his voice sounded hoarse. The coffee table rattled; the candle danced. Another book flew across the room, hitting the wall with a thud. The whispers were now so pronounced that Nina could barely hear anything else.

"You know what it is?" Tony said, crackling. "I didn't bless the wine. My parents always told me to bless my food or it would do bad things to me." His voice cracked as he sang a prayer in Hebrew.

Nina's pain was fading. She sniffed; the air, so heavy before, now smelled clean. "What's going on?"

"I don't know," Tony replied.

"Keep praying," Andrew said. Tony sang another prayer. "That's it. If we only had some batteries—we could play more Bach."

"What's that got to do with it?" Rosalie asked.

"It's sacred music. Didn't you notice? When the cassette was on, we were okay. Now Tony's praying, and I can't hear those voices anymore."

"You heard them too?"

"I think we all did."

Nina reached for Andrew's hand. Tony paused for breath; Rosalie began to sing "Rock of Ages." "It's the power failure," Andrew went on. "It's as if electricity is some sort of white magic, keeping things in check. Now we have to use older magic."

Nina trembled. An unseen hand pressed against her head, waiting to crush her when the songs failed. She had always dismissed her grandparents' lore, and even they had not taken it all that seriously. Now she recalled their tales of objects flying across rooms, of occasional murders which usually happened at night, of people barring their doors against the darkness.

"I can't believe it," Tony said. "This is the twentieth century, for God's sake." Rosalie was now singing "Amazing Grace"; her voice faltered on the high notes.

Out in the kitchen a dish smashed to the floor. The candle on the coffee table went out.

Nina felt as though she were at the center of a vortex; unseen beings whirled around her. Rosalie continued to sing as Andrew lit the candle. The walls, Nina felt, would cave in on her; whatever was with them would not be held off by a few simple songs and prayers.

"We have to get out of here," Andrew said. "The South Side still has power. We ought to be safe there."

"We can't," Jill replied. "It's too risky. They told people to stay off the roads unless it's an emergency."

"This is an emergency. I think we should get into our cars and go."

"No," Rosalie said as Tony began to sing. "We're safer here."

"As long as you keep singing." Books hopped on the shelves. "And maybe not even then."

"Andy's right," Nina said. A cushion of cold air seemed to swallow her words. "Please come with us." She glanced at the sofa. "At least let us take Melanie."

"No," Jill said, moving toward the child and shielding her with one arm.

Nina retreated to the door with Andrew. At the end of the hall the refrigerator rattled; more dishes fell. She reached for her purse, pulling it off a hook. "I'd better drive. You can't with all that wine in you." The words sounded harsher than she had intended; the pain was returning.

Andrew opened the door. Nina looked back at her neighbors, who were huddled around the candle; a misty barrier now separated her from them. She crept into the hall and down the darkened stairway, clinging to the railing. There was an ominous silence behind the O'Haras' door.

As she opened the front door, the wind nearly tore it from her grasp; she hung on. Andrew took her purse, fumbling for the car keys. She pushed the door shut.

He threw her the purse and sprinted toward the car, which was parked across the street. A large puddle had formed on the lawn, reaching to the sidewalk. Rain poured over her, plastering her clothes against her body. Next door, a man stood outside his house, screaming at the porch. Nina could not see the rest of the street; the sky, dark as it was, seemed lighter than the black earth below it.

Lightning lit her way. A shape was crouching near the building; it barked. "Oscar," she murmured, recognizing the O'Haras' dachshund, and wondering what it was doing outside. "Poor thing."

The dog leapt at her, biting at her leg. Claws and teeth tore at her jeans. She swung her purse, hitting the animal in the head and knocking it against the door.

"Come on, Nina!" She ran for the car, climbing in next to Andrew, and started the engine. Windshield wipers fanned back and forth, but the rain was so heavy she could see nothing else.

She turned on the headlights. The car crawled down the road. A tree had fallen, blocking the left side of the street; a group of people were in the right lane. Some were grinning; the headlights caught the white of their teeth and made their eyes gleam.

Nina honked her horn. The crowd rushed the car. She braked. Fists beat against the windows; the car rocked.

"Get going!" Andrew shouted.

She gunned the motor. The car shot forward; the people dropped away. She made a right turn, toward the south. "We'll make it," Andrew said. "Not much farther to go."

The car stalled. Nina turned the key, pumping the pedal. "Damn." The motor turned over and died. "What's wrong with it?"

"I don't know."

"You forgot to take it to the garage. I told you, and you forgot."

"I didn't have time."

"Dammit, Andy!" She struck at him; he grabbed her fists, holding her back. She tried to kick.

"Nina!" He shook her. "We'll have to walk, that's all."

"Out there?"

"You're already soaked. Come on."

They got out of the car. As they ran to the sidewalk, the wind howled, nearly knocking Nina to the ground. She heard a sharp crack. A tree toppled over, smashing the abandoned car.

Andrew grabbed her arm, leading her down the darkened street.

A dark mass milled in front of the shopping center; Nina heard the sound of shattering glass. Two men brushed past her, carrying a case of bourbon; a boy hurried by with a portable television set.

A crowd had gathered in front of the blacked-out stores. Several people were inside, hurling clothes, small appliances, and bottles through the broken windows to those in the parking lot.

Andrew stopped. Nina tugged at his arm. "We'd better get going!" she shouted. "The police will be here pretty soon." Alarms powered by batteries whined and clanged; the crowd cheered as a microwave oven hurtled through one window. She looked around hastily, wondering where the police were.

Another mob was running toward them; Nina and Andrew were suddenly in the midst of the crowd, being pushed toward the stores. She reached for her husband and clutched air.

"Andy!" She struggled to stay on her feet, afraid she would be trampled if she fell. "Andy!"

A toaster flew past her, hitting another woman, who dropped out of sight. A few people were carrying flashlights, holding them as if they were torches. A young girl raced past, her arms filled with jeans. Nina reached out for a post and held on as the crowd surged toward the liquor store.

Several people were lying on the walkway; she heard groans. Lightning lit up the scene; Nina imagined that she saw a black pool of blood near one man's head. "Andy!"

"Nina."

Andrew was near her, sprawled on the ground. She leaned over, pulling at him. He moaned. "My leg—it's hurt."

She pulled him up; he leaned against her heavily. More people ran past them, joining the crowd looting the nearby hardware store. "I don't think I can make it. You'd better leave me."

"Save yourself," the voice whispered.

"I won't!" Nina shouted. She said a prayer as she hauled Andrew through the parking lot and toward the road.

The wind had died down; the rain was falling more slowly. Trees threatened Nina with their branches as she passed, swatting at her as she struggled along with the limping Andrew. She was muttering prayers almost automatically, surprised that she, who had not said them in years, could remember so many.

They passed a lawn littered with furniture, and heard a distant scream. A beam blinded her for a moment; pebbles struck her as children laughed. Nina flailed at the air with her free arm. The flashlight fled from her as the children retreated.

She peered through the rain, seeing a hazy golden glow. "Light," she said. "We're almost there." She could now make out streetlights and tried to move faster; Andrew was slowing her down. She said, "You won't get me." A lighted road wound up a hill; an electric company truck was blocking it. She moved toward the truck.

A police car was parked under a streetlight, near the truck. Leading Andrew toward it, she approached the boundary between darkness and light, then stopped.

She tried to step forward and could not; something was holding her back. She pushed; her knees locked.

"No!" she screamed.

A door opened on one side of the police car; a man in a slicker hurried toward her. "What are you doing out here?" he shouted.

"Help us," she said, stretching out an arm. She couldn't reach him. He grabbed at her, then fell back.

"We can't get in," the policeman said. "We've tried. We're still trying."

"And you can't get out," the voice whispered.

She tried to step forward again, and felt herself stumble back; Andrew slipped to the ground.

"I can't help you, lady." The policeman waved his arms helplessly. "I wish I could."

She sank to the ground, cradling Andrew in her arms. The night was suddenly brighter; she was having delusions, seeing the light she longed for. The wind howled its rage. Arms seized her; she held on to Andrew.

"Come on, lady!" The policeman was holding her; he had reached her somehow. He let go and pulled Andrew up. She stumbled to her feet and followed the two men to the car, where the policeman's partner was waiting.

"Look!" the partner shouted.

Nina turned. Her side of town was now starry with light. A solid blackness lifted from the ground, then began to roll back toward the hills in the north. "We're safe," she said to Andrew. "We're safe." The policeman was shaking his head as he gazed at the ebony fog.

Sparks danced along a power line overhead; the line snapped, writhing down at them like a snake. They dragged Andrew to the car. The North Side was once again dark, and growing darker; soon the impenetrable darkness was so thick that Nina, safe in the light, could not see through the blackness at all.

She had dozed off. Nina awoke with a start, shook herself, and got out of the police car.

The rain had stopped. In the dim light she could see a medic wrapping a bandage around Andrew's leg. A crowd stood in the street, staring at the black veil before them.

"It's on!" a man's voice shouted. "Power's back!"

As the sun peeped over the hills to Nina's right, the black wall rolled away, defeated by the light. Someone cried out. Only blackened earth lay where the darkness had been; the gloom had taken everything away, leaving only a vast, scarred plain. Only the power lines, the town's humming sentries, remained on the ravaged North Side.

Nina thought of her friends, trapped forever in the dark. Where, she wondered, would the darkness go? She knew. It would retreat to the edge of the world, and into the people she knew, and into her; she could feel it lurking there even now, hiding in her mind's shadows with her fears. It would wait for the white magic to fail.

THE NIGHT
OF WHITE BHAIRAB

LUCIUS SHEPARD

Lucius Shepard is probably the best new short-fiction writer
of the 1980s. His novella "R & R" received a Nebula award
in 1987, and his stories were recently collected in a book
titled *Jaguar Hunter*. The most noticeable feature of his
tales is the exotic settings, which are gleaned from his own
travels. "The Night of White Bhairab" first appeared in *F
& SF* in October 1984 and is set in Nepal. It is the story of
a young American in Katmandu searching for enlightenment, only to fall in love and into a supernatural adventure.
In the tale, Lucius Shepard utilizes not only the landscape
of Nepal but also its myths and legends to create an eerie
entanglement in and with the "mysterious" East.

Whenever Mr. Chatterji went to
Delhi on business, twice yearly, he would leave Eliot Blackford in charge
of his Katmandu home, and prior to each trip, the transfer of keys and
instructions would be made at the Hotel Anapurna. Eliot—an angular,
sharp-featured man in his mid-thirties, with thinning blond hair and a
perpetually ardent expression—knew Mr. Chatterji for a subtle soul, and
he suspected that this subtlety had dictated the choice of meeting place.
The Anapurna was the Nepalese equivalent of a Hilton, its bar equipped
in vinyl and plastic, with a choirlike arrangement of bottles fronting the

mirror. Lights were muted, napkins monogrammed. Mr. Chatterji, plump and prosperous in a business suit, would consider it an elegant refutation of Kipling's famous couplet ("East is East," etc.) that he was at home here, whereas Eliot, wearing a scruffy robe and sandals, was not; he would argue that not only the twain met, they had actually exchanged places. It was Eliot's own measure of subtlety that restrained him from pointing out what Mr. Chatterji could not perceive: that the Anapurna was a skewed version of the American Dream. The carpeting was indoor-outdoor runner; the menu was rife with ludicrous misprints (*Skotch Miss*, *Screwdriver*), and the lounge act—two turbaned, tuxedoed Indians on electric guitar and traps—was managing to turn "Evergreen" into a doleful raga.

"There will be one important delivery." Mr. Chatterji hailed the waiter and nudged Eliot's shot glass forward. "It should have been here days ago, but you know these customs people." He gave an effeminate shudder to express his distaste for the bureaucracy, and cast an expectant eye on Eliot, who did not disappoint.

"What is it?" he asked, certain that it would be an addition to Mr. Chatterji's collection: he enjoyed discussing the collection with Americans; it proved that he had an overview of their culture.

"Something delicious!" said Mr. Chatterji. He took the tequila bottle from the waiter and—with a fond look—passed it to Eliot. "Are you familiar with the Carversville Terror?"

"Yeah, sure." Eliot knocked back another shot. "There was a book about it."

"Indeed," said Mr. Chatterji. "A best seller. The Cousineau mansion was once the most notorious haunted house of your New England. It was torn down several months ago, and I've succeeded in acquiring the fireplace, which"—he sipped his drink—"which was the locus of power. I'm very fortunate to have obtained it." He fitted his glass into the circle of moisture on the bar and waxed scholarly. "Aimée Cousineau was a most unusual spirit, capable of a variety of. . . ."

Eliot concentrated on his tequila. These recitals never failed to annoy him, as did—for different reasons—the sleek western disguise. When Eliot had arrived in Katmandu as a member of the Peace Corps, Mr. Chatterji had presented a far less pompous image: a scrawny kid dressed in jeans that he had wheedled from a tourist. He'd been one of the hangers-on—mostly young Tibetans—who frequented the grubby tea rooms on Freak Street, watching the American hippies giggle over their hash yogurt, lusting after their clothes, their women, their entire culture. The hippies had respected the Tibetans: they were a people of legend,

symbols of the occultism then in vogue, and the fact that they like James
Bond movies, fast cars, and Jimi Hendrix had increased the hippies' self-
esteem. But they had found laughable the fact that Ranjeesh Chatterji
—another westernized Indian—had liked these same things, and they
had treated him with mean condescension. Now, thirteen years later,
the roles had been reversed; it was Eliot who had become the hanger-
on.

He had settled in Katmandu after his tour was up, his idea being to
practice meditation, to achieve enlightenment. But it had not gone well.
There was an impediment in his mind—he pictured it as a dark stone,
a stone compounded of worldly attachments—that no amount of practice
could wear down, and his life had fallen into a futile pattern. He would
spend ten months of the year living in a small room near the temple of
Swayambhunath, meditating, rubbing away at the stone; and then, during
March and September, he would occupy Mr. Chatterji's house and de-
bauch himself with liquor and sex and drugs. He was aware that Mr.
Chatterji considered him a burnout, that the position of caretaker was
in effect a form of revenge, a means by which his employer could exercise
his own brand of condescension; but Eliot minded neither the label nor
the attitude. There were worse things to be than a burnout in Nepal. It
was beautiful country, it was inexpensive, it was far from Minnesota
(Eliot's home). And the concept of personal failure was meaningless here.
You lived, died, and were reborn over and over until at last you attained
the ultimate success of nonbeing: a terrific consolation for failure.

"Yet in your country," Mr. Chatterji was saying, "evil has a sultry
character. Sexy! It's as if the spirits were adopting vibrant personalities
in order to contend with pop groups and movie stars."

Eliot thought of a comment, but the tequila backed up on him and
he belched instead. Everything about Mr. Chatterji—teeth, eyes, hair,
gold rings—seemed to be gleaming with extraordinary brilliance. He
looked as unstable as a soap bubble, a fat little Hindu illusion.

Mr. Chatterji clapped a hand to his forehead. "I nearly forgot. There
will be another American staying at the house. A girl. Very shapely!"
He shaped an hourglass in the air. "I'm quite mad for her, but I don't
know if she's trustworthy. Please see she doesn't bring in any strays."

"Right," said Eliot. "No problem."

"I believe I will gamble now," said Mr. Chatterji, standing and gazing
toward the lobby. "Will you join me?"

"No, I think I'll get drunk. I guess I'll see you in October."

"You're drunk already. Eliot." Mr. Chatterji patted him on the shoulder. "Hadn't you noticed?"

Early the next morning, hung over, tongue cleaving to the roof of his mouth, Eliot sat himself down for a final bout of trying to visualize the Avalokitesvara Buddha. All the sounds outside—the buzzing of a motor scooter, birdsong, a girl's laughter—seemed to be repeating the mantra, and the gray stone walls of his room looked at once intensely real and yet incredibly fragile, papery, a painted backdrop he could rip with his hands. He began to feel the same fragility, as if he were being immersed in a liquid that was turning him opaque, filling him with clarity. A breath of wind could float him out the window, drift him across the fields, and he would pass through the trees and mountains, all the phantoms of the material world . . . but then a trickle of panic welled up from the bottom of his soul, from that dark stone. It was beginning to smolder, to give off poison fumes: a little briquette of anger and lust and fear. Cracks were spreading across the clear substance he had become, and if he didn't move soon, if he didn't break off the meditation, he would shatter.

He toppled out of the lotus position and lay propped on his elbows. His heart raced, his chest heaved, and he felt very much like screaming his frustration. Yeah, that was a temptation. To just say the hell with it and scream, to achieve through chaos what he could not through clarity: to empty himself into the scream. He was trembling, his emotions flowing between self-hate and self-pity. Finally, he struggled up and put on jeans and a cotton shirt. He knew he was close to a breakdown, and he realized that he usually reached this point just before taking up residence at Mr. Chatterji's. His life was a frayed thread stretched tight between those two poles of debauchery. One day it would snap.

"The hell with it," he said. He stuffed the remainder of his clothes into a duffel bag and headed into town.

Walking through Durbar Square—which wasn't really a square but a huge temple complex interspersed with open areas and wound through by cobbled paths—always put Eliot in mind of his brief stint as a tour guide, a career cut short when the agency received complaints about his eccentricity ("As you pick your way among the piles of human waste and fruit rinds, I caution you not to breathe too deeply of the divine afflatus; otherwise, it may forever numb you to the scent of Prairie Cove or Petitpoint Gulch or whatever citadel of gracious living it is that you call home. . . .") It had irked him to have to lecture on the carvings and history of the square, especially to the just-plain-folks who only wanted a Polaroid of Edna or Uncle Jimmy standing next to that weird monkey god on the pedestal. The square was a unique place, and, in Eliot's opinion, such unenlightened tourism demeaned it.

Pagoda-style temples of red brick and dark wood towered on all sides, their finials rising into brass lightning bolts. They were alien-looking— you half expected the sky above them to be of an otherworldly color and figured by several moons. Their eaves and window screens were ornately carved into the images of gods and demons, and behind a large window screen on the temple of White Bhairab lay the mask of that god. It was almost ten feet high, brass, with a fanciful headdress and long-lobed ears and a mouth full of white fangs; its eyebrows were enameled red, fiercely arched, but the eyes had the goofy quality common to Newari gods— no matter how wrathful they were, there was something essentially friendly about them, and they reminded Eliot of cartoon germs. Once a year— in fact, a little more than a week from now—the screens would be opened, a pipe would be inserted into the god's mouth, and rice beer would jet out into the mouths of the milling crowds; at some point a fish would be slipped into the pipe, and whoever caught it would be deemed the luckiest soul in the Katmandu Valley for the next year. It was one of Eliot's traditions to make a try for the fish, though he knew that it wasn't luck he needed.

Beyond the square, the streets were narrow, running between long brick buildings three and four stories tall, each divided into dozens of separate dwellings. The strip of sky between the roofs was bright, burning blue—a void color—and in the shade the bricks looked purplish. People hung out the windows of the upper stories, talking back and forth: an exotic tenement life. Small shrines—wooden enclosures containing statuary of stucco or brass—were tucked into wall niches and the mouths of alleys. The gods were everywhere in Katmandu, and there was hardly a corner to which their gaze did not penetrate.

On reaching Mr. Chatterji's, which occupied half a block-long building, Eliot made for the first of the interior courtyards; a stair led up from it to Mr. Chatterji's apartment, and he thought he would check on what had been left to drink. But as he entered the courtyard—a phalanx of jungly plants arranged around a lozenge of cement—he saw the girl and stopped short. She was sitting in a lawn chair, reading, and she was indeed very shapely. She wore loose cotton trousers, a T-shirt, and a long white scarf shot through with golden threads. The scarf and the trousers were the uniform of the young travelers who generally stayed in the expatriate enclave of Temal: it seemed that they all bought them immediately upon arrival in order to identify themselves to one another. Edging closer, peering between the leaves of a rubber plant, Eliot saw that the girl was doe-eyed, with honey-colored skin and shoulder-length brown hair interwoven by lighter strands. Her wide mouth had relaxed into a glum expression. Sensing him, she glanced up, startled; then she waved and set down her book.

"I'm Eliot," he said, walking over.

"I know. Ranjeesh told me." She stared at him incuriously.

"And you?" He squatted beside her.

"Michaela." She fingered the book, as if she were eager to get back to it.

"I can see you're new in town."

"How's that?"

He told her about the clothes, and she shrugged. "That's what I am," she said. "I'll probably always wear them." She folded her hands on her stomach: it was a nicely rounded stomach, and Eliot—a connoisseur of women's stomachs—felt the beginnings of arousal.

"Always?" he said. "You plan on being here that long?"

"I don't know." She ran a finger along the spine of the book. "Ranjeesh asked me to marry him, and I said maybe."

Eliot's infant plan of seduction collapsed beneath this wrecking ball of a statement, and he failed to hide his incredulity. "You're in love with Ranjeesh?"

"What's that got to do with it?" A wrinkle creased her brow: it was the perfect symptom of her mood, the line a cartoonist might have chosen to express petulant anger.

"Nothing. Not if it doesn't have anything to do with it." He tried a grin, but to no effect. "Well," he said after a pause. "How do you like Katmandu?"

"I don't get out much," she said flatly.

She obviously did not want conversation, but Eliot wasn't ready to give up. "You ought to," he said. "The festival of Indra Jatra's about to start. It's pretty wild. Especially on the night of White Bhairab. Buffalo sacrifices, torchlight. . . ."

"I don't like crowds," she said.

Strike two.

Eliot strained to think of an enticing topic, but he had the idea it was a lost cause. There was something inert about her, a veneer of listlessness redolent of Thorazine, of hospital routine. "Have you seen the Khaa?" he asked.

"The what?"

"The Khaa. It's a spirit . . . though some people will tell you it's partly animal, because over here the animal and spirit worlds overlap. But whatever it is, all the old houses have one, and those that don't are considered unlucky. There's one here."

"What's it look like?"

"Vaguely anthropomorphic. Black, featureless. Kind of a living shadow. They can stand upright, but they roll instead of walk."

She laughed. "No, I haven't seen it. Have you?"

"Maybe," said Eliot. "I thought I saw it a couple of times, but I was pretty stoned."

She sat up straighter and crossed her legs; her breasts jiggled and Eliot fought to keep his eyes centered on her face. "Ranjeesh tells me you're a little cracked," she said.

Good ol' Ranjeesh! He might have known that the son of a bitch would have sandbagged him with his new lady. "I guess I am," he said, preparing for the brush-off. "I do a lot of meditation, and sometimes I teeter on the edge."

But she appeared more intrigued by this admission than by anything else he had told her; a smile melted up from her carefully composed features. "Tell me some more about the Khaa," she said.

Eliot congratulated himself. "They're quirky sorts," he said. "Neither good nor evil. They hide in dark corners, though now and then they're seen in the streets or in the fields out near Jyapu. And the oldest ones, the most powerful ones, live in the temples in Durbar Square. There's a story about the one here that's descriptive of how they operate . . . if you're interested."

"Sure." Another smile.

"Before Ranjeesh bought this place, it was a guesthouse, and one night a woman with three goiters on her neck came to spend the night. She had two loaves of bread that she was taking home to her family, and she stuck them under her pillow before going to sleep. Around midnight the Khaa rolled into her room and was struck by the sight of her goiters rising and falling as she breathed. He thought they'd make a beautiful necklace, so he took them and put them on his own neck. Then he spotted the loaves sticking out from her pillow. They looked good, so he took them as well and replaced them with two loaves of gold. When the woman woke, she was delighted. She hurried back to her village to tell her family, and on the way she met a friend, a woman who was going to market. This woman had four goiters. The first woman told her what had happened, and that night the second woman went to the guesthouse and did exactly the same things. Around midnight the Khaa rolled into her room. He'd grown bored with his necklace, and he gave it to the woman. He'd also decided that bread didn't taste very good, but he still had a loaf and he figured he'd give it another chance. So in exchange for the necklace, he took the woman's appetite for bread. When she woke, she had seven goiters, no gold, and she could never eat bread again the rest of her life."

Eliot had expected a response of mild amusement, and had hoped that the story would be the opening gambit in a game with a foregone and pleasurable conclusion; but he had not expected her to stand, to become walled off from him again.

"I've got to go," she said, and with a distracted wave she made for the front door. She walked with her head down, hands thrust into her pockets, as if counting the steps.

"Where are you going?" called Eliot, taken back.

"I don't know. Freak Street, maybe."

"Want some company?"

She turned back at the door. "It's not your fault," she said, "but I don't really enjoy your company."

Shot down!

Trailing smoke, spinning, smacking into the hillside, and blowing up into a fireball.

Eliot didn't understand why it had hit him so hard. It had happened before, and it would again. Ordinarily he would have headed for Temal and found himself another long white scarf and pair of cotton trousers, one less morbidly self-involved (that, in retrospect, was how he characterized Michaela), one who would help him refuel for another bout of trying to visualize Avalokitesvara Buddha. He did, in fact, go to Temal; but he merely sat and drank tea and smoked hashish in a restaurant, and watched the young travelers pairing up for the night. Once he caught the bus to Patan and visited a friend, an old hippie pal named Sam Chipley who ran a medical clinic; once he walked out to Swayambhunath, close enough to see the white dome of the stupa, and, atop it, the gilt structure on which the all-seeing eyes of Buddha were painted: they seemed squinty and mean-looking, as if taking unfavorable notice of his approach. But mostly over the next week he wandered through Mr. Chatterji's house, carrying a bottle, maintaining a buzz, and keeping an eye on Michaela.

The majority of the rooms were unfurnished, but many bore signs of recent habitation: broken hash pipes, ripped sleeping bags, empty packets of incense. Mr. Chatterji let travelers—those he fancied sexually, male and female—use the rooms for up to months at a time, and to walk through them was to take a historical tour of the American counterculture. The graffiti spoke of concerns as various as Vietnam, the Sex Pistols, women's lib, and the housing shortage in Great Britain, and also conveyed personal messages: "Ken Finkel please get in touch with me at Am. Ex. in Bangkok . . . love Ruth." In one of the rooms was a complicated mural depicting Farrah Fawcett sitting on the lap of a Tibetan demon, throttling his barbed phallus with her fingers. It all conjured up the image of a moldering, deranged milieu. Eliot's milieu. At first the tour amused him, but eventually it began to sour him on himself, and he took to spending more and more time on a balcony overlooking the courtyard that was shared with the connecting house, listening to the Newari women sing at their chores and reading books from Mr. Chatterji's library. One of the books was titled *The Carversville Terror*.

". . . bloodcurdling, chilling. . . ." said the *New York Times* on the front flap. ". . . the Terror is unrelenting. . . ." commented Stephen King. ". . . riveting, gut-wrenching, mind-bending horror. . . ." gushed *People* magazine. In neat letters, Eliot appended his own blurb: ". . . piece of crap. . . ." The text—written to be read by the marginally literate—was a fictionalized treatment of purportedly real events dealing with the experiences of the Whitcomb family, who had attempted to renovate the Cousineau mansion during the sixties. Following the usual buildup of apparitions, cold spots, and noisome odors, the family—Papa David, Mama Elaine, young sons Tim and Randy, and teenage Ginny—had met to discuss the situation.

Even the kids, thought David, had been aged by the house. Gathered around the dining room table, they looked like a company of the damned—haggard, shadows under their eyes, grim-faced. Even with the windows open and the light streaming in, it seemed there was a pall in the air that no light could dispel. Thank God the damned thing was dormant during the day!

"Well," he said, "I guess the floor's open for arguments."

"I wanna go home!" Tears sprang from Randy's eyes, and on cue, Tim started crying too.

"It's not that simple," said David. "This *is* home, and I don't know how we'll make it if we do leave. The savings account is just about flat."

"I suppose I could get a job," said Elaine unenthusiastically.

"I'm not leaving!" Ginny jumped to her feet, knocking over her chair. "Every time I start to make friends, we have to move!"

"But Ginny!" Elaine reached out a hand to calm her. "You were the one. . . ."

"I've changed my mind!" She backed away, as if she had just recognized them all to be mortal enemies. "You can do what you want, but I'm staying!" And she ran from the room.

"Oh, God," said Elaine wearily. "What's gotten into her?"

What had gotten into Ginny, what was in the process of getting into her and was the only interesting part of the book, was the spirit of Aimée Cousineau. Concerned with his daughter's behavior, David Whitcomb had researched the house and learned a great deal about the spirit. Aimée Cousineau, née Vuillemont, had been a native of St. Berenice, a Swiss village at the foot of the mountain known as the Eiger (its photograph, as well as one of Aimée—a coldly beautiful woman with black hair and cameo features—was included in the central section of the book). Until the age of fifteen, she had been a sweet, unexceptional child; however, in the summer of 1889, while hiking on the slopes of the Eiger, she had become lost in a cave.

The family had all but given up hope, when, to their delight—three weeks later—she had turned up on the steps of her father's store. Their delight was short-lived. This Aimée was far different from the one who had entered the cave. Violent, calculating, slatternly.

Over the next two years, she succeeded in seducing half the men of the village, including the local priest. According to his testimony, he had been admonishing her that sin was not the path to happiness, when she began to undress. "I'm wed to Happiness," she told him. "I've entwined my limbs with the God of Bliss and kissed the scaly thighs of Joy." Throughout the ensuing affair, she made cryptic comments concerning "the God below the mountain," whose soul was now forever joined to hers.

At this point the book reverted to the gruesome adventures of the Whitcomb family, and Eliot, bored, realizing it was noon and that Michaela would be sunbathing, climbed to Mr. Chatterji's apartment on the fourth floor. He tossed the book onto a shelf and went out onto the balcony. His continued interest in Michaela puzzled him. It occurred to him that he might be falling in love, and he thought that would be nice. Though it would probably lead nowhere, love would be a good kind of energy to have. But he doubted this was the case. Most likely his interest was founded on some fuming product of the dark stone inside him. Simple lust. He looked over the edge of the balcony. She was lying on a blanket—her bikini top beside her—at the bottom of a well of sunlight: thin, pure sunlight like a refinement of honey spreading down and congealing into the mold of a little gold woman. It seemed her heat that was in the air.

That night Eliot broke one of Mr. Chatterji's rules and slept in the
master bedroom. It was roofed by a large skylight mounted in a ceiling
painted midnight blue. The normal display of stars had not been sufficient
for Mr. Chatterji, and so he'd had the skylight constructed of faceted
glass that multiplied the stars, making it appear that you were at the heart
of a galaxy, gazing out between the interstices of its blazing core. The
walls consisted of a photomural of the Khumbu Glacier and Chomolungma; and, bathed in the starlight, the mural had acquired the illusion
of depth and chill mountain silence. Lying there, Eliot could hear the
faint sounds of Indra Jatra: shouts and cymbals, oboes and drums. He
was drawn to the sounds; he wanted to run out into the streets, become
an element of the drunken crowds, be whirled through torchlight and
delirium to the feet of an idol stained with sacrificial blood. But he felt
bound to the house, to Michaela. Marooned in the glow of Mr. Chatterji's
starlight, floating above Chomolungma and listening to the din of the
world below, he could almost believe he was a bodhisattva awaiting a
call to action, that his watchfulness had some purpose.

The shipment arrived late in the afternoon of the eighth day. Five
enormous crates, each requiring the combined energies of Eliot and three
Newari workmen to wrangle up to the third-floor room that housed Mr.
Chatterji's collection. After tipping the men, Eliot—sweaty, panting—
sat down against the wall to catch his breath. The room was about twenty-
five feet by fifteen, but looked smaller because of the dozens of curious
objects standing around the floor and mounted one above the other on
the walls. A brass doorknob, a shattered door, a straight-back chair whose
arms were bound with a velvet rope to prevent anyone from sitting, a
discolored sink, a mirror streaked by a brown stain, a slashed lampshade.
They were all relics of some haunting or possession, some grotesque
violence, and there were cards affixed to them testifying to the details
and referring those who were interested to materials in Mr. Chatterji's
library. Sitting surrounded by these relics, the crates looked innocuous.
Bolted shut, chest-high, branded with customs stamps.

When he had recovered, Eliot strolled around the room, amused by
the care that Mr. Chatterji had squandered on his hobby; the most
amusing thing was that no one except Mr. Chatterji was impressed by
it: it provided travelers with a footnote for their journals. Nothing more.

A wave of dizziness swept over him—he had stood too soon—and he
leaned against one of the crates for support. Jesus, he was in lousy shape!
And then, as he blinked away the tangles of opaque cells drifting across
his field of vision, the crate shifted. Just a little shift, as if something

inside had twitched in its sleep. But palpable, real. He flung himself toward the door, backing away. A chill mapped every knob and articulation of his spine, and his sweat had evaporated, leaving clammy patches on his skin. The crate was motionless. But he was afraid to take his eyes off it, certain that if he did, it would release its pent-up fury. "Hi," said Michaela from the doorway.

Her voice electrified Eliot. He let out a squawk and wheeled around, his hands outheld to ward of attack.

"I didn't mean to startle you," she said. "I'm sorry."

"Goddamn!" he said. "Don't sneak up like that!" He remembered the crate and glanced back at it. "Listen, I was just locking. . . ."

"I'm sorry," she repeated, and walked past him into the room. "Ranjeesh is such an idiot about all this," she said, running her hand over the top of the crate. "Don't you think?"

Her familiarity with the crate eased Eliot's apprehension. Maybe he had been the one who had twitched: a spasm of overstrained muscles. "Yeah, I guess."

She walked over to the straight-back chair, slipped off the velvet rope, and sat down. She was wearing a pale brown skirt and a plaid blouse that made her look schoolgirlish. "I want to apologize about the other day," she said; she bowed her head, and the fall of her hair swung forward to obscure her face. "I've been having a bad time lately. I have trouble relating to people. To anything. But since we're living here together, I'd like to be friends." She stood and spread the folds of her skirt. "See? I even put on different clothes. I could tell the others offended you."

The innocent sexuality of the pose caused Eliot to have a rush of desire. "Looks nice," he said with forced casualness. "Why've you been having a bad time?"

She wandered to the door and gazed out. "Do you really want to hear about it?"

"Not if it's painful for you."

"It doesn't matter," she said, leaning against the doorframe. "I was in a band back in the States, and we were doing okay. Cutting an album, talking to record labels. I was living with the guitarist, in love with him. But then I had an affair. Not even an affair. It was stupid. Meaningless. I still don't know why I did it. The heat of the moment, I guess. That's what rock 'n' roll's all about, and maybe I was just acting out the myth. One of the other musicians told my boyfriend. That's the way bands are—you're friends with everyone, but never at the same time. See, I told this guy about the affair. We'd always confided. But one day he got mad at me over something. Something else stupid and meaningless."

Her chin was struggling to stay firm; the breeze from the courtyard drifted fine strands of hair across her face. "My boyfriend went crazy and beat up my. . . ." She gave a dismal laugh. "I don't know what to call him. My lover. Whatever. My boyfriend killed him. It was an accident, but he tried to run, and the police shot him."

Eliot wanted to stop her; she was obviously seeing it all again, seeing blood and police flashers and cold white morgue lights. But she was riding a wave of memory, borne along by its energy, and he knew that she had to crest with it, crash with it.

"I was out of it for a while. Dreamy. Nothing touched me. Not the funerals, the angry parents. I went away for months, to the mountains, and I started to feel better. But when I came home, I found that the musician who'd told my boyfriend had written a song about it. The affair, the killings. He'd cut a record. People were buying it, singing the hook when they walked down the street or took a shower. Dancing to it! They were dancing on blood and bones, humming grief, shelling out $5.98 for a jingle about suffering. Looking back, I realize I was crazy, but at the time everything I did seemed normal. More than normal. Directed, inspired. I bought a gun. A ladies' model, the salesman said. I remember thinking how strange it was that there were male and female guns, just like with electric razors. I felt enormous carrying it. I had to be meek and polite or else I was sure people would notice how large and purposeful I was. It wasn't hard to track down Ronnie—that's the guy who wrote the song. He was in Germany, cutting a second album. I couldn't believe it, I wasn't going to be able to kill him! I was so frustrated that one night I went down to a park and started shooting. I missed everything. Out of all the bums and joggers and squirrels, I hit leaves and air. They locked me up after that. A hospital. I think it helped, but. . . ." She blinked, waking from a trance. "But I still feel so disconnected, you now?"

Eliot carefully lifted away the strands of hair that had blown across her face and laid them back in place. Her smile flickered. "I know," he said. "I feel that way sometimes."

She nodded thoughtfully, as if to verify that she had recognized this quality in him.

They ate dinner in a Tibetan place in Temal; it had no name and was a dump with flyspecked tables and rickety chairs, specializing in water buffalo and barley soup. But it was away from the city center, which meant they could avoid the worst of the festival crowds. The waiter was a young Tibetan wearing jeans and a T-shirt that bore the legend MAGIC IS THE ANSWER; the earphones of personal stereo dangled about his neck.

The walls—visible through a haze of smoke—were covered with snap-shots, most featuring the waiter in the company of various tourists, but a few showing an older Tibetan in blue robes and turquoise jewelry, carrying an automatic rifle; this was the owner, one of the Khampa tribesmen who had fought a guerrilla war against the Chinese. He rarely put in an appearance at the restaurant, and when he did, his glowering presence tended to dampen conversation.

Over dinner, Eliot tried to steer clear of topics that might unsettle Michaela. He told her about Sam Chipley's clinic, the time the Dalai Lama had come to Katmandu, the musicians at Swayambhunath. Cheer-ful, exotic topics. Her listlessness was such an inessential part of her that Eliot was led to chip away at it, curious to learn what lay beneath; and the more he chipped away, the more animated her gestures, the more luminous her smile became. This was a different sort of smile than she had displayed on their first meeting. It came so suddenly over her face, it seemed an autonomic reaction, like the opening of a sunflower, as if she were facing not you but the principle of light upon which you were grounded. It was aware of you, of course, but it chose to see past the imperfections of the flesh and know the perfected thing you truly were. It boosted your sense of worth to realize that you were its target, and Eliot—whose sense of worth was at low ebb—would have done pratfalls to sustain it. Even when he told his own story, he told it as a joke, a metaphor for American misconceptions of Oriental pursuits.

"Why don't you quit it?" she asked. "The meditation, I mean. If it's not working out, why keep on with it?"

"My life's in perfect suspension," he said. "I'm afraid that if I quit practicing, if I change anything, I'll either sink to the bottom or fly off." He tapped his spoon against his cup, signaling for more tea. "You're not really going to marry Ranjeesh, are you?" he asked, and was surprised at the concern he felt that she actually might.

"Probably not." The waiter poured their tea, whispery drumbeats is-suing from his earphones. "I was just feeling lost. You see, my parents sued Ronnie over the song, and I ended up with a lot of money—which made me feel even worse. . . ."

"Let's not talk about it," he said.

"It's all right." She touched his wrist, reassuring, and the skin remained warm after her fingers had withdrawn. "Anyway," she went on, "I decided to travel, and all the strangeness . . . I don't know. I was starting to slip away. Ranjeesh was a kind of sanctuary."

Eliot was vastly relieved.

Outside, the streets were thronged with festivalgoers, and Michaela took Eliot's arm and let him guide her through the crowds. Newar wearing Nehru hats and white trousers that bagged at the hips and wrapped tightly around the calves; groups of tourists, shouting and waving bottles of rice beer; Indians in white robes and saris. The air was spiced with incense, and the strip of empurpled sky above was so regularly patterned with stars that it looked like a banner draped between the roofs. Near the house, a wild-eyed man in a blue satin robe rushed past, bumping into them, and he was followed by two boys dragging a goat, its forehead smeared with crimson powder: a sacrifice.

"This is crazy!" Michaela laughed.

"It's nothing. Wait'll tomorrow night."

"What happens then?"

"The night of White Bhairab." Eliot put on a grimace. "You'll have to watch yourself. Bhairab's a lusty, wrathful sort."

She laughed again and gave his arm an affectionate squeeze.

Inside the house, the moon—past full, blank, and golden—floated dead center of the square of night sky admitted by the roof. They stood close together in the courtyard, silent, suddenly awkward.

"I enjoyed tonight," said Michaela; she leaned forward and brushed his cheek with her lips. "Thank you," she whispered.

Eliot caught her as she drew back, tipped her chin, and kissed her mouth. Her lips parted, her tongue darted out. Then she pushed him away. "I'm tired," she said, her face tightened with anxiety. She walked off a few steps, but stopped and turned back. "If you want to . . . to be with me, maybe it'll be all right. We could try."

Eliot went to her and took her hands. "I want to make love with you," he said, no longer trying to hide his urgency. And that *was* what he wanted: to make love. Not to ball or bang or screw or any other inelegant version of the act.

But it was not love they made.

Under the starlit blaze of Mr. Chatterji's ceiling, she was very beautiful, and at first she was very loving, moving with a genuine involvement; then abruptly, she quit moving altogether and turned her face to the pillow.

Her eyes were glistening. Left alone atop her, listening to the animal sound of his breathing, the impact of his flesh against hers, Eliot knew he should stop and comfort her. But the months of abstinence, the eight days of wanting her, all this fused into a bright flare in the small of his back, a reactor core of lust that irradiated his conscience, and he continued to plunge into her, hurrying to completion. She let out a gasp when he withdrew, and curled up, facing away from him.

"God, I'm so sorry," she said, her voice cracked.

Eliot shut his eyes. He felt sickened, reduced to the bestial. It had been like two mental patients doing nasty on the sly, two fragments of people who together didn't form a whole. He understood now why Mr. Chatterji wanted to marry her: he planned to add her to his collection, to enshrine her with the other splinters of violence. And each night he would complete his revenge, substantiate his cultural overview, by making something less than love with this sad, inert girl, this American ghost. Her shoulders shook with muffled sobs. She needed someone to console her, to help her find her own strength and capacity for love. Eliot reached out to her, willing to do his best. But he knew it shouldn't be him.

Several hours later, after she had fallen asleep, unconsolable, Eliot sat in the courtyard, thoughtless, dejected, staring at a rubber plant. It was mired in shadow, its leaves hanging limp. He had been staring for a couple of minutes, when he noticed that a shadow in back of the plant was swaying ever so slightly; he tried to make it out, and the swaying subsided. He stood. The chair scraped on the concrete, sounding unnaturally loud. His neck prickled, and he glanced behind him. Nothing. Ye Olde Mental Fatigue, he thought. Ye Olde Emotional Strain. He laughed, and the clarity of the laugh—echoing up through the empty well—alarmed him; it seemed to stir little flickers of motion everywhere in the darkness. What he needed was a drink! The problem was how to get into the bedroom without waking Michaela. Hell, maybe he should wake her. Maybe they should talk more before what had happened hardened into a set of unbreakable attitudes.

He turned toward the stairs . . . and then, yelling out in panic, entangling his feet with the lawn chairs as he leapt backward midstep, he fell onto his side. A shadow—roughly man-shaped and man-sized—was standing a yard away; it was undulating the way a strand of kelp undulates in a gentle tide. The patch of air around it was rippling, as if the entire image had been badly edited into reality. Eliot scrambled away, coming to his knees. The shadow melted downward, puddling on the cement; it bunched in the middle like a caterpillar, folded over itself, and flowed after him: a rolling sort of motion. Then it reared up, again assuming its manlike shape, looming over him.

Eliot got to his feet, still frightened, but less so. If he had previously been asked to testify as to the existence of the Khaa, he would have rejected the evidence of his bleared senses and come down on the side of hallucination, folktale. But now, though he was tempted to draw that same conclusion, there was too much evidence to the contrary. Staring at the featureless black cowl of the Khaa's head, he had a sense of something staring back. More than a sense. A distinct impression of personality. It was as if the Khaa's undulations were producing a breeze that bore its psychic odor through the air. Eliot began to picture it as a loony, shy old uncle who liked to sit under the basement steps and eat flies and cackle to himself, but who could tell when the first frost was due and knew how to fix the tail on your kite. Weird, yet harmless. The Khaa stretched out an arm: the arm just peeled away from its torso, its hand a thumbless black mitten. Eliot edged back. He wasn't quite prepared to believe it was harmless. But the arm stretched farther than he had thought possible and enveloped his wrist. It was soft, ticklish, a river of furry moths crawling over his skin.

In the instant before he jumped away, Eliot heard a whining note inside his skull, and that whining—seeming to flow through his brain with the same suppleness that the Khaa's arm had displayed—was translated into a wordless plea. From it he understood that the Khaa was afraid. Terribly afraid. Suddenly it melted downward and went rolling, bunching, flowing up the stairs; it stopped on the first landing, rolled halfway down, then up again, repeating the process over and over. It came clear to Eliot (*Oh, Jesus! This is nuts!*) that it was trying to convince him to follow. Just like Lassie or some other ridiculous TV animal, it was trying to tell him something, to lead him to where the wounded forest ranger had fallen, where the nest of baby ducks was being threatened by the brush fire. He should walk over, rumple its head, and say, "What's the matter, girl? Those squirrels been teasing you?" This time his laughter had a sobering effect, acting to settle his thoughts. One likelihood was that his experience with Michaela had been sufficient to snap his frayed connection with consensus reality; but there was no point in buying that. Even if that were the case, he might as well go with it. He crossed to the stairs and climbed toward the rippling shadow on the landing.

"Okay, Bongo," he said. "Let's see what's got you so excited."

On the third floor, the Khaa turned down a hallway, moving fast, and Eliot didn't see it again until he was approaching the room that housed Mr. Chatterji's collection. It was standing beside the door, flapping its arms, apparently indicating that he should enter. Eliot remembered the crate.

"No, thanks," he said. A drop of sweat slid down his rib cage, and he realized that it was unusually warm next to the door.

The Khaa's hand flowed over the doorknob, enveloping it, and when the hand pulled back, it was bulging, oddly deformed, and there was a hole through the wood where the lock mechanism had been. The door swung open a couple of inches. Darkness leaked out of the room, adding an oily essence to the air. Eliot took a backward step. The Khaa dropped the lock mechanism—it materialized from beneath the formless black hand and clattered to the floor—and latched onto Eliot's arm. Once again he heard the whining, the plea for help, and, since he did not jump away, he had a clearer understanding of the process of translation. He could feel the whining as a cold fluid coursing through his brain, and as the whining died, the message simply appeared—the way an image might appear in a crystal ball. There was an undertone of reassurance to the Khaa's fear, and though Eliot knew this was the mistake people in horror movies were always making, he reached inside the room and fumbled for the wall switch, half expecting to be snatched up and savaged. He flicked on the light and pushed the door open with his foot.

And wished that he hadn't.

The crates had exploded. Splinters and shards of wood were scattered everywhere, and the bricks had been heaped at the center of the room. They were dark red, friable bricks like crumbling cakes of dried blood, and each was marked with black letters and numbers that signified its original position in the fireplace. But none were in their proper position now, though they were quite artfully arranged. They had been piled into the shape of a mountain, one that—despite the crudity of its building blocks—duplicated the sheer faces and chimneys and gentle slopes of a real mountain. Eliot recognized it from its photograph. The Eiger. It towered to the ceiling, and under the glare of the lights it gave off a radiation of ugliness and barbarity. It seemed alive, a fang of dark red meat, and the charred smell of the bricks was like a hum in Eliot's nostrils.

Ignoring the Khaa, who was again flapping its arms, Eliot broke for the landing; there he paused, and after a brief struggle between fear and conscience, he sprinted up the stairs to the bedroom, taking them three at a time. Michaela was gone! He stared at the starlit billows of the sheets. Where the hell . . . her room! He hurtled down the stairs and fell sprawling on the second-floor landing. Pain lanced through his kneecap, but he came to his feet running, certain that something was behind him.

A seam of reddish orange light—not lamplight—edged the bottom of Michaela's door, and he heard a crispy chuckling in a hearth. The wood was warm to the touch. Eliot's hand hovered over the doorknob. His heart seemed to have swelled to the size of a basketball and was doing a fancy dribble against his chest wall. The sensible thing to do would be to get out quick, because whatever lay beyond the door was bound to be too much for him to handle. But instead he did the stupid thing and burst into the room.

His first impression was that the room was burning, but then he saw that though the fire looked real, it did not spread; the flames clung to the outlines of things that were themselves unreal, that had no substance of their own and were made of the ghostly fire: belted drapes, an over-stuffed chair and sofa, a carved mantelpiece, all of antique design. The actual furniture—production-line junk—was undamaged. Intense red-dish-orange light glowed around the bed, and at its heart lay Michaela. Naked, her back arched. Lengths of her hair lifted into the air and tangled, floating in an invisible current; the muscles of her legs and abdomen were coiling, bunching, as if she were shedding her skin. The crackling grew louder, and the light began to rise from the bed to form into a column of even brighter light; it narrowed at the midpoint, bulged in an approximation of hips and breasts, gradually assuming the shape of a burning woman. She was faceless, a fiery silhouette. Her flickering gown shifted as with the movements of walking, and flames leapt out behind her head like windblown hair.

Eliot was pumped full of terror, too afraid to scream or run. Her aura of heat and power wrapped around him. Though she was within arm's length, she seemed a long way off, inset into a great distance and walking toward him down a tunnel that conformed exactly to her shape. She stretched out a hand, brushing his cheek with a finger. The touch brought more pain than he had ever known. It was luminous, lighting every circuit of his body. He could feel his skin crisping, cracking, fluids leaking forth and sizzling. He heard himself moan: a gush of rotten sound like something trapped in a drain.

Then she jerked back her hand, as if *he* had burned *her*.

Dazed, his nerves screaming, Eliot slumped to the floor and—through blurred eyes—caught sight of a blackness rippling by the door. The Khaa. The burning woman stood facing it a few feet away. It was such an uncanny scene, this confrontation of fire and darkness, of two super-natural systems, that Eliot was shocked to alertness. He had the idea that neither of them knew what to do. Surrounded by its patch of disturbed air, the Khaa undulated; the burning woman crackled and flickered, embedded in her eerie distance. Tentatively, she lifted her hand; but before she could complete the gesture, the Khaa reached with blinding swiftness and its hand enveloped hers.

A shriek like tortured metal issued from them, as if some ironclad principle had been breached. Dark tendrils wound through the burning woman's arm, seams of fire striped the Khaa, and there was a high-pitched humming, a vibration that jarred Eliot's teeth. For a moment he was afraid that spiritual versions of antimatter and matter had been brought into conjunction, that the room would explode. But the hum was sheared off as the Khaa snatched back its hand: a scrap of reddish-orange flame glimmered within it. The Khaa melted downward and went rolling out the door. The burning woman—and every bit of flame in the room—shrank to an incandescent point and vanished.

Still dazed, Eliot touched his face. It felt burned, but there was no apparent damage. He hauled himself to his feet, staggered to bed, and collapsed next to Michaela. She was breathing deeply, unconscious. "Michaela!" He shook her. She moaned, her head rolled from side to side. He heaved her over his shoulder in a fireman's lift and crept out into the hall. Moving stealthily, he eased along the hall to the balcony overlooking the courtyard and peered over the edge . . . and bit his lip to stifle a cry. Clearly visible in the electric-blue air of the predawn darkness, standing in the middle of the courtyard, was a tall, pale woman wearing a white nightgown. Her black hair fanned across her back. She snapped her head around to stare at him, her cameo features twisted by a gloating smile, and that smile told Eliot everything he had wanted to know about the possibility of escape. Just try to leave, Aimée Cousineau was saying. Go ahead and try. I'd like that. A shadow sprang erect about a dozen feet away from her, and she turned to it. Suddenly there was a wind in the courtyard: a violent, whirling wind of which she was the calm center. Plants went flapping up into the well like leathery birds; pots shattered, and the shards flew toward the Khaa. Slowed by Michaela's weight, wanting to get as far as he could from the battle, Eliot headed up the stairs toward Mr. Chatterji's bedroom.

It was an hour later, an hour of peeking down into the courtyard, watching the game of hide-and-seek that the Khaa was playing with Aimée Cousineau, realizing that the Khaa was protecting them by keeping her busy . . . it was then that Eliot remembered the book. He retrieved it from the shelf and began to skim through it, hoping to learn something helpful. There was nothing else to do. He picked up at the point of Aimée's rap about her marriage to Happiness, passed over the transformation of Ginny Whitcomb into a teenage monster, and found a second section dealing with Aimée.

In 1895 a wealthy Swiss-American named Armand Cousineau had returned to St. Berenice—his birthplace—for a visit. He was smitten with Aimée Vuillemont, and her family, seizing the opportunity to be rid of her, allowed Cousineau to marry Aimée and sail her off to his home in Carversville, New Hampshire. Aimée's taste for seduction had not been curbed by the move. Lawyers, deacons, merchants, farmers: they were all grist for her mill. But in the winter of 1905 she fell in love—obsessively, passionately in love—with a young schoolmaster. She believed that the schoolmaster had saved her from her unholy marriage, and her gratitude knew no bounds. Unfortunately, when the schoolmaster fell in love with another woman, neither did her fury. One night while passing the Cousineau mansion, the town doctor spotted a woman walking the grounds. "A woman of flame, not burning but composed of flame, her every particular a fiery construct. . . ." Smoke was curling from a window; the doctor rushed inside and discovered the schoolmaster wrapped in chains, burning like a log in the vast fireplace. He put out the small blaze spreading from the hearth, and on going back onto the grounds, he stumbled over Aimée's charred corpse.

It was not clear whether Aimée's death had been accidental, a stray spark catching on her nightgown, or the result of suicide; but it *was* clear that thereafter the mansion had been haunted by a spirit who delighted in possessing women and driving them to kill their men. The spirit's supernatural powers were limited by the flesh, but were augmented by immense physical strength. Ginny Whitcomb, for example, had killed her brother Tim by twisting off his arm, and then had gone after her other brother and her father, a harrowing chase that had lasted a day and a night: while in possession of a body, the spirit was not limited to nocturnal activity. . . .

Christ!

The light coming through the skylight was gray.

They were safe!

Eliot went to the bed and began shaking Michaela. She moaned, her eyes blinked open. "Wake up!" he said. "We've got to get out!"

"What?" She batted at his hands. "What are you talking about?"

"Don't you remember?"

"Remember what?" She swung her legs onto the floor, sitting with her head down, stunned by wakefulness; she stood, swayed, and said, "God, what did you do to me? I feel. . . ." A dull, suspicious expression washed over her face.

"We have to leave." He walked around the bed to her. "Ranjeesh hit the jackpot. Those crates of his had an honest-to-God spirit packed in with the bricks. Last night it tried to possess you." He saw her disbelief. "You must have blanked out. Here." He offered the book. "This'll explain. . . ."

"Oh, God!" she shouted. "What did you do? I'm all raw inside!" She backed away, eyes wide with fright.

"I didn't do anything." He held out his palms as if to prove he had no weapons.

"You raped me! While I was asleep!" She looked left, right, in a panic.

"That's ridiculous!"

"You must have drugged me or something! Oh, God! Go away!"

"I won't argue," he said. "We have to get out. After that you can turn me in for rape or whatever. But we're leaving, even if I have to drag you."

Some of her desperation evaporated, her shoulders sagged.

"Look," he said, moving closer. "I didn't rape you. What you're feeling is something that goddamn spirit did to you. It was. . . ."

She brought her knee up into his groin.

As he writhed on the floor, curled up around the pain, Eliot heard the door open and her footsteps receding. He caught at the edge of the bed, hauled himself to his knees, and vomited all over the sheets. He fell back and lay there for several minutes, until the pain had dwindled to a powerful throbbing, a throbbing that jolted his heart into the same rhythm; then, gingerly, he stood and shuffled out into the hall. Leaning on the railing, he eased down the stairs to Michaela's room and lowered himself into a sitting position. He let out a shuddering sigh. Actinic flashes burst in front of his eyes.

"Michaela," he said. "Listen to me." His voice sounded feeble: the voice of an old, old man.

"I've got a knife," she said from just behind the door. "I'll use it if you try to break in."

"I wouldn't worry about that," he said. "And I sure as hell wouldn't worry about being raped. Now, will you listen?"

No response.

He told her everything, and when he was done, she said, "You're insane. You raped me."

"I wouldn't hurt you. I . . ." He had been on the verge of telling her he loved her, but decided it probably wasn't true. He probably just wished that he had a good, clean truth like love. The pain was making him nauseated again, as if the blackish-purple stain of his bruises were seeping up into his stomach and filling him with bad gases. He struggled to his feet and leaned against the wall. There was no point in arguing, and there was not much hope that she would leave the house on her own, not if she reacted to Aimée like Ginny Whitcomb. The only solution was to go to the police, accuse her of some crime. Assault. She would accuse him of rape, but with luck they would both be held overnight. And he would have time to wire Mr. Chatterji . . . who would believe him. Mr. Chatterji was by nature a believer: it simply hadn't fit his notion of sophistication to give credence to his native spirits. He'd be on the first flight from Delhi, eager to document the Terror.

Himself eager to get it over, Eliot negotiated the stairs and hobbled across the courtyard; but the Khaa was waiting, flapping its arms in the shadowed alcove that led to the street. Whether it was an effect of the light or of its battle with Aimée, or, specifically, of the pale scrap of fire visible within its hand, the Khaa looked less substantial. Its blackness was somewhat opaque, and the air around it was blurred, smeary, like waves over a lens: it was as if the Khaa were being submerged more deeply in its own medium. Eliot felt no compunction about allowing it to touch him; he was grateful to it, and his relaxed attitude seemed to intensify the communication. He began to see images in his mind's eye: Michaela's face, Aimée's, and then the two faces were superimposed. He was shown this over and over, and he understood from it that the Khaa wanted the possession to take place. But he didn't understand why. More images. Himself running, Michaela running, Durbar Square, the mask of White Bhairab, the Khaa. Lots of Khaa. Little black hieroglyphs. These images were repeated, too, and after each sequence the Khaa would hold its hand up to his face and display the glimmering scrap of Aimée's fire. Eliot thought he understood, but whenever he tried to convey that he wasn't sure, the Khaa merely repeated the images.

At last, realizing that the Khaa had reached the limits of its ability to communicate, Eliot headed for the street. The Khaa melted down, reared up in the doorway to block his path, and flapped its arms desperately. Once again Eliot had a sense of its weird-old-man-ness. It went against logic to put his trust in such an erratic creature, especially in such a dangerous plan; but logic had little hold on him, and this was a permanent solution. If it worked. If he hadn't misread it. He laughed. The hell with it!

"Take it easy, Bongo," he said. "I'll be back as soon as I get my shootin' iron fixed."

The waiting room of Sam Chipley's clinic was crowded with Newari mothers and children, who giggled as Eliot did a bowlegged shuffle through their midst. Sam's wife led him into the examination room, where Sam—a burly, bearded man, his long hair tied in a ponytail—helped him onto a surgical table.

"Holy shit!" he said after inspecting the injury. "What you been into, man?" He began rubbing ointment into the bruises.

"Accident," gritted Eliot, trying not to cry out.

"Yeah, I bet," said Sam. "Maybe a sexy little accident who had a change of heart when it come down to strokes. You know, not gettin' it steady might tend to make you a tad intense for some ladies, man. Ever think about that?"

"That's not how it was. Am I all right?"

"Yeah, but you ain't gonna be superstud for a while." Sam went to the sink and washed his hands. "Don't gimme that innocent bullshit. You were tryin' to slip it to Chatterji's new squeeze, right?"

"You know her?"

"He brought her over one day, showin' her off. She's a head case, man. You should know better."

"Will I be able to run?"

Sam laughed. "Not hardly."

"Listen, Sam." Eliot sat up, winced. "Chatterji's lady. She's in bad trouble, and I'm the only one who can help her. I have to be able to run, and I need something to keep me awake. I haven't slept for a couple of days."

"I ain't givin' you pills, Eliot. You can stagger through your doper phase without my help." Sam finished drying his hands and went to sit on a stool beside the window; beyond the window was a brick wall, and atop it a string of prayer flags snapped in the breeze.

"I'm not after a supply, dammit! Just enough to keep me going tonight. This is important, Sam!"

Sam scratched his neck. "What kind of trouble she in?"

"I can't tell you now," said Eliot, knowing that Sam would laugh at the idea of something as metaphysically suspect as the Khaa. "But I will tomorrow. It's not illegal. Come on, man! There's got to be something you can give me."

"Oh, I can fix you up. I can make you feel like King Shit on Coronation Day." Sam mulled it over. "Okay, Eliot. But you get your ass back here tomorrow and tell me what's happenin'." He gave a snort of amusement. "All I can say is it must be some strange damn trouble for you to be the only one who can save her."

After wiring Mr. Chatterji, urging him to come home at once, Eliot returned to the house and unscrewed the hinges of the front door. He was not certain that Aimée would be able to control the house, to slam doors and make windows stick as she had with her house in New Hampshire, but he didn't want to take any chances. As he lifted the door and set it against the wall of the alcove, he was amazed by its lightness; he felt possessed of a giddy strength, capable of heaving the door up through the well of the courtyard and over the roofs. The cocktail of painkillers and speed was working wonders. His groin ached, but the ache was distant, far removed from the center of his consciousness, which was a fount of well-being. When he had finished with the door, he grabbed some fruit juice from the kitchen and went back to the alcove to wait.

In midafternoon Michaela came downstairs. Eliot tried to talk to her, to convince her to leave, but she warned him to keep away and scuttled back to her room. Then, around five o'clock, the burning woman appeared, floating a few feet above the courtyard floor. The sun had withdrawn to the upper third of the well, and her fiery silhouette was inset into slate-blue shadow, the flames of her hair dancing about her head. Eliot, who had been hitting the painkillers heavily, was dazzled by her: had she been a hallucination, she would have made his all-time top ten. But even realizing that she was not, he was too drugged to relate to her as a threat. He snickered and shied a piece of broken pot at her. She shrank to an incandescent point, vanished, and that brought home to him his foolhardiness. He took more speed to counteract his euphoria, and did stretching exercises to loosen the kinks and to rid himself of the cramped sensation in his chest.

Twilight blended the shadows in the courtyard, celebrants passed in the street, and he could hear distant drums and cymbals. He felt cut off from the city, the festival. Afraid. Not even the presence of the Khaa, half merged with the shadows along the wall, served to comfort him. Near dusk, Aimée Cousineau walked into the courtyard and stopped about twenty feet away, staring at him. He had no desire to laugh or throw things. At this distance he could see that her eyes had no whites or pupils or irises. They were dead black. One moment they seemed to be the bulging head of black screws threaded into her skull; the next they seemed to recede into blackness, into a cave beneath a mountain where something waited to teach the joys of hell to whoever wandered in. Eliot sidled closer to the door. But she turned, climbed the stairs to the second landing, and walked down Michaela's hallway.

Eliot's waiting began in earnest.

An hour passed. He paced between the door and the courtyard. His mouth was cottony; his joints felt brittle, held together by frail wires of speed and adrenaline. This was insane! All he had done was to put them in worse danger. Finally, he heard a door close upstairs. He backed into the street, bumping into two Newari girls, who giggled and skipped away. Crowds of people were moving toward Durbar Square.

"Eliot!"

Michaela's voice. He'd expected a hoarse, demon voice, and when she walked into the alcove, her white scarf glowing palely against the dark air, he was surprised to see that she was unchanged. Her features held no trace of anything other than her usual listlessness.

"I'm sorry I hurt you," she said, walking toward him. "I know you didn't do anything. I was just upset about last night."

Eliot continued to back away.

"What's wrong?" She stopped in the doorway.

It might have been his imagination, the drugs, but Eliot could have sworn that her eyes were much darker than normal. He trotted off a dozen yards or so and stood looking at her.

"Eliot!"

It was a scream of rage and frustration, and he could scarcely believe the speed with which she darted toward him. He ran full tilt at first, leaping sideways to avoid collisions, veering past alarmed, dark-skinned faces; but after a couple of blocks he found a more efficient rhythm and began to anticipate obstacles, to glide in and out of the crowd. Angry shouts were raised behind him. He glanced back. Michaela was closing the distance, beelining for him, knocking people sprawling with what seemed effortless blows. He ran harder. The crowd grew thicker, and he kept near the walls of the houses, where it was thinnest; but even there it was hard to maintain a good pace. Torches were waved in his face; young men—singing, their arms linked—posed barriers that slowed him further. He could no longer see Michaela, but he could see the wake of her passage. Fists shaking, heads jerking. The entire scene was starting to lose cohesiveness to Eliot. There were screams of torchlight, bright shards of deranged shouts, jostling waves of incense and ordure. He felt like the only solid chunk in a glittering soup that was being poured through a stone trough.

At the edge of Durbar Square, he had a brief glimpse of a shadow standing by the massive gilt doors of Degutale Temple. It was larger and a more anthracitic black than Mr. Chatterji's Khaa: one of the old ones, the powerful ones. The sight buoyed his confidence and restored his equilibrium. He had not misread the plan. But he knew that this was the most dangerous part. He had lost track of Michaela, and the crowd was sweeping him along; if she caught up to him now, he would not be able to run. Fighting for elbow room, struggling to keep his feet, he was borne into the temple complex. The pagoda roofs sloped up into darkness like strangely carved mountains, their peaks hidden by a moonless night; the cobbled paths were narrow, barely ten feet across, and the crowd was being squeezed along them, a lava flow of humanity. Torches bobbed everywhere, sending wild licks of shadow and orange light up the walls, revealing scowling faces on the eaves. Atop its pedestal, the gilt statue of Hanuman—the monkey god—looked to be swaying. Clashing cymbals and arrhythmic drumming scattered Eliot's heartbeat; the sinewy wail of oboes seemed to be graphing the fluctuations of his nerves.

As he swept past Hanuman Dhoka Temple, he caught sight of the brass mask of White Bhairab shining over the heads of the crowd like the face of an evil clown. It was less than a hundred feet away, set in a huge niche in a temple wall and illuminated by light bulbs that hung down among strings of prayer flags. The crowd surged faster, knocking him this way and that; but he managed to spot two more Khaa in the doorway of Hanuman Dhoka. Both melted downward, vanishing, and Eliot's hopes soared. They must have located Michaela, they must be attacking! By the time he had been carried to within a few yards of the mask, he was sure that he was safe. They must have finished her exorcism by now. The only problem left was to find her. That, he realized, had been the weak link in the plan. He'd been an idiot not to have foreseen it. Who knows what might happen if she were to fall in the midst of the crowd. Suddenly he was beneath the pipe that stuck out of the god's mouth; the stream of rice beer arching from it looked translucent under the lights, and as it splashed his face (no fish), its coldness acted to wash away his veneer of chemical strength. He was dizzy, his groin throbbed. The great face, with its fierce fangs and goofy, startled eyes, appeared to be swelling and rocking back and forth. He took a deep breath. The thing to do would be to find a place next to a wall where he could wedge himself against the flow of the crowd, wait until it had thinned, and then search for her. He was about to do that very thing, when two powerful hands gripped his elbows from behind.

Unable to turn, he craned his neck and peered over his shoulder. Michaela smiled at him: a gloating "gotcha!" smile. Her eyes were dead-black ovals. She shaped his name with her mouth, her voice inaudible above the music and shouting, and she began to push him ahead of her, using him as a battering ram to forge a path through the crowd. To anyone watching, it might have appeared that he was running interference for her, but his feet were dangling just off the ground. Angry Newar yelled at him as he knocked them aside. He yelled too. No one noticed. Within seconds they had gotten clear into a side street, threading between groups of drunkards. People laughed at Eliot's cries for help, and one guy imitated the funny, loose-limbed way he was running.

Michaela turned into a doorway, carrying him down a dirt-floored corridor whose walls were carved into ornate screens; the dusky orange lamplight shining through the screens cast a lacework of shadow on the dirt. The corridor widened to a small courtyard, the age-darkened wood of its walls and doors inlaid with intricate mosaics of ivory. Michaela stopped and slammed him against a wall. He was stunned, but he recognized the place to be one of the old Buddhist temples that surrounded the square. Except for a life-size statue of a golden cow, the courtyard was empty.

"Eliot." The way she said it, it was more of a curse than a name.

He opened his mouth to scream, but she drew him into an embrace; her grip on his right elbow tightened, and her other hand squeezed the back of his neck, pinching off the scream.

"Don't be afraid," she said. "I only want to kiss you."

Her breasts crushed into his chest, her pelvis ground against him in a mockery of passion, and inch by inch she forced his face down to hers. Her lips parted, and—*oh, Christ Jesus!*—Eliot writhed in her grasp, enlivened by a new horror. The inside of her mouth was as black as her eyes. She wanted him to kiss that blackness, the same she had kissed beneath the Eiger. He kicked and clawed with his free hand, but she was irresistible, her hands like iron. His elbow cracked, and brilliant pain shot through his arm. Something else was cracking in his neck. Yet none of that compared to what he felt as her tongue—a burning black poker —pushed between his lips. His chest was bursting with the need to scream, and everything was going dark. Thinking this was death, he experienced a peevish resentment that death was not—as he'd been led to believe—an end to pain, that it merely added a tickling sensation to all his other pain. Then the searing heat in his mouth diminished, and he thought that death must just have been a bit slower than usual.

Several seconds passed before he realized that he was lying on the ground, several more before he noticed Michaela lying beside him, and—because darkness was tattering the edges of his vision—it was considerably longer before he distinguished the six undulating darknesses that had ringed Aimée Cousineau. They towered over her; their blackness gleamed like thick fur, and the air around them was awash with vibration. In her fluted white nightgown, her cameo face composed in an expression of calm, Aimée looked the antithesis of the vaguely male giants that were menacing her, delicate and finely worked in contrast to their crudity.

Her eyes appeared to mirror their negative color. After a moment, a little wind kicked up, swirling about her. The undulations of the Khaa increased, becoming rhythmic, the movements of boneless dancers, and the wind subsided. Puzzled, she darted between two of them and took a defensive stance next to the golden cow; she lowered her head and stared up through her brows at the Khaa. They melted downward, rolled forward, sprang erect, and hemmed her in against the statue. But the stare was doing its damage. Pieces of ivory and wood were splintering, flying off the walls toward the Khaa, and one of them was fading, a mist of black particles accumulating around its body; then, with a shrill noise that reminded Eliot of a jet passing overhead, it misted away.

Five Khaa remained in the courtyard. Aimée smiled and turned her stare on another. Before the stare could take effect, however, the Khaa moved close, blocking Eliot's view of her; and when they pulled back, it was Aimée who showed signs of damage. Rills of blackness were leading from her eyes, webbing her cheeks, making it look as if her face were cracking. Her nightgown caught fire, her hair began to leap. Flames danced on her fingertips, spread to her arms, her breast, and she assumed the form of the burning woman.

As soon as the transformation was complete, she tried to shrink, to dwindle to her vanishing point; but, acting in unison, the Khaa extended their hands and touched her. There was that shriek of tortured metal, lapsing to a high-pitched hum, and to Eliot's amazement the Khaa were sucked inside her. It was a rapid process. The Khaa faded to a haze, to nothing, and veins of black marbled the burning woman's fire; the blackness coalesced, forming into five tiny stick figures, a hieroglyphic design patterning her gown. With a fuming sound, she expanded again, regaining her normal dimensions, and the Khaa flowed back out, surrounding her. For an instant she stood motionless, dwarfed: a schoolgirl helpless amidst a circle of bullies. Then she clawed at the nearest of them. Though she had no features with which to express emotion, it seemed to Eliot there was desperation in gesture, in the agitated leaping of her fiery hair. Unperturbed, the Khaa stretched out their enormous mitten hands, hands that spread like oil and enveloped her.

The destruction of the burning woman, of Aimée Cousineau, lasted only a matter of seconds; but to Eliot it occurred within a bubble of slow time, a time during which he achieved a speculative distance. He wondered if—as the Khaa stole portions of her fire and secreted it within their bodies—they were removing disparate elements of her soul, if she consisted of psychologically distinct fragments: the girl who had wandered into the cave, the girl who had returned from it, the betrayed lover. Did she embody gradations of innocence and sinfulness, or was she a contaminated essence, an unfractionated evil? While still involved in this speculation, half a reaction to pain, half to the metallic shriek of her losing battle, he lost consciousness, and when he reopened his eyes, the courtyard was deserted. He could hear music and shouting from Durbar Square. The golden cow stared contentedly into nowhere.

He had the idea that if he moved, he would further break all the broken things inside him; but he inched his left hand across the dirt and rested it on Michaela's breast. It was rising and falling with a steady rhythm. That made him happy, and he kept his hand there, exulting in the hits of her life against his palm. Something shadowy above him. He strained to see it. One of the Khaa . . . No! It was Mr. Chatterji's Khaa. Opaquely black, scrap of fire glimmering in its hand. Compared to its big brothers, it had the look of a skinny, sorry mutt. Eliot felt a camaraderie toward it.

"Hey, Bongo," he said weakly. "We won."

A tickling at the top of his head, a whining note, and he had an impression not of gratitude—as he might have expected—but of intense curiosity. The tickling stopped, and Eliot suddenly felt clear in his mind. Strange. He was passing out once again, his consciousness whirling, darkening, and yet he was calm and unafraid. A roar came from the direction of the square. Somebody—the luckiest somebody in the Katmandu Valley—had caught the fish. But as Eliot's eyelids fluttered shut, as he had a last glimpse of the Khaa looming above them and felt the warm measure of Michaela's heartbeat, he thought maybe that the crowd was cheering the wrong man.

Three weeks after the night of White Bhairab, Ranjeesh Chatterji divested himself of all worldly possessions (including the gift of a year's free rent at his house to Eliot) and took up residence at Swayambhunath where—according to Sam Chipley, who visited Eliot in the hospital—he was attempting to visualize the Avalokitesvara Buddha. It was then that Eliot understood the nature of his newfound clarity. Just as it had done long ago with the woman's goiters, the Khaa had tried his habituation to meditation on for size, had not cared for it, and had sloughed it off in a handy respository: Ranjeesh Chatterji.

It was such a delicious irony that Eliot had to restrain himself from telling Michaela when she visited that same afternoon; she had no memory of the Khaa, and news of it tended to unsettle her. But otherwise she had been healing right along with Eliot. All her listlessness had eroded over the weeks, her capacity for love was returning and was focused solely on Eliot. "I guess I needed someone to show me that I was worth an effort," she told him. "I'll never stop trying to repay you." She kissed him. "I can hardly wait till you come home." She brought him books and candy and flowers; she sat with him each day until the nurses shooed her away. Yet being the center of her devotion disturbed him. He was still uncertain whether or not he loved her. Clarity, it seemed, made a man dangerously versatile, his conscience flexible, and instituted a cautious approach to commitment. At least this was the substance of Eliot's clarity. He didn't want to rush into anything.

When at last he did come home, he and Michaela made love beneath the starlight glory of Mr. Chatterji's skylight. Because of Eliot's neck brace and cast, they had to manage the act with extreme care, but despite that, despite the ambivalence of his feelings, this time it *was* love they made. Afterward, lying with his good arm around her, he edged nearer to commitment. Whether or not he loved her, there was no way this part of things could be improved by any increment of emotion. Maybe he'd give it a try with her. If it didn't work out, well, he was not going to be responsible for her mental health. She would have to learn to live without him.

"Happy?" he asked, caressing her shoulder.

She nodded and cuddled closer and whispered something that was partially drowned out by the crinkling of the pillow. He was sure he had misheard her, but the mere thought that he hadn't was enough to lodge a nugget of chill between his shoulder blades.

"What did you say?" he asked.

She turned to him and propped herself on an elbow, silhouetted by the starlight, her features obscured. But when she spoke, he realized that Mr. Chatterji's Khaa had been true to its erratic traditions on the night of White Bhairab; and he knew that if she were to tip back her head ever so slightly and let the light shine into her eyes, he would be able to resolve all his speculations about the composition of Aimée Cousineau's soul.

"I'm wed to Happiness," she said.

SALVAGE RITES

IAN WATSON

British writer Ian Watson is one of the most significant writers and critics to emerge in the last twenty years. From the publication in 1974 of his first novel, *The Embedding*, for which he was runner-up for the John W. Campbell Award, he has been lauded for his excellent and thought-provoking writing. In much of his writing reality often appears to be a subjective matter, and one could interpret "Salvage Rites" from this perspective. On first glance, "Salvage Rites" is the story of an innocent foray to the town dump. Quite obviously, however, Ian Watson has considered the matter of rubbish and comes up with a dark vision indeed of a trip to the junkyard.

Tim and Rosy had cleared out their spare room ruthlessly. They had almost emptied it of the various categories of things that haunt spare rooms: surplus things, fatigued things, souvenir things, exiled things, scraps of things, things that might conceivably be repaired or cannibalized, things that might one day come in handy—all the time vault of twenty years.

"Trouble with being poor," Rosy said while they were loading the car, "is the way you store rubbish like treasure." As if she blamed him for the accumulation.

"We aren't exactly poor," Tim said awkwardly. "Compared with, say, someone in Africa, we're well off. We get by."

Yes, they got by, on the income from the grocery shop. They were able to pay the interest on their debts, which lodged with them like a greedy, infirm uncle; like a senile, crippled mother who stopped them from ever going on vacation. Tim's poetry earned a bit of extra money. His short, fierce lyrics could be roughed out during slack half hours— jotted down like customers' grocery lists—then polished before bed. Two small collections had been published and well received. And of course he was working on his sustained mock epic set in an imaginary Central European country, forever adding ten lines, crossing out five. The country in question needed to be imaginary since he and Rosy couldn't afford to travel abroad.

"Modern life is rubbish," said Rosy. "I saw that sprayed on the front of the cinema. It's perfectly true."

"It's the fault of the recession," he replied.

"It always costs more to be poor, doesn't it? We buy the cheapest, so it's trash. We wear clothes from charity shops, so we look like paupers and people try to swindle us. The poor always rob the poor. This car's a heap of junk; it costs more to keep on the road than a Rolls."

Their car was over ten years old, and rust was eating the bottoms of the doors. The hydraulics of the hatchback had failed; thus the hatch had to be propped up with a broom handle when open. The erratic engine guzzled oil.

When the car, with its rear seats lowered, had been crammed with off cuts of carpet, underfelt, old curtains and coats, bags of lank sweaters and sad shoes, tatty toys, a sick television set, and such, Tim felt oddly refreshed and clean. Whenever he scraped out the last smears of marmalade or pickle from a jar, whenever he emptied out a cereal box, he would feel a similar minor surge of satisfaction, as though now something new and different might happen. Freud might explain this as a babyish pleasure in the expulsion of feces. True, Freud also spoke about anal retention. Next to nothing had been retained in the spare room.

The clearout coincided with Daughter Emma's departure to college. Her choice of geography to study wasn't so much a poignant comment on her parents' immobility as due to geography being regarded academically as an easy option. Emma would probably become an underpaid teacher in a mediocre school; she might marry another teacher. Emma didn't know this yet. Kids were as bouncy as bunnies, before the fox ate them or the winter froze them. Nature pumped the hormone of optimism into each generation. In recent years, Tim had reconciled himself at last to dwelling in the geography of the imagination.

So the house above the shop was doubly empty. It was empty of accumulated clutter; and empty of Emma. Sadly, yet somehow refreshingly empty, like the late-autumn Sunday itself. The sun shone brightly on the empty street. People were still in bed, sleeping in. But the public dump five miles away would be open. Dawn till dusk.

"Junk," repeated Rosy. Tim hoped she wasn't going to turn bitter when it came time to throw their past away.

He removed the broom handle, let the hatchback slam itself, and patted it reassuringly. "Don't discourage the old thing."

Rosy plucked at a loop in her saggy sweater and eyed a box of Emma's childhood toys inside.

"Well, we've got rid of her at last," she said, apparently changing the subject. "Now we can start living, I suppose. If we still know how. Before we're too old."

Automatically, Tim smoothed his hair around the tonsure of his bald patch. They climbed into the car, which started without too much fuss.

As they drove off, Rosy said, "If we won a fortune, I shouldn't be able to spend it, you know. I could never bring myself to buy a coat at *new* prices. Or a meal in a restaurant. Or a proper hairdo. It would seem obscene. I've been trained."

"Me too. I wonder how we'd win a fortune." He spoke flatly, not asking. Most houses and gardens they passed were blank and lifeless, but one man was out washing a car with last year's registration. Tim hardly knew what model it was. He failed to imagine himself driving it. He and Rosy had originally started the shop with help from parents, back in the days when he had dreamed of becoming an internationally regarded poet who traveled places. Parents were now all dead. Legacies had gone to assuage the upward-creeping debts.

"Beautiful day."

Rosy said nothing in reply. She pulled down the sun visor briefly and sought wrinkles in the mirror on the back.

"My hair needs cutting," she said presently.

"Go to a hairdresser's," he murmured.

"I'll do it myself. As usual."

Tim thought he needed a haircut too. When you wore cheap old clothes, short hair was best.

"The roots are showing," she said.

"That's fashionable nowadays. Look, you said we ought to start living.

If you couldn't ever splash out in a restaurant, how can we start living? A bit of a contradiction, isn't it?"

"An economic contradiction. Why should we have to own a shop? The state should own everything. There shouldn't be private cars either. There should be enough good buses and railways."

"True. But there aren't. The services have been castrated."

A poem occurred to him: about eunuchs in Arabian robes driving harems of passengers who peered not through windows but through intricate lattices.

The dump would be open today because the dump was a market too. A bazaar of sorts. Just as charity shops sprouted like fungi in any temporarily empty commercial premises in town, selling the rags of richer people to poorer people to send aid to the totally poor in the Third World, so, with the deliberate decline of the economy, rubbish dumps had changed their nature. Concessionaires bid for the salvage rights. Anything reusable was sold back to the public. Ecological recycling? Logic of poverty? One or the other.

Tim and Rosy had visited the dump outside town a year before and bought a washing machine for a song. The machine worked for three months before breaking down. Cheaper than renting with an option to buy. Now the carcass, with holes cut in it, acted as a compost bin in their patch of back garden. According to gossips visiting the shop, the dump had since undergone a further metamorphosis. A hot-drink vending machine had been installed so that browsers could refresh themselves with a plastic cup of coffee. That summer an ice cream van had visited the dump most weekends.

"Next thing," he said, "people will be having picnics at the dump. There'll be a play area for kids. Tours of the infill. Bulldozer rides. Déjeuner sur le dump."

"What?"

"The Manet painting. Imagine that fellow and his naked mistress sitting on the dump drinking champagne. I presume she'd have to wear a bikini."

A poem? "Manet at the dump." Maybe. What word rhymed with "rubbish"?

Driving along the two-lane road between the first plowed empty fields of the countryside, Tim spotted a cloud of gulls milling in the sky over the sprawling infill acres of the dump, like so many scraps of white paper. Rusty corrugated iron sheets walled off the visitors' zone.

Which they entered, in low gear, the suspension creaking ominously as the car humped itself over the sleeping-policeman ramp.

•

A large concrete yard was lined with bulky rubbish bins into which their car could probably have fit. Down one side the high bins were already loaded with rubble. Those along the opposite side were empty; however, most were roped off with a notice prohibiting use. An arrow pointed to the far end, where several bins stood behind notice boards indicating "glass," "garden refuse," "metal." Those bins were already full; sunlight glared from a pile of windows.

A battered bulk-shipping container the size of a railway carriage blocked the view beyond, though another mounted wooden arrow pointed behind it.

Nearer to hand stood a black oil sump, and a bottle bank painted camouflage green that resembled an armored car, with slots for clear and colored bottles reminiscent of muzzles from which howitzer shells could be fired. A score of ripped-off doors were stacked against one end.

Tim stopped the car by a truck trailer that was packed with a mound of old clothes and rags. Shirt-sleeves hung down as if they had tried to climb out and failed, all the breath crushed out of them.

Beside this trailer, another huge shipping container, open at one end, was labeled "shop." Within, Tim saw clothes on racks, shelves of paperback books, electrical goods. A fat, vacant-faced woman of indeterminate middle age, wearing a pink parka, occupied a deck chair outside. The shop forecourt displayed collections of tools, lamp bases and shades, mirrors, ambiguous metal paraphernalia, a cocktail cabinet with the veneer peeling.

Inside a makeshift pen, cobbled together from car roof racks, an Alsatian guard bitch woke to life when Tim opened his door. The powerful animal reared, barking, raving.

"Jilly!" screamed the fat woman. She ignored Tim. The Alsatian slumped, and whined.

Apart from their own car, the yard was deserted. Too early in the day, perhaps. By this afternoon the bazaar of rubbish might be buzzing; then the beast wouldn't be on edge. Tim stepped nervously round to the hatchback, raised it, and inserted the broom handle. He carried the first plastic bag of clothes to the open trailer, and swung. The bag landed high up the hill of garments, jamming against the roof. He noticed a movement in the inner gloom. Some rags shifting, knocked off balance?

Rosy wound her window down. "Why can't you save the bags?"

"Oh," he said stupidly, measuring the height of the trailer floor, the incline of the clothes hill. Should he climb up and empty the bag? "There's no space left at the front. Our stuff would fall out."

Supposing you tried to repossess a coat you'd thrown away—having changed your mind about discarding it—would the Alsatian be within its rights to rip your throat out? Because you no longer owned that coat? A sign fixed to the dog pen forbade visitors from taking anything, except by way of the shop. Salvage rights had been granted. To a firm called Griffiths Scavenging. Associates of the fat woman in the deck chair.

"Tim, come back here!"

He hurried to the car window.

"Someone inside there," Rosy whispered.

In the dim interior of the trailer, almost hidden by the summit of fabrics, Tim spotted a skinny girl with ratty hair. As he watched, she ripped open the bag he had thrown, and tossed the contents this way and that, examining, sorting.

"It's obscene," said Rosy, "having your socks and knickers picked over before your very eyes."

"Maybe we should have washed all our old clothes before we threw them away?"

"That isn't funny. Find somewhere else, will you? Down there by those signs."

Leaving the hatchback propped, Tim got in and started the engine. He drove down toward the other freight container and followed the arrow round behind it.

Another arrow pointed the way down a long lane lined by bins. As Tim and Rosy entered the lane, shadow fell upon them from the high metal sides and suddenly the day was cold. The occasional freestanding notice announced "plastic," "rubber & tires." As well as being inconveniently tall, the bins were mostly full.

Heeding a further arrow, he turned the car along a side lane similarly walled with bins and intermittent notices.

"Carpeting," he read. "Here we are. Get rid of *that*, at any rate."

On his second attempt, he managed to raise their rolled threadbare carpet to head height and tumble it over the metal lip. It fell dully within. From the car, he hauled the first bundle of heavy underfelt, which they had stored for years on the off chance.

"That isn't exactly *carpet*," called Rosy.

"Undercarpet. Same thing. What do they expect? We should sort out everything for them? Bother that. I'll toss the lot in here, clothes and all. Who cares?"

Another plump, empty-faced woman, in raggy woolens and baggy trousers—an obvious sister of the deck chair occupant—squeezed her way from between two bins and stood watching. A boy of five or six in shorts and black zipper jacket followed her, clutching a torn picture book.

Tim walked over to the woman. "Is it all right if I throw underfelt in that one?" Her skin oozed grease.

"Wha'?" she said after a while.

He repeated himself.

"Uh," she said, which might have meant anything. He realized that the woman was stupid, moronic. Maybe she had no connection with Griffiths Scavenging, after all. She might just be wandering around.

"Well, I will, then." So Tim disposed of all the underfelt, awkwardly heaving and hurling aloft while the woman stared silently at him.

He got back into the car. "There'll be bins for clothes and stuff farther on."

True enough. The next arrow directed them into another long, narrow roadway of bins, all brimful of different categories of clothing. Signs were hardly necessary. Suits. Shirts. Skirts. Underwear. Boots and shoes. Buttons; there was even a bin full of buttons, a mountain height of multicolored shingle.

He cruised at walking pace. "Must be their storeroom, hmm? Maybe they export to poor countries. Or places hit by disaster. Cyclones, earthquakes. We oughtn't to have come so far. We should have dumped the lot back in the yard."

A pair of acne-scarred youths in jeans, heavy steel-tipped boots, and bomber jackets emerged. One slapped a hand on the front of the car, forcing Tim to brake. The other strolled grinning round to the open backside.

"Yelp yer, mate?" The youth tore a bag open and pulled out an old skirt of Rosy's. He ran and tossed this up into a bin of skirts, returned, and burrowed, while his companion joined him.

"Hey," objected Tim. "Get out of our car. Now."

As though instinctively alert to the contents, the youths grabbed the other clothes bags out of the back and ripped them open to sort on the ground. Tim immediately drove on and soon rounded another corner. Yet another lane of bins—all apparently empty—stretched ahead, with an arrow indicating a turning halfway along.

"Stop and reverse," said Rosy. "Go back the way we came."

"We still have the TV to dump, and the—"

"Stop! Back up and turn. Unload the rest in the yard. Anywhere! Drive away. Home."

Home. That house above a shop that fed them and imprisoned them.

The house with an empty daughter's room. And now with an empty spare room. Tim experienced an odd feeling of certainty that before leaving that morning they had emptied the entire house—of furniture, stove, refrigerator, everything—and that there was nothing left any longer to connect them to the place. As if they had cleared all the shelves in the shop, too, leaving bare boards. They were free; they had escaped—hadn't they? Something new could begin.

Vacant shop, vacant house, vacant debts. As vacant as this street of empty bins; as vacant as the rear of the car was fast becoming. He wished he had closed the hatchback down. Otherwise something more precious than junk might escape, might be snatched or simply drift away into the chilly air here between these looming steel boxes that mockingly imitated a decrepit city street—from the future, perhaps, after a war.

He halted the car and shook his head to clear a cold fog of apprehension from his brain. Before he could engage reverse gear, he saw in the rearview mirror the high front of a truck loom around the corner behind. Piston arms, at attention, dangled chains embracing the steel bin on its flatbed back. Somehow the bin truck negotiated the turn. He wondered how it could ever maneuver to pick up or deposit any of the bins ranged on either side. Maybe there was a turntable built into the chassis. Standing in the bin as though navigating the vehicle was the moronic woman. Suddenly the sight of her terrified him. The truck slowly approached, and honked.

"It must be one-way-only, Rosy." Tim drove forward to the next intersection and swung down a lane of close-packed bins containing scrap metal. By the time they reached another arrow, and another turn, the bin truck had already entered the scrap metal street.

Tim took another turn, then another, losing the truck way behind. *If* it had been deliberately following, to begin with.

Arrow followed arrow. Turn followed turn. Lane of bins succeeded lane of bins. Once they turned into the street of clothing bins, yet this led to a street of scrap metal bins, not a street where the bins were empty. Unless his memory was deceiving him. No, it wasn't. The clothes bins must have been different ones. They were lost in a maze.

"This is ridiculous," he told Rosy. "There isn't space for all these lanes."

"We've entered the world of rubbish," Rosy whispered back. "Where we've been heading for the past twenty years."

The engine coughed and missed a couple of times. Tim pulled the choke half out, racing the engine, though of necessity still driving slowly.

"It's all this damn crawling in first gear. The plugs soot up."

The very next lane opened into a long concrete yard walled in by bins. It wasn't the yard that housed the shop. Slamming the choke back in, Tim gunned the car toward the arrow marking the exit at the far end, hoping to burn the plugs clean. He braked violently in time to enter the next narrow alley.

Six lanes later the engine quit. Tim couldn't restart the car.

"What do we do now?" asked Rosy.

"Walk. I'll leave the keys in the ignition."

The bins on either side stood shoulder to shoulder. They seemed twice as large as previously. You couldn't even squeeze sideways between bins, though you might just manage to crawl on your belly. The only route was the concrete road.

"I wonder if this was once an old airfield?"

Then Tim remembered the gulls flocking above the infill. But no gulls flapped in the sky now.

"What's in the bins, Tim?"

Not since that second yard had they passed a single sign announcing the contents. He peered up. Suddenly he understood the assorted shapes peering over the lips of the containers.

Car doors.

Farther along . . . a forest of exhaust pipes like several church organs jumbled by a bomb blast.

"Bits of cars," he said, opening his door.

Two lanes later they heard from somewhere behind them the whine of a power tool, then the clanging of metal. He felt sure that their stalled car was being broken up into parts. Taking Rosy's hand, he hurried her onward and along another lane. Faintly, he heard a thump of boots and a silly, idiotic giggling.

Clothes bins again! Jackets, shirts, sandals, nightdresses loomed over bin tops. Before they could reach the next corner, the moronic woman waddled out from it ahead of them. She was accompanied by a big, bony, overall-clad man in his mid-forties, his thick black hair slicked back in waves, his nose an absurdly small squash blob in a large, battered face.

"Yer need a hand, squire?"

Tim jerked around. One of the youths sat perched on the edge of a shirt bin behind them. The youth dropped to the ground just as his partner came wading over the bin of summer dresses opposite. He leapt down too.

"Show us the way out of here!" cried Rosy. "No, go away! Leave us alone!"

The two youths rushed and clamped Rosy by the arms. At the same moment the man seized Tim, who struggled uselessly; the grip was like granite.

"Yer need a hand," the youth repeated.

The plump woman ambled forward. While the man manipulated Tim like a toy or a life-size doll, the woman undressed him, taking her time about it, tossing his clothes up into various bins. Soon Tim shivered nakedly, still held tight.

Then it was Rosy's turn.

Their captors led Tim and Rosy, both stripped naked, to the turn and released them, thrusting them into the next steel and concrete lane.

"Ge' on, now, squire!"

The woman and her three companions remained at the intersection, blocking any return to the bins where Tim's and Rosy's clothes and shoes had been discarded. Shaking with cold and shock, Tim and Rosy ran along numbly to the next turn, as much to hide their nakedness from the blankly watchful eyes and chilly breeze as to escape.

Tim's teeth chattered. "We'll f-find something to wear. F-farther on. Any old rags. Or c-curtains."

The bins in this new lane were loaded with sheets of cardboard, rolls of wallpaper, bundles of old magazines. Tim wondered whether he could scale the side of a bin with bare feet. He would have to!

Rosy wailed, "I thought they were going to rape—!" Her breast bounced. "They did! They did. It was the same."

"Listen, this is all a vicious joke. Next we'll come across some rags to put on. Then we'll reach the yard where the shop is, looking like scarecrows. And we'll find our car waiting for us—with our clothes folded on the seats. Nobody will believe us, but . . ." He had to believe it. "They could have hurt us. They didn't."

"You think they didn't hurt us? I'm hurt forever."

The bins in the next lane all looked empty; nothing peeped over the tops. Tim rapped his knuckles against several; all rang hollowly. He didn't feel inclined to try to climb, to check.

They walked in cold shade. Whichever direction a lane led, sunlight seemed excluded. At last an arrow pointed the way down between rows of bins full of broken furniture, to a concrete-surfaced yard.

"It's the way out," he said. "We've arrived."

However, the yard, lined with more giant bins, was only as large as a tennis court, and no arrow pointed to an exit. There was only an entrance. Half of the yard was bathed in sunshine, where Rosy ran to warm herself.

Her bare flesh quivering, the breeze still nipped her. Whatever these bins contained couldn't be seen from ground level. A car roof rack rested against one. Side-on, its metal bars were steps.

"I'll see the way out!" Wincing, then planting her feet sideways so as to spread her weight along the thin steel bars, Rosy ascended.

Shading her eyes, she stared around helplessly.

She looked down inside the bin itself. And screamed. Screamed.

Tim scaled the bars; there was room alongside. Clutching her cold shoulders with a chilly arm, he, too, gazed down.

For a few seconds he hardly understood what he saw. A layer of slime-coated Ping-Pong balls? Hundreds of hard-boiled eggs?

No. Eyes. The optic cords sprouted like tiny lengths of electric cord torn out of plugs.

Sheep's eyes? No, he didn't think so. Not the eyes of sheep, or any other animal. Rosy had stopped screaming, out of breath. She shook convulsively, clutching the top of the bin, screwing her own eyes tight shut as if to hide them.

He could see into the neighboring bin as well. A heap of french fries? Baby parsnips? No.

Fingers. Chopped-off human fingers.

He stared wildly around the yard. What did all the other bins hide in their depths? Toes, tongues, lungs? Arms and loins and brains? The parts of the body, sorted out . . . Yes! He knew this was so, even before the grind of an engine dragged his gaze to the entrance of the little yard.

The bin truck heaved into view and halted in the entrance, completing the circuit of metal walls. The front jutted sufficiently into the yard that the truck doors would be free to open. Crowded side by side in the cab were the man, at the wheel; the two youths; the moronic woman with her boy on her knee; the blank-faced fat woman in the pink parka; and the skinny, ratty girl. All of the passengers, even the little boy, were clutching assorted tools. Saws. Pincers. A gouge. A small ax.

The truck engine died.

"For God's sake, climb on top, Rosy!! Walk along the side of the bin beyond. We must get out of here."

Beyond the yard for as far as he could see in all directions were endless rows of bins.

Desperately, bruising his naked body, almost crippling a toe, Tim scrambled on top, struggling to balance, half helping, half dragging Rosy with him. The top edge was far too narrow ever to walk along with bare feet, tightrope-style. Nude, he knew they couldn't even slide along, astride. That would be like riding a blunt steel blade. After a while it would cut up through them, between their legs. Instead, he slid down inside, pulling Rosy howling with him.

"We'll climb out the back way into the next one! And the next!"

Jelly lumps squelched underfoot. He skidded in the six-inch-deep pool of eyes and fell, nauseated. Scrambling up, he waded, then leapt at the high rear edge of the bin. He did catch hold, with outstretched fingers, his front smashing against the metal, but he couldn't pull himself up. He hadn't enough of a grip. There was no purchase. His feet were slipping on soft marbles.

"Yer need a hand?"

A crowd of heads popped up behind. Vacant faces smiled vaguely. The man, the women, the youths, the ratty girl, even the little boy.

Hands rose into view, displaying a gouge, an ax, pincers, saws.

TEST

THEODORE L. THOMAS

Theodore L. Thomas, patent attorney, science columnist and lecturer, and scuba diver, began publishing in 1952 both under his own name and under the pseudonym of Leonard Lockhardt. In addition to his short stories, he has written two novels in collaboration with Kate Wilhelm, *The Clone* (1965) and *The Year of the Cloud* (1970). "Test," first published in *F & SF* in 1962, is a curt and chilling tale which, despite its brevity, is one of the best action stories you will ever read. It poses a question that—once asked—readers will recognize as having echoed in their own minds forever.

Robert Proctor was a good driver for so young a man. The turnpike curved gently ahead of him, lightly traveled on this cool morning in May. He felt relaxed and alert. Two hours of driving had not yet produced the twinges of fatigue that appeared first in the muscles in the base of the neck. The sun was bright but not glaring, and the air smelled fresh and clean. He breathed it deeply, and blew it out noisily. It was a good day for driving.

He glanced quickly at the slim, gray-haired woman sitting in the front seat with him. Her mouth was curved in a quiet smile. She watched the trees and the fields slip by on her side of the pike. Robert Proctor immediately looked back at the road. He said, "Enjoying it, Mom?"

"Yes, Robert." Her voice was as cool as the morning. "It is very pleasant to sit here. I was thinking of the driving I did for you when you were little. I wonder if you enjoyed it as much as I enjoy this."

He smiled, embarrassed. "Sure I did."

She reached over and patted him gently on the arm, and then turned back to the scenery.

He listened to the smooth purr of the engine. Up ahead he saw a great truck, spouting a geyser of smoke as it sped along the turnpike. Behind it, not passing it, was a long blue convertible, content to drive in the wake of the truck. Robert Proctor noted the arrangement and filed it in the back of his mind. He was slowly overtaking them, but he would not reach them for another minute or two.

He listened to the purr of the engine, and he was pleased with the sound. He had tuned that engine himself over the objections of the mechanic. The engine idled rough now, but it ran smoothly at high speed. You needed a special feel to do good work on engines, and Robert Proctor knew he had it. No one in the world had a feel like his for the tune of an engine.

It was a good morning for driving, and his mind was filled with good thoughts. He pulled nearly abreast of the blue convertible and began to pass it. His speed was a few miles per hour above the turnpike limit, but his car was under perfect control. The blue convertible suddenly swung out from behind the truck. It swung out without warning and struck his car near the right front fender, knocking his car to the shoulder on the left side of the turnpike lane.

Robert Proctor was a good driver, too wise to slam on the brakes. He fought the steering wheel to hold the car on a straight path. The left wheels sank into the soft left shoulder, and the car tugged to pull to the left and cross the island and enter the lanes carrying the cars heading in the opposite direction. He held it, then the wheel struck a rock buried in the soft dirt, and the left front tire blew out. The car slewed, and it was then that his mother began to scream.

The car turned sideways and skidded part of the way out into the other lanes. Robert Proctor fought against the steering wheel to straighten the car, but the drag of the blown tire was too much. The scream ran steadily in his ears, and even as he strained at the wheel one part of his mind wondered coolly how a scream could so long be sustained without a breath. An oncoming car struck his radiator from the side and spun him viciously, full into the left-hand lanes.

He was flung into his mother's lap, and she was thrown against the right door. It held. With his left hand he reached for the steering wheel and pulled himself erect against the force of the spin. He turned the wheel to the left, and tried to stop the spin and career out of the lanes of oncoming traffic. His mother was unable to right herself; she lay against the door, her cry rising and falling with the eccentric spin of the car.

The car lost some of its momentum. During one of the spins he twisted the wheel straight, and the car wobblingly stopped spinning and headed down the lane. Before Robert Proctor could turn it off the pike to safety, a car loomed ahead of him, bearing down on him. There was a man at the wheel of that other car, sitting rigid, unable to move, eyes wide and staring and filled with fright. Alongside the man was a girl, her head against the back of the seat, soft curls framing a lovely face, her eyes closed in easy sleep. It was not the fear in the man that reached into Robert Proctor; it was the trusting helplessness in the face of the sleeping girl. The two cars sped closer to each other, and Robert Proctor could not change the direction of his car. The driver of the other car remained frozen at the wheel. At the last moment Robert Proctor sat motionless, staring into the face of the onrushing, sleeping girl, his mother's cry still sounding in his ears. He heard no crash when the two cars collided head-on at a high rate of speed. He felt something push into his stomach, and the world began to go gray. Just before he lost consciousness he heard the scream stop, and he knew then that he had been hearing a single, short-lived scream that had only seemed to drag on and on. There came a painless wrench, and then darkness.

Robert Proctor seemed to be at the bottom of a deep black well. There was a spot of faint light in the far distance, and he could hear the rumble of a distant voice. He tried to pull himself toward the light and the sound, but the effort was too great. He lay still and gathered himself and tried again. The light grew brighter and the voice louder. He tried harder, again, and he drew closer. Then he opened his eyes full and looked at the man sitting in front of him.

"You all right, son?" asked the man. He wore a blue uniform, and his round, beefy face was familiar.

Robert Proctor tentatively moved his head, and discovered he was seated in a reclining chair, unharmed, and able to move his arms and legs with no trouble. He looked around the room, and he remembered.

The man in the uniform saw the growing intelligence in his eyes and he said, "No harm done, son. You just took the last part of your driver's test."

Robert Proctor focused his eyes on the man. Though he saw the man clearly, he seemed to see the faint face of the sleeping girl in front of him.

The uniformed man continued to speak. "We put you through an accident under hypnosis—do it to everybody these days before they can get their driver's licenses. Makes better drivers of them, more careful drivers the rest of their lives. Remember it now? Coming in here and all?"

Robert Proctor nodded, thinking of the sleeping girl. She never would have awakened; she would have passed right from a sweet, temporary sleep into the dark heavy sleep of death, nothing in between. His mother would have been bad enough; after all, she was pretty old. The sleeping girl was downright waste.

The uniformed man was still speaking. "So you're all set now. You pay me the ten-dollar fee, and sign this application, and we'll have your license in the mail in a day or two." He did not look up.

Robert Proctor placed a ten-dollar bill on the table in front of him, glanced over the application, and signed it. He looked up to find two white-uniformed men, standing one on each side of him, and he frowned in annoyance. He started to speak, but the uniformed man spoke first. "Sorry, son. You failed. You're sick; you need treatment."

The two men lifted Robert Proctor to his feet, and he said, "Take your hands off me. What is this?"

The uniformed man said, "Nobody should want to drive a car after going through what you just went through. It should take months before you can even think of driving again, but you're ready right now. Killing people doesn't bother you. We don't let your kind run around loose in society anymore. But don't you worry now, son. They'll take good care of you, and they'll fix you up." He nodded to the two men, and they began to march Robert Proctor out.

At the door he spoke, and his voice was so urgent the two men paused. Robert Proctor said, "You can't really mean this. I'm still dreaming, aren't I? This is still part of the test, isn't it?"

The uniformed man said, *"How do any of us know?"* And they dragged Robert Proctor out the door, knees stiff, feet dragging, his rubber heels sliding along the two grooves worn into the floor.

THE LITTLE BLACK TRAIN

MANLY WADE WELLMAN

When Manly Wade Wellman died in 1986, the world of American fiction was lessened. Manly Wade Wellman began publishing in 1927, capturing the southern American spirit in all his tales. His most famous sequence of tales, of which "The Little Black Train" is but one, concerned the roving ballad singer, John. These stories were published in *F & SF* from 1951 to 1962 and collected as *Who Fears the Devil?* (1963). John is a character who seems just bound to meet up with odd people in odder places. We find these tales particularly attractive both for Manly Wade Wellman's faithful recording of one type of regional speech and for his rewarding explorations in American folklore. "The Little Black Train" is one of Manly Wade Wellman's most compelling tales. In it, John once again confronts evil in an attempt to turn aside—with his silver-stringed guitar—a curse of twenty years.

There in the High Fork country, with peaks saw-toothing into the sky and hollows diving away down and trees thicketed every which way, you'd think human foot had never stepped. Walking the trail between high pines, I touched my guitar's silver strings for company of the sound. But then a man squandered into sight around a bend—younglike, red-faced, baldy-headed. Gentlemen, he was as drunk as a hoot. I gave him good evening.

"Can you play that thing?" he gobbled at me and, second grab of his shaky hand, he got hold of my hickory shirt-sleeve. "Come to the party, friend. Our fiddle band, last moment, they got scared out. We got just only a mouth harp to play for us."

"What way was the fiddle band scared?" I asked him to tell.

"Party's at Miss Donie Carawan's," he said, without replying me. "Bobbycue pig and chicken, bar'l of good stump-hole whisky."

"Listen," I said, "ever hear tell of the man invited a stranger fiddler, he turned out to be Satan?"

"Shoo," he snickered, "Satan plays the fiddle, you play the guitar, I don't pay your guitar no worry. What's your name, friend?"

"John. What's yours?"

But he'd started up a narrow, grown-over, snaky-turny path you'd not notice. I reckoned the party'd be at a house, where I could sleep the night that was coming, so I followed. He nearly fell back top of me, he was so stone drunk, but we got to a notch on the ridge, and the far side was a valley of trees, dark and secret-looking. Going down, I began to hear loud laughing talk. Finally we reached a yard at the bottom. There was a house there, and it looked like enough men and women to swing a primary election.

They whooped at us; so loud it rang my ears. The drunk man waved both his hands. "This here's my friend John," he bawled out, "and he's a-going to play us some music!"

They whooped louder at that, and easiest thing for me to do was start picking "Hell Broke Loose in Georgia"; and, gentlemen, right away they danced up a storm.

Wildlike, they whipped and whirled. Most of them were young folks dressed their best. One side, a great big man called the dance, but you couldn't much hear him, everybody laughed and hollered so loud. It got in my mind that children laugh and yell thataway, passing an old burying ground where ghosts could be. It was the way they might be trying to dance down the nervouses; I jumped myself, between picks, when something started moaning beside me. But it was just a middling-old fellow with a thin face, playing his mouth harp along with my guitar.

I looked to the house—it was new and wide and solid, with white-washed clay chinking between the squared logs of it. Through a dog-trot from front to back I saw clear down valley, west to where the sunball dropped red toward a far string of mountains. The valley bottom's trees were spaced out with a kind of path or road, the whole length. The house windows began to light up as I played. Somebody was putting a match to lamps, against the night's fall.

End of the tune, everybody clapped me loud and long. "More! More!" they hollered, bunched among the yard trees, still fighting their nervouses.

"Friends," I managed to be heard, "let me make my manners to the one who's giving this party."

"Hi, Miss Donie!" yelled out the drunk man. "Come meet John!"

From the house she walked through the crowded-around folks, stepping so proud, she looked taller than she was. A right much stripy skirt swished to her high heels; but she hadn't such a much dress above, and none at all on her round arms and shoulders. The butter yellow of her hair must have come from a bottle, and the doll pink of her face from a box. She smiled up to me, and her perfume tingled my nose. Behind her followed that big dance-caller, with his dead black hair and wide teeth, and his heavy hands swinging like balance weights.

"Glad you came, John," she said, deep in her round throat.

I looked at her robin-egg-blue eyes and her butter hair and her red mouth and her bare pink shoulders. She was maybe thirty-five, maybe forty, maybe more and not looking it. "Proud to be here," I said, my politest. "Is this a birthday, Miss Donie Carawan?"

Folks fell quiet, swapping looks. An open cooking fire blazed up as the night sneaked in. Donie Carawan laughed deep.

"Birthday of a curse," and she widened her blue eyes. "End of the curse, too, I reckon. All tonight."

Some mouths came open, but didn't let words out. I reckoned that whatever had scared out the fiddle band was nothing usual. She held out a slim hand, with green-stoned rings on it.

"Come eat and drink, John," she bade me.

"Thanks," I said, for I hadn't eaten ary mouthful since crack of day.

Off she led me, her fingers pressing mine, her eye corners watching me. The big dance-caller glittered a glare after us. He was purely jealoused up that she'd made me so welcome.

Two dark-faced old men stood at an iron rack over a pit of coals, where lay two halves of a slow-cooking hog. One old man dipped a stick with a rag ball into a kettle of sauce and painted it over the brown roast meat. From a big pot of fat over yet another fire, an old woman forked hush puppies into pans set ready on a plank table.

"Line up!" called Donie Carawan out, like a bugle. They lined up, talking and hollering again, smiles back on their faces. It was some way like dreams you have, folks carrying on loud and excited, and something bad coming on to happen.

Donie Carawan put her bare arm through my blue-sleeved elbow while an old man sliced chunks of barbecued hog on paper plates for us. The old woman forked on a hush puppy and a big hobby of cole slaw. Eating, I wondered how they made the barbecue sauce—wondered, too, if all these folks really wanted to be here for what Donie Carawan called the birthday of a curse.

"John," she said, the way you'd think she read what I wondered, "don't they say a witch's curse can't work on a pure heart?"

"They say that," I agreed her, and she laughed her laugh. The big dance-caller and the skinny mouth harp man looked up from their barbecue.

"An old witch cursed me for guilty twenty years back," said Donie Carawan. "The law said I was innocent. Who was right?"

"Don't know how to answer that," I had to say, and again she laughed, and bit into her hush puppy.

"Look around you, John," she said. "This house is my house, and this valley is my valley, and these folks are my friends, come to help me pleasure myself."

Again I reckoned, she's the only one here that's pleasured, maybe not even her.

"Law me," she laughed, "it's rough on a few folks, holding their breath all these years to see the curse light on me. Since it wouldn't light, I figured how to shoo it away." Her blue eyes looked up. "But what are you doing around High Fork, John?"

The dance-caller listened, and the thin mouth harp man. "Just passing through," I said. "Looking for songs. I heard about a High Fork song, something about a little black train."

Silence quick stretched all around, the way you'd think I'd been impolite. Yet again she broke the silence with a laugh.

"Why," she said, "I've known that song as long as I've known about the curse, near to. Want me to sing it for you?"

Folks were watching, and, "Please, ma'am," I asked her.

She sang, there in the yellow lamplight and red firelight, among the shady-shadowy trees and the mountain dark, without ary slice of moon overhead. Her voice was a good voice. I put down my plate and, a line or two along, I made out to follow her with the guitar.

> I heard a voice of warning,
> A message from on high,
> "Go put your house in order
> For thou shalt surely die.
> Tell all your friends a long farewell
> And get your business right—
> The little black train is rolling in
> To call for you tonight."

"Miss Donie, that's a tuneful thing," I said. "Sounds right like a train rolling."

"My voice isn't high enough to sound the whistle part," she smiled at me, red-mouthed.

"I might could do that," said the mouth harp man, coming close and speaking soft. And folks were craning at us, looking sick, embarrassed, purely distasted. I began to wonder why I shouldn't have given a name to that black train song.

But then rose up a big holler near the house, where a barrel was set. The drunk man that'd fetched me was yelling mad at another man near about as drunk, and they were trying to grab a drinking gourd from each other. Two, three other men on each side hoorawed them on to squabble more.

"Jeth!" called Donie Carawan to the big dance-caller. "Let's stop that before they spill the whiskey, Jeth."

Jeth and she headed for the bunch by the barrel, and everybody else was crowding to watch.

"John," said a quiet somebody—the mouth harp man, with firelight showing lines in his thin face, salty gray in his hair. "What you really doing here?"

"Watching," I said, while big Jeth hauled those two drunk men off from each other, and Donie Carawan scolded them. "And listening," I said. "Wanting to know what way the black train song fits in with this party and the tale about the curse. You know about it?"

"I know," he said.

We carried out food out of the firelight. Folks were crowding to the barrel, laughing and yelling.

"Donie Carawan was to marry Trevis Jones," the mouth harp man told me. "He owned the High Fork Railroad to freight the timber from this valley. He'd a lavish of money, is how he got to marry her. But"— and he swallowed hard—"another young fellow loved her. Cobb Richardson, who ran Trevis Jones's train on the High Fork Railroad. And he killed Trevis Jones."

"For love?" I asked.

"Folks reckoned that Donie Carawan decided against Trevis and love-talked Cobb into the killing; for Trevis had made a will and heired her all his money and property—the railroad and all. But Cobb made confession. Said Donie had no part in it. The law let her go, and killed Cobb in the electric chair, down at the state capital."

"I declare to never," I said.

"Fact. And Cobb's mother—Mrs. Amanda Richardson—spoke the curse."

"Oh," I said, "is she the witch that—"

"She was no witch"—he broke me off—"but she cursed Donie Carawan, that the train that Cobb had engine drove, and Trevis had heired to her, would be her death and destruction. Donie laughed. You've heard her laugh. And folks started the song, the black train song."

"Who made it?" I asked him.

"Reckon I did," he said, looking long at me. He waited to let me feel that news. Then he said, "Maybe it was the song decided Donie Carawan to deal with the Hickory River Railroad, agreeing for an income of money not to run the High Fork train no more."

I'd finished my barbecue. I could have had more, but I didn't feel like it. "I see," I told him. "She reckoned that if no train ran on the High Fork tracks, it couldn't be her death and destruction."

He and I put our paper plates on one of the fires. I didn't look at the other folks, but it seemed to me they were quieting their laughing and talking as the night got darker.

"Only thing is," the mouth harp man went on, "folks say the train runs on that track. Or it did. A black train runs some nights at midnight, they say, and when it runs a sinner dies."

"You ever see it run?"

"No, John, but I've sure God heard it. And only Donie Carawan laughs about it."

She laughed right then, joking the two men who'd feathered up to fight. Ary man's neck craned at her, and women looked the way you'd figure they didn't relish that. My neck craned some itself.

"Twenty years back, the height of her bloom," said the mouth harp man, "law me, you'd never call to look at anything else."

"What does she mean, no more curse?"

"She made another deal, John. She sold off the rails of the High Fork Road, that's stood idle for twenty years. Today the last of them was torn up and carried off. Meanwhile, she's had this house built, across where the right of way used to be. Looky yonder, through the dog-trot. That's where the road ran."

So it was the old road bed made that dark dip amongst the trees. Just now it didn't look so wide a dip.

"No rails," he said. "She figures no black train at midnight. Folks came at her invite—some because they rent her land, some because they owe her money, and some—men folks—because they'll do anything she bids them."

"And she never married?" I asked.

"If she done that, she'd lose the money and land she heired from Trevis

Jones. It was in his will. She just takes men without marrying, one and then another. I've known men kill theirselves because she'd put her heart back in her pocket on them. Lately, it's been big Jeth. She acts tonight like picking herself a new beau lover."

She walked back through the lamplight and firelight. "John," she said, "these folks want to dance again."

What I played them was "Many Thousands Gone," with the mouth harp to help, and they danced and stomped the way you'd think it was a many thousands dancing. In its thick, Donie Carawan promenaded left and right and do-si-doed with a fair-haired young fellow, and Jeth the dance-caller looked pickle sour. When I'd done, Donie Carawan came swishing back.

"Let the mouth harp play," she said, "and dance with me."

"Can't dance no shakes," I told her. "Just now, I'd relish to practice the black train song."

Her blue eyes crinkled. "All right. Play, and I'll sing."

She did. The mouth harp man blew whistle moanings to my guitar, and folks listened, goggling like frogs.

> *A bold young man kept mocking,*
> *Cared not for the warning word,*
> *When the wild and lonely whistle*
> *Of the little black train he heard.*
> *"Have mercy, Lord, forgive me!*
> *I'm cut down in my sin!*
> *O death, will you not spare me?"*
> *But the little black train rolled in.*

When she'd sung that much, Donie Carawan laughed like before, deep and bantering. Jeth the dance-caller made a funny sound in his bull throat.

"What I don't figure," he said, "was how you all made the train sound like coming in, closer and closer."

"Just by changing the music," I said. "Changing the pitch."

"Fact," said the mouth harp man. "I played the change with him."

A woman laughed, nervous. "Now, I think, that's true. A train whistle sounds higher and higher while it comes up to you. Then it passes and goes off, sounding lower and lower."

"But I didn't hear the train go away in the song," allowed a man beside her. "It just kept coming." He shrugged, maybe he shivered.

"Donie," said the woman, "reckon I'll go along."

"Stay on, Lettie," began Donie Carawan, telling her instead of asking.

"Got a right much walking to do, and no moon," said the woman. "Reuben, you come too."

She left. The man looked back just once at Donie Carawan, and followed. Another couple, and then another, went with them from the firelight. Maybe more would have gone, but Donie Carawan snorted, like a horse, to stop them.

"Let's drink," she said. "Plenty for all, now those folks I reckoned to be my friends are gone."

Maybe two, three others faded away, between there and the barrel. Donie Carawan dipped herself a drink, watching me over the gourd's edge. Then she dipped more and held it out.

"You drink after a lady," she whispered, "and get a kiss."

I drank. It was good stump-hole whiskey. "Tasty," I said.

"The kiss?" she laughed. But the dance-caller didn't laugh, or either the mouth harp man, or either me.

"Let's dance," said Donie Carawan, and I picked "Sourwood Mountain" and the mouth harp moaned.

The dancers had got to be few, just in a short while. But the trees they danced through looked bigger, and more of them. It minded me of how I'd heard, when I was a chap, about day-trees and night-trees, they weren't the same things at all; and the night-trees can crowd all round a house they don't like, pound the shingles off the roof, bust in the window glass and the door panels; and that's the sort of night you'd better never set your foot outside. . . .

Not so much clapping at the end of "Sourwood Mountain." Not such a holler of "More!" Folks went to take another drink at the barrel, but the mouth harp man held me back.

"Tell me," he said, "about that business. The noise sounding higher when the train comes close."

"It was explained out to me by a man I know, place in Tennessee called Oak Ridge," I said. "It's about what they call sound waves, and some way it works with light too. Don't rightly catch on how, but they can measure how far it is to the stars thataway."

He thought, frowning. "Something like what's called radar?"

I shook my head. "No, no machinery to it. Just what they name a principle. Fellow named Doppler—Christian Doppler, a foreigner—got it up."

"His name was Christian," the mouth harp man repeated me. "Then I reckon it's no witch stuff."

"Why you worrying it?" I asked him.

"I watched through the dog-trot while we were playing the black train song, changing pitch, making it sound like coming near," he said. "Looky yonder, see for yourself."

I looked. There was a streaky shine down the valley. Two streaky shines, though nary moon. I saw what he meant—it looked like those pulled-up rails were still there, where they hadn't been before.

"That second verse Miss Donie sang," I said. "Was it about—"

"Yes," he said before I'd finished. "That was the verse about Cobb Richardson. How he prayed for God's forgiveness, night before he died."

Donie Carawan came and poked her hand under my arm. I could tell that good strong liquor was feeling its way around her insides. She laughed at almost nothing whatever. "You're not leaving, anyway." She smiled at me.

"Don't have anyplace special to go," I said.

She upped on her pointed toes. "Stay here tonight," she said in my ear. "The rest of them will be gone by midnight."

"You invite men like that?" I said, looking into her blue eyes. "When you don't know them?"

"I know men well enough," she said. "Knowing men keeps a woman young." Her finger touched my guitar where it hung behind my shoulder, and the strings whispered a reply. "Sing me something, John."

"I still want to learn the black train song."

"I've sung you both verses," she said.

"Then," I told her, "I'll sing a verse I've just made up inside my head." I looked at the mouth harp man. "Help me with this."

Together we played, raising pitch gradually, and I sang the new verse I'd made, with my eyes on Donie Carawan.

> Go tell that laughing lady
> All filled with worldly pride,
> The little black train is coming,
> Get ready to take a ride.
> With a little black coach and engine
> And a little black baggage car,
> The words and deeds she has said and done
> Must roll to the judgment bar.

When I was through, I looked up at those who'd stayed. They weren't more than half a dozen now, bunched up together like cows in a storm; all but Big Jeth, standing to one side with eyes stabbing at me, and Donie Carawan, leaning tiredlike against a tree with hanging branches.

"Jeth," she said, "stomp his guitar to pieces."

I switched the carrying cord off my neck and held the guitar at my side. "Don't try such a thing, Jeth," I warned him.

His big square teeth grinned, with dark spaces between them. He looked twice as wide as me.

"I'll stomp you and your guitar both," he said.

I put the guitar on the ground, glad I'd had but the one drink. Jeth ran and stooped for it, and I put my fist hard under his ear. He hopped two steps away to keep his feet.

Shouldn't anybody name me what he did then, and I hit him twice more, harder yet. His nose flatted out under my knuckles and when he pulled back away, blood trickled.

The mouth harp man grabbed up my guitar. "This here'll be a square fight!" he yelled, louder than he'd spoken so far. "Ain't a fair one, seeing Jeth's so big, but it'll be square! Just them two in it, and no more!"

"I'll settle you later," Jeth promised him, mean.

"Settle me first," I said, and got betwixt them.

Jeth ran at me. I stepped sidewise and got him under the ear again as he went shammocking past. He turned, and I dug my fist right into his belly-middle, to stir up all that stump-hole whiskey he'd been drinking, then the other fist under the ear yet once more, then on the chin and the mouth, under the ear, on the broken nose—ten licks like that, as fast and hard as I could fetch them in, and eighth or ninth he went slack, and the tenth he just fell flat and loose, like a coat from a nail. I stood waiting, but he didn't move.

"Gentlemen," said the drunk man who'd fetched me, "looky yonder at Jeth laying there! Never figured to see the day! Maybe that stranger-man calls himself John is Satan, after all!"

Donie Carawan walked across, slow, and gouged Jeth's ribs with the pointy toe of her high-heeled shoe. "Get up," she bade him.

He grunted and mumbled and opened his eyes. Then he got up, joint by joint, careful and sore, like a sick bull. He tried to stop the blood from his nose with the back of his big hand. Donie Carawan looked at him and then she looked at me.

"Get out of here, Jeth," she ordered him. "Off my place."

He went, cripplylike, with his knees bent and his hands swinging and his back humped, the way you'd think he carried something heavy.

The drunk man hiccuped. "I reckon to go too," he said, maybe just to himself.

"Then go!" Donie Carawan yelled at him. "Everybody can go, right now, this minute! I thought you were my friends—now I see I don't have a friend among the whole bunch! Hurry up, get going! Everybody!"

Hands on hips, she blared it out. Folks moved off through the trees, a sight faster than Jeth had gone. But I stood where I was. The mouth harp man gave me back my guitar, and I touched a chord of its strings. Donie Carawan spun around like on a swivel to set her blue eyes on me.

"You stayed," she said, the way she thought there was something funny about it.

"It's not midnight yet," I told her.

"But near to," added the mouth harp man. "Just a few minutes off. And it's at midnight the little black train runs."

She lifted her round bare shoulders. She made to laugh again, but didn't.

"That's all gone. If it ever was true, it's not true anymore. The rails were taken up—"

"Looky yonder through the dog-trot," the mouth harp man broke in. "See the two rails in place, streaking along the valley."

Again she swung around and she looked, and seemed to me she swayed in the light of the dying fires. She could see those streaky rails, all right.

"And listen," said the mouth harp man. "Don't you all hear something?"

I heard it, and so did Donie Carawan, for she flinched. It was a wild and lonely whistle, soft but plain, far down valley.

"Are you doing that, John?" she squealed at me in a voice gone all of a sudden high and weak and old. Then she ran at the house and into the dog-trot, staring down along what looked like railroad track.

I followed her, and the mouth harp man followed me. Inside the dog-trot was a floor of dirt, stomped hard as brick. Donie Carawan looked back at us. Lamplight came through a window, to make her face look bright pale, with the painted red of the mouth gone almost black against it.

"John," she said, "you're playing a trick, making it sound like—"

"Not me," I swore to her.

It whistled again, *wooooooeeeee!* And I, too, looked along the two rails, shining plain as plain in the dark, moonless night, to curve off around a valley bend. A second later the engine itself sounded, *chukchukchuk-chuk*, and the whistle, *wooooooeeeee!*

"Miss Donie," I said, close behind her, "you'd better go away."

I pushed her gently.

"No!" She lifted her fists, and I saw cordy lines on their backs—they weren't a young woman's fists. "This is my house and my land, and it's my railroad!"

"But—" I started to say.

"If it comes here," she broke me off, "where can I run to from it?"

The mouth harp man tugged my sleeve. "I'm going," he said. "You and me raised the pitch and brought the black train. Thought I could stay, watch it, and glory in it. But I'm not man enough."

Going, he blew a whistle moan on his mouth harp, and the other whistle blew back an answer, louder and nearer.

And higher in the pitch.

"That's a real train coming," I told Donie Carawan, but she shook her yellow head.

"No," she said, deadlike. "It's coming, but it's no real train. It's heading right to this dog-trot. Look, John. On the ground."

Rails looked to run there, right through the dog-trot like through a tunnel. Maybe it was some peculiar way of the light. They lay close together, like narrow-gauge rails. I didn't feel like touching them with my toe to make sure of them, but I saw them. Holding my guitar under one arm, I put out my other hand to take Donie Carawan's elbow. "We'd better go," I said again.

"I can't!"

She said it loud and sharp and purely scared. And taking hold of her arm was like grabbing the rail of a fence, it was so stiff and unmoving.

"I own this land," she was saying. "I can't leave it."

I tried to pick her up, and that couldn't be done. You'd have thought she'd grown to the ground inside that dog-trot, spang between what looked like the rails, the way you'd figure roots had come from her pointy toes and high heels. Out yonder, where the track marks curved off, the sound rose louder, higher, *chukchukchukchuk—wooooooe eeee!* And light was coming from round the curve, like a headlight maybe, only it had some blue to its yellow.

The sound of the coming engine made the notes of the song in my head:

> *Go put your house in order*
> *For thou shalt surely die—*

Getting higher, getting higher, changing pitch as it came close and closer—

I don't know when I began picking the tune on my guitar, but I was playing as I stood there next to Donie Carawan. She couldn't flee. She was rooted there, or frozen there, and the train was going to come in sight in just a second.

The mouth harp man credited us, him and me, with bringing it, by that pitch-changing. And, whatever anybody deserved, wasn't for me to bring their deservings on them. I thought things like that. Also:

Christian Doppler was the name of the fellow who'd thought out the why and wherefore of how pitch makes the sound closeness. Like what the mouth harp man said, his name showed it wasn't witch stuff. An honest man could try . . .

I slid my fingers back up the guitar neck, little by little, as I picked the music, and the pitch sneaked down.

"Here it comes, John," whimpered Donie Carawan, standing solid as a stump.

"No," I said. "It's going—listen!"

I played so soft you could pick up the train noise with your ear. And the pitch was dropping, like with my guitar, and the whistle sounded *woooooeeeee*! Lower it sounded.

"The light—dimmer—" she said. "Oh, if I could have the chance to live different—"

She moaned and swayed.

Words came for me to sing as I picked:

> *Oh, see her standing helpless,*
> *Oh, hear her shedding tears.*
> *She's counting these last moments*
> *As once she counted years.*
> *She'd turn from proud and wicked ways,*
> *She'd leave her sin, O Lord!*
> *If the little black train would just back up*
> *And not take her aboard.*

For she was weeping, all right. I heard her breath catch and strangle and shake her body, the way you'd look for it to tear her ribs loose from her backbone. I picked on, strummed on, lower and lower.

Just for once, I thought I could glimpse what might have come at us.

It was little, all right, and black under that funny cold-blue light it carried. And the cars weren't any bigger than coffins, and some way the shape of coffins. Or maybe I just sort of imagined that, dreamed it up while I stood there. Anyway, the light grew dim, and the *chukchuk-chukchuk* went softer and lower, and you'd guess the train was backing off, out of hearing.

I stopped my hand on the silver strings. We stood there in a silence like what there must be in some lifeless, airless place like on the moon.

Then Donie Carawan gave out one big, broken sob, and I caught her with my free arm as she fell.

She was soft enough then. All the tight was gone from her. She lifted one weak, round, bare arm around my neck, and her tears wet my hickory shirt.

"You saved me, John," she kept saying. "You turned the curse away."

"Reckon I did," I said, though that sounded like bragging. I looked down at the rails, and they weren't there, in the dog-trot or beyond. Just the dark of the valley. The cooking fires had burned out, and the lamps in the house were low.

Her arm tightened around my neck. "Come in," she said. "Come in, John. You and me, alone in there."

"It's time for me to head off away," I said.

Her arm dropped from me. "What's the matter? Don't you like me?" she asked.

I didn't even answer that one, she sounded so pitiful. "Miss Donie," I said, "you told a true thing. I turned the curse from you. It hadn't died. You can't kill it by laughing at it, or saying there aren't such things, or pulling up rails. If it held off tonight, it might come back."

"Oh!" She half raised her arms to me again, then put them down.

"What must I do?" she begged me.

"Stop being a sinner."

Her blue eyes got round in her pale face.

"You want me to live," she said, hopeful.

"It's better for you to live. You told me that folks owe you money, rent land from you, and such. How'd they get along if you got carried off?"

She could see what I meant, maybe the first time in her life.

"You'd be gone," I minded her, "but the folks would stay behind, needing your help. Well, you're still here, Miss Donie. Try to help the folks. There's a thousand ways to do it. I don't have to name them to you. And you act right, you won't be so apt to hear that whistle at midnight."

I started out of the dog-trot.

"John!" My name sounded like a wail in her mouth.

"Stay here tonight, John," she begged me. "Stay with me! I want you here, John, I need you here!"

"No, you don't need me, Miss Donie," I said. "You've got a right much of thinking and planning to do. Around about the up of sun, you'll have done enough, maybe, to start living different from this on."

She started to cry. As I walked away I noticed how, farther I got, lower her voice-pitch sounded.

I sort of stumbled on the trail. The mouth harp man sat on a chopped-down old log.

"I listened, John," he said. "Think you done right?"

"Did the closest I could to right. Maybe the black train was bound to roll, on orders from whatever station it starts from; maybe it was you and me, raising the pitch the way we did, brought it here tonight."

"I left when I did, dreading that thought." He nodded.

"The same thought made me back it out again," I said.

"Anyway, I kind of glimmer the idea you all can look for a new Donie Carawan hereabouts, from now forward."

He got up and turned to go up trail. "I never said who I was."

"No, sir," I agreed him. "And I never asked."

"I'm Cobb Richardson's brother. Wyatt Richardson. Dying, my mother swore me to even things with Donie Carawan for what happened to Cobb. Doubt if she meant this sort of turnout, but I reckon it would suit her fine."

We walked into the dark together.

"Come stay at my house tonight, John," he made the offer. "Ain't much there, but you're welcome to what there is."

"Thank you kindly," I said. "I'd be proud to stay."

THE AUTOPSY

MICHAEL SHEA

Californian Michael Shea often mixes science fiction with horror in his writings to produce (paradoxically) literate, rational terror. His novel *Nifft the Lean* (1982) is set in the future, yet it is a horrific future. "The Autopsy" uses a similar mix of sf and horror. This story—in which Dr. Carl Winters, a fifty-seven-year-old pathologist, arrives at a mountain town to perform autopsies on the victims of a suspicious mining explosion—is about the business of death; and so be warned that it is in some ways a grim tale. However, it is ultimately a positive, even touching story. You won't soon forget Dr. Winters and what he finds in a defunct ice plant on the edge of the town known as Bailey.

Dr. Winters stepped out of the tiny Greyhound station and into the midnight street that smelt of pines and the river, though the street was in the heart of the town. But then, it was a town of only five main streets in breadth, and these extended scarcely a mile and a half along the rim of the gorge. Deep in that gorge though the river ran, its blurred roar flowed, perfectly distinct, between the banks of dark shop windows. The station's window showed the only light, save for a luminous clock face several doors down and a little neon beer logo two blocks farther on. When he had walked a short distance, Dr. Winters set his suitcase down, pocketed his hands, and looked at the stars—thick as cobblestones in the black gulf.

"A mountain hamlet—a mining town," he said. "Stars. No moon. We are in Bailey."

He was talking to his cancer. It was in his stomach. Since learning of it, he had developed this habit of wry communion with it. He meant to show courtesy to this uninvited guest, Death. It would not find him churlish, for that would make its victory absolute. Except, of course, that its victory would *be* absolute, with or without his ironies.

He picked up his suitcase and walked on. The starlight made faint mirrors of the windows' blackness and showed him the man who passed: lizard-lean, white-haired (at fifty-seven), a man traveling on death's business, carrying his own death in him, and even bearing death's wardrobe in his suitcase. For this was filled—aside from his medical kit and some scant necessities—with mortuary bags. The sheriff had told him on the phone of the improvisations that presently enveloped the corpses, and so the doctor had packed these, laying them in his case with bitter amusement, checking the last one's breadth against his chest before the mirror, as a woman will gauge a dress before donning it, and telling his cancer: "Oh, yes, that's plenty roomy enough for both of us!"

The case was heavy and he stopped frequently to rest and scan the sky. What a night's work to do, probing soulless filth, eyes earthward, beneath such a ceiling of stars! It had taken five days to dig them out. The autumnal equinox had passed, but the weather here had been uniformly hot. And warmer still, no doubt, so deep in the earth.

He entered the courthouse by a side door. His heels knocked on the linoleum corridor. A door at the end of it, on which was lettered NATE CRAVEN, COUNTY SHERIFF, opened well before he reached it, and his friend stepped out to meet him.

"Dammit, Carl, you're *still* so thin they could use you for a whip. Gimme that. You're in too good a shape already. You don't need the exercise."

The case hung weightless from his hand, imparting no tilt at all to his bull shoulders. Despite his implied self-derogation, he was only moderately paunched for a man his age and size. He had a rough-hewn face and the bulk of brow, nose, and jaw made his greenish eyes look small until one engaged them and felt the snap and penetration of their intelligence. He half filled two cups from a coffee urn and topped both off with bourbon from a bottle in his desk. When they had finished these, they had finished trading news of mutual friends. The sheriff mixed another round, and sipped from his in a silence clearly prefatory to the work at hand.

"They talk about rough justice," he said. "I've sure seen it now. One of those . . . patients of yours that you'll be working on? He was a killer. 'Killer' don't even half say it, really. You could say that *he* got justly executed in that blast. That much was justice for damn sure. But rough as hell on those other nine. And the rough don't just stop with their being dead either. That kiss-ass boss of yours! He's breaking his god-damned back touching his toes for Fordham Mutual. How much of the picture did he give you?"

"You refer, I take it, to the estimable Coroner Waddleton of Fordham County." Dr. Winters paused to sip his drink. With a delicate flaring of his nostrils he communicated all the disgust, contempt, and amusement he had felt in his four years as pathologist in Waddleton's office. The sheriff laughed.

"Clear pictures seldom emerge from anything the coroner says," the doctor continued. "He took your name in vain. Vigorously and repeatedly. These expressions formed his opening remarks. He then developed the theme of our office's strict responsibility to the letter of the law, and of the workmen's compensation law in particular. Death benefits accrue only to the dependents of decedents whose death arise *out of the course of* their employment, not merely *in* the course of it. Victims of a maniacal assault, though they die on the job, are by no means necessarily compensable under the law. We then contemplated the tragic injustice of an insurance company—*any* insurance company—having to pay benefits to unentitled persons, solely through the laxity and incompetence of investigating officers. Your name came up again."

Craven uttered a bark of mirth and fury. "The impartial public servant! Ha! The impartial brown-nose, flimflam and bullshit man is what he *is*. Ten to one, Fordham Mutual will slip out of it *without* his help, and those widows won't see a goddamn nickel." Words were an insufficient vent; the sheriff turned and spat into his wastebasket. He drained his cup, and sighed. "I beg your pardon, Carl. We've been five days digging those men out and the last two days sifting half that mountain for explosive traces, with those insurance investigators hanging on our elbows, and the most they could say was that there was 'strong presumptive evidence' of a bomb. Well, I don't budge for that because I don't have to. Waddleton can shove his 'extraordinary circumstances.' If you don't find anything in those bodies, then that's all the autopsy there is to it, and they get buried right here where their families want 'em."

The doctor was smiling at his friend. He finished his cup and spoke with his previous wry detachment, as if the sheriff had not interrupted.

"The honorable coroner then spoke with remarkable volubility on the subject of autopsy consent forms and the malicious subversion of private citizens by vested officers of the law. He had, as it happened, a sheaf of such forms on his desk, all signed, all with a rider clause typed in above the signatures. A cogent paragraph. It had, among its other qualities, the property of turning the coroner's face purple when he read it aloud. He read it aloud to me three times. It appeared that the survivors' consent was contingent on two conditions: that the autopsy be performed *in locem mortis*, that is to say in Bailey, and that only if the coroner's pathologist found concrete evidence of homicide should the decedents be subject either to removal from Bailey or to further necropsy. It was well written. I remember wondering who wrote it."

The sheriff nodded musingly. He took Dr. Winters's empty cup, set it by his own, filled both two thirds with bourbon, and added a splash of coffee to the doctor's. The two friends exchanged a level stare, rather like poker players in the clinch. The sheriff regarded his cup, sipped from it.

"*In locem mortis*. What-all does that mean exactly?"

" 'In the place of death'."

"Oh. Freshen that up for you?"

"I've just started it, thank you."

Both men laughed, paused, and laughed again, some might have said immoderately.

"He all but told me that I *had* to find something to compel a second autopsy," the doctor said at length. "He would have sold his soul—or taken out a second mortgage on it—for a mobile X-ray unit. He's right, of course. If those bodies have trapped any bomb fragments, that would be the surest and quickest way of finding them. It still amazes me your Dr. Parsons could let his X ray go unfixed for so long."

"He sets bones, stitches wounds, writes prescriptions, and sends anything tricky down the mountain. Just barely manages that. Drunks don't get much done."

"He's gotten that bad?"

"He hangs on and no more. Waddleton was right there, not deputizing him pathologist. I doubt he could find a cannonball in a dead rat. I wouldn't say it where it could hurt him, as long as he's still managing, but everyone here knows it. His patients sort of look after *him* half the time. But Waddleton would have sent you, no matter who was here. Nothing but his best for party contributors like Fordham Mutual."

The doctor looked at his hands and shrugged. "So. There's a killer in the batch. *Was* there a bomb?"

Slowly, the sheriff planted his elbows on the desk and pressed his hands against his temples, as if the question had raised a turbulence of memories. For the first time the doctor—half harkening throughout to the never-quite-muted stirrings of the death within him—saw his friend's exhaustion: the tremor of hand, the bruised look under the eyes.

"I'm going to give you what I have, Carl. I told you I don't think you'll find a damn thing in those bodies. You're probably going to end up assuming what I do about it, but assuming is as far as anyone's going to get with this one. It is truly one of those nightmare specials that the good Lord tortures lawmen with and then hides the answers to forever.

"All right then. About two months ago, we had a man disappear—Ronald Hanley. Mine worker, rock steady, family man. He didn't come home one night, and we never found a trace of him. Okay, that happens sometimes. About a week later, the lady that ran the Laundromat, Sharon Starker, *she* disappeared, no trace. We got edgy then. I made an announcement on the local radio about a possible weirdo at large, spelled out special precautions everybody should take. We put both our squad cars on the night beat, and by day we set to work knocking on every door in town collecting alibis for the two times of disappearance.

"No good. Maybe you're fooled by this uniform and think I'm a law officer, protector of the people, and all that? A natural mistake. A lot of people were fooled. In less than seven weeks, six people vanished, just like that. Me and my deputies might as well have stayed in bed round the clock, for all the good we did." The sheriff drained his cup.

"Anyway, at last we got lucky. Don't get me wrong now. We didn't go all hog wild and actually prevent a crime or anything. But we *did* find a body—except it wasn't the body of any of the seven people that had disappeared. We'd took to combing the woods nearest town, with temporary deputies from the miners to help. Well, one of those boys was out there with us last week. It was hot—like it's been for a while now—and it was real quiet. He heard this buzzing noise and looked around for it, and he saw a bee swarm up in the crotch of a tree. Except he was smart enough to know that that's not usual around here—beehives. So it wasn't bees. It was bluebottle flies, a goddamned big cloud of them, all over a bundle that was wrapped in a tarp."

The sheriff studied his knuckles. He had, in his eventful life, occasionally met men literate enough to understand his last name and rash enough to be openly amused by it, and the knuckles—scarred knobs—were eloquent of his reactions. He looked back into his old friend's eyes.

"We got that thing down and unwrapped it. Billy Lee Davis, one of my deputies, he was in Vietnam, been near some bad, bad things and held on. Billy Lee blew his lunch all over the ground when we unwrapped that thing. It was a man. Some of a man. We knew he'd stood six-two because all the bones were there, and he'd probably weighed between two fifteen and two twenty-five, but he folded up no bigger than a big-size laundry package. Still had his face, both shoulders, and the left arm, but all the rest was clean. It wasn't animal work. It was knife work, all the edges neat as butcher cuts. Except butchered meat, even when you drain it all you can, will bleed a good deal afterward, and there wasn't one goddamned drop of blood on the tarp, nor in that meat. It was just as pale as fish meat."

Deep in his body's center, the doctor's cancer touched him. Not a ravening attack—it sank one fang of pain, questioningly, into new, un-tasted flesh, probing the scope for its appetite there. He disguised his tremor with a shake of the head.

"A cache, then."

The sheriff nodded. "Like you might keep a pot roast in the icebox for making lunches. I took some pictures of his face, then we put him back and erased our traces. Two of the miners I'd deputized did a lot of hunting, were woods-smart. So I left them on the first watch. We worked out positions and cover for them, and drove back.

"We got right on tracing him, sent out descriptions to every town within a hundred miles. He was no one I'd ever seen in Bailey, nor anyone else either, it began to look like, after we'd combed the town all day with the photos. Then, out of the blue, Billy Lee Davis smacks himself on the forehead and says, 'Sheriff, I seen this man somewhere in town, and not long ago!'

"He'd been shook all day since throwing up, and then all of a sudden he just snapped to. Was dead sure. Except he couldn't remember where or when. We went over and over it and he tried and tried. It got to where I wanted to grab him by the ankles and hang him upside down and shake him till it dropped out of him. But it was no damn use. Just after dark we went back to that tree—we'd worked out a place to hide the cars and a route to it through the woods. When we were close we walkie-talkied the men we'd left for an all-clear to come up. No answer at all. And when we got there, all that was left of our trap was the tree. No body, no tarp, no special assistant deputies. Nothing."

This time Dr. Winters poured the coffee and bourbon. "Too much coffee," the sheriff muttered, but drank anyway. "Part of me wanted to chew nails and break necks. And part of me was scared shitless. When we got back I got on the radio station again and made an emergency broadcast and then had the man at the station rebroadcast it every hour. Told everyone to do everything in groups of three, to stay together at night in threes at least, to go out little as possible, keep armed, and keep checking up on each other. It had such a damn-fool sound to it, but just pairing up was no protection if half of one of those pairs was the killer. I deputized more men and put them on the streets to beef up the night patrol.

"It was next morning that things broke. The sheriff of Rakehell called—he's over in the next county. He said our corpse sounded a lot like a man named Abel Dougherty, a mill hand with Con Wood over there. I left Billy Lee in charge and drove right out.

"This Dougherty had a crippled older sister he always checked back to by phone whenever he left town for long, a habit no one knew about, probably embarrassed him. Sheriff Peck there only found out about it when the woman called him, said her brother'd been four days gone for vacation and not rung her once. Without that Peck might not've thought of Dougherty just from our description, though the photo I showed him clinched it, and one would've reached him by mail soon enough. Well, he'd hardly set it down again, when a call came through for me. It was Billy Lee. He'd remembered.

"When he'd seen Dougherty was the Sunday night three days before we found him. Where he'd seen him was the Trucker's Tavern outside the north end of town. The man had made a stir by being jolly drunk and latching on to a miner who was drinking there, man named Joe Allen, who'd started at the mine about two months back. Dougherty kept telling him that he wasn't Joe Allen, but Dougherty's old buddy named Sykes that had worked with him at Con Wood for a coon's age, and what the hell kind of joke was this, come have a beer old buddy and tell me why you took off so sudden and what the hell you been doing with yourself.

"Allen took it laughing. Dougherty'd clap him on the shoulder, Allen'd clap him right back and make every kind of joke about it, say 'Give this man another beer, I'm standing in for a long-lost friend of his.' Dougherty was so big and loud and stubborn, Billy Lee was worried about a fight starting, and he wasn't the only one worried. But this Joe Allen was a natural good ol' boy, handled it perfect. We'd checked him out weeks back along with everyone else, and he was real popular with the other miners. Finally Dougherty swore he was going to take him on to another bar to help celebrate the vacation Dougherty was starting out on. Joe

Allen got up grinning, said goddammit, he couldn't accommodate Dougherty by being this fellow Sykes, but he could sure as hell have a glass with any serious drinking man that was treating. He went out with him, and gave everyone a wink as he left, to the general satisfaction of the audience."

Craven paused. Dr. Winters met his eyes and knew his thought, two images: the jolly wink that roused the room to laughter, and the thing in the tarp aboil with bright blue flies.

"It was plain enough for me," the sheriff said. "I told Billy Lee to search Allen's room at the Skettles' boardinghouse and then go straight to the mine and take him. We could fine-polish things once we had him. Since I was already in Rakehell, I saw to some of the loose ends before I started back. I went with Sheriff Peck down to Con Wood and we found a picture of Eddie Sykes in the personnel files. I'd seen Joe Allen often enough, and it was his picture in that file.

"We found out Sykes lived alone, was an on-again off-again worker, private in his comings and goings, and hadn't been around for a while. But one of the sawyers there could be pretty sure of when Sykes left Rakehell because he'd gone to Sykes's cabin the morning after a big meteor shower they had out there about nine weeks back, since some thought the shower might have reached the ground, and not far from Sykes's side of the mountain. He wasn't in that morning, and the sawyer hadn't seen him since.

"It looked sewed up. It *was* sewed up. After all those weeks, I was less than a mile out of Bailey, had the pedal floored. Full of rage and revenge. I felt . . . like a *bullet*, like I was one big thirty-caliber slug that was going to go right through that blood-sucking cannibal, tear the whole truth right out of his heart, enough to hang him a hundred times. That was the closest I got. So close that I *heard* it when it all blew to shit.

"I sound squirrelly. I know I do. Maybe all this gave me something I'll never shake off. We had to put together what happened. Billy Lee didn't have my other deputy with him. Travis was out with some men on the mountain dragnetting around that tree for clues. By luck, he was back at the car when Billy Lee was trying to raise him. He said he'd just been through Allen's room and had gotten something we could maybe hold him on. It was a sphere, half again big as a basketball, heavy, made of something that wasn't metal or glass but was a little like both. He could half-see into it and it looked to be full of some kind of circuitry and components. If someone tried to spring Allen, we could make a theft rap out of this thing, or say we suspected it was a bomb. Jesus! Anyway, he said it was the only strange thing he found, but it was plenty strange. He told Travis to get up to the mine for backup. He'd be there first and should already have Allen by the time Travis arrived.

"Tierney, the shift boss up there, had an assistant that told us the rest. Billy Lee parked behind the offices where the men in the yard wouldn't see the car. He went upstairs to arrange the arrest with Tierney. They got half a dozen men together. Just as they came out of the building, they saw Allen take off running from the squad car with the sphere under his arm.

"The whole compound's fenced in and Tierney'd already phoned to have all the gates shut. Allen zigged and zagged some but caught on quick to the trap. The sphere slowed him, but he still had a good lead. He hesitated a minute and then ran straight for the main shaft. A cage was just going down with a crew, and he risked every bone in him jumping down after it, but he got safe on top. By the time they got to the switches, the cage was down to the second level, and Allen and the crew had got out. Tierney got it back up. Billy Lee ordered the rest back to get weapons and follow, and him and Tierney rode the cage right back down. And about two minutes later half the goddamned mine blew up."

The sheriff stopped as if cut off, his lips parted to say more, his eyes registering for perhaps the hundredth time his amazement that there was no more, that the weeks of death and mystification ended here, with this split-second recapitulation: more death, more answerless dark, sealing all.

"Nate."

"What."

"Wrap it up and go to bed. I don't need your help. You're dead on your feet."

"I'm not on my feet. And I'm coming along."

"Give me a picture of the victims' position relative to the blast. I'm going to work and you're going to bed."

The sheriff shook his head absently. "They're mining in shrinkage stopes. The adits—levels—branch off lateral from the vertical shaft. From one level they hollow out overhand up to the one above. Scoop out big chambers and let most of the broken rock stay inside so they can stand on the heaps to cut the ceilings higher. They leave sections of support wall between stopes, and those men were buried several stopes in from the shaft. The cave-in killed *them*. The mountain just folded them up in their own hill of tailings. No kind of fragments reached them. I'm dead sure. The only ones they *found* were of some standard charges that the main blast set off, and those didn't even get close. The big one blew out where the adit joined the shaft, right where, and right when Billy Lee and Tierney got out of the cage. And there is *nothing* left there, Carl. No sphere, no cage, no Tierney, no Billy Lee Davis. Just rock blown fine as flour."

Dr. Winters nodded and, after a moment, stood up.

"Come on, Nate. I've got to get started. I'll be lucky to have even a few of them done before morning. Drop me off and go to sleep, till then at least. You'll still be there to witness most of the work."

The sheriff rose, took up the doctor's suitcase, and led him out of the office without a word, concession in his silence.

The patrol car was behind the building. The doctor saw a crueller beauty in the stars than he had an hour before. They got in, and Craven swung them out onto the empty street. The doctor opened the window and harkened, but the motor's surge drowned out the river sound. Before the thrust of their headlights, ranks of old-fashioned parking meters sprouted shadows tall across the sidewalks, shadows which shrank and were cut down by the lights' passage. The sheriff said: "All those extra dead. For nothing! Not even to . . . *feed* him! If it *was* a bomb, and he made it, he'd know how powerful it was. He wouldn't try some stupid escape stunt with it. And how did he even know the thing was there? We worked it out that Allen was just ending a shift, but he wasn't even up out of the ground before Billy Lee'd parked out of sight."

"Let it rest, Nate. I want to hear more, but after you've slept. I know you. All the photos will be there, and the report complete, all the evidence neatly boxed and carefully described. When I've looked things over I'll know exactly how to proceed by myself."

Bailey had neither hospital nor morgue, and the bodies were in a defunct ice plant on the edge of town. A generator had been brought down from the mine, lighting improvised, and the refrigeration system reactivated. Dr. Parsons's office, and the tiny examining room that served the sheriff's station in place of a morgue, had furnished this makeshift with all the equipment that Dr. Winters would need beyond what he carried with him. A quarter-mile outside the main body of the town, they drew up to it. Tree-flanked, unneighbored by any other structure, it was a double building; the smaller half—the office—was illuminated. The bodies would be in the big, windowless refrigerator segment. Craven pulled up beside a second squad car parked near the office door. A short, rake-thin man wearing a large white Stetson got out of the car and came over. Craven rolled down his window.

"Trav. This here's Dr. Winters."

" 'Lo, Nate. Dr. Winters. Everything's shipshape inside. Felt more comfortable out here. Last of those newshounds left two hours ago."

"They sure do hang on. You take off now, Trav. Get some sleep and be back at sunup. What temperature we getting?"

The pale Stetson, far clearer in the starlight than the shadow face beneath it, wagged dubiously. "Thirty-six. She won't get lower—some kind of leak."

"That should be cold enough," the doctor said.

Travis drove off and the sheriff unlocked the padlock on the office door. Waiting behind him, Dr. Winters heard the river again—a cold balm, a whisper of freedom—and overlying this, the stutter and soft snarl of the generator behind the building, a gnawing, remorseless sound that somehow fed the obscure anguish which the other soothed. They went in.

The preparations had been thoughtful and complete. "You can wheel 'em out of the fridge on this and do the examining in here," the sheriff said, indicating a table and a gurney. "You should find all the gear you need on this big table here, and you can write up your reports on that desk. The phone's not hooked up—there's a pay phone at that last gas station if you have to call me."

The doctor nodded, checking over the material on the larger table: scalpels, post-mortem and cartilage knives, intestine scissors, rib shears, forceps, probes, mallet and chisels, a blade saw and electric bone saw, scale, jars for specimens, needles and suture, sterilizer, gloves. . . . Beside this array were a few boxes and envelopes with descriptive sheets attached, containing the photographs and such evidentiary objects as had been found associated with the bodies.

"Excellent," he muttered.

"The overhead light's fluorescent, full spectrum or whatever they call it. Better for colors. There's a pint of decent bourbon in that top desk drawer. Ready to look at 'em?"

"Yes."

The sheriff unbarred and slid back the big metal door to the refrigeration chamber. Icy, tainted air boiled out of the doorway. The light within was dimmer than that provided in the office—a yellow gloom wherein ten oblong heaps lay on trestles.

The two stood silent for a time, their stillness a kind of unpremeditated homage paid the eternal mystery at its threshold. As if the cold room were in fact a shrine, the doctor found a peculiar awe in the row of veiled forms. The awful unison of their dying, the titan's grave that had been made for them, conferred on them a stern authority, death's chosen ones.

His stomach hurt, and he found he had his hand pressed to his abdomen. He glanced at Craven and was relieved to see that his friend, staring wearily at the bodies, had missed the gesture.

"Nate. Help me uncover them."

Starting at opposite ends of the row, they stripped the tarps off and piled them in a corner. Both were brusque now, not pausing over the revelation of the swelled, pulpy faces—most three-lipped with the gaseous burgeoning of their tongues—and the fat, livid hands sprouting from the filthy sleeves. But at one of the bodies Craven stopped. The doctor saw him look, and his mouth twist. Then he flung the tarp on the heap and moved to the next trestle.

When they came out Dr. Winters took out the bottle and glasses Craven had put in the desk, and they had a drink together. The sheriff made as if he would speak, but shook his head and sighed.

"I *will* get some sleep, Carl. I'm getting crazy thoughts with this thing." The doctor wanted to ask those thoughts. Instead, he laid a hand on his friend's shoulder.

"Go home, Sheriff Craven. Take off the badge and lie down. The dead won't run off on you. We'll all still be here in the morning."

When the sound of the patrol car faded, the doctor stood listening to the generator's growl and the silence of the dead, resurgent now. Both the sound and the silence seemed to mock him. The after-echo of his last words made him uneasy. He said to his cancer: "What about it, dear colleague? We *will* still be here tomorrow? All of us?"

He smiled, but felt an odd discomfort, as if he had ventured a jest in company and roused a hostile silence. He went to the refrigerator door, rolled it back, and viewed the corpses in their ordered rank, with their strange tribunal air. "What, sirs?" he murmured. "Do you judge me? Just who is to examine whom tonight, if I may ask?"

He went back into the office, where his first step was to examine the photographs made by the sheriff, in order to see how the dead had lain at their uncovering. The earth had seized them with terrible suddenness. Some crouched, some partly stood, others sprawled in crazy, free-fall postures. Each successive photo showed more of the jumble as the shovels continued their work between shots. The doctor studied them closely, noting the identifications inked on the bodies as they came completely into view.

One man, Roger Willet, had died some yards from the main cluster. It appeared he had just straggled into the stope from the adit at the moment of the explosion. He should thus have received, more directly than any of the others, the shockwaves of the blast. If bomb fragments were to be found in any of the corpses, Mr. Willet's seemed likeliest to contain them. Dr. Winters pulled on a pair of surgical gloves.

He lay at one end of the line of trestles. He wore a thermal shirt and overalls that were strikingly new beneath the filth of burial. Their tough fabrics jarred with that of his flesh—blue, swollen, seeming easily torn or burst, like ripe fruit. In life Willet had grease-combed his hair. Now it was a sculpture of dust, spikes, and whorls shaped by the head's last grindings against the mountain that clenched it.

Rigor had come and gone—Willet rolled laxly onto the gurney. As the doctor wheeled him past the others, he felt a slight self-consciousness. The sense of some judgment flowing from the dead assembly—unlike most such vagrant emotional embellishments of experience—had an odd tenacity in him. This stubborn unease began to irritate him with himself, and he moved more briskly.

He put Willet on the examining table and cut the clothes off him with shears, storing the pieces in an evidence box. The overalls were soiled with agonal waste expulsions. The doctor stared a moment with unwilling pity at his naked subject.

"You won't ride down to Fordham in any case," he said to the corpse. "Not unless I find something pretty damned obvious." He pulled his gloves tighter and arranged his implements.

Waddleton had said more to him than he had reported to the sheriff. The doctor was to find, and forcefully to record that he had found, strong "indications" absolutely requiring the decedents' removal to Fordham for X ray and an exhaustive second post mortem. The doctor's continued employment with the coroner's office depended entirely on his compliance in this. He had received this stipulation with a silence Waddleton had not thought it necessary to break. His present resolution was all but made at that moment. Let the obvious be taken as such. If the others showed as plainly as Willet did the external signs of death by asphyxiation, they would receive no more than a thorough external exam. Willet he would examine internally as well, merely to establish in depth for this one what should appear obvious in all. Otherwise, only when the external exam revealed a clearly anomalous feature—and clear and suggestive it must be—would he look deeper.

He rinsed the caked hair in a basin, poured the sediment into a flask, and labeled it. Starting with the scalp, he began a minute scrutiny of the body's surfaces, recording his observations as he went.

The characteristic signs of asphyxial death were evident, despite the complicating effects of autolysis and putrefaction. The eyeballs' bulge and the tongue's protrusion were by now at least partly due to gas pressure as well as the mode of death, but the latter organ was clamped between locked teeth, leaving little doubt as to that mode. The coloration of degenerative change—a greenish-yellow tint, a darkening and mapping-out of superficial veins—was marked, but not sufficient to obscure the blue of syanosis on the face and neck, nor the pinpoint hemorrhages freckling neck, chest, and shoulders. From the mouth and nose the doctor scraped matter he was confident was the blood-tinged mucus typically ejected in the airless agony.

He began to find a kind of comedy in his work. What a buffoon death made of a man! A blue, popeyed, three-lipped thing. And there was himself, his curious, solicitous intimacy with this clownish carrion. Excuse me, Mr. Willet, while I probe this laceration. How does it feel when I do this? Nothing? Nothing at all? Fine, now what about these nails. Split them clawing at the earth, did you? Yes. A nice blood blister under this thumbnail I see—got it on the job a few days before your accident no doubt? Remarkable calluses here, still quite tough. . . .

The doctor looked for an unanalytic moment at the hands—puffed, dark paws, gestureless, having renounced all touch and grasp. He felt the wastage of the man concentrated in the hands. The painful futility of the body's fine articulation when it is seen in death—this poignancy he had long learned not to acknowledge when he worked. But now he let it move him a little. This Roger Willet, plodding to his work one afternoon, had suddenly been scrapped, crushed to a nonfunctional heap of perishable materials. It simply happened that his life had chanced to move too close to the passage of a more powerful life, one of those inexorable and hungry lives that leave human wreckage—known or undiscovered—in their wakes. Bad luck, Mr. Willet. Naturally, we feel very sorry about this. But this Joe Allen, your coworker. Apparently he was some sort of . . . cannibal. It's complicated. We don't understand it all. But the fact is we have to dismantle you now to a certain extent. There's really no hope of your using these parts of yourself again, I'm afraid. Ready now?

The doctor proceeded to the internal exam with a vague eagerness for Willet's fragmentation, for the disarticulation of that sadness in his natural form. He grasped Willet by the jaw and took up the post-mortem knife. He sank its point beneath the chin and began the long, gently sawing incision that opened Willet from throat to groin.

In the painstaking separation of the body's laminae, Dr. Winters found absorption and pleasure. And yet throughout he felt, marginal but insistent, the movement of a stream of irrelevant images. These were of the building that contained him, and of the night containing it. As from outside, he saw the plant—bleached planks, iron roofing—and the trees crowding it, all in starlight, a ghost-town image. And he saw the refrigerator vault beyond the wall as from within, feeling the stillness of murdered men in a cold yellow light. And at length a question formed itself, darting in and out of the weave of his concentration as the images did: Why did he still feel, like some stir of the air, that sense of mute vigilance surrounding his action, furtively touching his nerves with its inquiry as he worked? He shrugged, overtly angry now. Who else was attending but Death? Wasn't he Death's hireling, and this Death's place? Then let the master look on.

Peeling back Willet's cover of hemorrhage-stippled skin, Dr. Winters read the corpse with an increasing dispassion, a mortuary text. He confined his inspection to the lungs and mediastinum and found there unequivocal testimony to Willet's asphyxial death. The pleurae of the lungs exhibited the expected ecchymoses—bruised spots in the glassy, enveloping membrane. Beneath, the polyhedral surface lobules of the lungs themselves were bubbled and blistered—the expected interstitial emphysema. The lungs, on section, were intensely and bloodily congested. The left half of the heart he found contracted and empty, while the right was overdistended and engorged with dark blood, as were the large veins of the upper mediastinum. It was a classic picture of death by suffocation, and at length the doctor, with needle and suture, closed up the text again.

He returned the corpse to the gurney and draped one of his mortuary bags over it in the manner of a shroud. When he had help in the morning, he would weigh the bodies on a platform scale the office contained and afterward bag them properly. He came to the refrigerator door, and hesitated. He stared at the door, not moving, not understanding why.

Run. Get out, now.

The thought was his own, but it came to him so urgently, he turned around as if someone behind him had spoken. Across the room a thin man in smock and gloves, his eyes shadows, glared at the doctor from the black windows. Behind the man was a shrouded cart, behind that, a wide metal door.

Quietly, wonderingly, the doctor asked, "Run from what?" The eyeless man in the glass was still half crouched, afraid.

Then, a moment later, the man straightened, threw back his head, and laughed. The doctor walked to the desk and sat down shoulder to shoulder with him. He pulled out the bottle and they had a drink together, regarding each other with identical bemused smiles. Then the doctor said, "Let me pour you another. You need it old fellow. It makes a man himself again."

Nevertheless, his reentry of the vault was difficult, toilsome, each step seeming to require a new summoning of the will to move. In the freezing half light, all movement felt like defiance. His body lagged behind his craving to be quick, to be done with this molestation of the gathered dead. He returned Willet to his pallet and took his neighbor. The name on the tag wired to his boot was Ed Moses. Dr. Winters wheeled him back to the office and closed the big door behind him.

With Moses his work gained momentum. He expected to perform no further internal necropsies. He thought of his employer, rejoicing now in his seeming submission to Waddleton's ultimatum. The impact would be dire. He pictured the coroner in shock, a sheaf of pathologist's reports in one hand, and smiled.

Waddleton could probably make a plausible case for incomplete examination. Still, a pathologist's discretionary powers were not well defined. Many good ones would approve the adequacy of the doctor's method, given his working conditions. The inevitable litigation with a coalition of compensation claimants would be strenuous and protracted. Win or lose, Waddleton's venal devotion to the insurance company's interest would be abundantly displayed. Further, immediately on his dismissal the doctor would formally disclose its occult cause to the press. A libel action would ensue, which he would have as little cause to fear as he had to fear his firing. Both his savings and the lawsuit would long outlast his life.

Externally, Ed Moses exhibited a condition as typically asphyxial as Willet's had been, with no slightest mark of fragment entry. The doctor finished his report and returned Moses to the vault, his movements brisk and precise. His unease was all but gone. That queasy stirring of the air—had he really felt it? It had been, perhaps, some new reverberation of the death at work in him, a psychic shudder of response to the cancer's stealthy probing for his life. He brought out the body next to Moses in the line.

Walter Lou Jackson was big, six-two from heel to crown, and would surely weigh out at more than two hundred pounds. He had writhed mightily against his million-ton coffin with an agonal strength that had torn his face and hands. Death had mauled him like a lion. The doctor set to work.

His hands were fully themselves now—fleet, exact, intricately testing the corpse's character as other fingers might explore a keyboard for its latent melodies. And the doctor watched them with an old pleasure, one of the few that had never failed him, his mind at one remove from their busy intelligence. All the hard deaths! A worldful of them, time without end. Lives wrenched kicking from their snug meat frames. Walter Lou Jackson had died very hard. Joe Allen brought this on you, Mr. Jackson. We think it was part of his attempt to escape the law.

But what a botched flight! The unreason of it—more than baffling—was eerie in its colossal futility. Beyond question, Allen had been cunning. A ghoul with a psychopath's social finesse. A good old boy who could make a tavernful of men laugh with delight while he cut his victim from their midst, make them applaud his exit with the prey, who stepped jovially into the darkness with murder at his side clapping him on the shoulder. Intelligent, certainly, with a strange technical sophistication as well, suggested by the sphere. Then what of the lunacy yet more strongly suggested by the same object? In the sphere was concentrated all the lethal mystery of Bailey's long nightmare.

Why the explosion? Its location implied an ambush for Allen's pursuers, a purposeful detonation. Had he aimed at a limited cave-in from which he schemed some inconceivable escape? Folly enough in this—far more if, as seemed sure, Allen had made the bomb himself, for then he would have to know its power was grossly inordinate to the need.

But if it was not a bomb, had a different function and only incidentally an explosive potential, Allen might underestimate the blast. It appeared the object was somehow remotely monitored by him, for the timing of events showed he had gone straight for it the instant he emerged from the shaft—shunned the bus waiting to take his shift back to town and made a beeline across the compound for a patrol car that was hidden from his view by the office building. This suggested something more complex than a mere explosive device, something, perhaps, whose destruction was itself more Allen's aim than the explosion produced thereby.

The fact that he risked the sphere's retrieval at all pointed to this interpretation. For the moment he sensed its presence at the mine, he must have guessed that the murder investigation had led to its discovery and removal from his room. But then, knowing himself already liable to the extreme penalty, why should Allen go to such lengths to recapture evidence incriminatory of a lesser offense, possession of an explosive device?

Then grant that the sphere was something more, something instrumental to his murders that could guarantee a conviction he might otherwise evade. Still, his gambit made no sense. Since the sphere—and thus the lawmen he could assume to have taken it—were already at the mine office, he must expect the compound to be sealed at any moment. Meanwhile, the gate was open, escape into the mountains a strong possibility for a man capable of stalking and destroying two experienced and well-armed woodsmen lying in ambush for him. Why had he all but insured his capture to weaken a case against himself that his escape would have rendered irrelevant? Dr. Winters saw his fingers, like a hunting pack round a covert, converge on a small puncture wound below Walter Lou Jackson's xiphoid process, between the eighth ribs.

His left hand touched its borders, the fingers' inquiry quick and tender. The right hand introduced a probe, and both together eased it into the wound. It inched unobstructed deep into the body, curving upward through the diaphragm toward the heart. The doctor's own heart accelerated. He watched his hands move to record the observation, watched them pause, watched them return to their survey of the corpse, leaving pen and page untouched.

Inspection revealed no further anomaly. All else he observed the doctor recorded faithfully, wondering throughout at the distress he felt. When he had finished, he understood it. Its cause was not the discovery of an entry wound that might bolster Waddleton's case. For the find had, within moments, revealed to him that, should he encounter anything he thought to be a mark of fragment penetration, he was going to ignore it. The damage Joe Allen had done was going to end here, with this last grand slaughter, and would not extend to the impoverishment of his victims' survivors. No more internals. The externals, will they nill-they, would from now on explicitly contraindicate the need for them.

The problem was that he did not believe the puncture in Jackson's thorax *was* a mark of fragment entry. Why? And, finding no answer to this question, why was he, once again, afraid? Slowly, he signed the report on Jackson, set it aside, and took up the post-mortem knife.

First the long, sawing slice, unzippering the mortal overcoat. Next, two great, square flaps of flesh reflected, scrolled laterally to the armpits' line, disrobing the chest: one hand grasping the flap's skirt, the other sweeping beneath it with the knife, flensing through the glassy tissue that joined it to the chest wall, and shaving all muscles from their anchorages to bone and cartilage beneath. Then the dismantling of the strongbox within. Rib shears—so frank and forward a tool, like a gardener's. The steel beak bit through each rib's gristle anchor to the sternum's centerplate. At the sternum's crownpiece the collarbones' ends were knifed, pried, and sprung free from their sockets. The coffer unhasped, unhinged, a knife teased beneath the lid and levered it off.

Some minutes later the doctor straightened up and stepped back from his subject. He moved almost drunkenly, and his age seemed scored more deeply in his face. With loathing haste he stripped his gloves off. He went to the desk, sat down, and poured another drink. If there was something like horror in his face, there was also a hardening in his mouth's line, and the muscles of his jaw. He spoke to his glass: "So be it, Your Excellency. Something new for your humble servant. Testing my nerve?"

Jackson's pericardium, the shapely capsule containing his heart, should have been all but hidden between the big blood-fat loaves of his lungs. The doctor had found it fully exposed, the lungs flanking it wrinkled lumps less than a third their natural bulk. Not only they, but the left heart and the superior mediastinal veins—all the regions that should have been grossly engorged with blood—were utterly drained of it.

The doctor swallowed his drink and got out the photographs again. He found that Jackson had died on his stomach across the body of another worker, with the upper part of a third trapped between them. Neither these two subjacent corpses nor the surrounding earth showed any stain of a blood loss that must have amounted to two liters.

Possibly the pictures, by some trick of shadow, had failed to pick it up. He turned to the investigator's report, where Craven would surely have mentioned any significant amounts of bloody earth uncovered during the disinterment. The sheriff recorded nothing of the kind. Dr. Winters returned to the pictures.

Ronald Pollack, Jackson's most intimate associate in the grave, had died on his back, beneath and slightly askew of Jackson, placing most of their torsos in contact, save where the head and shoulder of the third interposed. It seemed inconceivable Pollock's clothing should lack any trace of such massive drainage from a death mate thus embraced.

The doctor rose abruptly, pulled on fresh gloves, and returned to Jackson. His hands showed a more brutal speed now, closing the great incision temporarily with a few widely spaced sutures. He replaced him in the vault and brought out Pollock, striding, heaving hard at the dead shapes in the shifting of them, thrusting always—so it seemed to him— just a step ahead of urgent thoughts he did not want to have, deformities that whispered at his back, emitting faint, chill gusts of putrid breath. He shook his head—denying, delaying—and pushed the new corpse onto the worktable. The scissors undressed Pollock in greedy bites.

But at length, when he had scanned each scrap of fabric and found nothing like the stain of blood, he came to rest again, relinquishing that simplest, desired resolution he had made such haste to reach. He stood at the instrument table, not seeing it, submitting to the approach of the half-formed things at his mind's periphery.

The revelation of Jackson's shriveled lungs had been more than a shock. He had felt a stab of panic, too, in fact that same curiously explicit terror of this place that had urged him to flee earlier. He acknowledged now that the germ of that quickly suppressed terror had been a premonition of this failure to find any trace of the missing blood. Whence the premonition? It had to do with a problem he had steadfastly refused to consider: the mechanics of so complete a drainage of the lungs' densely reticulated vascular structure. Could the earth's crude pressure by itself work so thoroughly, given only a single vent both slender and strangely curved? And then the photograph he had studied. It frightened him now to recall the image—some covert meaning stirred within it, struggling to be seen. Dr. Winters picked the probe up from the table and turned again to the corpse. As surely and exactly as if he had already ascertained the wound's presence, he leaned forward and touched it: a small, neat puncture, just beneath the xiphoid process. He introduced the probe. The wound received it deeply, in a familiar direction.

The doctor went to the desk, and took up the photograph again. Pollock's and Jackson's wounded areas were not in contact. The third man's head was sandwiched between their bodies at just that point. He searched out another picture, in which this third man was more central, and found his name inked in below his image: Joe Allen.

Dreamingly, Dr. Winters went to the wide metal door, shoved it aside, entered the vault. He did not search, but went straight to the trestle, where his friend had paused some hours before, and found the same name on its tag.

The body, beneath decay's spurious obesity, was trim and well muscled. The face was square cut, shelf-browed, with a vulpine nose skewed by an old fracture. The swollen tongue lay behind the teeth, and the bulge of decomposition did not obscure what the man's initial impact must have been—handsome and open, his now-waxen black eyes sly and convivial. Say, good buddy, got a minute? I see you comin' on the swing shift every day, don't I? Yeah, Joe Allen. Look, I know it's late, you want to get home, tell the wife you ain't been in there drinkin' since you got off, right? Oh, yeah, I hear that. But this damn disappearance thing's got me so edgy, and I'd swear to God just as I was coming here I seen someone moving around back of that frame house up the street. See how the trees thin out a little down back of the yard, where the moonlight gets in? That's right. Well, I got me this little popper here. Oh, yeah, that's a beauty, we'll have it covered between us. I knew I could spot a man ready for some trouble—couldn't find a patrol car anywhere on the street. Yeah, just down in here now, to that clump of pine. Step careful, you can barely see. That's right. . . .

The doctor's face ran with sweat. He turned on his heel and walked out of the vault, heaving the door shut behind him. In the office's greater warmth he felt the perspiration soaking his shirt under the smock. His stomach rasped with steady oscillations of pain, but he scarcely attended it. He went to Pollock and seized up the post-mortem knife.

The work was done with surreal speed, the laminae of flesh and bone recoiling smoothly beneath his desperate but unerring hands, until the thoracic cavity lay exposed, and in it, the vampire-stricken lungs, two gnarled lumps of gray tissue.

He searched no deeper, knowing what the heart and veins would show. He returned to sit at the desk, weakly drooping, the knife, forgotten, still in his left hand. He looked at the window, and it seemed his thoughts originated with that fainter, more tenuous Dr. Winters hanging like a ghost outside.

What was this world he lived in? Surely, in a lifetime, he had not begun to guess. To feed in such a way! There was horror enough in this alone. But to feed thus *in his own grave*. How had he accomplished it —leaving aside how he had fought suffocation long enough to do anything at all? How was it to be comprehended, a greed that raged so hotly it would glut itself at the very threshold of its own destruction? That last feast was surely in his stomach still.

Dr. Winters looked at the photograph, at Allen's head snugged into the others' middles like a hungry suckling nuzzling to the sow. Then he looked at the knife in his hand. The hand felt empty of all technique. Its one impulse was to slash, cleave, obliterate the remains of this gluttonous thing, this Joe Allen. He must do this, or flee it utterly. There was no course between. He did not move.

"I *will* examine him," said the ghost in the glass, and did not move. Inside the refrigeration vault there was a slight noise.

No. It had been some hitch in the generator's murmur. Nothing in there could move. There was another noise, a brief friction against the vault's inner wall. The two old men shook their heads at each other. A catch clicked and the metal door slid open. Behind the staring image of his own amazement, the doctor saw that a filthy shape stood in the doorway and raised its arms toward him in a gesture of supplication. The doctor turned in his chair. From the shape came a whistling groan, the decayed fragment of a human voice.

Pleadingly, Joe Allen worked his jaw and spread his purple hands. As if speech were a maggot struggling to emerge from his mouth, the blue, tumescent face toiled, the huge tongue wallowed helplessly between the viscid lips.

The doctor reached for the telephone, lifted the receiver. Its deadness to his ear meant nothing—he could not have spoken. The thing confronting him, with each least movement that it made, destroyed the very frame of sanity in which words might have meaning, reduced the world itself around him to a waste of dark and silence, a starlit ruin where already, everywhere, the alien and unimaginable was awakening to its new dominion. The corpse raised and reached out one hand as if to stay him—turned, and walked toward the instrument table. Its legs were leaden, it rocked its shoulders like a swimmer, fighting to make its passage through gravity's dense medium. It reached the table and grasped it exhaustedly. The doctor found himself on his feet, crouched slightly, weightlessly still. The knife in his hand was the only part of himself he clearly felt, and it was like a tongue of fire, a crematory flame. Joe Allen's corpse thrust one hand among the instruments. The thick fingers, with a queer simian ineptitude, brought up a scalpel. Both hands clasped the little handle and plunged the blade between the lips, as a thirsty child might a Popsicle, then jerked it out again, slashing the tongue. Turbid fluid splashed down to the floor. The jaw worked stiffly, the mouth brought out words in a wet, ragged hiss: "Please. Help me. Trapped in *this.*" One dead hand struck the dead chest. "Starving."

"What are you?"

"Traveler. Not of earth."

"An eater of human flesh. A drinker of human blood."

"No. No. Hiding only. Am small. Shape hideous to you. Feared death."

"You brought death." The doctor spoke with the calm of perfect disbelief, himself as incredible to him as the thing he spoke with. It shook its head, the dull, popped eyes glaring with an agony of thwarted expression.

"Killed none. Hid in this. Hid in this not to be killed. Five days now. Drowning in decay. Free me. Please."

"No. You have come to feed on us, you are not hiding in fear. We are your food, your meat and drink. You fed on those two men within your grave. *Their* grave. For you, a delay. In fact, a diversion that has ended the hunt for you."

"No! No! Used men already dead. For me, five days, starvation. Even less. Fed only from necessity. Horrible necessity!"

The spoiled vocal instrument made a mangled gasp of the last word

—an inhuman, snake-pit noise the doctor felt as a cold flicker of ophidian tongues within his ears—while the dead arms moved in a sodden approximation of the body language that swears truth.

"No," the doctor said. "You killed them all. Including your . . . tool—this man. *What are you?*" Panic erupted in the question which he tried to bury by answering himself instantly. "Resolute, yes. That surely. You used death for an escape route. You need no oxygen perhaps."

"Extracted more than my need from gasses of decay. A lesser component of our metabolism."

The voice was gaining distinctness, developing makeshifts for tones lost in the agonal rupturing of the valves and stops of speech, more effectively wrestling vowel and consonant from the putrid tongue and lips. At the same time, the body's crudity of movement did not quite obscure a subtle, incessant experimentation. Fingers flexed and stirred, testing the give of tendons, groping the palm for the old points of purchase and counterpressure there. The knees, with cautious repetitions, assessed the new limits of their articulation.

"What was the sphere?"

"My ship. Its destruction our first duty facing discovery." (Fear touched the doctor, like a slug climbing his neck; he had seen, as it spoke, a sharp, spastic activity of the tongue, a pleating and shrinkage of its bulk as at the tug of some inward adjustment.) "No chance to reenter. Leaving this take far too long. Not even time to set for destruct—must extrude a cilium, chemical key to broach hull shield. In shaft my only chance to halt host."

The right arm tested the wrist, and the scalpel the hand still held cut white sparks from the air, while the word "host" seemed itself a little knife prick, a teasing abandonment of fiction—though the dead mask showed no irony—preliminary to attack.

But he found that fear had gone from him. The impossibility with which he conversed, and was about to struggle, was working in him an overwhelming amplification of his life's long, helpless rage at death. He found his parochial pity for earth alone stretched to the tranststellar scope this traveler commanded, to the whole cosmic trash yard with its bulldozed multitudes of corpses; galactic wheels of carnage—stars, planets with their most majestic generations—all trash, cracked bones and foul rags that pooled, settled, reconcatenated in futile symmetries gravid with new multitudes of briefly animate trash.

And this, standing before him now, was the death it was given him particularly to deal—his mite was being called in by the universal Treasury of death, and Dr. Winters found himself, an old healer, on fire to

pay. His own, more lethal blade, tugged at his hand with its own sharp
appetite. He felt entirely the Examiner once more, knew the precise cuts
he would make, swiftly and without error. *Very soon now*, he thought,
and coolly probed for some further insight before its onslaught.

"Why must your ship be destroyed, even at the cost of your host's life?"

"We must not be understood."

"The livestock must not understand what is devouring them."

"Yes, Doctor. Not all at once. But one by one. You will understand
what is devouring you. That is essential to my feast."

The doctor shook his head. "You are in your grave already, Traveler.
That body will be your coffin. You will be buried in it a second time,
for all time."

The thing came one step nearer and opened its mouth. The flabby
throat wrestled as with speech, but what sprang out was a slender white
filament, more than whip-fast. Dr. Winters saw only the first flicker of
its eruption, and then his brain novaed, thinning out at light-speed to a
white nullity.

When the doctor came to himself, it was in fact to a part of himself only.
Before he had opened his eyes he found that his wakened mind had
repossessed proprioceptively only a bizarre truncation of his body. His
head, neck, left shoulder, arm, and hand declared themselves—the rest
was silence.

When he opened his eyes, he found that he lay supine on the gurney,
and naked. Something propped his head. A strap bound his left elbow
to the gurney's edge, a strap he could feel. His chest was also anchored
by a strap, and this he could not feel Indeed, save for its active remnant,
his entire body might have been bound in a block of ice, so numb was
it, and so powerless was he to compel the slightest movement from the
least part of it.

The room was empty, but from the open door of the vault there came
slight sounds: the creak and soft frictions of heavy tarpaulin shifted to
accommodate some business involving small clicking and kissing noises.

Tears of fury filled the doctor's eyes. Clenching his one fist at the starry
engine of creation that he could not see, he ground his teeth and whispered in the hot breath of strangled weeping: "Take it back, this dirty
little shred of life! I throw it off gladly like the filth it is." The slow knock
of boot soles loudened from within the vault, and he turned his head.
From the vault door Joe Allen's corpse approached him.

It moved with new energy, though its gait was grotesque, a ducking,
hitching progress, jerky with circumventions of decayed muscle, while

above this galvanized, struggling frame, the bruise-colored face hung inanimate, an image of detachment. With terrible clarity it revealed the thing for what it was—a damaged hand puppet vigorously worked from within. And when that frozen face was brought to hang above the doctor, the reeking hands, with the light, solicitous touch of friends at sickbeds, rested on his naked thigh.

The absence of sensation made the touch more dreadful than it felt. It showed him that the nightmare he still desperately denied at heart had annexed his body while he—holding head and arm free—had already more than half drowned in its mortal paralysis. There lay his nightmare part, a nothingness freely possessed by an unspeakability. The corpse said: "Rotten blood. Thin nourishment. Only one hour alone before you came. Fed from neighbor to my left—barely had strength to extend siphon. Fed from the right while you worked. Tricky going—you are alert. Expected Dr. Parsons. Energy needs of animating this"—one hand left the doctor's thigh and smote the dusty overalls— "and of host-transfer, very high. Once I have you synapsed, will be near starvation again."

A sequence of unbearable images unfolded in the doctor's mind, even as the robot carrion turned from the gurney and walked to the instrument table: the sheriff's arrival just after dawn, alone, of course, since Craven always took thought for his deputies' rest and because on this errand he would want privacy to consider any indiscretion on behalf of the miners' survivors that the situation might call for; his finding his old friend, supine and alarmingly weak; his hurrying over, his leaning near. Then, somewhat later, a police car containing a rack of still-wet bones might plunge off the highway above some deep spot in the gorge.

The corpse took an evidence box from the table and put the scalpel in it. Then it turned and retrieved the mortuary knife from the floor and put that in as well, saying as it did so, without turning, "The sheriff will come in the morning. You spoke like close friends. He will probably come alone."

The coincidence with his thoughts had to be accident, but the intent to terrify and appall him was clear. The tone and timing of that patched-up voice were unmistakably deliberate—sly probes that sought his anguish specifically, sought his mind's personal center. He watched the corpse —back at the table—dipping an apish but accurate hand and plucking up rib shears, scissors, clamps, adding all to the box. He stared, momentarily emptied by shock of all but the will to know finally the full extent of the horror that had appropriated his life. Joe Allen's body carried the box to the worktable beside the gurney, and the expressionless eyes met the doctor's.

"I have gambled. A grave gamble. But now I have won. At risk of personal discovery we are obliged to disconnect, contract, hide as well as possible in host body. Suicide in effect. I disregarded situational imperatives, despite starvation before disinterment and subsequent autopsy all but certain. I caught up with crew, tackled Pollock and Jackson microseconds before blast. Computed five days' survival from this cache, could disconnect at limit of strength to do so, but otherwise would chance autopsy, knowing doctor was alcoholic incompetent. And now see my gain. You are a prize host, can feed with near impunity even when killing too dangerous. Safe meals delivered to you still warm."

The corpse had painstakingly aligned the gurney parallel to the worktable but offset, the table's foot extending past the gurney's, and separated from it by a distance somewhat less than the reach of Joe Allen's right arm. Now the dead hands distributed the implements along the right edge of the table, save for the scissors and the box. These the corpse took to the table's foot, where it set down the box and slid the scissors' jaws round one strap of its overalls. It began to speak again, and as it did, the scissors dismembered its cerements in unhesitating strokes.

"The cut must be medical, forensically right, though a smaller one easier. Must be careful of the pectoral muscles or arms will not convey me. I am no larva anymore—over fifteen hundred grams."

To ease the nightmare's suffocating pressure, to thrust out some flicker of his own will against its engulfment, the doctor flung a question, his voice more cracked than the other's now was: "Why is my arm free?"

"The last, fine neural splicing needs a sensory-motor standard, to perfect my brain's fit to yours. Lacking this eye–hand coordinating check, much coarser motor control of host. This done, I flush out the paralytic, unbind us, and we are free together."

The grave clothes had fallen in a puzzle of fragments, and the cadaver stood naked, its dark, gas-rounded contours making it seem some sleek marine creature, ruddered with the black-veined, gas-distended sex. Again the voice had teased for his fear, had uttered the last word with a savoring protraction, and now the doctor's cup of anguish brimmed over; horror and outrage wrenched his spirit in brutal alternation as if trying to tear it naked from its captive frame. He rolled his head in this deadlock, his mouth beginning to split with the slow birth of a mind-emptying outcry.

The corpse watched this, giving a single nod that might have been approbation. Then it mounted the worktable and, with the concentrated caution of some practiced convalescent reentering his bed, lay on its back. The dead eyes again sought the living and found the doctor staring back, grinning insanely.

"Clever corpse!" the doctor cried. "Clever, carnivorous corpse! Able alien! Please don't think I'm criticizing. Who am I to criticize? A mere arm and shoulder, a talking hand, just a small piece of a pathologist. But I'm confused." He paused, savoring the monster's attentive silence and his own buoyancy in the hysterical levity that had unexpectedly liberated him. "You're going to use your puppet there to pluck you out of itself and put you on me. But once he's pulled you from your driver's seat, won't he go dead, so to speak, and drop you? You could get a nasty knock. Why not set a plank between the tables—the puppet opens the door, and you scuttle, ooze, lurch, flop, slither, as the case may be, across the bridge. No messy spills. And in any case, isn't this an odd, rather clumsy way to get around among your cattle? Shouldn't you at least carry your own scalpels when you travel? There's always the risk you'll run across that one host in a million that isn't carrying one with him."

He knew his gibes would be answered to his own despair. He exulted, but solely in the momentary bafflement of the predator—in having, for just a moment, mocked its gloating assurance to silence and marred its feast.

Its right hand picked up the post-mortem knife beside it, and the left wedged a roll of gauze beneath Allen's neck, lifting the throat to a more prominent arch. The mouth told the ceiling: "We retain larval form till entry of the host. As larvae we have locomotor structures, and sense buds usable outside our ships' sensory amplifiers. I waited coiled round Joe Allen's bed leg till night, entered by his mouth as he slept." Allen's hand lifted the knife, held it high above the dull, quick eyes, turning it in the light. "Once lodged, we have three instars to adult form," the voice continued absently—the knife might have been a mirror from which the corpse read its features. "Larvally we have only a sketch of our full neural tap. Our metamorphosis cued and determined by host's endosomatic ecology. I matured in three days." Allen's wrist flexed, tipping the knife's point downmost. "Most supreme adaptations purchased at the cost of inessential capacities." The elbow pronated and slowly flexed, hooking the knife body-wards. "Our hosts are all sentients, eco-dominants, are already carrying the baggage of coping structures for the planetary environment. Limbs, sensory portals"—the fist planted the fang of its tool under the chin, tilted it and rode it smoothly down the throat, the voice proceeding unmarred from under the furrow that the steel plowed—"somatic envelopes, instrumentalities"—down the sternum, diaphragm, abdomen the stainless blade painted its stripe of gaping, muddy tissue—"with a host's brain we inherit all these, the mastery of any planet, netted in its dominant's cerebral nexus. Thus our genetic codings are now all but disencumbered of such provisions."

So swiftly the doctor flinched, Joe Allen's hand slashed four lateral cuts from the great wound's axis. The seeming butchery left two flawlessly drawn thoracic flaps cleanly outlined. The left hand raised the left flap's hem, and the right coaxed the knife into the aperture, deepening it with small stabs and slices. The posture was a man's who searches a breast pocket, with the dead eyes studying the slow recoil of flesh. The voice, when it resumed, had geared up to an intenser pitch.

"Galactically, the chordate nerve/brain paradigm abounds, and the neural labyrinth is our dominion. Are we to make plank bridges and worm across them to our food? Are cockroaches greater than we for having legs to run up walls and antennae to grope their way! All the quaint, hinged crutches that life sports! The stilts, fins, fans, springs, stalks, flippers, and feathers, all in turn so variously terminating in hooks, clamps, suckers, scissors, forks, or little cages of digits! And besides all the gadgets it concocts for wrestling through its worlds, it is all knobbed, whiskered, crested, plumed, vented, spiked, or measeled over with perceptual gear for combing pittances of noise or color from the environing plentitude."

Invincibly calm and sure, the hands traded tool and tasks. The right flap eased back, revealing ropes of ingeniously spared muscle while promising a genuine appearance once sutured back in place. Helplessly the doctor felt his delirious defiance bleed away and a bleak fascination rebind him.

"We are the taps and relays that share the host's aggregate of afferent nerve impulse precisely at its nodes of integration. We are the brains that peruse these integrations, integrate them with our existing banks of host-specific data, and, lastly, let their consequences flow down the motor pathway—either the consequences they seek spontaneously, or those we wish to graft upon them. We are besides a streamlined alimentary/circulatory system and a reproductive apparatus. And more than this we need not be."

The corpse had spread its bloody vest, and the feculent hands now took up the rib shears. The voice's sinister coloration of pitch and stress grew yet more marked—the phrases slid from the tongue with a cobra's seeking sway, winding their liquid rhythms round the doctor till a gap in his resistance should let them pour through to slaughter the little courage left him.

"For in his form we have inhabited the densest brainweb of three hundred races, lain intricately snug within them like thriving vine on trelliswork. We've looked out from too many variously windowed masks to regret our own vestigial senses. None read their worlds definitely. Far better then our nomad's range and choice than an unvarying tenancy of one poor set of structures. Far better to slip on as we do whole living beings and wear at once all of their limbs and organs, memories and powers—wear all as tightly congruent to our wills as a glove is to the hand that fills it."

The shears clipped through the gristle, stolid, bloody jaws monotonously feeding, stopping short of the sternoclavicular joint in the manubrium where the muscles of the pectoral girdle have an important anchorage.

"No consciousness of the chordate type that we have found has been impermeable to our finesse—no dendritic pattern so elaborate we could not read its stitchwork and thread ourselves to match, precisely map its each synaptic seam till we could loosen it and retailor all to suit ourselves. We have strutted costumed in the bodies of planetary autarchs, venerable manikins of moral fashion, but cut of the universal cloth: the weave of fleet electric filaments of experience which we easily reshuttled to the warp of our wishes. Whereafter—newly hemmed and gathered—their living fabric hung obedient to our bias, investing us with honor and influence unlimited."

The tricky verbal melody, through the corpse's deft, unfaltering self-dismemberment—the sheer neuromuscular orchestration of the compound activity—struck Dr. Winters with the detached enthrallment great keyboard performers could bring him. He glimpsed the alien's perspective—a Gulliver waiting in a brobdingnagian grave, then marshaling a dead giant against a living, like a dwarf in a huge mechanical crane, feverishly programming combat on a battery of levers and pedals, waiting for the robot arms' enactments, the remote, titanic impact of the foes—and he marveled, filled with a bleak wonder at life's infinite strategy and plasticity. Joe Allen's hands reached into his half-opened abdominal cavity, reached deep below the uncut anterior muscle that was exposed by the shallow, spurious incision of the epidermis, till by external measure they were extended far enough to be touching his thighs. The voice was still as the forearms advertised a delicate rummaging with the buried fingers. The shoulders drew back. As the steady withdrawal brought the wrists into view, the dead legs tremored and quaked with diffuse spasms.

"You called your kind our food and drink, Doctor. If you were merely that, an elementary usurpation of your motor tracts alone would satisfy us, give us perfect cattle-control—for what rarest word or subtlest behavior is more than a flurry of varied muscles? That trifling skill was ours long ago. It is not mere blood that feeds this lust I feel now to tenant you, this craving for an intimacy that years will not stale. My truest feast lies in compelling you to feed in that way and in the utter deformation of your will this will involve. Had gross nourishment been my prime need, then my gravemates—Pollock and Jackson—could have eked out two weeks of life for me or more. But I scorned a cowardly parsimony in the face of death. I reinvested more than half the energy that their blood gave me in fabricating chemicals to keep their brains alive, and fluid-bathed with oxygenated nutriment."

Out of the chasmed midriff the smeared hands dragged two long tresses of silvery filament that writhed and sparkled with a million simultaneous coilings and contractions. The legs jittered with faint, chaotic pulses throughout their musculature, until the bright vermiculate tresses had gathered into two spheric masses which the hands laid carefully within the incision. Then the legs lay still as death.

"I had accessory neural taps only to spare, but I could access much memory, and all of their cognitive responses, and having in my banks all the organ of Coti's electrochemical conversions of English words, I could whisper anything to them directly into the eighth cranial nerve. Those are our true feast, Doctor, such bodiless electric storms of impotent cognition as I tickled up in those two little bone globes. I was forced to drain them yesterday, just before disinterment. They lived till then and understood everything—*everything* I did to them.

When the voice paused, the dead and living eyes were locked together. They remained so a moment, and then the dead face smiled.

It recapitulated all the horror of Allen's first resurrection—this waking of expressive soul from those grave-mound contours. And it was a demon-soul the doctor saw awaken: the smile was barbed with fine, sharp hooks of cruelty at the corners of the mouth, while the barbed eyes beamed fond, languorous anticipation of his pain. Remotely, Dr. Winters heard the flat sound of his own voice asking: "And Joe Allen?"

"Oh, yes, Doctor. He is with us now, has been throughout. I grieve to abandon so rare a host! He is a true hermit-philosopher, well-read in four languages. He is writing a translation of Marcus Aurelius—he was, I mean, in his free time. . . ."

Long minutes succeeded of the voice accompanying the surreal self-autopsy, but the doctor lay stilled, emptied of reactive power. Still, the full understanding of his fate reverberated in his mind—an empty room though which the voice, not heard exactly but somehow implanted directly as in the subterranean torture it had just described, sent aftershocks of realization, amplifications of the Unspeakable.

The parasite had traced and tapped the complex interface between cortical integration of input and the consequent neural output shaping response. It had interposed its brain between, sharing consciousness while solely commanding the pathways of reaction. The host, the bottled personality; was mute and limbless for any least expression of its own will, while hellishly articulate and agile in the service of the parasite's. It was the host's own hands that bound and wrenched the life half out of his prey, his own loins that experienced the repeated orgasms crowning his other despoliations of their bodies. And when they lay, bound and shrieking still, ready for the consummation, it was his own strength that hauled the smoking entrails from them, and his own intimate tongue and guzzling mouth he plunged into the rank, palpitating feast.

And the doctor had glimpses of the history behind this predation, that of a race so far advanced in the essentializing, the inexorable abstraction of their own mental fabric that through scientific commitment and genetic self-cultivation they had come to embody their own model of perfected consciousness, streamlined to permit the entry of other beings and the direct acquisition of their experiental worlds. All strictest scholarship at first, until there matured in the disembodied scholars their long-germinal and now blazing, jealous hatred for all 'lesser' minds rooted and clothed in the soil and sunlight of solid, particular worlds. The parasite spoke of the "cerebral music" the "symphonies of agonized paradox" that were its invasion's chief plunder. The doctor felt the truth behind this grandiloquence: its actual harvest from the systematic violation of encoffined personalities was the experience of a barren supremacy of means over lives more primitive, perhaps, but vastly wealthier in the vividness and passionate concern with which life for them was imbued.

Joe Allen's hands had scooped up the bunched skeins of alien nerve, with the wrinkled brain node couched amidst them, and for some time had waited the slow retraction of a last major trunkline which seemingly had followed the spine's axis. At last, when only a slender subfiber of this remained implanted, the corpse, smiling once more, held up for him to view its reconcatenated master. The doctor looked into its eyes then and spoke—not to their controller, but to the captive who shared them with it, and who now, the doctor knew, neared his final death.

"Good-bye, Joe Allen. Eddie Sykes. You are guiltless. Peace be with you at last."

The demon smile remained fixed, the right hand reached its viscid cargo across the gap and over the doctor's groin. He watched the hand set the glittering medusa's head—his new self—upon his flesh, return to the table, take up the scalpel, and reach back to cut in his groin a four-inch incision—all in eerie absence of tactile stimulus. The line that had remained plunged into the corpse suddenly whipped free of the mediastinal crevice, retracted across the gap, and shortened to a taut stub on the seething organism atop the doctor.

Joe Allen's body collapsed, emptied, all slack. He was a corpse again entirely, but with one anomalous feature to his posture. His right arm had not dropped to the nearly vertical hang that would have been natural. At the instant of the alien's unplugging, the shoulder had given a fierce shrug and wrenching of its angle, flinging the arm upward as it died so that it now lay in the orientation of an arm that reaches up for a ladder's next rung. The slightest tremor would unfix the joints and dump the arm back into the gravitational bias; it would also serve to dump the scalpel from the proferred, upturned palm that implement still precariously occupied.

The man had repossessed himself one microsecond before his end. The doctor's heart stirred, woke, and sang within him, for he saw that the scalpel was just in reach of his fingers at his forearm's fullest stretch from the bound elbow. The horror crouched on him and, even now slowly feeding its trunkline into his groin incision, at first stopped the doctor's hand with a pang of terror. Then he reminded himself that, until implanted, the enemy was a senseless mass, bristling with plugs, with input jacks for senses, but, until installed in the physical amplifiers of eyes and ears, an utterly deaf, blind monad that waited in a perfect solipsism between two captive sensory envelopes.

He saw his straining fingers above the bright tool of freedom, thought with an insane smile of God and Adam on the Cistine ceiling, and then, with a life span of surgeon's fine control, plucked up the scalpel. The arm fell and hung.

"Sleep." The doctor said. "Sleep revenged."

But he found his retaliation harshly reined in by the alien's careful provisions. His elbow had been fixed with his upper arm almost at right angles to his body's long axis; his forearm could reach his hand inward and present it closely to the face, suiting the parasite's need of an eye-hand coordinative check, but could not, even with the scalpel's added reach, bring its point within four inches of his groin. Steadily the parasite fed in its tap line. It would usurp motor control in three or four minutes at most, to judge by the time its extrication from Allen had taken.

Frantically the doctor bent his wrist inward to its limit, trying to pick through the strap where it crossed his inner elbow. Sufficient pressure was impossible, and the hold so awkward that even feeble attempts threatened the loss of the scalpel. Smoothly the root of alien control sank into him. It was a defenseless thing of jelly against which he lay lethally armed, and he was still doomed—a preview of all his thrall's impotence-to-be.

But of course there was a way. Not to survive. But to escape, and to have vengeance. For a moment he stared at his captor, hardening his mettle in the blaze of hate it lit in him. Then, swiftly, he determined the order of his moves, and began.

He reached the scalpel to his neck and opened his superior thyroid vein—his inkwell. He laid the scalpel by his ear, dipped his finger in his blood, and began to write on the metal surface of the gurney, beginning by his thigh and moving toward his armpit. Oddly, the incision of his neck, though this was muscularly awake, had been painless, which gave him hopes that raised his courage for what remained to do.

When he had done the message read:

> MIND PARASITE
> FM ALLEN IN ME
> CUT *ALL* TILL
> FIND
> 1500 GM MASS
> NERVE FIBER

He wanted to write good-bye to his friend, but the alien had begun to pay out smaller, auxiliary filaments collaterally with the main one, and all now lay in speed.

He took up the scalpel, rolled his head to the left, and plunged the blade deep in his ear.

Miracle! Last, accidental mercy! It was painless. Some procedural, highly specific anesthetic was in effect. With careful plunges, he obliterated the right inner ear and then thrust silence, with equal thoroughness, into the left. The slashing of the vocal chords followed, then the tendons in the back of the neck that hold it erect. He wished he were free to unstring knees and elbows, too, but it could not be. But blinded, with centers of balance lost, with only rough motor control—all these conditions should fetter the alien's escape, should it in the first place manage the reanimation of a bloodless corpse in which it had not yet achieved a fine-tuned interweave. Before he extinguished his eyes, he paused, the scalpel poised above his face, and blinked them to clear his aim of tears. The right, then the left, both retinas meticulously carved away, the yolk of vision quite scooped out of them. The scalpel's last task, once it had tilted the head sideways to guide the blood flow absolutely clear of possible effacement of the message, was to slash the external carotid artery.

When this was done, the old man sighed with relief and laid his scalpel down. Even as he did so, he felt the deep inward prickle of an alien energy—something that flared, crackled, flared, *groped for* but did not quite find its purchase. And inwardly, as the doctor sank toward sleep— cerebrally, as a voiceless man must speak—he spoke to the parasite these carefully chosen words: "Welcome to your new house. I'm afraid there's been some vandalism—the lights don't work, and the plumbing has a very bad leak. There are some other things wrong as well—the neighborhood is perhaps a little *too* quiet, and you may find it hard to get around very easily. But it's been a lovely home to me for fifty-seven years, and somehow I think you'll stay. . . ."

The face, turned toward the body of Joe Allen, seemed to weep scarlet tears, but its last movement before death was to smile.